The Exploits of
Professor Tornada
(Volume 1)

André Couvreur

The Exploits of Professor Tornada
Volume 1:
An Invasion of Macrobes
The Androgyne

translated, annotated and introduced by
Brian Stableford

A Black Coat Press Book

Visit our website at www.blackcoatpress.com

TABLE OF CONTENTS

Introduction

Une Invasion de Macrobes by André Couvreur, here translated as "An Invasion of Macrobes," was originally published in four parts in November 1909 in the weekly literary supplement of the newspaper *L'Illustration*, and reprinted in book form, in a revised version, the following year by Pierre Lafitte. The serial version was reprinted twice, firstly in a cheap edition in 1940, and then in an undated small press edition in the early years of the present century; the book version was reprinted in paperback in 1998.

L'Androgyne, here translated as "The Androgyne," was originally published in *Oeuvres Libres* no. 7 (January 1922), and was reprinted in book form the following year by Albin Michel, the book version being dedicated to J.-H. Rosny Aîné. Couvreur went on to publish four more novellas featuring Professor Tornada in that periodical, plus two other long stories, none of which were ever reprinted in book form, even though the author had apparently signed a four-book contract with Albin Michel for a series featuring Tornada.

It is unclear why Albin Michel did not publish the further items in the series that he had commissioned. Given the he had published *L'Androgyne* and was apparently sufficiently enthused by it to request more work of a similar nature it is unlikely that he was put off by the flagrant and perverse erotic content of the next item in the series, "Le Valseur phosphorescent" (1923)[1], which is no more explicit or perverse than that in *L'Androgyne* or Couvreur's earlier mad scientist story *Caresco, surhomme* (1904)[2]. It is possible that public or offi-

---

[1] translated in the second volume of the present series as "The Phosphorescent Waltzer."

[2] translated as *Caresco, Superman*, Black Coat Press, ISBN 978-1-61227-254-2.

cial reaction to *L'Androgyne* deterred the publication of a similar work, although it is hard to believe that there could have been any threat of prosecution on the grounds of obscenity at such a late date. It is, however, notable that none of the subsequent stories in the Tornada sequence reproduce the erotic fascinations of *L'Androgyne* and "Le Valseur phosphorescent," seeming distinctly prim by comparison.

It might also be worth noting that there appears to have been something of a marketplace backlash against speculative fiction in the early 1920s. Maurice Renard, who tried to return to the production of such work once his military service in the war was over ran into similarly rapid difficulties marketing his work, and ultimately had to switch to the writing to anodyne detective stories, while J.-H. Rosny's endeavors in the genre, having similarly flattered only to deceive, soon began to flounder. Like Couvreur, Rosny sold one ambitious item of *roman scientifique* to *Oeuvres Libres* in "Les Navigateurs de l'infini" (1925)[3] but aborted its advertised sequel and never produced anything as imaginatively ambitious again—and *Oeuvres Libres* never published anything else in the genre thereafter, except for the later Professor Tornada stories.

The Tornada stories constitute a sequence rather than a series because they present the rather unusual feature of seemingly reinventing their central character from scratch every time. Although certain aspects of his physical appearance—the short legs, the long beard, the pointed ears and the multiple tics—are faithfully reproduced every time, there is no sense in which the six stories can add up to a biography; none of the stories make any substantial reference to any events in the earlier ones, and two of them feature large-scale world-shaking events that cannot possibly have occurred in the back-stories of the scenarios featured within the subsequent texts. The last story in the series contains a sentence referring to the plots of three of the earlier adventures, with footnoted refer-

---

[3] translated as *The Navigators of Space*, Black Coat Press, ISBN 978-1-935558-35-4.

ences, but the events of at least one of those stories could not possibly have occurred in the world forming the backcloth to the current story, and the sentence is probably included as an advertisement, thought necessary because of a twelve-year gap between the story and its predecessor in the series. Tornada is, therefore, not so much a person as an idea, perhaps even a symbol.

It is noticeable too that, although he is not the same character as Armand Caresco, similarly reinvented by the author in *Caresco, surhomme*—which is also unusually disconnected from the earlier novel in which he is the protagonist, *Le Mal nécessaire* (1899)[4]—Tornada does take on some of Caresco's key attributes. Although he is not a surgeon when first introduced, in *Une Invasion de Macrobes*, he is most definitely a surgeon in *L'Androgyne*, when he undertakes an experiment credited to Caresco in in *Caresco, surhomme*, and that becomes his primary specialty again in the fifth story of the series, "Le Biocole" (1927)[5], in which he goes so far in emulation of Caresco as to found his own heavily-defended utopian enclave and to begin styling himself "le Surhomme," just as his predecessor had done. It is probably safe to say, therefore, that not only is Tornada an idea, and perhaps a symbol, but that he is much the same idea, carrying a similar symbolic value, as Armand Caresco.

At any rate, there is a sense in which all five of the volumes in the present set are connected, albeit in a rather peculiar, and perhaps unique, fashion. The fact that the stories they contain extend over a period of forty years, from 1899 to 1939, also adds interest to the endeavor in terms of the possibility of deriving some insight therefrom into the evolution in the author's mind of the idea that Caresco and Tornada represent. At its simplest, the idea in question is that of the "mad

---

[4] translated as *The Necessary Evil*, Black Coat Press, ISBN 978-1-61227-253-5.
[5] translated in the third volume of the present series as "The Biocole."

scientist"—which, of course, implies that the correlations between the two terms is somehow intrinsic, in that genius is inherently close to madness and that scientific genius is not only uniquely close but uniquely dangerous, especially in the contexts of biological and medical science, where the discoveries of genius might have social and personal implications that are not merely sweeping but intimate. Put crudely, whereas physics and chemistry can dramatically increase the ways in which people can travel, communicate and kill one another, biology has the potential to transform us in ways that are both much more radical and much more insidious.

There is, however, far more to Caresco and Tornada than madness and genius, at least once the volumes that introduce the characters are out of the way. The madness and the genius alike place them outside the ranks of commonplace humankind, able to pass scathing judgment on its faults, but also able to explore ways of ameliorating these faults. Tornada's claim that the surgical sex-changes affected in *L'Androgyne* are carried out with a view to enhancing human choice rather than simply out of curiosity to see what will happen might ring false, and the experiment he carries out in "Le Valseur phosphorescent" also looks suspiciously like curiosity for curiosity's sake, but the humanitarian excuses offered for such further quests as the development of technologies of suspended animation, the resurrection of the dead, and the photographing of thought do seem to have some authentic weight.

Be that as it may, the two short novels combined in the present volume definitely show the mercurial professor in his most unflattering light, and the first of them also does the same for humankind. *Une Invasion de macrobes* is the nearest thing to a conventional thriller that Couvreur ever wrote, and for much of the horrific climax—especially the scenes in the sewer—it is easy to forget the story is actually a comedy; its graphic action is very effective, because rather than in spite of its garishness. Although it is not a thriller or a horror story, the same is true of the second story, in that the author becomes

10

genuinely wrapped up in his thought-experiment, fascination frequently taking precedence over satire.

Like many of Couvreur's works, *L'Androgyne* was genuinely ground-breaking in its depiction of a sex-swap—it appeared nine years in advance of Thorne Smith's *Turnabout*, a much broader farce—and the author had every reason to become fascinated by the extrapolation of the notion, which still has the potential to intrigue modern readers who have had the opportunity to read or view other adaptations of the same idea. The title might seem odd, but the central character is indeed a genuine androgyne, combining an exceedingly masculine mind with a completely female physique; although the extrapolation of that notion embodies all the sexist assumptions of the day (Couvreur was certainly no feminist) it is by no means lacking in acuity, or in eccentricity and peculiar perversity, all of which combine to make it a remarkable work.

The second volume of the present set contains translations of "Le Valseur phosphorescent" (1923), as "The Phosphorescent Waltzer," and "Les Mémoires d'un immortel" (1924), as "The Memoirs of an Immortal." The third volume completes the Tornada sequence with translations of "Le Biocole" (1927), as "The Biocole," and "Les Cas de la baronne Sasoitsu" (1939), as "The Case of Baronne Sasoitsu," and also includes, by way of a bonus, a translation of the unrelated novella "En Au-delà" (1937), as "In the Afterlife." All of those stories appeared in *Oeuvres Libres*, and none has previously been reprinted in book form.

The following translation of *Une Invasion de Macrobes* was made from a copy of the 1998 paperback edition published in Toulouse by Éditions Ombres, which reproduces the revised Lafitte text rather than the serial version. The translation of "L'Androgyne" was made from the London Library's copy of *Oeuvres Libres* no. 7.

Brian Stableford

AN INVASION OF MACROBES

I

I shall never forget the evening of May the eleventh. It marked the beginning of an event so extraordinary that our posterity, when it remembers it, will have the right to wonder whether an entire people might not have been carried away by madness at a particular moment of its social history. However, what I am going to consign to this memoir, I lived through, suffering frightful emotions, and if I was mad, along with everyone else, at least I am sincere in writing.

I was then in charge of a laboratory at the Institut Pasteur, and I had just become engaged to Mademoiselle Suzanne Vernet, the daughter of the celebrated biologist Vernet, a member of the Académie des Sciences. Suzanne was a young woman of the elite, nobly raised by a father who had been widowed for a long time. Her ash-blonde hair would have been sufficient to render her remarkable even if the regularity of her features, the limpid flame of her blue eyes and all the harmonious grace of her person had not added a surplus of beauty that everyone admired. We had adored one another since adolescence—which explains how delightful that initial familiarity was, in which propriety permitted us to hold hands, when she ceased to address me ceremoniously as "Monsieur Gérard" in order to call me Jean, while I responded by calling her Suzanne.

Oh, that exquisite spring evening! I remember that, in order to escape the compliments of the habitués of the house, we had gone into the garden and sat down on a bench. A pale moonlight inundated us; the lilacs, asleep in the warmth, sent us their perfumes; and there was a universal caress. Although the open window allowed us to overhear the conversation of Monsieur Vernet's guests, we were only listening to one another.

There were, however, many interesting people among those who had come to my future father-in-law's weekly gathering: scientists, artists and political men. They included Commandant Junisseau, the pilot of the dirigible *France*; the chemist Serviat, a member of the Institut and the inventor of fracassite, an incomparable explosive; General Gramont of the artillery; Dardant, the editor of the *Parisien*, the great twice-daily paper; Vigueur, the Undersecretary of State for Posts and Telegraphs; and others equally notorious. But what did those celebrities matter, compared with our simple love? Was all of human glory worth as much as one of Suzanne's smiles? Was all that enlightenment as dazzling as her soft gaze—touched, at that moment, one might have thought, by a celestial tint? And what eloquence could match that of our future projects?

I must admit, however, that one name, suddenly pronounced by the others, extracted us from our delicious intimacy. I don't know what frightful presentiment made us prick up our ears when it was pronounced. It even seemed to us that the evocation of Tornada, the individual who was mentioned, threw a malaise equal to ours into the salon, for silence fell abruptly as soon as the chemist Serviat, the inventor of fracassite, resumed speaking, in order to denigrate that man he had just named, violently.

"Tornada—what a strange name![6] Do you know him?" my fiancée asked me then.

---

[6] Slightly strange, indeed, as a name for a scientist (but no more so than Caresco). A *tornada*, in Occitan literature, is a supplementary stanza to a lyric poem, which sometimes served in the days of the troubadours as a kind of "punch-line," sometimes as an explanatory footnote or dedication, and sometimes, especially in Italian Renaissance adaptations— perhaps most significantly, in the present context—as a fresh voice commenting on the substance of the lyric.

"I do, indeed, know him, my dear Suzanne," I replied. "This Tornada is a scientist who is as eccentric as he is rich: an unorthodox worker whose research, toward whatever branch of science he directs it, has always been marked by a hint of genius. He has occupied himself successively with telepathy, the problems of unknown forces, biology, astronomy and everything connected with the occult. Notably, we owe to him the discovery of a certain microbe living in alkaline environments, which he named *Micrococcus aspirator*—a discovery denied by Monsieur Serviat, who is speaking at present. But what has put his name in lights most of all is a paper on 'The Abnormal Development of Organisms Favored by Culture Media,' which generated a lot of discussion in the scientific world, and even in the newspapers when he presented it at the Académie des Science."

"Abnormal Development?" queried Suzanne.

"That language is incomprehensible for you, isn't it? What it means is that, according to Tornada, one can transform certain organisms, such as microbes, causing them to grow to extraordinary dimensions, simply by placing them in conditions of life and nutrition appropriate to their development..."

"Making giants with microbes?"

"I don't think that's Tornada's ambition," I replied, smiling, "but he seems to be promising that. In any case, the paper made the learned assembly to which it was submitted sit up. It was considered as the work of a maniac who had yielded himself to a Darwinist fantasy—and it's precisely because of the kind of anxiety provoked by his very special intelligence that Tornada was denied a seat at the Académie when he offered himself as a candidate last year. Since then, he's disappeared, swearing that he'll have his revenge."

"Yes, I remember now," Suzanne said. "Papa was very sorry about his failure. Unlike Monsieur Serviat, he appreciates Tornada's inventive genius, and he had supported his candidature..."

We would have liked to get back to our amorous conversation, but the suggestion of the individual haunted us, and we went back into the drawing room to listen to the discussion that had sprung up on his account. His bad temper was being assessed there without indulgence. Monsieur Vernet was the only one to defend him, and to protest against the jesting calumnies suggesting, on the part of some, that he has succumbed to an attack of furious madness and, on the part of others, that he had gone to China to stir up racial hatred.

Suddenly, however, the voice of Commandant Junisseau rose up: "Permit me, Messieurs, to tell you what has become of Tornada."

He was surrounded, and in absolute silence, he continued: "Do you know the forest of Rosny, near Mantes? There exists therein, not far from the Seine, a region little known to holiday-makers. No road takes automobiles there, and an entire estate, hidden in the trees, attached to the Château de Chambure, is invisible—one might even say inaccessible. It's there that, three days ago, passing over it in my dirigible, I was surprised to see a large building, occupying about ten thousand square meters, about a hundred meters high, which had risen up as if by enchantment. Extremely intrigued, I landed, and made a tour on foot of a kind of hangar. I observed that it was closed everywhere, except for one place where there was an enormous iron door. I then sought information from the local peasants, and bit by bit—for the people seemed to be afraid of saying too much—I got it out of them that the edifice had been constructed in secret by an individual whose description fits that of Professor Tornada."

"Is it plausible that such an edifice can sprout from the ground without the press finding out about it?" protested Monsieur Dardant, the editor of the *Parisien*, shrugging his shoulders skeptically.

"My dear Monsieur, that's precisely what renders the thing interesting—that you haven't even suspected it. It's high time that you put the dirigible at the service of your reporters. Know, then, what I heard from a reliable source. The materials of the gigantic hall were ordered from abroad: the iron from America, the cement from Holland, the bricks from England, the wood from Norway—even the workmen, who were introduced in gangs, weren't French. Having arrived by steamer, they went home the same way, without making contact with the indigenes, of whose language they were, in any case, completely ignorant. The proximity of the railways and the Seine facilitated these transportations."

"It's very improbable...." someone else objected.

"What is even more improbable," Junisseau went on, turning toward his interlocutor, "is that unknown machines comparable to laboratory apparatus—giant laboratory apparatus, for Titans—have been brought piece by piece and assembled in place as soon as the construction was finished. Commentaries, naturally, have taken wing; the rumor has gone around that Tornada has installed a distillery; and the locals—who are, I repeat, terrorized—haven't been able to learn any more, for the massive door, functioning by means of a electrical mechanism, is always closed to their curiosity."

"But Tornada isn't living in his hangar on his own?" queried Monsieur Serviat, again.

"So it's believed."

"It's a fairy tale!" the chemist scoffed.

His irony was aborted by the sound of voices. What did it all mean? Was Tornada completely mad, or an utter genius? Was he attempting his promised vengeance? Monsieur Vernet recalled, in order to excuse him, that it was after having lost his wife and daughter—both of whom he adored—in a single night that the inventor had shown the first signs of strangeness.

And it was while a few instances of that strangeness were being cited that that a manservant opened the drawing room door and announced: "Monsieur le Professeur Tornada!"

17

II

There was a stir. One might have thought that the bizarre name fell upon the room like the announcement of a catastrophe. Instinctively, obedient to a protective impulse, I moved closer to my fiancée.

The sight of the newcomer was, in any case, conducive to some malaise. He was a short, simian man, of whom one only noticed at first the black beard, so thick that it hung down in two carefully-combed sections all the way to his legs. By contrast, the head was almost completely bald, and the polished cranium permitted observation of the abnormal conformation of the head, which one might have thought kneaded by the Devil, undulating with excessive bumps that must have lodged a particular intelligence. The rest of the physiognomy, when one took inventory of it, did not attenuate in the least the surprise provoked by those first impressions. The ears stuck out like the appendages of a wolf, twitching at the slightest sonorities. The exceedingly dark eyes, very small and mobile, filled with flashes at times, and retreated behind the eyelids at others. Finally, numerous tics, some more singular than others, continually shook the head, the arms and the legs, testifying to incessant convulsions beneath that Hoffmannesque exterior.

Nevertheless, my future father-in-law welcomed Tornada deferentially. He introduced him, not without malice, to the influential individuals present who had just been heaping their criticism on his inventive genius. The little man accompanied each handshake he gave with a snigger. When it was Monsieur Serviat's turn, he turned away with a manifest disgust and immediately came toward Suzanne and me.

I was surprised then by the transformation that had overtaken him. His nervous phenomena seemed suddenly to have calmed down. He gazed with an undisguised and thoroughly paternal admiration at my fiancée's lovely face. He took us to one side and complimented us with a softness of voice all the more surprising because we might have expected to hear nothing other than inarticulate sounds issuing from such a scarcely human face.

He questioned us about the tenderness of our idyll, and seemed very sensitive to it. He confided to us, wiping away a tear, that his daughter would also have been of an age to get married, if destiny had not snatched her away. Then, to dissipate that sadness, he offered Suzanne a book of verses that he had composed for her—and I recall that my fiancée, seduced by the gesture, requested silence, and read a few agreeably-turned lines, which drew applause addressed as much to the reader as to the poet.

That incident had effaced the bitterness and malevolence of the words that had preceded the professor's arrival. Tea was served, and he accepted it, like everyone else, with a good grace, while elegantly stroking his beard. He even made a few witty remarks. And the rest of the soirée would have gone by normally, in an inattention salutary for everyone, had it not be for the fact that, exactly at midnight, at the first stroke of the clock, Tornada began to show signs of anxiety.

He grimaced several times; his legs launched kicks into empty space; his hands described a very particular gesticulation, which I compared to the ameboid movements of certain animalcules. One sensed that a crisis was brewing. Although the conversations continued with an apparent indifference, the attention of the entire salon was nevertheless fixed on him.

Finally, at the last stroke of midnight, he uttered a more resounding snigger, bounded on to a sofa, and declared: "Messieurs, it's exactly a year since I was rejected by the Académie. Illustrious, jealous individuals—you were one of them, Serviat—considered my paper on 'The Abnormal Development of Organisms Favored by Culture Media' as the work of a poorly equilibrated mind. Come on, look at me—do I look like a madman?"

His tics had returned, more frightfully. Taking pity on him, fearing an attack that might cause him to fall down, I made a movement as if to catch him in my arms, but the particularly alarming expression of his eyes at that moment stopped me.

He went on: "No, I'm not mad! I'm merely a misunderstood and insulted genius. And I'll have my revenge, my good friends! I'll savor a terrible revenge! Look! It's beginning at this moment. In an hour's time, I'll open the door, and they'll go forth, they'll go forth! On your way, my lovely macrobes! On your way! Feast! There's flesh! There's blood! Flesh, and blood!"

He was shouting. Dolorously amazed, we were already thinking about putting him in a straitjacket—but he calmed down somewhat, in order to address himself to a few of us for whom he seemed to have a particular hatred.

"You, Commandant Junisseau, heave been spying on me: prepare your dirigible for flight! You, Dardant, your paper has ridiculed me; do you think you can laugh much longer? It's my turn now! In a week's time you'll no longer have a single one of those readers whose minds you've perverted. You, Duverdon the banker, you've supported my competitors with your influence: quickly, close your counters, for you'll have no clients...and in any case, the Bourse will be destroyed! You, Minister Vigueur, no more posts, no more telegraphs! You, Serviat, ha ha! you... prepare tons of fracassite! My children are going to eat you, Serviat On your way! On your way! They're going forth! They're going forth! On your way, my lovely macrobes!"

Everyone around him had fallen silent, shivering with an instinctive fear, resulting not from the incomprehensible threats that the orator was uttering but from the malady that had afflicted him to such an extent. Monsieur Vernet tried to calm him down. He helped him to get down from the sofa and drew him gently toward the door.

In any case, Tornada had suddenly calmed down again, and I was not far from thinking that he was trying to attenuate, by a reasonable attitude, the amazement and alarm that he had read on my fiancée's face. As he went out he beckoned to us, and we followed him into the antechamber, drawn as if by a magnetism.

There he put his hands together to make a plea.

"My children, and you, Vernet, are the only ones I want to spare, so listen to my advice and follow it. I'm lucid, and I'm fonder of you than you can believe. Listen to me. Within a week, Paris will be devastated. There won't be a single Frenchman left alive in a fortnight's time. Flee! Flee! Arrange your affairs swiftly, and leave by the first steamer. Flee tomorrow! The day after, it will be too late!"

"My good friend, would you like me to take you home?" Monsieur Vernet proposed.

"He thinks I'm mad too!" Tornada lamented. "Oh, if I didn't love you" Look, you know me, right? Reread my book. You know that my *Micrococcus aspirator* lives in alkaline environments, and that my culture media enable it to develop abnormally. So, then, what do you think, eh? If, all of a sudden...ha ha!"

He became furiously exited again, brandishing his umbrella. "In an hour they go forth! Flesh screams! Blood flows! Everything crumbles! Flee!"

He slipped away, without our being able to make a move to stop him and care for him. He plunged into the dim light of the boulevard. We went to the door and saw him go to an automobile without a chauffeur, into which he bounded, and drove off furiously.

We went back to the drawing room, dolorously impressed. People there were laughing, without any commiseration for that brain afflicted with disequilibrium. Monsieur Serviat declared that a madhouse would collect him before much longer. Then we finished taking tea, talking about the threat of a railway strike that was causing Undersecretary Vigueur far more anxiety than Tornada's predictions.

III

As soon as the soirée was over I went home. My apartment was in the Chaussée de la Muette, in the delightful quarter of Paris bordering the Bois de Boulogne. I plunged into my sheets, but although I was very tired, I could not go to sleep at first. A nagging thought was running through my head, which one word dropped into Tornada's rambling summarized in its entirety.

What was the meaning of the term "macrobe," which he had pronounced several times? Not that I had any trouble establishing its etymology. *Macrobe* was obviously the term opposite to *microbe*, signifying very large, in the same way that the latter term signifies very small. It wasn't necessary to be much of a Hellenist to deduce that. But how big had those animals been able to grow, assuming that the scientist really had developed them abnormally? Would they have a destructive effect as phenomenal as his sinister prophecy indicted?

No! It would become slightly unhinged oneself even to dream of it. And I strove to drive away that stupid anxiety. As it did not cease to recur, I thought about my fiancée, and then about my automobile, which I had just changed in order to buy a more powerful one. My imagination placed Suzanne in the vehicle by my side, while Monsieur Vernet was in the back seat, and I finally departed for a delightful excursion that occupied my entire slumber.

The next morning, I woke up feeling very spry. It required the perception of my newspaper to remind me of the incidents of the previous day. I opened it unhurriedly, without even searching for some sensational headline. Anyway, the rag contained nothing new, except that the railway strike was still threatening. I got dressed and had breakfast cheerfully, and went out under a radiant sky in order to go to the Institut Pasteur on foot.

I felt less enthusiasm than usual to devote myself to my customary tasks that day. Those who love the atmosphere of a laboratory know the veritable satisfaction one experiences in going into rooms bathed with light, putting on the long white smock that is like a uniform for pupils and their masters alike, and sitting down amid the greetings of comrades at the glass-topped table garnished with the hundred various utensils whose precious mechanism and ingenious complication aids bacteriological research. In truth, I felt that I was a very small and very modest cog in the vast factory of health to which the great Pasteur gave the initial impetus, but it seemed that the scientist's memory encouraged my efforts, and that his glorious past was prolonged in my humble labor.

That day, as I said, I took longer than usual to make the journey. I would gladly have let myself idle. The weather was so conducive to dreaming, and nature was putting such seduction into everything! The young leaves on the trees had never been as green, the air was calm, as fluid as the celestial spaces. Everything was vibrant with the joy of spring, and the Seine, which I crossed by the Pont de la Concorde, deliberately extending my route in order to savor the terrestrial beauty more fully, was nothing but a vast crucible in which a thousand diamonds were glittering, given birth by a breeze that was adorable to breathe.

My hopes as a fiancé came into unison with the tenderness scattered over the city; I saw myself a few months older—our marriage was arranged for the middle of August—holding Suzanne in my arms, walking beside the river, initiating her into the marvels of the great liquid way, renewed at every hour of the day, adopting, in accordance with the influence of the light—mist, sunshine, darkness, even rain and storms—such diverse and ever-seductive appearances. The quays silent or animated; the water peaceful with the slumber of boats, or noisy with the bustle of barges, the smoky and whistling passage of steamboats; the bridges crowded of deserted; the reflections of grave monuments or the pure profiles of domes, towers, belfries—yes, the whole river was a poem that I would read with Suzanne, and no power in the world, save for death, would be able to prevent me from traveling it with her.

But I perceived that I was late. I hailed a cab; and, rapidly transported to the Institut Pasteur, I went through the door and reached my laboratory.

As I went in I was surprised to find a highly unusual animation there. Twenty students were surrounding one of my colleagues, who was leaning over a microscope, listening to him pronounce words whose meaning I could not grasp, but to which bursts of laughter replied. I advanced toward them. It was only then that the name of Tornada, which was stimulating their gaiety, reached my ears and reminded me, with a disagreeable—even painful—sentiment, of the previous evening's scene, to which I had not given another thought, so much had my thought built me an ivory tower inaccessible to the actions of others.

"Here's Gérard!" exclaimed my colleague, perceiving me. "You've arrived just in time, my dear friend, to give us your opinion. Put your eye to this microscope..."

I did as I was asked; taking his place, I interrogated the field of the apparatus, which was extremely powerful. I saw there, moving between the two transparent slivers of the preparation, several animalcules of a form that was unknown to me. Magnified a thousand times, they presented a swollen central section with seeming extremities, one a tail and one a head, the latter rather elongated and endowed with a few vibratile movements. The ensemble was, moreover, rather confused, for one can imagine how tiny an animal is that has to be magnified to that extent for one to begin to make it out.

"Do you recognize that dirty beast?" joked my colleague, addressing himself to me.

"No."

"What might it be?" he asked, again.

I consulted the objective again.

"I don't know."

"Well, no, my dear chap; it's the famous *Micrococcus aspirator* of alkaline environments described by Tornada, which we're trying to fatten up by means of his method. I believe, in truth, that we've only succeeded in making it thinner..."

At the tone of his response, and the laughter that broke out around me, I thought he was trying to trick me, by presenting me with one of those microorganisms that abound in nature but that science has not yet classified. Although my research was not orientated in that direction, I did not want, even so, to appear ignorant, and I joined in with the gaiety. However, a sharp interior disturbance contradicted the amusement on my lips, and it was further accentuated when my knowledgeable comrade went on, more seriously: "Yes, that wretched little beast has remained inexorable to all our attempts; we've cared for it and pampered it for months on end, rigorously following Tornada's method—but nothing; it gives its belly the cold shoulder; our cooking isn't to its taste, and I firmly believe that Tornada's paper is nothing but a joke in rather poor taste."

He turned to the students. "Messieurs let's not waste any more of our time on this joke; let's go on to other exercises. If I ever see Tornada again, I'll ask him whether he's making fun of the Institut Pasteur. To work, Messieurs!

A few further ludicrous reflections by the pupils saluted the definitive burial of that research. One offered the straight-faced suggestion that the scientist ought to be trepanned in order to discover the microbes that were inspiring such delirium in his brain. Another proposed extracting therefrom a serum usable in the treatment of madness, although wisdom was also a very tedious malady. A third, finally, regretted the failure of the experiment, because it would have been amusing and lucrative to exhibit the *Micrococcus aspirator* in a menagerie.

"Shutting Tornada in with it dressing him as an animal-tamer, eh? What receipts!"

A new order from my colleague extinguished the juvenile jokes pitilessly, however. Soon, there was nothing to be heard in the room but the discreet noises of a laborious anthill.

For my part, the failure of the scientist's method, and the buffooneries that had been its consequence, had dissipated the malaise and the puerile presentiment that had oppressed me briefly. I started to smile at the vague dread to which the threats of the madman and Commandant Junisseau's revelations concerning the giant laboratory had given a kind of logical consistency.

I resumed my ordinary occupations serenely, and at six o'clock in the evening, satisfied with my day, I escaped from the Institut, like a bird drunk on liberty, in order to go to Monsieur Vernet's house the Boulevard de Sebastopol, where I was to dine.

I was scarcely in the street when I heard a special edition being advertized. I approached the crier, and was able to read in the huge characters of the headline news that stupefied me:

A scientific phenomenon! Public danger! Appearance of giant man-eating animals near Mantes!

I could scarcely believe my ears. I bought the paper and discovered, in no time, quite simply what the newsvendor had just been howling. The paper gave no further details, and the few lines that related the circumstance would have passed unnoticed if the headline had not printed them in such large letters.

I must confess that a little frisson ran through me at first, but the idea occurred to me at the same time that Dardant, the editor of the *Parisien*, had heard Tornada's declaration, and that he was occasionally wont to print "hoaxes"—a hoax excusable on this occasion, to deflect attention from worries about the impending strike. Those reflections reassured me.

I took the Metro, and became even more confident when, having reached the great boulevards, I observed that my opinion was shared by the public. On the sidewalks, on the terraces of the cafés, everywhere, people were reading the newspaper and welcoming the dispatch with bursts of laughter and shrugs.

I bought a bouquet, and it was with a light heart that I crossed my future father-in-law's threshold. I kissed my fiancée's hand and gave her my flowers, and we sat down at the dining-table. That family meal, with its admirable intimacy, distanced me so completely from the external world that it was only at dessert that I thought of unfolding the *Parisien* to show her the news.

It produced the same effect on Suzanne as it had had on me. It seemed to her to be an amusing invention, significant of Dardant's prodigious mercantile talent. But as Monsieur Vernet remained pensive, I was surprised, and asked him what he was thinking.

"Who can tell?" he replied. "Perhaps Tornada isn't completely mad. His paper has merit..."

"So you believe, Monsieur Vernet...?"

"I don't believe anything, my friend; I don't know anything. But..."

He concluded his thought with a vague gesture, which was not very reassuring. As Suzanne was becoming anxious, I said: "Doesn't your friend Marceline Colais live in Mantes? Couldn't she tell us something? Would you care to telephone her?"

"Right away! Right away!" Suzanne approved.

The apparatus was brought to the table, and I obtained a connection easily. My fiancée took one earpiece while I put the other to my own ear. An anxious attention attached us to the apparatus. Suzanne spoke,

"Hello! It's Suzanne Vernet who's telephoning. What's this that the newspapers are saying about anthropophagic animals in your region?"

A burst of laughter replied to us. The young woman did not know anything, had not heard anything, and made fun of our credulity. Just as she said goodbye, however, Suzanne and I went pale. We had heard, quite clearly, a very singular sound coming from the earpiece. It resembled the whistle of a siren, which was followed by a noise similar to that produced by a collapsing house—all dominated by a scream of terror, the sound of a woman panicking.

We were stunned. What drama was unfolding out there, on the other end of the wire?

"My God! What can have happened?" asked Suzanne, shivering.

Then, after a pause that we employed in looking at one another interrogatively, she continued: "My friend's scream…that racket… it's all inconceivable… don't you think so?"

"Try to restore the connection," said Monsieur Vernet.

I tried to interrogate the apparatus again, in vain. Three times, in a nervous voice, I begged for the connection to be restored, but the operator told us that it was impossible to obtain one. A fourth appeal met with the same response.

That episode had bowled us over. We strove, however, to find a reassuring interpretation. We criticized the incompetence of the switchboards and the improbable noises that were heard crackling on the line even in times when they were functioning normally. In truth, out explanations were only designed to make us feel better. The dinner was concluded without enthusiasm, and Suzanne and I bid one another goodnight, with the emotion of lovers whose tenderness is threatened by an evil destiny.

"If ever something happens," she confided to me in a whisper, "come here quickly to find me…"

I promised her that. Once outside, I wanted to clarify the matter. In the splendid nocturnal weather, a trip to Mantes in my forty horsepower Motobloc was a simple excursion. I would therefore go to Mantes. I turned into the boulevard, heading for the Metro that ought to take me to the Chaussée de la Muette. The great artery immediately filled me with anxiety. At a distance, I heard ominous noises, and I saw an agitated crowd swelling. When I arrived at the location of the tumult, however, I found that it was only a demonstration by strikers.

It passed by, and life became normal again at that spot. The theater audiences were spilling out during the intermissions; the display windows of the cafés were ablaze. Some displays imposed their luxury in an orgy of electricity. Open air phonographs and cinematographs in windows gathered spectators. Nothing had changed. It was nocturnal Paris, the elegant good humor of which was not even eroded by the strike.

I went home. I dressed for the road and went to the garage next door to my apartment. My chauffeur, his day's work completed, had gone. At first, I hesitated to undertake the excursion on my own, but, incapable of resisting my curiosity, I switched on two powerful headlights, took my place in the driving-seat, and sped away in my machine, which was soon beyond the toll-booths.

The Bois and the hill to Suresnes were traversed in no time. My powerful and docile vehicle, which had recently been delivered to me by the famous manufacturer Page, carried me along with a magnificent surge, and I listened delightedly to the palpitations of its mechanical heart, as calm and regular going up the hills as coming down them. I passed through the pretty towns on my route—which form an almost uninterrupted border of gracious houses all the way to Saint-Germain—like a whirlwind. After going through Saint-Germain I perceived that I had unwittingly taken the road to Poissy. I was in the middle of deserted woodland, framed by two walls of trees split overhead by a palpitating sky.

No one who has not undertaken such nocturnal escapades can imagine the emotions and the fantastic suggestions imposed by the landscape—to which my obsession gave a particular force. I required all that preoccupation not to get carried away and to retain a measure of composure, and the full glare of my headlights not to mistake for extraordinary animals the foliage that I went past on my route, and the air stirred up by the speed of my passage for their breath. The moon was hidden; I could only see the obstacles revealed by

29

my headlights, and when I had gone past them I thought I was leaving behind an immensity populated by phantoms.

I arrived in Poissy at about half past eleven. I was very glad, after traversing a few silent streets, to come into the middle of a party. A musical competition was keeping the town awake; multicolored illuminations were running along the façades; the main square was animated by an open air ball; and a brass band, playing on a stage covered with garlands, was guiding the gesticulations of uniforms and bright dresses. The sight of that enthusiasm and gaiety made me appreciate the puerility of my fears. Would these people be amusing themselves in that fashion if danger threatened them? Could they be unaware of it?

I stopped my auto in front of a tavern, in order to draw off some moral rearmament more than to warm myself up with a cup of coffee, and I hesitated briefly as to whether to continue my journey. However, as I had promise myself to dissipate my nightmare completely, I got back into the driving seat and stepped on the accelerator again, making a detour in order to rejoin the direct road from Saint-Germain to Mantes.

Now, let me collect my impressions, because the next hour became stupefying, and it was at that moment that I entered veritably into the drama. I remember perfectly that I had completely forgotten the macrobes, and that I had no other thought than savoring the charm of nocturnal tourism, when I arrived within six kilometers of Mantes. My first anxiety was in observing that there were no lights indicating the location of the town—a sign that led me at first to think that I had missed my way.

Surprised to have gone astray on a road that I knew very well, I had stopped to consult my map when a strange echo, coming from a few kilometers away, interrupted my research. It was the roar of a siren, but a very particular roar, deeper in the middle and more highly pitched at the end than the sound produced by the warning devices fashionable to indicate the approach of automobiles. The clamor reminded me exactly of the one I had heard over the telephone. A short silence followed, more frightening than the din, which held me in suspense. Then a second blast burst forth, soon followed by a third, then a fourth, then five and then ten, twenty, in an enormous, frightful concert.

No, there could not be as many automobiles as that. And a terrible suspicion took possession of my mind again. Shivering, I turned my machine round, dimmed my headlights, and climbed up on my seat, directing my eyes toward the enigma of the obscurity. I waited, ready to flee.

I did not have to wait long. My senses, their acuity multiplied tenfold by an anxious curiosity, soon enabled me to perceive that an extraordinary phenomenon was occurring in the vicinity. The roaring had ceased, but it was replaced by sounds that I had great difficulty at first comparing to sounds that I knew. I heard: *Frott…! Frott…! Frott…! Frott..! Frott…!* as if immense iron brooms were being swept over stone. Yes, it resembled gigantic sweeps of a broom clearing the distant ground—and it was getting nearer, without any obvious great rapidity.

Frott…! Frott..! Frott…! the air repeated.

What was happening out there? What hallucinatory horde was raking the terrestrial crust like that? What monstrosities were approaching?

To interrogate the mystery, I knelt down on the seat of my vehicle, and, with my hand clutching the back, I looked in bewilderment in the direction of the town whose lights were extinct.

I had not discovered anything there when my eyes, adapting slightly better to the gloom, distinguished some three kilometers away, surging from a place where I knew there was a dip in the terrain, a confused phosphorescent form, moving unevenly off the road, sometimes to the right and sometimes to the left.

It was impossible for me to estimate the dimensions of the moving object at that distance, but it was certainly very large. In sum I could only compare the visual impression to the one that a green mist would have given me, seen from a long way off, at the moment when it emerged from the ground in order to displace itself by performing zigzags.

In the limpid firmament, the stars stood out without losing any of their brightness—which proved to me that the radiation of the mass as not very vivid. The glimmer sank into a dip in the terrain, then reappeared, closer and more extended, accompanied by several others, whose number gradually increased until I counted a dozen of them. Finally, the entire horizon was occupied by those phosphorescent presences, and the rumble that they allowed to be heard, heavier and more sonorous, soon demonstrated to me that I was dealing with colossal solid displacements.

To describe my terror is an impossible task. The most elementary prudence would have advised me to flee, but an invincible need to know attached me to the unreal spectacle. The creatures drew nearer. The more distinct they came, the more convinced I was that a kind of gigantic arm emerging from them was accomplishing circular gyratory movement, reminiscent of those described by an elephant's trunk, very rapidly.

They were still a good kilometer away, and yet I thought that I could already perceive their breath—unless it was an improbable displacement of air provoked by the rotations of their appendages. And I stayed there, paralyzed and stupid, entirely focused on their luminous progress, only retaining the vaguest consciousness of the fact that they were now approaching with greater rapidity.

Yes, I was still there, hypnotized, when suddenly the sky was filled with the fall of an immense green bolide, which came to land fifty meters away from me, to my right, while I was deafened by the roar of a siren, and a violent blast of air nearly tore me out of my seat.

Then, finally obedient to terror, conscious that I had just escaped death, but that death was still threatening me, I turned round, stamped on the accelerator of my Motobloc and, clinging to my steering-wheel, sped away frantically.

How did I not crash twenty times during that flight at a hundred kilometers an hour? How, with the feeble glare of my dimmed headlights, was I able to avoid ditches and avoid run-ning off the road at bends? It was a pure miracle. Fortunately, French roads are admirable. My whole machine was quiver-ing, creaking and lurching. One might have thought that my panic had infected it.

I went through several silent villages. I remember slow-ing down, as I passed a belated peasant, and shouting at him: "Run! The macrobes are coming!" But he looked at me un-comprehendingly. He must have thought I was mad. Had I not thought Tornada was mad myself? And I resumed my flight. The road seemed to sink behind me, becoming a gulf as soon as I had passed over it.

Before arriving at the forest of Saint-Germain, however, I was ashamed of my cowardice and wanted to make amends with a little humanity. Confident in the advance I had over the fantastic animals, I took the turning toward Poissy again, in order to raise the alarm. Oh, what a fatal inspiration! It must have been half past one when I got there; the nocturnal fête was coming to an end, the dances were languishing, the illu-minations going out. Recognizing a gendarme in the middle of the crowd I asked him to take me to the Maire.

I shall never forget the indignation of that honest munic-ipal officer when, disturbed in his legitimate slumber, he ap-peared at his window still half-asleep, wearing a red headscarf.

"What do you want?" he growled.

"I need to talk to you urgently, Monsieur le Maire," I re-plied. "It's a very serious matter. The life of our fatherland might depend on it."

"Have you put our hand on a spy?"

"No, Monsieur le Maire, it's much more serious, much more serious..."

I divined that he was hesitant, but the presence of the gendarme undoubtedly reassured him, for he closed his win-dow in order to open his door to me soon thereafter, holding a candle-tray in his hand. I followed him into a banal drawing room, and the only memory I have of it that that a Japanese tapestry hanging on one wall immediately attracted my curiosity. It represented a warrior with bristling moustaches aiming his spear at a fantastic animal, the silhouette of which, by an apposite freak of chance, adopted the form of a *Micrococcus aspirator* to which a thick furry pelt had been added. In the state of preoccupation that I was in, that coincidence frightened me, and I spent the entire beginning of my visit—all the time that the Maire took to light an oil lamp—hypnotizing myself with that exotic work of art, not without noticing that my attitude was making the good bourgeois anxious, for he stopped several times to look at me from the corner of his eyes.

"I'm listening," he said, finally, offering me a chair protected by a dust-cover, while he sat down on a sofa, hiding his bare legs under the flaps of a vast dressing-gown.

"Monsieur," I began, forcing myself to speak calmly, "I regret to disturb you at this undue hour, but the peril is at your gates; the macrobes are coming, and as they might invade your town at any moment..."

"The macrobes?"

No, you cannot imagine the physiognomy that the honorable representative of the citizens of Poissy adopted at that moment. I do not know any actor, the funniest of all the buffoons of out theatrical stages, or the most tragic tragedian among the great stars of drama, who could have imprinted his features with such a mixture of bewilderment, stupor and terror. Yes, terror—not of the danger that I had just related to him, but of me. That is, moreover, understandable. I was trembling like an alcoholic; my hair retained the disorder of my flight in the auto, and my eyes were hallucinated by the Japanese tapestry. I must have looked as if I had just emerged from a straitjacket.

"Let's see!" he said, getting up and prudently putting the table between us. "What are macrobes?"

"They're giant animals, Monsieur le Maire, quite similar to the one your tapestry represents---there, you see, on the wall..."

"And where are these animals?"

"Half way along the road from Mantes to Poissy."

"You've seen them?"

"Just now. I was in my car...my car...I had to turn round. You do believe me, Monsieur le Maire?"

"Certainly, my good friend!"

"And you'll warn your fellow citizens, advise them to flee?"

"Certainly—right away..."

How did I not guess that the stupid old man was not planning at that moment a means of immobilizing me? He took a few more steps around the table, still to get away from me—for in my ardor to convince him I had attempted to get closer to him. Then, suddenly, he bounded outside, saying: "Wait here, I'll warn them...I'll be back!"

And he disappeared, turning the key in the lock on the door. Stupefied, I remained patient for a moment; then, finally, understanding my interlocutor's intentions, I became indignant, shaking the door violently. The sound of footfalls responded to my anger. The door opened again; three gendarmes grabbed hold of me, and would not let me go.

A grave individual with long hair, his expression clouded by sleep, was accompanying them. He examined me, looked at my pupils, took my pulse, listened momentarily to the arbitrary vociferations that the arbitrary violence was causing me to utter, and then, taking a few steps back, he held a discussion with the Maire. I could hear what they were saying.

"Yes, yes, he's very excited. A fit, probably, perhaps *delirium tremens*..."

"What shall we do, my dear Doctor?" the Maire asked, anxiously.

"Put him in a safe place! We can't let him go...he might be capable..."

"Where, in a safe place? We don't have a hospital."

"I can only think of the prison."

"Obviously."

"Obviously."

"You'll make your report tomorrow, won't you?" the Maire concluded. "You'll not that we were obliged to lock him up because he's a danger to public safety?" Turning toward me, he added: "Poor fellow."

His testimony of pity did not pacify me. On the contrary, I covered the municipal officer and the physician with the most violent imprecations, which increased their certainty that I was quite mad. The gendarmes shook their heads dolorously. I tried to escape their grip, in vain. The more I struggled, the tighter the vice of their fingers became. I had to confess myself defeated, and allow myself to be tied up with a cord whose knots dug into my flesh. Finally, I was lifted up on to the shoulders of a gendarme in order to be carried to a cell.

The prison was next door to the Maire's house, so we only had a short street to cross. My guardians opened a massive door, dragged me along a corridor and threw me into a square redoubt reeking of ordure and brightly enough lit by a gas-lamp for me to make out a drunkard snoring on the straw.

"Isn't it dangerous to leave them together?" asked the Maire.

"Have no fear," said one of the gendarmes, "given that we've tied him up like a chicken for the oven."

"As for the other, he's out for the count; he'll sleep until tomorrow," added a second uniform.

"And then again, if one of them kills the other, it'll be no great loss to society," the doctor philosophized.

"In that case, my friend, let's go to bed," the ministerial officer concluded, serenely.

The lock grated, my despots' footsteps drew away, and I was left alone with the drunkard.

All these incidents might seem amusingly picturesque to those who are reading them, but I can assure you that I retain an exceedingly melancholy memory of them. During the first few minutes in which I found myself claustrated in that infamous company, my anger dissipated to give way to an anxiety, of which Suzanne and her father, as you can imagine, were the sole objects. I anticipated that I would be locked in that cell for at least a day, the time for a medical investigation to repair the gross error of the Poissy practitioner. What would happen during those twenty-four hours of detention? What formidable events, the menace of which was sweeping the ground out there, in the direction of Mantes—events inaccessible to human will—might prevent me from rejoining my pure fiancée and my venerable friend.

I reflected, fearfully. All the incredible things that I had seen on that sinister evening returned to stand out with irrefutable clarity on the screen of my memory.

Obviously, the mystery still subsisted, with its frightful horror, but there was no doubt that I had been close to those phosphorescent monstrosities; that they were solid bodies of incalculable dimensions; that their whistling, like the noise of a siren, signified an enormous displacement of air; that their progress was accomplished without great rapidity.

One sole point left me hesitant, with regard to that last remark, which was that one roaring mass, the one that had determined my flight at the moment when I perceived the others, had seemed to me to fall from the sky, as if a trampoline had projected it to land beside me. I had then had the deafening sound of its fall in my ears; I remembered having felt the earth vacillate. Did not that fact permit the conclusion that the fantastic animals were, at certain moments, capable of speed, of progressing by means of prodigious bounds?

But those few seconds had gone by in such confusion, and a legitimate terror had attenuated the veritable impression to such an extent, that on reflection, I no longer dared affirm that fall, and that the apparition might, instead of descending from on high, have surged forth from below, when a caprice of the terrain had hid it from me. No, I no longer knew. In my uncertainty, I preferred to rally to the latter hypothesis, inasmuch as my need for personal tranquility also concerned the two dear distant beings, Suzanne and her father, whom my absence tomorrow was bound to torment.

My absence? Why could I not find myself close to them? Why could I not demand of my ingenuity, and my muscular strength, the means of escaping, of getting back to them? My eyes made a tour of the cell; I sounded the thickness of the walls that isolated me from the rest of humankind.

No chance of escape that way; Hercules himself could not have shaken the imposing resistance of the massive stones; a pick-ax, which I did not possess, would have taken days to bite into them.

As for the narrow window that I observed above my head, its orifice was defended by iron bars so voluminous and so solid that I could not even think of separating them—and in any case, the rope that bound me from head to foot was reminding me dolorously of my impotence.

No, before thinking about getting through the door, the only issue that I recognized as possible, it was first necessary for me to get rid of my bonds, and they were laboring my flesh violently enough for me to recognize that there was nothing for me to do but bow to fatality and await the implacable unfurling of events.

I lay my head on the straw that served me as a bed, and a long shiver of distress, as might be caused by the fall into an abyss, ran through me.

"Want summat?" growled a quavering voice, at that moment, beside me.

It was my drunkard. He had just woken up, and after having propped himself up on his elbow, he was looking at me with a blissful smile. He was clad in a dirty, threadbare chestnut-colored costume, some cast-off from a well-to-do wardrobe. His graying hair sent dusty wisps in all directions. His wild and unkempt beard was varnished, under the chin, by a trickle of drool.

"Y'thirsty?" he asked, again.

I turned my head away, sickened. Was I, on top of everything else, to be subjected to the amiability of that repulsive individual?

He seemed, in fact, to be full of the most fraternal intentions toward me. He was still smiling. He belched. Then, interpreting my silence in favor of his sentiments, he tried to move closer to me. He got up, fell back on the straw, and attempted a new thrust, which brought him on to all fours—after which, holding on to a ring sealed into the wall, he succeeded in standing up. Tottering, with his hands in his pocket like a satisfied landowner, he came over to me, studied me for a moment, rejoiced noisily in the inferiority that retained me tied up at his feet, then hiccupped: "Yer a bugeois, no? Not on the social? Me, I am. But so what? All brudders. Ever'thin' aff t'turn upside-down for us all t'be equil. Eh? Get it, m'dear— no mo' bosses…no mo' workus…equility f'r all! And feet for'ard! Eh? What'yer say?"

Oh, that ignoble language, which might perhaps have moved me to pity on any other occasion, but which took on I don't know what prophetic significance that night! Evidently, if the nightmare that I had lived near Mantes for intense minutes were ever realized, if I were not dreaming, if I were not mad, all the democratic ambition of my drunkard, the great social leveling that was the obsession of the humble, was about to be accomplished before long, as the normal conclusion of a biological adventure. Evidently, from one moment to the next, the classes might no longer exist, wealth no longer differentiating people, and parallelism would be established under the threat of a common danger. Would they be effective, then, the theories that I had heard emerging from other mouths than those of libertarians, when sociologists had predicted in my presence that science would accomplish the egalitarian work rejected by charity? Alas, could I imagine that the hour might offer itself so precociously, in circumstances so dramatic, under the influence of a laboratory discovery?

And once again, I was brought back to thinking about Tornada by the divagations of my cellmate.

I decided, however, that I ought to be obedient to circumstances, and perhaps make use of my occasional philosopher. I turned my gaze toward him. He was pitiful, repulsive and terrible. In the gaslight that struck his face, the expression of his physiognomy was suddenly modified. His smile was transformed into a rictus; he passed from affection to hatred.

His beard bristled, his eyes filled with an evil gleam. I understood that I had become the focal point of a long rancor.

"Bastard!" he howled, raising his fist. "No mo' bugeois! Absint' for ev'ry cit'zen, f'rever!" Drawing closer to me, he added: "Say: death t'cops!"

And when I remained obstinately silent, he repeated the order: "Gwan, say death t'cops!"

I would certainly have granted him that exclamation in order to have peace. I even began to pronounce it, when my complaisance froze on my lips. The drunkard, obedient to his interior rage, had just taken out a knife, and was leaning toward me. I confess that I felt a rather disagreeable frisson pass through me.

"Y'don'wanter? Well, I'm gwant'bleed yer."

He made the gesture. I saw the flash of the blade heading toward my immobility.

But the knife, fortunately misdirected by the alcoholic, missed its target and lodged instead in the gap between my torso and my arm, while the effort projected my would-be murderer on to the ground, from which he tried in vain to get up again. Fearful, nevertheless, of a further attempt, using the only means of avoidance permissible to me, I rolled over and over for several meters—and at that moment I had the particularly intoxicating impression of being liberated from my bonds.

It had in fact, been the case that, while my adversary's weapon had not succeeded in stabbing me, it had severed the rope that wound around me, in such a fashion that, by a blessed hazard, instead of annihilating me, his action had freed me.

I conceived such gratitude for the drunk that my first sentiment, once I was untied, was to put my hand to my fob-pocket, in order to recompense him generously for his failed crime—but I did not have to carry out the intention; the drunkard had fallen asleep where he was, arching his lips into a new smile, as if the soul of justice were translated on his face.

From then on, my escape plan was easy to conceive and carry out. At daybreak, when one of the gendarmes came to check on the condition of his two prisoners, I pounced on him and, planting my head in his chest, sent him flying into the corridor. I stepped over the representative of order, without taking pity on his groans, and found myself running in the open air.

A few peasants arriving for the market saw me pass by with amazement. Needless to say, they put down their baskets in order to pursue me, for the mentality of the crowd is so formulated that any man running without a reason immediately inspires the idea that he is a criminal, but I had a sufficient start on them to give myself the infantile satisfaction of breaking a few windows in the mayor's house; after which I leapt into my Motobloc—which, fortunately, was still parked under his windows—and took the road to Paris without worrying any further about sparing such stupidly-governed citizens from the disaster.

Amazingly, the great city was waking up in absolute calm. In the Chaussée de la Muette, the shops were opening as usual, the little people were setting off for their customary work. I parked my auto at the sidewalk, ran to buy the newspapers, and observed with surprise that they had no information. Even the *Parisien* had fallen silent about the event and had retracted the news that it had published the day before, attributing it to the work of a practical joker. On the other hand, it devoted a great deal of space to the railway strike, and I learned thus that the Nord, the Est and the Orléans had suspended their departures for lack of staff.

"The work of a practical joker!" I sniggered, crumpling the newspaper

Those words immediately dilated before me with a sinister amplitude. I could not leave them with the banal significance that the reporter had wanted to give them, and they provoked a new bitterness within me. A practical joke was, indeed, about to be played on the nation, but what a joke, concluding with what consequences!

The silhouette of the man who had planned it sprang forth again in my memory. I saw him again, coming into my future father-in-law's drawing room, devoting himself during the early part of the evening to placid conversation, welcoming the homage of those who venerated his science, shunning his detractors, offering my fiancée, in the form of poetry, the adornment of a mind that was able to detach itself from the arid problems of biology, and also seemed to be accessible to charm, tenderness, pity and dolor—and suddenly, at the moment when the clock had announced the opening of another day, rising up like a horrible prophet, declaiming to a elite with an incoherence of language, a dementia of gestures, at which, alas, I could to longer be content to smile pityingly.

Yes, it was a joke: a horrible joke.

I could not free my memory from it. I gazed with dazed eyes at the unfortunate traders who had no suspicion of the menace, and who would soon become its victims. The street, whose picturesque bustle ordinary offered me so much attraction at that hour, when the great city placidly prepares for its daily work, filled me this time with an unprecedented dolorous melancholy.

While I generally held the effort of those laborious shopkeepers in high esteem, deeming a social benefit their promptitude in rising early, running to the Les Halles, making their purchases and coming back just as rapidly to display their wares, organize their deliveries, decorate their windows and satisfy the needs of their clientele; while I admired their tenacious economy, their savings acquired sou by sou, which, converted into shares and bonds, constituted the fortune and strength of our nation relative to foreign nations; while they confirmed the impression in me that the fate of a people is subordinate to the work of the humble, and that the initiative from below takes precedence over everything that radiates from above—that morning, by contrast, their tranquil energy exasperated me. Were they not about to be the turkeys of that formidable practical joke, tomorrow, or perhaps today?

Veritably, their gait seemed to me to have taken on something turkey-like: they were heavy and flat, waddling like poultry—and if they had been warned, they would certainly have started uttering the incredulous clucking of a poultry-yard!

I remained on the pavement momentarily, in that disconcerting contemplation. An open bakery dispatched the flavorsome aroma of fresh warm loaves in my direction. I breathed it in without allowing myself to be tempted. I soon saw a shopgirl come out, her hair tousled, her expression still clouded by sleep, holding a piece of paper in her hands, wrapped around a few croissants just out of the oven. She was graceful; she characterized in her modest garments the elegance particular to young Parisiennes. Simply by the way she tucked up her skirt, she testified to the artistic character of her race.

She considered my appearance with astonishment—my animal skin and the dirt on my face. Before stepping off the sidewalk to cross the road she paused beside my auto and examined the bodywork with a knowing expression, approving of it with a nod of the head. One last glance that she darted at me seemed to demand a place in the vehicle, evocative of open spaces, rapid travel beneath the blue sky, through landscapes caressed by the sun. The she drew away, hurrying to work.

Little shopgirl, if you had known the terror that reigned within me, would you have implored me with that tacit prayer?

I consulted my watch. It was not yet seven o'clock. A sentiment of reserve, incomprehensible in the circumstances, a dread of disturbing my friends so early, advised me to put off for a little while the moment when I would arrive to throw fear into their peaceful intimacy. I sat outside a café and ordered a glass of milk, which I forgot to drink.

Weary of the earth, of everything that moved upon it and everything that was in preparation for it, I looked up momentarily at the sky. What a contrast! Up there, everything expanded in a delightful fluidity. A blaze of dawn light flowed from the adorably blue infinity over the rooftops, bringing out against a golden background the jutting balconies of a recently-constructed tall building, proud of its novelty among others more ancient. Would that order still subsist tomorrow? Would that architectural décor, terminating a centuries-of esthetic tradition, edified by the genius of a people, be standing much longer? Would it not crumble, collapse and fall apart, like Messina in its recent convulsion,[7] under the brutal effect of monsters?

But no; that was implausible, and I had to smile at my dread. And I focused, as the objective of my illusions and my hopes, on a little curly cloud drifting in the celestial softness. Its tranquility comforted me. I could not imagine disaster surging from such placid harmony, beneath such a reassuring firmament.

I swallowed my glass of milk; I called the waiter to settle up with a ten franc piece, and while waiting for him to bring me my change I picked up my newspaper again in order to confirm my quietude—for it seemed implausible to me that a calamity as redoubtable as the one whose advent I dreaded could be unsuspected in its columns.

Again, my search was in vain; all the reportage, from the masthead to the stop press, was taken up by calculating the effects of the rail strike. And I became indignant that the Nord, the East and the Orléans had suspended their traffic for lack of personnel.

"It's truly a fine time for those animals to go on strike!" I could not help saying to the waiter, who came back carrying a saucer containing coins.

He looked me up and down. I judged him to be a rude and frustrated citizen, one of those people who judge the enemy by the cut of his waistcoat and would make a meal of a well-dressed man. God knows, however, what my costume

---

[7] The city of Messina, in Sicily, was almost completely destroyed by an earthquake on 28 December 1908.

looked like! But my auto was there, testifying to my wealth and the privilege of my class.

The waiter cleaned the marble table-top with swipe of a dish-cloth and riposted: "Isn't it always the moment? Demands have no time limit. The longer the proletariat waits, the more they'll suffer. Why shouldn't they profit from the occasion, citizen?"

"What occasion, my friend?"

I expected a response that related to my inner anguish.

"Well, the occasion..."

"Again, what?"

"You want me to spell it out? You know very well."

"I don't know anything," I insisted.

"Citizen Bitard, secretary of the C.G.T. has been arrested," he declared.[8]

"Oh, my friend, he's not the one that it's necessary to arrest!"

He expressed his surprise with a violent swipe of his dish-cloth. "Who, then?"

"It's them."

"Them?"

"Yes, them... the others... out there!"

I remember his disdainful, indignant expression, and the manner in which he expressed his opinion of how I had spent the night, simulating the gesture of drinking to imply that I was drunk. I neglected to make him revise his sentiment, for I got up abruptly and abandoned the table, forgetting to pick up my change.

The railway strike suddenly appeared to me as a further complication aggravating the probable situation. The social catastrophe, even if it did not spread to other lines, would immobilize and paralyze an entire city just at the moment when an exodus might become necessary. What would become of those people without a means of flight at the time when it was

---

[8] La Confédération Générale du Travail was—and still is—one of the principal trade unions in France.

necessary to flee? What an untimely obstacle, due to the imbecilic pressure of a few troublemakers!

I felt the need to get back to my fiancée as soon as possible. Having climbed back into my vehicle I took the quickest and least encumbered route to reach the Boulevard de Sebastopol—but I had reckoned without the vicissitudes that still awaited me.

Thinking that the streets would be deserted at that early hour I was going along the Seine, intending, once I reached the Châtelet, to make a turn that would bring me directly to the house of my future father-in-law, when, having reached the level of the Quai d'Orsay railway station, I ran into a violent crowd that the police were having difficulty containing. I don't know how many thousands of hotheads were there, inflamed by anger and alcohol, thundering imprecations and raising arms at the ends of which cudgels where twirling, while, in the distance, a black mass disposed in six ranks—a cohort of the central brigades—were waiting to be given orders by a short Prefect of Police surrounded by a general staff of peace officers and conferring with them.

My car had reached the outer eddies of that crowd, and, perched in my seat, I contemplated the spectacle with all the more passion because I wanted to find therein a confirmation of my secret dread, to believe that I was facing a people conscious of the danger that threatened them and preparing the resistance. But I soon had to abandon that idea when I had interrogated by a gamin who, having climbed up on to a streetlight, was encouraging the demonstration with his acidulated clamors. Just as he was about to reply to me, I saw him suddenly go pale, direct his arm westwards and shout: "There they are! There they are!"

I turned round, expecting giant apparitions, but I only perceived a sparkle of helmets dominating the stature of warhorses. It was the dragoons, summoned to bar the strikers' route as they were preparing the cross the Seine and sack the Quai d'Orsay station. Their mass, projecting the flashes of weapons, soon stopped behind me, an opaque and menacing

46

animal barrier, toward which the central brigades, suddenly going into action, began to drive the demonstrators, herding them with a reckless savagery—with the result that I was trapped between the two parties, cursing the fury of both, watching, with the sole desire to escape as quickly as possible from the pitiless impacts of whirling sabers and cudgels, the cries of the wounded, the falling bodies and the splashes of blood that thrusts directed at heads and faces caused to spring forth.

Soon, a frantic revolutionary brandishing a stick at the end of which hung a red handkerchief leapt on to my car to rally his companions, and I became the center of the battle. Fortunately, the agents could only succeed in making roads into the first ranks of the crowd; an armor composed of ten human tampons protected me from their ranks. My mudguard and headlights gave way under the pressure, I heard their splintering mingled with the vociferations, and I was already fearing for the more precious mechanisms of my engine when, before a more desperate charge by the strikers, the police yielded, broke ranks and retreated. I took advantage of it to back up slowly, heading toward the dragoons, who were charging in their turn, and who, when they reached me, divided their ranks in order to let me through.

From then on, I was uninterested in the outcome of the collision. I scarcely noticed it when a fanatic with the face of a boar grabbed a horse by the nostrils and unsaddled the rider, who was trampled by other horses, and when a peace officer of giant stature, shaking off a cluster of hooligans intent on destroying him, was cut down by a saber-thrust that a maladroit dragoon had intended for one of his adversaries. I had only one urgency: to escape as quickly as possible and get back to my fiancée; and after having turned the vehicle round, I was about to depart, leaving those stupid energies at odds when a female voice emerging from a group of spectators planted on the sidewalk called to me: "Monsieur Gérard! Monsieur Gérard!"

Your name, shouted from the middle of a crowd—especially a crowd subject to such a delirium—is always somewhat impressive. I turned round.

"You, Madame Danielli!" I exclaimed.

I had just recognized a celebrated pythoness. Madame Danielli hosted a famous salon simultaneous frequented by naïve spiritists, skeptical scientists and a few artists and satirical writers. One could not, however, resist her elegant youthfulness and her tragic mask, afflicted by numerous successes of second sight. Combining cleverness and distinction with her remarkable gifts of mediumship, she was welcomed in the best society, and fished for her clients in the troubled open waters of worldly credulity. She announced everyone's destiny after reading the lines on their hands, and, it was said, the fate of peoples did not escape her when she consulted the reflection of the stars by night in the transparency of a lake she owned in Italy. She adapted to her prophecies the phenomena and the instrumentation of recent discoveries in science; radium was in her domain; she applied it by some unknown method to the materialization of the perispirit and the astral body.[9] In sum, she offered a curious complication of good faith and trickery that I had detected on the two evenings when I had allowed myself to be dragged to her house by one of my friends, a professor in the Faculté de Médecine.

"You here, Madame?" I repeated.

"Do you blame me for having got up early to come and observe an event that I had predicted a long time ago?"

---

[9] "Perispirit" was a term frequently employed French spiritism, having been invented by its most influential pioneer, Allen Kardec. It refers to a hypothetical "fluid body": a subtle substance improvised by a spirit in order to connect with the sensory perceptions of observers. Basically a refinement of the idea of a ghost, it has some kinship with the Theosophist notion of an "astral body," which was a later invention than Kardec's and was more widely popularized.

She was triumphant; her physiognomy did not reveal any compassion for the outrages that were being perpetrated before her eyes. On the contrary; her teeth were dazzling in a radiant smile, all the more so because a flattering approval, emitted by the snobs surrounding her, was supporting her victory.

"Ah! You predicted it!"

The most suspicious intelligences pass through phases of credulity. It is at moments of sentimental crisis, when nerves tensed for too long leave you in a kind of psychic inferiority. You then become prey to a confidence for which you will criticize yourself in calmer moments; you allow yourself to submit to puerile investigations of your self—and history reports such weakness among great captains and the most notorious political schemers. Suddenly, that was my case.

"Is this the only event you predicted for the present epoch?" I asked her, awaiting her response with such an expression of interest that she understood immediately that I was about to fall under her influence.

"No."

Then, taking a further step, I said: "Can you tell me something I know, which perhaps I'm the only person to know, which will be manifest today or tomorrow?"

"Certainly," she affirmed, with conviction.

"I'm listening."

With a gesture, she asked her entourage to move aside. She seemed to isolate herself from the external world. Her features dressed themselves with mystical suffering. Her gaze widened, became hallucinated, and penetrated mine. It also seemed to me that my brain received some kind of fluid discharge sent by hers, and I shivered.

"What I have to tell you," she murmured, her lips almost joined, leaning her suddenly-stiffened silhouette toward me, "is that it's necessary for you to get out of Paris as soon as possible, taking those who are dear to you with you."

"Why?"

"A peril is in preparation for you....it's coming...it's getting closer..."

"What?"

"An incredible event...yes, truly incredible..."

"Once again, what?"

She hesitated. Her throat appealed for air as if a hand were blocking its entrance. I noticed that the veins of her neck were distended, tracing blue lines beneath the nacre of her skin. Her eyebrows coming together, her forehead furrowed, she continued: "What? I can't tell you, exactly. It's a phenomenon so unfamiliar, so strange..."

"I want to know," I insisted.

"Well, I see large arms reminiscent of elephants' trunks...but are they really arms? Can arms terminate in shocks of long hair divided in two? I can see them, though; they're agitating...they're agitating in front of a green terrain...but a green that isn't that of nature...one might rather take it for a green fog...and I can see little animals...yes, tiny, very tiny...as tiny microbes running over a sofa...in a drawing room where a young woman is smiling..."

"Go on! Go on!" I begged, observing that her nervous exaltation seemed to be coming to an end.

I did not obtain anything more. Suddenly, she went pale, and her eyes wandered. She tottered, and her companions only just had time to leap forward to catch her in their arms. That was the way that her divinatory crises usually concluded.

I did not stay to care for her. Subject to the suggestion of her prediction, in which I detected, among the incoherence of its imagery, a confused fraction of truth, I fled; I spend toward the Boulevard de Sebastopol, going via the Place de la Concorde and the main roads.

I have often reflected since then about the curious oracle of the young pythoness. I do not believe in occultism or any supernatural manifestation, but it is certain that an order of divinatory phenomena exists, which science is already attempting to explain, and of which it will succeed one day or another in unraveling the threads of the mystery.

With regard to my own case, I believe I can confirm that Madame Danielli—who, it will be noted, told me nothing that I did not already know—had extracted the elements of her prediction from me. How? Simply by reading the thoughts that my disorientated mind had delivered to her as easily as a book recounts an individual's sentiments. Endowed with a particularly sensitive nervous system, the perspicacity of which is not attenuated by the location or the circumstances, she penetrated my soul, received its impressions by means of the same mechanism by which wireless telegraphy puts two distant poles in communication; she only repeated back to me what she had discovered within me.

That conviction is also inspired in me by the disjointed and baroque fashion in which she translated the images which, at that emotional moment, were vibrant within my skull. When she embellished the microbes' trunks with "shocks of long hair divided in two" it's probable that I was thinking at that moment about the characteristic shape of Tornada's beard, and that the seeress only glimpsed that particularity, which she grafted on to the appendices of the giant animals. In the same way, the green terrains and green fog that she had mentioned were a confusion of two impressions I had retained from my nocturnal excursion, one resulting from the monsters' phosphorescence, the other from the extent of the ground over which they were moving. And the same explanation appeared to me to attach to the final phrase of her discourse, for the "tiny microbes running over a sofa in a drawing room where a young woman is smiling" doubtless derived from the memory I hastily invoked, while she was reading me, of the original soirée of the drama, when my fiancée and I had discussed Tornada's scientific pretensions and the madman had announced their realization by bounding on to a sofa in the middle of my future father-in-law's drawing room.

In order to make the matter even more comprehensible, I will say that my mind, at the moment when the pythoness was documented it, was similar to a disordered cinematograph, turning at such a speed, and so incoherently, that the person

51

reading its impressions could only transmit them in the form of blurred visions superimposed on one another.

At any rate, what the young woman had said had troubled me strangely. I added it to all the supernatural aspects of that frightful adventure, and began to feel an indescribable distress. It seemed to me that my reason was tottering on the brink of an abyss, and I began to wonder seriously whether the diagnosis of the physician who had had me locked up in the prison at Poissy as a madman might not offer some appearance of logic after all. The sentiment that persisted from that descent into doubt was fear, an atrocious fear, which made my hand tremble on the steering-wheel of my auto, distilling a cold sweat on my temples.

I passed furiously through the Place de la Concorde, the Rue de la Paix and the great boulevards. At the corner of the Boulevard Sebastopol I scraped another automobile; it was a miracle that I did not reduce my vehicle to smithereens. I greeted the accusations and insults of the people who witnessed the collision with a snigger; I passed on, and finally arrived at my friends' house.

I found Monsieur Vernet and my adorable fiancée there, well rested by a good night's sleep, finishing their breakfast. What a sovereign peace there was in that interior, where those two elite individuals lived! What comfort and consolation there was in that familial vision! Succeeding the anxieties that I had just traversed, and preceding a drama whose horror I could foresee, I knew the price of the gentle intimacy of that hearth. I went into it with the wonderment of a disaster-victim escaping from devouring flames or engulfing waters.

The table was set in the dining room; a clean tablecloth with red stripes forming rectangles, covered the tabletop; the white bowls and metal receptacles exhaled the flavorsome odor of milky coffee; crusty bread-rolls rounded their backs in the vicinity of delicate butter; the silverware gleamed placidly. Around the meal there was a restful ambience: a Provençal dresser dormant beneath its centenarian patina, supporting red-tinted copper pans; a bread-basket like a cage with lustrous bars; the antique clock, with the regular tick-tock of its swinging pendulum; the preciously polychromatic plates decorating the walls; the modernized chandelier still opposing its candles to the electric switch; and the deep, shaggy, soft Orient carpet, into which the feet sank, easing the difficulty of walking, making you forget that elsewhere, it was necessary to crush in order to advance in life...

There, in that limpid décor, my friends were inaugurating their day. Suzanne had tied back her hair in a hasty torsade; a mauve peignoir liberally espoused her harmonious figure; she was imparting the confidences of her young heart to her father with a happy loquacity: the impressions of a fiancée's happiness, which the night had cradled and appeared in the morning fresher and even more radiant.

Monsieur Vernet, already dressed in order to give his lecture, attenuating by the gentleness and bounty of his venerable face the austerity offered by his costume of frock-coat and black cravat, was listening, with his elbows on the table, reflecting in the adoration of his eyes the charm to which he was subject. Oh, how far they were from the implausible peril with which I was about to poison their conversation, when I irrupted into the dining room, and threw myself, utterly exhausted by fatigue and emotion, on to a chair that Suzanne offered me.

I stammered my odyssey; I recounted my frightful night, my adventure in the darkness, my peril in confrontation with the phosphorescent monsters; and the tragic voice of the sirens, and the fall of the green bolide, which must have been a monster's leap; and my return amid the abysm of the roads, and my sojourn in prison.

I glimpsed an anxious interrogation in their eyes; I understood that they too were beginning to doubt my mental condition.

"Come on, my boy, are you quite certain of what you're saying?" Monsieur Vernet asked, to begin with.

"Unless I've gone mad," I objected.

"Oh no, it isn't that, thank God, that I'm supposing...but you might, while accomplishing the journey that you've described to us, have been influenced by a suggestion from the previous evening. The mysterious troubles the bravest, and the imagination is exasperated under the influence of fatigue. It's a physiological phenomenon noted by science, and it has been observed that dreams are thus transported into reality. Come on, think hard: ask yourself whether you were not asleep in the seat of your car when you stopped before Mantes?"

"It's possible...it sometimes happens, in sleep..." Suzanne added, trying to soften the impact.

When I sketched a negative gesture, Monsieur Vernet continued.

"I remember that during the war of 1870, one night when I was posted as an advance sentinel, I went to sleep under the exhaustion of overwork. In my mind, haunted by the invasion, a suggestion was then produced in which I mingled the enemy—who, however, were not occupying the département in which we were camped. I saw an entire Prussian army pass by in the moonlight, and imagined that it was accomplishing a flanking movement with the intention of surrounding us and crushing us.

"I only experienced that dream for about five minutes, during which I remained upright, with my back against a tree, but when I woke up, the impression of it was so clear, so persistent, so absolute that I confused my orders with my imagination and fired a rifle shot to warn my companions of the danger; after which I flew to the advance posts, where I recounted with the greatest sincerity—as you have just done, my friend—what my mind had created during my brief slumber. The regiment moved off, ready to do battle, but it was observed the following morning that no Prussians were there—any more, I hope than monsters were there last night, in the vicinity of Mantes."

"No!" I exclaimed. "I swear to you that I have not been the victim of a hallucination of that kind! I had full mastery of my brain when I saw what I've reported to you."

I resumed my story; I put so much effort into convincing them, brought forth so many plausible details, so many precise memories, and supported them with scientific reflections establishing so clearly the integrity of my faculties, that they finally allowed themselves to be infected by my anguish.

We discussed the consequences of the event at length. They did not seem to me to be as frightful as I had been led at first to imagine them.

"In the twentieth century, damn it, it would be very surprising if people couldn't defend themselves against animals!" asserted Monsieur Vernet, raising his head with a challenging expression.

"Evidently, we have cannons whose force of projection is incalculable," agreed my fiancée.

"We have explosives that can blast through the walls of fortresses and the steel of armor-plate," Monsieur Vernet insisted.

"We have toxins, we have all the treasures of chemistry!" I enthused, adding another dimension of possibility to the measures of destruction.

"The government will take action!" the scientist affirmed.

"Has it even been alerted?" I said, doubtfully.

"It seems implausible to me that it hasn't, my friend."

And, deciding the employment of my morning, which I had intended to spend waiting with my fiancée, the worthy man gave me his advice: "Go to the Ministry of Posts. See Vigueur on my behalf; demand the truth, which he might perhaps be hiding from the public, and get him to tell you exactly how grave the danger is. We'll decide what to do thereafter."

"But what if it's too late?" I objected.

Nevertheless, I did as the scientist said.

My driving costume, which I had not had time to change, caused the ushers some disquiet; I had a great deal of difficulty getting as far as the minister. Fortunately, a cabinet attaché recognized me under my animal-skin and had the doors opened for me.

I was had only just arrived in the minister's office, and had begun to tell him about my adventure, to which he was listening with the pitying indulgence that the language of lunatics provokes, when a communication from the telegraph office informed us that after Mantes, communication by wire with Le Havre had been cut off.

"There must have been a storm," said the minister, with absurd confidence.

"No, Monsieur, it's the macrobes."

He looked at me with even more pity. This time, however, I was convinced. I no longer had the right to doubt my reason. Was not the interruption of telegrams a further proof that had just been added to all those I had accumulated during my mysterious nocturnal encounter?

I left the minister, searching feverishly for a means of escaping the terrible approach. It seemed to me to be utterly imprudent to await events and to depend on human resistance. Was it not a legitimate egotism that commanded me, first of all, to ensure the retreat of my future family, and my own?

Spurred on by the memory of what Tornada had said— "Flee! Flee without losing a minute! Flee tomorrow!"—and regretting that we had already lost one day, it was under the lash of a whip that I returned to my fiancée's home.

Suzanne was alone, Monsieur Vernet having thought that he ought not to miss his lecture at the Collège de France. I had never seen the dear child so tenderly emotional, and simultaneously so resolute in the face of the decision to be made.

"Listen, my dear Jean," she said, "I don't know what these macrobes are, or what real danger they pose, but my heart—and you know very well what renders it vigilant— advises me that we should leave. At the rate at which you tell me they're advancing, they probably won't reach Paris for two days. We still have time, therefore. Would you like us to leave together, tomorrow?"

"This evening, Suzanne, this evening!"

"Well, all right then, this evening! It will be our anticipated honeymoon voyage, and I'll easily convince Papa to leave..."

She smiled, adorably sad. Confident in her good sense, I asked her: "In what direction shall we go, my dear Suzanne?"

"Southwards, eastwards or northwards, since the west is occupied by the enemy."

"Alas, Suzanne the railways to the north and east are on strike."

"The P.L.M., then," she said, trenchantly. "We'll meet at seven o'clock in the buffet at the Gare de Lyon, shall we? We'll take the nine o'clock express to Marseilles."

I accepted enthusiastically. If she had been taking me toward Mantes I would still have followed her. Each of her words was a command, which I accepted while blessing her.

IV

Immediately after leaving Suzanne, I went in haste to the garage in which I had put my car a short while before. I wanted to be ready for any eventuality, and I had a notion that my auto might be useful.

The garage was not far from my apartment, and I had hired a compartment therein reserved for my exclusive use. Do I have any need to say that Jules, my chauffeur, was one of those ingenious and shady Parisians, of whom automobilism has cultivated so many? But he adored his car, and made it a point of honor to look after it in such a way that it was always ready to take to the road. Every morning he cleaned it and checked the engine, and as the task was generally finished before ten o'clock, I hoped to be able to count on my machine that day.

It was a great disappointment to me when I found my mechanic still hard at work. Clad in a blue smock, his arms bare and his face stained with grease, he had taken off the dashboard and was striving to repair one of the components. As soon as he saw me he raised his arms in the air.

"There you are!" he proclaimed. "I don't know what Monsieur was doing with his auto last night, and I don't know where Monsieur went, but Monsieur must surely have run into a few ditches. All the bolts are loose, the float isn't working..." He pointed at the rear of the vehicle: "And Monsieur had broken a spring!"

I was on the point of telling him about my nocturnal excursion and the extraordinary surprise that had motivated my flight at a hundred kilometers an hour, without headlights, along dark roads, to the point that he would be surprised that my machine had not been completely demolished, but an instinctive prudence, compounded out of egotism and lack of confidence in my servant's discretion arrested the confidence on my lips. Anyway, was I sure of what I had been about to tell him? Had I not undergone a fantastic adventure of which I was still in doubt myself?

My story would only have aroused the incredulity and laughter of the workers surrounding me. Everyone is aware of the camaraderie, the kind of freemasonry, that unites the workers of the sport, and my revelations would not have taken long to be passed around, covering me with ridicule. I had too much to repent of my loquaciousness in Poissy; that first experiment had been too fertile in disappointment, and I was still aching from it. So I preferred to keep silent, while resolving to take Jules with me.

"How long will the repairs take?" I asked.

"They'll require a good two or three hours, Monsieur; and that's not counting the spring, which will probably take me all afternoon. Strictly speaking, though, that can wait until tomorrow, if Monsieur isn't taking passengers."

"But I'm taking Monsieur and Mademoiselle Vernet, Jules, and we're leaving for a long journey?"

"Monsieur can't put it off?"

"That's impossible."

Desperately, I turned my anxiety toward the other mechanics, nodding my head in their direction. "Will they help you? I'll pay what's necessary."

"Monsieur can see that they're all busy."

I lowered my head—but what my chauffeur said next caused me to raise it again instantly.

"Then again," he said, "I don't know what's going on…it's definitely the day for things to go wrong…two of my mates who left for Rouen with their bosses and should have returned this morning haven't come back. They've probably had a breakdown."

I had a frightful vision. In spite of my uncertainty, my ignorance of the reality of the dancer, and the confusion of my nocturnal impressions, I immediately created a frightful legend. I imagined the unfortunates encountering the monsters, and being subject to assaults whose nature I could not conceive, but in which were mingled effusions of blood and the crushing of flesh, as Tornada had announced in Monsieur Vernet's house during his fit of prophetic madness. That thought contracted my physiognomy to such an extent that my chauffeur perceived it,

"Is Monsieur in pain?" he asked.

"Yes, Jules, I'm not very well."

"Monsieur would do better to rest instead of wanting to go out on the road."

"Rest? No, Jules, I can't, because..." I didn't finish. An atrocious anxiety, even more than an interested reserve, caused me to change the tenor of my reply. "You're right, Jules; I'll go to bed." And one last time, I urged him: "Hurry up, my friend, hurry up!"

I left and headed for home. Not being able to depend on my car, I decided to take a fiacre to the Gare de Lyon at the appointed hour. In the meantime I would have time to pack my bags and repair the heavy insomnia that was weighing down on me. I went along the street slowly, without thinking about getting something to eat in a restaurant, although it was lunch time.

What astonished me most of all was the placidity of people who were continuing their indolent existence, when so much anxiety was eating me up inside. They didn't know anything, then? They didn't suspect anything? They were going past me, rubbing shoulders with me, with an air of indifference. Some were reading their newspapers; others were walking dogs; others were displaying themselves in open carriages and deeming it normal that their coachmen were not whipping the horses in order to flee, that their chauffeurs were filling up their gas tanks in order to reach distant regions.

I had a temptation to run to them, to shout at them to get ready to leave, to protect their loved ones. I was like a drunken man irritated by the tranquility of the crowd, an anarchist awaiting the disaster who also wants to let the secret of his vengeance explode. A fat woman who was putting on airs beneath a mauve umbrella annoyed me to the point that I wanted to slap her face. When my concierge called to me to hand me my letters as I passed her lodge, I shuddered and looked at her with a fearful expression.

"Monsieur didn't come home last night," she said, suggestively, with an indulgent smile.

I reached the elevator and pressed the button for the third floor. Curiously enough, the fact of being lifted off the ground caused my ideas to change. Once I was in the cage, I gradually yielded to a confidence as calm as my fears had been agonizing a minute before. No, it wasn't possible that the century that utilized electricity so easily as a means of transport, which challenged distance by the manipulation of steam, perfected destruction by inventing terrible weapons, and reckoned with air and water by the simple use of gasoline-powered propellers, could be incapable of responding to an invasion of animals emerged from a test-tube in a laboratory. Oh, how illogical I was being, given my science! My cerebral mechanism must have been disrupted by insomnia and emotion!

Having reached my apartment I was glad to observe the absence of my domestic, and also irritated by it. Remembering that I had given him orders that would keep him out all day, I went to the lumber-room, seized a leather trunk of respectable dimensions, dragged it into my room and got ready to start filling it.

But what should I put in the trunk? Where were we going? How long would we be away? Would we be cold or hot? Oh, a curious engagement voyage. I piled in clothes at random. One detail, which makes me smile now, and demonstrates the extent to which Suzanne was occupying my thoughts: I equipped myself, in anticipation of a long sojourn in her company, with three pairs of silk pajamas in pastel shades, which I had bought to adorn the coquetry of the first days of our marriage.

Nevertheless, while occupying myself with these garments, my mind never ceased to envisage the cruel problem of the moment. From time to time I stopped, went to stand in front of my mirror, and considered the lines engraved in my face by worry. I was pale, my forehead striped by two furrows; sweat that was not engendered by the temperature moistened the roots of my hair; a feverish tremor agitated my fingers. I no longer recognized in that image the calm fellow who, two days previously, had counted so radiantly on the future embellished by the promises of his marriage.

I was in the middle of my preparations when I heard carriages passing by heading for the races at Saint-Cloud. That exodus in the direction of the danger returned all my uncertainty. I could not conceive that, in twelve hours, and event of such importance had not reached the ears of Parisians, when Mantes was scarcely fifty kilometers away from the capital. Obviously, the strike on the westbound railway, the interruption of the telephone and telegraph wires, went some way to explaining the slowness with which the news was traveling, but were the roads not teeming with numerous excursionists? Did not a continuous coming-and-going of private couriers, local trams and even pedestrians establish a kind of chain between those two points, capable of transmitting such grave information? Were there not dirigibles, and carrier pigeons?

I reflected on that with an insistence near to obsession. I strayed over those ideas to the point of calculating the time it would take for a good horseman to bring a dispatch from a prefect to the government. Veritably, nothing seemed simpler. Then why—yes, why—this silence?

Of course! Because the couriers, the autos, the trams, the pedestrians and the riders—the entire chain of communication—had been broken by the monsters! Because the latter had a destructive radius of which I envisaged the full amplitude; because they had absorbed or paralyzed everything that moved, everything that transmitted social life.

"We're doomed" I couldn't help murmuring at my image in the mirror.

"No, we have time to escape," the same image replied, "because our enemies are only moving with an appreciable slowness. Even supposing that their progress were less rapid, and that they were only advancing, in a straight line, at three kilometers an hour—the pace of a slow walker, taking into account the unevenness of the terrain—wouldn't they already be at the gates of Paris? Wouldn't our ears be deafened by their roars, at least? Come on, Jean my friend! Calm down; finish your packing calmly, and then replenish your energy with a few hours sleep!"

Those reflections by my double calmed me down. I comforted myself with a light snack, and, overcome by fatigue, threw myself on to my bed fully dressed, in order to get a little salutary sleep before leaving.

V

At four o'clock in the afternoon I was woken up by a tumult in the street. I went to the window and saw people running and shouting, in an extraordinary disorder. Autos went by, and then large carriages, crammed with people.

As soon as I went down into the street to make enquiries, I learned that in the middle of the horse races at Saint-Cloud, the news had arrived that the macrobes had been seen in the forest of Saint-Germain. Descriptions of the animals were being given that were obviously exaggerated—magnified, I assumed, by popular imagination, It was said that they were as tall as the first platform of the Eiffel Tower, equipped with three long gyratory arms and endowed with a veracity that did not spare anything, swallowing livestock and people alike.

I concluded that the tales were implausible, but the progress of the monsters, more rapid than I had thought, alarmed me. Could I not change our plan of escape, and go to the Boulevard de Sebastopol by car in order to carry away those who were dear to me in a vehicle as rapid as the train?

I returned to the garage and found that my chauffeur had dismantled two of the most important components, and that the reassembly would take several more hours. Disconcerted, unable to think of any other course of action than to attend the arranged rendezvous at the railways station, I wasted time telling him to hurry, stunning him with futile words, in order that he would not interrupt his work to listen to the noises in the street. But as, in any case, he would not be able to finish before the end of the day, I left him to return to my apartment. I loaded my baggage into an odious fiacre, and took my place therein as well, without becoming too indignant at the fact that the coachman demanded fifty francs for the trip, paid in advance,

My carriage progressed with difficulty in the midst of an excited crowd filling the street. As soon as it had crossed the

Seine, by the Pont Henri IV, I found the causeway invaded by an extraordinary melee of vehicles trying to reach the railway station, and the sidewalks were no less cluttered with a population of travelers of all conditions, the majority carrying parcels as if moving house. The news of the invasion must have spread like wildfire and inspired everyone with the same idea as us. To get out of Paris and flee was the sovereign determination of that entire crowd.

I felt a vivid annoyance. Would we get a seat on the train? I could see other carriages racing from everywhere, and the express was not due to leave for two hours, so I abandoned my fiacre, leaving the coachman my trunk by way of a tip. Furnished only with a small bag, which permitted me to cleave a path through the crowd, I succeeded, with infinite difficult, in reaching the station buffet. I saw Suzanne and her father immediately, sitting at a table. They seemed consternated.

"Do you know what I've just heard?" declared Monsieur Vernet, immediately. "The trains aren't leaving! A P.L.M. strike was called this afternoon at the Bourse du Travail!"

"What are we going to do?" asked Suzanne, anxiously.

"Well," I replied, "we'll leave by automobile."

I had already drawn up a plan of my route and mentally traced the route that we would follow, drawing away from the enemy, to reach the south of France. I had driven around the suburbs of Paris so extensively, and knew the slightest byroads so well, that the map was, so to speak, encrusted in my memory.

"My forty horse-power ought to be ready. I'll go fetch it and come back to collect you."

"No! Don't leave us, we'll lose one another," she objected, tenderly fearful.

My proposal has reassured my friends. They got up in order to follow it, and we went back into the crowd. It was becoming increasingly dense and increasingly hostile. We understood that news of the strike had spread. We saw fists raised, faced grimacing their hatred. Voices were shouting: "Death to the strikers!" at a uniformed employee who was trying to calm them down—in vain, for his supplications had no effect on the stupidity of hooligans who were beginning to smash innocent baggage-carts and set fire to them.

The arrival of a flock of newsvendors suspended the tumult, however. Imitating everyone else, so powerful was our curiosity, we bought several evening editions at inflated prices. They related frightening details about the macrobes. In spite of contradictory descriptions of their origin, their form, their size and their color, they were in accord in recognizing their voracity and their taste for human flesh. There was talk of hecatombs. They had destroyed Mantes, consumed Poissy, and it was said that their weight was so colossal that no monument could resist them, that they crushed or toppled everything in their path. And the papers reported other rumors too; they announced a council of ministers, urgently convened, to organize defenses against this new kind of invasion.

Those stories distressed us deeply.

"Let's hurry to the auto!" Suzanne begged.

But how could we get back to the Muette quarter? How could we get out of that crowd, for a start? The entire population, it seemed to us, was outside, rushing futilely toward the station, agitated by contrary currents that were swirling toward the inaccessible Metro, while carriages, immobilized, stagnated in the middle of that human sea. We saw a child crushed in front of us, and I had to protect Suzanne, who was suffocating. Love rendered me ferocious; I would have knocked down the people who were daring to crowd my fiancée and hinder her progress.

Finally, with extraordinary difficulty, we escaped from the brutal turbulence and headed for the Seine in order to take a boat. Alas, there was another hitch when we got there; there was a queue at the pontoons for the departure to Charenton, but the steamboats for the Point-du-Jour had suspended their service. An empty fiacre, which we hailed, went past us at a fast gallop, without the coachman even turning his head. We decided them to get to my quarter by means of our own resources, and set off at a hasty walk, following the Boulevard Saint-Germain and the quays.

Night was falling already. A lamplighter, faithful to his task, was automatically spreading light over the almost-deserted streets. In the sky, the firmament exhibited a grave and limpid purity.

We were pressing our pace when, before crossing the Pont d'Iéna, uniformed officers appeared in the dim light. We followed them momentarily, and understood from what they were saying that they were a commission appointed by the Minister of War to go to the top of the Eiffel Tower in order to reconnoiter the macrobes' positions and project fire at them.

"What's the point of going up?" said one of them. "The electrical workers have stopped work. We won't have any light."

That reflection inspired us with an even greater desire to reach our liberating vehicle. But one might have thought that destiny was against us. When we went into the garage, exhausted by our journey, the automobile was no longer there. My chauffeur had disappeared, taking it away. My greatest dolor was observing Suzanne's despair.

"What are we going to do now?" he said.

We were in the road, facing my garage. The street was almost entirely deserted, save or certain places where panicky merchants were shuttering their shop windows, while others were trying to shift their furniture, as if they were afraid that it might fall victim to the macrobes' rapacity. An old woman went by, using a flap of her mantle to protect a cage occupied by a parrot. We also saw an entire family, including young children, collapse on the sidewalk. The little ones were carrying they toys, with fearful gestures. Everyone was protecting the things they loved in their own fashion. And that general desolation was in complete conformity with the sadness that reigned in us.

"I'll go ask a policeman is any measures have been taken," I proposed, feeling a need to do something.

I went to a policeman who, faithful to his orders, was on patrol outside the railway station at the boundary. He was a man of terrifying aspect, his forehead bulging, his lip barred with a thick moustache, clad in a badly-fitting uniform. Before even listening to me he cut off my question with a weary gesture and ordered me to move on.

"He doesn't know anything," I said, when I returned, crestfallen, to my friends.

"What are we going to do?" Suzanne repeated.

"Let's not lose our composure, my children," Monsieur Vernet advised. "Let's wait until tomorrow to make a decision, given that the gas is now going out too. What could we do in the dark, weary as we are?"

"Yes, I'm tired—very tired," admitted my fiancée.

"In any case," Monsieur Vernet went on, "are the macrobes as much to be feared as interested journalism proclaims? How do you expect these animals, emerged from a culture broth, as vastly developed as one can imagine, to nourish themselves on human flesh?"

"And to possess tissues sufficient compact to topple houses?" I added.

"It's pure fantasy, my future father-in-law insisted. "There are limits to science, and credulity also ought to exist therein. Let's not allow ourselves to be carried away by the folly of others. Moreover, I'd like to believe that our protection is being organized by our government. Let's have confidence in them, and offer ourselves hospitality, my dear child."

"Gladly!" I agreed.

I understood well enough that the scientist's rather banal reflections had been intended to reassure his daughter. I was of the same mind, and I hastened to take them home and offer them the honors of my domicile, with which they were not yet familiar.

The visit to my apartment, the presentation of family trinkets with so many precious memories attached to them and the organization of sleeping accommodation for the night soon provided a diversion for our obsession. My home emitted a kind of radiation from which my guests and I derived the greatest benefit. I had lit the candles in the candlesticks; their soft light threw golden glints into my fiancée's hair, and Monsieur Vernet's head was haloed by an even more respectable whiteness. We could not repress a smile when he agreed to quit his frock-coat in order to put on my indoor jacket in Pyrenean wool, whose sleeves were too short.

A dear family intimacy for which I had so often wished was inaugurated, restful in its little pleasantries, even in the midst of a tragic ambiance. I was not so far from feeling grateful for the events that had procured it for me.

"You can take my bed, my dear Suzanne," I proposed. "As for you, Monsieur Vernet, forgive me for only offering you the drawing room divan—but it's comfortable..."

"What about you?" the young woman asked.

"I'll be content with my manservant's bed, given that he hasn't come back. Would I not be comfortable anywhere, when it's a matter of blunting the cruelties of fate for you? And am I not the humblest of your servants, my dear Suzanne?"

I gave some plausibility to that last declaration by going to find something for them to eat. In the kitchen I discovered the remains of a ragout, dry bread and half a bottle of Bordeaux: the remains of my meal the day before last. I set the table; I put on an apron in order to warn up the food over a wood fire, and refused the aid that Suzanne offered me, having also put on an apron, with an adorable grace.

Our accoutrements inspired us with such good humor that we dined almost cheerfully, deliberately omitting to talk about the menace that was approaching from the west.

At ten o'clock, we parted, and I learned later that my fiancée slept heavily. I must confess that my slumber arrived rather belatedly, and was troubled by Tornada-like tics.

VI

I was already no longer asleep when an unusual sound of wheels, coming from the street, reverberated in the panes of my window at daybreak the next morning. I got dressed in haste and when downstairs to see what was happening. On the doorstep, in front of the concierge's lodge—deserted, like the rest of the house—I encountered Monsieur Vernet and Suzanne. They were already in conversation with General Gramont, whom I had met in their house many a time. He was a small, stiff, nervous man, notoriously energetic, whom the Ministry of War was sending to meet the enemy with two batteries of artillery. Monsieur Vernet had stopped him in order to question him, as he was passing by, taking his cannons to Mont-Valérien.

I went up to him. "Well, General?"

"Well, this is a strange business!" proclaimed the warrior, caressing the neck of his horse with his riding-crop. With a smile, he continued: "How could I have thought, my dear Monsieur, on the day when I was complimenting you on your engagement, that that epileptic specimen"—he meant Tornada—"had such a surprise in store for us in short order? To depart on campaign against macrobes, to mobilize the army, bring out our artillery, to destroy infusoria, that's out of the ordinary! Until now, for lack of a war, they've been using us as police; are they going to make us sweep the streets now? Oh, the twentieth century promises astonishment to those of our grandchildren who embark on a military career!"

"What news is there?" I asked, after having acquiesced to the generalities the general had pronounced.

"News? Rather curious, and even incomprehensible, if one can judge by the information that has reached the Ministry of War, which comes from a reconnaissance service ordered especially—for the observation post on top of the Eiffel Tower isn't functioning."

"Incomprehensible in what way, General?"

"In the sense that the danger that was menacing us solely in the west now seems to have circumscribed Paris. Yes, the macrobes have carried out a flanking maneuver and drawn a circle around the city. Their presence has been ascertained at Saint-Germain, at Saint-Cyr, at Versailles, at Palaiseau, at Corbeil, at Raincy and beyond the forest of Montmorency. A veritable investment, I tell you. And it's that plan of attack on their part which stupefies me, for it's a strategy, there's no doubt about it! So, one wonders what brain is communicating its orders, what genius has the inconceivable power to direct them, to organize them!"

"And one thinks of Tornada," said Monsieur Vernet, confessing the thought that was oppressing all of us.

"Of Tornada, obviously."

The sinister evocation silenced us for a few seconds. We contemplated the military apparatus that society was opposing to the beasts, the silhouettes of horsemen dancing with the trot of their mounts, the members of the gun crews shaken by the rude jolts of the ammunition-carts in which they had been placed and the menacing profiles of the cannons whose gray maws had been dispossessed of their covers. Hoofbeats, rumblings, threat; it really was war.

"They're advancing with an extraordinary speed, then?" Suzanne asked, tearfully.

"Everything leads us to think so, my child. Everything leads us to believe that they'd already be in Paris if their inconceivable discipline hadn't retained them long enough to besiege us."

"Are they as terrible as the reports indicate?" my fiancée persisted.

"They seem to be. I've been told that they're carnivores. Carnivores! Can you imagine that, Monsieur Vernet? It's amazing! Can you imagine that a squadron of cuirassiers sent against them in the direction of Raincy has disappeared in its entirety, with the exception of a few cavalrymen and the physician-major, who were manning the field hospital? Placed in the rear, they were able to escape, thanks to the restraint of the macrobes, which appeared not to want to surpass an attack zone. I met the major at the Ministry this morning, and held his report in my hands."

"What did it say? How do they operate?"

"He claims that the monsters possess a kind of cloaca underneath their abdomen, which opens to absorb their fodder. Once introduced into them, it's crushed, triturated and emptied of all its nutritive elements, while the non-alimentary substances—breastplates, for example, which are certainly rather indigestible—are expelled through the same cloaca, which opens again to reject them."

Monsieur Vernet interrupted the warrior. "That procedure," he remarked, is scarcely in accord with the idea I had formed of *Micrococcus aspirator*. If what Tornada told the Académie is accurate, the microbe possesses, by way of a nourishing arm, a kind of long appendage planted at the front of the individual."

Turning to me, he interrogated me with his gaze. I confirmed with a nod of the head that that detail was indeed what I had observed the night before last.

"I must admit," Gramont went on, "that the major was rather reserved concerning the accuracy of his report. You'll agree that it's a rather difficult time to make scientific observations when one is threatened with being sucked into the belly of a monster. A Jonah can't easily stand in for a Claude Bernard. One sees oneself more as *cuvé* than Cuvier!"[10]

On another occasion we would have appreciated the joke; on this one, it slid past our anxiety.

---

[10] This pun does not translate, obviously; *cuver*, of which *cuvé* is the past participle, refers to fermentation, with specific reference to wine-making; feminized, it become a noun referring to the vat in which such fermentation takes place, whereas the common noun *cuvier* refers to a copper washtub; the proper noun, of course, refers to the great biologist Georges Cuvier.

"The newspapers assert that their proportions are colossal, that they can crush houses beneath their weight?" I queried. More urgently, I added: "Is that true? In what fashion do they move in order to achieve such destructive effects?"

"One second, my friend," the general prevaricated. He leaned toward his orderly and shouted an order; the latter set off at a gallop to transmit the command to the head of the column. Soon, the cohort stopped; the members of the troop relaxed and the cannons ceased their deafening metallic rattle. We were more easily able to collect the general's information, which he transmitted to us while puffing nervously on a cigarette.

"I'm giving them a little rest," he explained. "The poor fellows spent the night on their feet, ready to saddle up at a moment's notice." Then, in reply to my question, he said: "How do they move? That's rather special. It's by rolling transversally—at least, so the major says. He also claims that the mode of progression in question hasn't yet been observed in nature."

"Pardon me!" said Monsieur Vernet, "but we know of some microorganisms that move in that fashion. I've seen them under the objective of my microscope. But again, that doesn't correspond with observations of *Micrococcus aspirator*, General."

"Then it's necessary to conclude, my dear Master, that the macrobes are other animals than those you believe to have been cultivated by Tornada."

That discussion of theoretical taxonomy scarcely suited the warrior. He preferred positive phenomena, obstacles that shells could attain and damage. While twirling his cigarette, however, he went on: "In any case, that explanation confirms the destructive power of the monsters. It's by rotating themselves, by virtue of their excessive mass, that they crush and flatten everything they encounter. Yesterday, at Mont-Valérien, where I'm going, the annihilation of the Château de Saint-German was observed through binoculars, and the town itself, through which we've all passed, where we've all paraded our reveries, collapsed and was flattened like a mere sand-dune."

"Will we ever stop them?" sighed Suzanne, veiling her eyes, as if to protect them from the image of that scene of ruination.

The general resumed smiling, with fine confidence. He threw away his cigarette and gathered up the reins of his mount.

"Certainly, my child. Artillery has been sent in all directions. You're going to hear the growling of new pieces, and you'll see how they comport themselves against the macrobes. We're going to puncture those bladders as easily as cutting through butter. Ours is a new therapeutics—mechanotherapy! Melinite—the medicament of the century, eh? Who would have believed it?" As Monsieur Vernet shook his head, worriedly, he went on: "You don't believe that we can smash them? Do you want me to show you? It's worth the trouble, I can assure you. We won't see a war as original as this for a long time..." And still joking, at the scientist's expense, he added: "Unless, my dear Master, you can grow a few infusoria yourself to attack the others?"

The proposition of accompanying the general to Mont-Valérien was seductive. What else did we have to do, anyway? We consulted one another with our gaze, admitting our temptation. What an appetite is greater than curiosity? Before the attraction of the spectacle, we lost all fear of danger. Furthermore, the combatant's final words had revived our courage.

"We'd like nothing better than to see the battle," said Monsieur Vernet, but how are we going to get there? How can we go with you?"

"I have two bicycles," I proposed. "One for you and the other for Suzanne."

"I don't know how to ride one, my boy."

"I can give you a place in an ammunition-cart."

"In that case, let's go."

We were soon ready to depart. Orders shouted at the top of the voice brought the weary men to their feet. A clink of sabers was mingled with the whinnying of the animals. Then the ground rumbled, the column moved off in martial fashion, and we left with that unexpected caravan, in the midst of the blinding dust raised by the heavy machines.

That whole suburban region, first the Bois de Boulogne, and then the hill of Suresnes, though which we passed to reach Fort Mont-Valérien, was abandoned.[11] We passed over a drawbridge, went through an old fortified wall and then, separating from the artillery, which took another path in order to position the guns, we followed a path leading to a barracks, which, once traversed, finally permitted us to reach, via a narrow staircase, a broad terrace from which the view extended all the way to the hills of Saint-Germain. Our eyes did not take long to savor the splendor of the panorama bathed in solar radiation, and the blue-tinted patches of terrain emerging from the mist.

We looked immediately for the fearful enigma, avid for information, but at first we could not see anything. The appearance of the region seemed normal.

"I can see them!" Monsieur Vernet suddenly exclaimed, his eyes glued to a pair of binoculars.

I seized his apparatus immediately, and inspected the horizon in my turn. Indeed, in the direction of Bezons, confused masses, melting into the gray background, had stopped behind a bridge newly built over the Seine, visible in that location in the middle of a devastated landscape. Their volume at that distance was inappreciable; they seemed, however, to be twice as tall as the only house that remained standing.

---

[11] Fort Mont-Valérien is of some symbolic significance in this context because it had played a major role in keeping the Prussians at bay for some time during the 1870 siege, withstanding heavy artillery bombardment. Its surrender was a key clause in the armistice signed in January 1871; it was effectively bartered for the food supplies that Bismarck let into the city to save the population from the threat of starvation.

Their form was that of an elongated oval, with one extremity that seemed to be the head, and another that might have been the tail. At the level of the head section, an appendage sprouted, of a dimension at least equal to half the length of the body, and it seemed to me that the appendage in question terminated in a wider section, waving limply in the air, idly raised like an elephant's trunk.

The animals did not have any other apparent limbs, and I was wondering how they could move forward when I saw one extend its prolongation, set it on the ground in order to obtain a point of support there, and—probably fixing itself by means of some kind of suction mechanism, drag the rest of its body after it, which elongated and then became compacted again. Their progress was thus a little like that of a snake whose body was obedient to a tentacle, and the physician's report, which General Gramont had mentioned a little while before, was erroneous in all points. On the contrary; the disposition adopted really was the one of which I had retained an impression in the wake of my nocturnal excursion.

I counted ten similar monsters.

"But it really is the *Micrococcus aspirator* of alkaline environments described by Tornada!" exclaimed Monsieur Vernet, his scientific interest coming to the fore in spite of everything. Then he added: "That's prodigious! The man is a genius! Now it's a matter of ascertaining whether the animal's appendage also serves to nourish them."

"Alas! As long as it's not at our expense..." Suzanne murmured.

I was about to reply when rapid orders shouted beneath us compelled us to silence.

A battery prepared to fire. The distance was calculated and I saw the officers lean over the apparatus. Then a din deafened us. Fortunately, I had advised my fiancée to block her ears, and she closed her eyes as the blast passed through the air.

The moment became tragic, anguishing. What would the shell do to the animals?

With my eyes to the binoculars, I took note of the effects. I saw the projectile land on the house that was still standing and hollow out a breach in it. Almost immediately, a second shot was dispatched, falling directly on to the bridge, which was half-demolished.

"Victory!" cried Monsieur Vernet. "They can't get across!"

What illusion! The scientist had scarcely prophesied than the macrobes moved into the water, which did not even cover two-thirds of their bodies. Their immersion caused the river to overflow and produced distant eddies. They stayed there for a while, as if bathing. Some of them plunged their trunks into the liquid, and launched torrents as they pulled them out again.

Finally, the first emerged, then a second, and a third was following them when another shell, more successfully aimed, landed on it. The extraordinary thing was that the shell, instead of striking it, slid over its tegument and went to burst against a tree on the other bank.

At first we thought the device had been badly-constructed, all the more so because something else very peculiar happened at the same instant. Just as the shell exploded, we saw an orange flash about a hundred meters above the enemy troop, so vivid that it eclipsed to solar radiation, and so strangely distributed in the sky that it was reminiscent of a firework rocket launched in broad daylight, of a previously unknown intensity.

I did not understand those phenomena at all. I attempted to reason them out by attributing them to defective powder being used by the artillery, but that explanation could not be true, for the shots that followed were no more fortunate. The projectiles touched the carapaces of the monsters, and the carapaces caused them to rebound.

"They're invulnerable, then!" Monsieur Vernet exclaimed. "Their consistency disrupts all my hypotheses!"

And it was true. All the more stimulated by the impacts they received, seemingly obedient to a mysterious order, the macrobes increased the rapidity of their progress and undulated more precipitately in our direction.

"My God! My God!" stammered Suzanne, seizing my arm. "They're coming!"

"Indeed..."

"Let's run! Run!"

"One more second," I said, my attention riveted by that unreal spectacle. But did I really see what followed? Did the binoculars, trembling in my hands, not deceive me? Did I really see that the colossi were employing a different fashion of movement, and that they were now proceeding by means of successive bounds, obtaining a point of support on the ground by means of their trunks and describing in the air, a long way from the ground, an enormous somersault, like the leap of a carp when it emerges from the water—and which caused them to advance hundreds of meters at each jump?

Our terror, following the failure of the artillery, was indescribable. We ran away, tumbling down the stairs any old how and running through the courtyard, and we found ourselves outside the fortifying wall. Officers, soldiers and civilians alike were frantic, stampeding. The guns had been abandoned in order to flee more rapidly.

The general tried in vain to organize an honorable retreat, but his voice was drowned out by the din. I saw his furious mouth howling incomprehensible orders. Nothing could have opposed the torrent of the panic.

I had not forgotten my dear Suzanne, however. I had taken care to put her on her bicycle and to support her during the descent of Suresnes. She was calling madly for her father when the scientist caught us up. He was fleeing at a rapid trot on a horse that he had mounted in haste. He had never learned to ride and was going downhill with his hair blowing in the wind, clinging to the saddle and the animal's mane, offering a spectacle that would have been hilarious if we had still had a sense of humor.

We found ourselves back in the Chaussée de la Muette without my remembering exactly how we got there. I dismounted just in time to catch Suzanne, who was about to faint. The dear child was exhausted by fear, fatigue and hunger.

I immediately thought of finding something for her to eat, but I had exhausted my provisions the previous evening. The quarter was deserted, none of the shops any longer being inhabited. I was cursing my impotence when hazard came to our aid.

The last runaways had scarcely disappeared into the Rue de Passy when a refrain sung in a tenor voice rose up behind us. The tune—*Viens, poupoule, viens!*—was familiar to us; it was one of those odious popular songs that invade the country like epidemics of stupidity from time to time.[12] The words, however, had been adapted to circumstances, and the parody "*Viens, macrobe, viens!*" rose with a stupefying insistence in the solitude of the place.

We turned round and perceived the singer. It was a little man with a hilarious physiognomy, dressed in the fashion of a Montmartre cabaret singer in a gray frock-coat and flared trousers. Installed before a display of brioches and licorice water, he was waiting for clients and seemed to be ironically enjoying the situation we were in. I went over to him, lured by his provisions.

"Just in time!" I said. "You're very philosophical..."

"Fatalistic, Monsieur," he replied. "Long experience of events has taught me that it does no good to get excited. It's necessary to await the course of destiny while singing. It's very French."

"And you're not afraid to stay here? You know that they're not far away?"

"Where would I go? Under the bridges? I'm familiar with them, thanks! They've sheltered my poor anatomy all too often. It's true that my place was marked out for me at the

---

[12] The song in question, whose title and chorus is roughly translatable as "Come, baby, come," was made famous by the popular music hall performer Félix Mayol. He can still be seen and heard singing it, thanks to YouTube.

Élysée…perhaps you don't know that there's been a change of government, and that I was offered the Undersecretariat of Fine Arts…but no, I refused. The position isn't sufficiently fruitful. I prefer selling brioches and coco, to cocos of your sort."[13]

And as my eyes were shining in response to the bait of suggestive bread rolls, with a golden patina that was already several days old, he added: "You want some?"

"Yes—how much?"

"Two hundred francs for three."

"Oh!"

"The macrobian price, Monsieur. And I'll throw in the nectar too!"

"Done," I said, exchanging two lovely banknotes for the brioches and a liter of the beverage.

I brought them back to my friends, and the singer retired, informing us that we were "mugs." I blessed him nonetheless.

---

[13] Another untranslatable pun; *coco* signifying both "licorice water"—also known in England as sugarelly, although the beverage has faded from popularity to such an extent that the term is no longer current—and "coconut," the latter being used as an argot term with the same implication as "block-head.".

VII

Hunger appeased, we discussed our distress. Who would save us? Having the good fortune to be a friend of the Voisin brothers, the constructors of the famous tailed biplane,[14] I thought briefly of going to their nearby factory to procure one of their aircraft, in order to carry us away. Their ingenious apparatus was familiar to me; I knew that they were now using aerial transport of proven security in several places, capable of long journeys without renewing contact with the ground. But a major aviation show in the Midi, I remembered, had attracted all of their available machines, and my desire was incapable of realization.

That further disappointment plunged us back into melancholy. The destruction of the incredible invaders appeared to us to be increasingly improbable. The cannon fire that we could now hear in all directions was scarcely reassuring; we knew its impotence. And we were allowing ourselves to go on to more cruel anticipations when a faint noise overhead caused us to look up.

Then our hearts dilated, for we had just perceived the presence in the sky of Commandant Junisseau, in his dirigible.

He had recognized us too. He came, with a consummate mastery, to hover ten meters above us. Very excited, he shouted to us, his voice vibrant: "I've followed all the vicissitudes of the artillery battle and observed the vain results of melinite. I'm going to employ the fracassite recently invented by Serviat. Unfortunately, I lack an aide. Would you like to come with me, Monsieur Gérard? It's for the fatherland!

---

[14] Gabriel and Charles Voisin bought out their collaborator Louis Blériot in 1906 in order to establish the first aircraft manufacturing company at Billancourt, accessible from the Chaussée de la Muette in Passy without too much difficulty, by bicycle or on horseback.

Oh, the cruel hesitation! To abandon my friends at such a moment! To leave Suzanne! I was about to refuse when my fiancée's gaze ordered me to depart.

"Go, Jean, go! You owe it to your country! We'll wait for you in your apartment. My heart won't leave you."

A rope hoisted me up. In order to reach the nacelle I had to accomplish a few gymnastic movements to which I was no longer accustomed, and which I executed with a certain difficulty. Encouraged by Junisseau, however, I succeeded, and we departed.

I shall not waste time describing the vast apparatus that carried me away, or explaining how the fabric envelope inflated by a gas lighter than air supported, by means of a network emanating therefrom, the cage set on an armed beam that had collected me. Nor shall I linger over an explanation of the role of the air-balloon, the stabilizers, the automatic valves, the pressure vent, the multiplier, the equilibrator, the bolt-rope and the suspension. In any case, such machines fly over every day, and the dirigible has lost the favor of curiosity since the airplane has completed the conquest of the fluid that we breathe. Let it suffice, therefore, for the reader to know that the nacelle was surrounded by an iron wire mesh stopping at a support-rail, and that I perceived at my feet, on the perforated floor, two carefully-stacked piles of shells.

Detaching my gaze from those destructive engines, I then observed the luminous circle described by the propeller in the play of the sunlight; then, after an empty space, the raised catwalk on which Junisseau was standing, close enough for conversation between us to be possible. Standing with superb authority, he was presiding, thanks to movements transmitted by a steering-column, over the evolution of his apparatus, while at the rear, a single assistant, the mechanic, was manning the engine, obedient to the orders that the commandant whistled to him by telephone. All these dispositions would have interested me prodigiously at another time, for it was my first ascent, but for the moment, I only retained the impression of a magnificent instrument utilizable in the defense of those I loved.

"Stay there, don't move, and understand clearly what I expect of you!" the aeronaut shouted to me from his catwalk, in the midst of the various sounds produced by the dirigible's flight.

He scanned the horizon with an imperious eye, and then communicated to his servant the orders that, once executed, produced a lurching that caused me to feel some nausea. I soon realized, however, that we had caught a favorable air current, for it appeared to me that we were moving faster, and my stomach settled. Looking down at my feet then, I perceived the ground through the gaps in the floor, drawing away beneath us. The branches of the Bois de Boulogne flew past confusedly, in a green harmony. Soon, the gray ribbon of the Seine was surpassed.

Junisseau's voice tore me away from that spectacle.

"In brief, this is what I want you to do. I've seen the futile contest of the artillery; I've observed the macrobes at length, and I've understood that there's only one means of thwarting them."

"What's that, Commandant?"

"It's blinding them."

"Blinding them?"

"Yes. I've noticed on their carapace, not far behind their appendage, a kind of circular patch, with two concentric rings, which seems to constitute the monsters' cyclopean eye. It's by that means that I think they're accessible. Although projectiles slide over and ricochet from their teguments—and see how nature protects them, since their visual apparatus is shielded by the invulnerable trunk!—our perpendicularity gives us the hope that we might get to them simply by depositing the explosive at the portal to the cerebral system. Can you imagine the purée that half a pound of fracassite will make of their insides!"

He rubbed his hands and pinched his nose, then remarked, with a loud laugh: "The anarchists haven't yet found anything like it, eh?"

"But what's my role, Commandant?" I asked. "How can I be useful to you?"

"You're brave, aren't you? You're not chicken? You won't tremble? You're not myopic?"

I reassured him on all these points. Then he continued: "You, my good friend, have simply, if I might express it thus, to put the salt on the sparrow's tail—in other words, to let the projectile fall on to the macrobe's eye at the moment that I cause the dirigible to hover above it. It's a game of massacre, an amusement for pretty ladies, and I truly regret not having invited any to partake of this new kind of sport. Once the first macrobe is destroyed, we'll pass on to the second, then the third, and so on, until the complete extermination of the race. I can stay in the air for ten hours and in my hangar at Moulineaux I have a reserve of five hundred shells, as many loaded with melinite as with fracassite, so it will be easy for us to restock."

What he said gave me pause for thought. I thought that handling bombs was a perilous business, and that I had thirty of them at my feet.

"Isn't there any danger at the moment of the explosion?" I asked. "I'd very much like to know."

"No—not the slightest! And then again, so what? It's for the fatherland!"

"Yes—for France!" I cried. And silently, I added: "For Suzanne." A noble heroic enthusiasm exalted me. I felt as brave as an ancient god taking to the serenity of the skies in order to smite the dragons delivered to my blows by another celestial power rivaling my own.

Entirely intent on the role I was to play, from then on I took a passionate interest in the movements of my two bold companions, ingeniously maneuvering the dirigible. The captain, consulting a compass, gave curt orders that his aide carried out phlegmatically. After having flown straight up into the sky, we allowed ourselves to descend with a vertiginous lightning rapidity. I could have sworn, however, that we were not moving, and that our balloon was suspended by an immense wire attached to a hook somewhere high in the sky.

Suddenly, the engine was not throbbing as rapidly. I understood that we were stationary, and leaned over the side.

"Rueil!" Junisseau specified.

How small the world seemed! And how derisory those monstrous gray masses were, that I had feared so much a little while before! I was surprised not to feel more distressed by the sight of them. They had changed location slightly, moving back in the direction of Rueil, and after having destroyed and pulverized everything in their path, they were taking a rest before tackling the rising ground that extends from Rueil to Suresnes and Mont-Valérien.

We drew closer still, and I was able to see that the idea I had formed from a distance had given me a reasonably exact idea of what they really were. They reproduced in colossal proportions, which I estimate to be thirty meters in height by ten broad and fifty long, the *Micrococcus aspirator* of alkaline environments described and depicted by Tornada. I saw that their carapace was constituted by overlapping scales, so harmonious in form that I thought that the scales, hardened by their special culture, must represent the cells of a tegument whose discrimination the microscope did not permit in tiny specimens, although there was no reason why it should not exist.

As for their gyratory tentacle, I confirmed that it served both as an organ of locomotion and if nutrition, as the baleful scientist had announced, for a poor field-worker who was obstinate in not fleeing, was caught by one of them before my eyes, and absorbed as a breadcrumb might be by a human mouth—or, to offer a better representation, sucked in by a current of air determined by the trunk while producing the siren-like sound, now significant for me as the roar of a vacuum-cleaner. The man disappeared head first, gesturing stiffly, reminiscent of one of the marionettes of a Punch-and-Judy show dragged off their miniature stage by an invisible string. He disappeared, and I heard his horrible screams...but the sentiment of my liberating mission filled me too much for me to pity him.

I was no longer thinking about anything but the strange destinies of the science capable of transforming the world in this fashion. Were these macrobes not the masters of the world? Oh, it was high time they were destroyed—that I directed my explosive vengeance toward that lidless eye, whose stupid pupil, round and black, with a green-tinted rim, seemed to be looking at us at that exact moment. And I calculated that I could let my projectile fall upon it without difficulty, even if their immobility did not last long.

We drew even closer. We were no more than a hundred meters or so above the leading macrobe when Junisseau said to me: "Look, Monsieur Gérard—there's another enigma! It's that indefinable entity that I observed for some time a little while ago, and which leads the macrobes in battle, whom they obey like a leader. Can you see it there, at the rear?"

I turned in the direction indicated by the Commandant, and did indeed perceive, unfortunately too far away to be able to make out its nature precisely, a kind of reddish animal, with the vague form of a little human whose upper body and head had been replaced by a sponge taller than it was wide, and equipped with an arm. Yes, a sponge-man, moving on two thin legs, running to the right and left to herd the giant animals, as a sheepdog does with a flock of sheep. It was steering them without making any sound, from a distance, making gestures like a sprinkler of holy water, and its orders were executed, it seemed to me, with the same fearful docility with which sheep obey the commands of the dog.

I confess that that little general of colossi intrigued me greatly, and I would gladly have lingered to watch its maneuvers if Junisseau had not raised his voice again.

"Pay attention! The time has come!" He pointed at the shells carefully stacked at my feet. "Take the first one from the right-hand pile, which is composed of fracassite. Place it on the exterior bar…carefully, without tilting it… it's a delicate operation."

A tremor ran through me, which he perceived, in spite of my attempt to repress it.

"Are you scared?"

I stiffened myself. "Not at all, Commandant."

And, with all my muscles tense, all my nervous strength deployed, I took hold of one of the voluminous steel cones, which weight approximately fifty kilos, and lifted it up to the rim of the nacelle.

"Have you a clear sight of the monster's eye?"

"Yes, Commandant."

"You won't miss the target?"

"I hope not."

"It's necessary not to hope, but to be sure. If the device falls anywhere but into the optical orifice, it's us who'll be blown up, my friend…and I'd rather it was them!"

"Me too, Commandant," I agreed, with a pale smile.

I was scarcely at ease. I was having infinite difficulty maintaining the explosive on the rail, all the more so as I had placed it on the very edge, in order not to miss the precise instant of release, and the fifty thousand grams were pulling on my nervous arms. The Commandant whistled into his telephone; the mechanic moved a lever. The engine throbbed less rapidly. We dropped toward the monster.

"Wait! Stay cool!" ordered the Commandant.

Another blast of the whistle resounded; the propeller stopped turning. This time, I perceived the colossal grey mass directly beneath my feet, the optical patch displayed thereon.

"Wait!"

I was only waiting for the word when the dirigible suddenly tilted, while a roar, two which an oath from the aviator replied, burst forth beneath our floor. We had made the mistake of not worrying about the seemingly-lazy trunk of the animal, which was swinging limply at the level of our mooring rope, and the monster had grabbed the rope, drawing us toward it with an improbable force.

Our vessel lurched. We were doomed.

"Above all, don't let go!" Junisseau shouted.

As he spoke, he launched himself off the catwalk. I thought at first he was making the move to escape the danger, to flee, at the risk of killing himself as he abandoned us, but my indignation was soon converted into a boundless admiration. Oh, what courage! What audacity! I saw him hang on by one arm to the iron framework like a veritable acrobat, above the void, and then seize with his other hand a knife that he was clutching in his teeth, and cut the rope. His liberating gesture, aided by the intelligence of the mechanic, who has restored thrust to the engine, caused us to rebound out of the monster's reach. We were saved.

"Commandant, that's admirable, what you did!" I shouted, when his athletic agility had brought him back to his steering-column.

Well, yes—he scarcely cared about my appreciation. In any case, he could hardly hear me amid the renewed purr of the engine and the propeller determined by our new thrust. Very calmly, he controlled his equilibrator, transmitted his instructions to the mechanic again with blasts of his whistle. Under the guidance of its helm, the dirigible circled around, bringing us back over the enemy. Junisseau's courageous deed had inspired me with a noble emulation. This time, it was without trembling that I approached the first macrobe, still motionless.

The maneuver was repeated with the same precision, and when I judged that I was situated vertically above the circular patch, I looked at the Commandant.

"Go!"

I relaxed my taut arms. I saw the steel thunderbolt reach the enemy. Then, for a second of intense emotion, I waited for the noise consecutive to my action.

What a surprise! Nothing! No bang! The detonation did not take place. And when, in spite of the maneuver that had taken the dirigible precipitately out of range of the anticipated explosion, I saw what had become of the shell, I perceived that it had slid over the monster and fallen on the ground without bursting.

"A dud! Another! Another!" Junisseau shouted at me, bringing us back to the battle.

"Another!"

With a new rage, I lifted a second device on to the rail. We approached again, and I propelled it into the void with the same care to aim exactly. Alas, once again the result was implausibly negative; all that I heard exploded was the Commandant's oath.

"Fracassite doesn't explode!" he said, with a cold wrath. "It's another one of Serviat's hoaxes!"

And, leaning on the equilibrator so hard that I thought we were going to crash on top of the monster, he added: "Get the melinite! It's the pile on the left! Perhaps, in the eye...the artillery shells didn't hit the eye…!"

I did as I was told. I got ready for a third time. Again the dirigible hovered above the enormous carapace.

"Let go!" Junisseau howled.

"Smack in the eye!" I exulted.

A frightful detonation accompanied my cry of victory. The floor, hit by shrapnel, was holed almost beneath my feet. Acrid fumes, which gripped the throat, enveloped us as we were carried sideways by a rapid thrust. It took perhaps a minute to dissipate the mist.

"This time, Commandant, I think..."

"This time? Look, my friend!"

Surprised by the irony of his tone, I leaned over the side to observe my massacre. What a disappointment! I had proclaimed the triumph too soon. My device had indeed hit the target, but the monster had not sustained the slightest damage. On the contrary: the shock seemed to have given it pleasure, as if tickling it, for it was continuing to swing its tentacle indolently.

Then, we realized that the "eye" was simply a variation of the carapace, something like an ornament, a beauty spot, as fantasists call them. At any rate, the invulnerability of the macrobes became a proven fact after we had attempted—from a greater height, in order to avoid the shrapnel—further shots at a second one, and then a third. The results were the same. They were definitely indestructible. A ferocious snigger, uttered by the sponge-man, who had drawn closer to us and had witnessed the duel, convinced us further still. Where had I heard that laughter before? Oh, why hadn't I thought of destroying that one?

I was overwhelmed. I hardly heard Junisseau ordering the return to Paris. What would become of us, now that combat was definitively impossible? Would the Commandant take pity on us? Would he be humane enough to take Monsieur Vernet, Suzanne and me away in his dirigible?

I was about to beg him to do that when a pain in my wrist suspended my request. Examining the place that was causing me to suffer, I saw that it was bleeding, with a gray-tinted body in the middle of the wound. I had been wounded without realizing it in the heat of the battle.

I took out the foreign body, and, after having observed that it was a fragment of a macrobian scale, a horny tissue as hard as iron, I bandaged my arm with my handkerchief and turned my imploring eyes toward Junisseau.

"Commandant! Commandant!" I begged, finally.

He had anticipated me. He shook his head, declaring that the engine was fatigued, that he could not overload it, and that his duty called him elsewhere, to the national defense.

Perhaps he also understood, by the anger in my eyes, that I was capable of a crime, capable of throwing him overboard in order to take possession of his dirigible. But what could I have done with it? I did not know how to fly it; and a circular glance cast over the region we were overlooking had just told me that Paris was surrounded on all sides by the gray masses, into the midst of which my inexperience would doubtless have steered us.

Furthermore, our enemies were progressing with prodigious rapidity. A curve that the pilot had described having brought us over Saint-Cloud, I saw that the town was already threatened with ruin. Its square was swarming with fugitives, and in an matter of seconds, its railway station, its bridge, its church, the entrance to its park and the taverns planted along its shore—an entire sunlit décor, picturesque, amusing, evocative of so many Parisian Sunday excursions—were nothing more than dust.

Then I lowered my head and waited for Junisseau to drop me off in the Chaussée de la Muette. He left without saying another word. With him, my last hope disappeared, as his dirigible paled and vanished in the azure.

VIII

I found Monsieur Vernet and my fiancée in my apartment. As soon as she perceived that I was injured, Suzanne threw herself into my arms, weeping. The dear heart! I would gladly have been hurt, more grievously, twenty times over to receive the dolorous charm of such an impulse.

"Oh, my dear Jean," she said you me, "here you are at last! If you knew what I'd gone through! I was mad with anxiety! The hope I invested in your expedition, of the annihilation of the macrobes due to your courage, couldn't dissipate my anguish! And Papa was no less troubled than me! We've spent the entire time of your absence leaning out of the window, looking at the horizon, listening for the noises that might have reached us from that frightful battle...and nothing! Nothing reached us, except once...three distant explosions. We understood, alas, when we did not hear the explosions repeated, that the battle was lost..."

"She ought to have added, to tell you everything," Monsieur Verne remarked, "that the silence of the explosives was even more difficult for her to bear than the echoes of the engagement..."

Suzanne placed her hand gently over her father's mouth, to stop the confession—but Monsieur Vernet continued: "Didn't she imagine that you had fallen prey to the monsters? I tried in vain to demonstrate the impossibility of that, by reason of the altitude accessible to the dirigible and the facility of the maneuvers favorable to your escape, but she didn't want to admit it. She objected, with a certain logic, that the leaping of the animals, which we observed a little while ago through the binoculars, was capable of carrying them within range of you. She could already see you..."

"In truth," I interjected, "it was very nearly true."

And I recounted, terrifying them with my story, how one of the animals had, at one time, seized the aerial vessel's mooring-rope, and how we had only escaped its attack thanks to the incredible gymnastic feat accomplished by Commandant Junisseau. Evidently, my language must have been imprinted with all the force of the sensations I had experienced—and never, I thought, had a storyteller been obliged to give such color, interest and sincerity to his story, for to every one of the episodes of the adventure, Suzanne responded with a facial expression of greater distress, and the tighter pressure of her mutually-clasped hands. I had to relate the same details ten times over, and retrace the silhouette of the monsters a hundred times, to satisfy curiosities that my own exhausted emotion no longer permitted me to envisage calmly. The incessant interjections of my friends continually suspended my confidences, and I scarcely had time to answer one question before another was posed.

"Are they really as big as that?"

"Is it conceivable that fracassite isn't able to damage them?"

"How long is their appendage?"

"What diameter?"

"Do they make a noise as they suck things in?"

"In sum, do they have the form of a leather bottle?"

"Of an elongated leather bottle?"

"Of a leather bottle whose anterior prolongation is their aspirator arm?"

"Their tentacle widens at the tip, doesn't it, like a conch?"

"And their carapace, let's talk about that—it's made of scales, like a crocodile's, you say?"

"Can you explain why their movement isn't jerky?"

"They crawl, then?"

"They crawl *and* they bound?"

"And the sponge-man—what can it be?"

"It's prodigious!"

"It's terrifying!"

I did my best to content their breathless curiosity; I re-read in them all my previous alarms. The listened to me with wide eyes, their hearts palpitating, and my explanations confirmed the proverb alleging that the truth can be stranger than fiction. In the fervor of my narration, I began to gesticulate, and in response to one movement my wrist started hurting and began to bleed. I could not suppress a whimper; my nervous system found its trigger in that physical dolor.

"How uncharitable we are, Father! Look, our poor friend's pale...he's hurt!"

Indeed, I had to sit down. A mist clouded my eyes. Mastering their fear, Suzanne and her father hastened to help me. They untied the handkerchief that I had hurriedly put over the wound.

I had a long cut, such as might have been produced by the edge of a sword, with astonishingly neat edges. The separated tissues revealed the nacreous trajectory of tendons, which, mercifully, had not been severed.

The conviction that my wound would have no further consequences, and would allow me to use my arm—at the cost of some pain, it is true—gave me strength, and permitted me to reassure my fiancée who had gone pale in her turn.

"It's nothing—nothing at all—my dear Suzanne...a mere scratch. In a few days it'll be completely gone."

"Are you sure?" asked Monsieur Vernet, "that the injury was produced by a splinter of a carapace?"

"Of course," I said, holding out the projectile, which I had put in my waistcoat pocket.

It was a precious piece of evidence, of which the scientist immediately took possession. He examined it, felt it and turned it over repeatedly, with a veritable avidity. Assuredly, none of his anatomical specimens, in which the power or bizarrerie of life was manifest, had ever procured him such joy as he manipulated it. He consulted its opacity, its color, its form. He took a magnifying-glass from his pocket and studied its contexture. A gem worth a million could not have put more emotion into the heart of a coquette.

"What's inconceivable," he ended up admitting, in a tone mingling delight and surprise, "is the consistency of the tissue.

I wonder what elements it's composed of. I'd never have believed that an anatomical parenchyma could acquire such cohesion in such a short time. No, that's never been observed in nature. Diamond, which is the most resistant substance known, is only carbon crystallized by the centuries…but centuries have passed over it, whereas a year, at the most, has transformed and solidified the epidermis of *Micrococcus aspirator*. It's a prodigy, my children. Ought we not to admire it…?"

But he fell silent. Our physiognomies had admitted that his enthusiasm seemed to us to be pure blasphemy. Holding the debris between his fingers, he went to the window and ran the cutting edge of the fragment over the pane.

"Ha! My word, it scratches glass! You see, my children—it scratches glass!"

Feverishly, his hand traced two words, and I realized that he was simply translating his scientific wonderment into those two words, because what he had written was: *Tornada genius*. He even took his enthusiasm so far as to remove from Suzanne's finger the superb solitaire that I had slipped on to it on the day of our engagement, and run the edge of the fragment over it.

"And that's more extraordinary still! My children, it scratches diamond!"

"Oh, Papa!" Suzanne protested.

Perhaps for the first time in his life, however, he became indignant. "What! A man has had conceptions vast enough to surpass the work of time, and you criticize me for checking its effects with what I have to hand? In what way does that diminish your affection? It has never been given to anyone to experiment with such a phenomenon! Damn it! Leave me to my admiration, my children! I'm free to admire! I'm the master of my veneration! Evil has its beauty, and its grandeur too! And I revolt, in the end, on observing that you don't appreciate, as I do, the creative power of a brain that has thrown down this challenge to nature! For he has created, one must admit…while we scientists have been content to translate and deduce, Tornada has created, at a stroke, formidable life! And that it scratches diamond, I can hardly believe!"

Soon, however, his daughter's distressed expression returned him to a more reasonable appreciation. He calmed down completely at the spectacle of his daughter completing the dressing of my wound, after having washed it with an antiseptic solution. He placed the projectile in his wallet, and began pacing back and forth with long strides—but he evidently continued in private the enthusiastic monologue that our dolorous task had interrupted—and when my wrist was finally bandaged, he did not wait any longer to give free rein to an interpretation that his scientific logic had inspired.

He turned to me: "Well, my friend, that patch that you mistook for the monster's eye, do you know what it is? It's the trace of the original segmentation of the macrobe."

"What does that mean?" Suzanne asked.

"To put it more prosaically, their navel, my dear child. These animalcules, which have been poorly observed at the Institut Pasteur, multiply by binary fission. They give live by virtue of their own resources. They bear their perpetuity in themselves alone. Hence, one can deduce their pullulation when one thinks that they have only to divide into two to make two individuals, and that those segmented fragments constitute, in their turn, individuals capable of multiplying themselves. And that's rather frightful...and quite interesting. Yes, prodigiously interesting. Oh, that Tornada!"

A plaint from Suzanne extinguished his admiration. The poor child went pale. Valiant as she had shown herself to be thus far, she could not resist the exigencies of hunger. For my part, I was no longer listening to my rancor against Tornada, already the cause of so much suffering and calamity, inasmuch as my fiancée's hunger had reached me, and my stomach, like those of my companions, was remembering that it had absorbed nothing in the last eighteen hours by a single brioche and a glass of licorice water. But where could we find something to eat? How could I get into the deserted shops, where provisions must still exit?

I went down into the street to search. I knocked on the iron shutters, which remained deaf to my appeals. Then, understanding the futility of my attempts, I went to my garage and equipped myself with a full set of burglar's tools, which I used to force the doors of the apartments in my house. I rushed to the larders; they were empty. On the fourth floor, however, I discovered a bag of chocolate in a bedroom, which I pocketed; and in the concierge's lodge, which I did not neglect, there was the remains of a cheese, some jam and stale bread. I brought it all back to my friends, and we feasted on it.

Then we went out, cocking our ears toward the west, without perceiving any abnormal noises. It was four o'clock in the afternoon. A delightful sun bathed that frightful day with its gentle warmth. No, the sky had never opposed such delights of spring to so much terrestrial devastation. We went along the Rue de Passy and headed toward the Seine.

Monsieur Vernet, aching from his unexpected morning ride, advanced with difficulty, his hand on his hack. Taking pity on his suffering and his white hair, Suzanne and I each lent him a supportive arm. On the way, haunted by the proximity of the macrobes, we discussed their ravages again, and their fashion of leaping into the air, crushing houses with their colossal mass as they fell back. We were surprised that the rapidity of their action had not yet introduced them into Paris. What were they waiting for? Why were they pausing before falling upon that colossal prey of two million inhabitants? Were they already sated? What order of suspension were they obeying? We could only imagine...

The danger, as frightening as could be, caused us to imagine the utility of our terror in escaping their reach.

"In a cellar!" Suzanne proposed.

"No," I said. "Their tentacle is long, and would surely suck us in."

"Of course! Let's go up the Eiffel Tower!" Monsieur Vernet exclaimed, pointing at the monument, which was nearby. "The appendage of the animals can't reckon with its solidity, and won't reach the first stage!"

We headed in that direction, swiftly, but on the Pont d'Iéna we were stopped by a battalion of infantry. Conserving their marvelous discipline amid the general panic, the troop had formed a barrage around the Chap-de-Mars. We tried in vain to negotiate a passage. We learned that the tower had been reserved for studies of the defense, and that the government had already appointed a committee, chaired by ministers, which would function up there, after having installed offices and a supply of paper.

"That puts the lid on it!" sniggered Monsieur Vernet, shrugging his shoulders.

"Let's go into the Metro," I suggested. "I think it will be safer underground than in the open, as long as we stay away from the tunnel openings."

My plan was agreed, and we resumed our route toward Marbeuf station. There, once again, our despair and indignation increased, when we found that the Metro, like the tower, was under military guard and that no one was allowed in.

Then, consternated, reduced to wandering without shelter, anticipating the end of everything, but nevertheless driven to seek out a crowd by an appetite of curiosity, a need to combine our misery with that of others, we went along the Champs-Élysées toward the Place de la Concorde.

The splendid avenue was less abandoned by human presence. In the gathering dust we observed a certain movement. There was traffic moving through open coaching entrances, carts waiting on the sidewalk; a dispute had just begun. That life, succeeding the solitude of my own quarter, warmed our hearts. We experienced the egotistical impression determining that the sight of the misery of others offers solace to our own.

We drew nearer, and I went up to a group of three individuals, of somewhat disquieting attitude, who were agitating around piled-up items of furniture. I thought that they had received instructions from a property-owner to clear a house whose vestibule announced a certain sumptuousness.

"What are you doing, my friends?" I asked. "How are you wasting your time? Do you realize the peril that threatens us? Since you have the good fortune to possess a carriage, only load it with yourselves, and leave!"

I hesitated for a moment before continuing. An absurd hope attached me o the fate of those fanatics, whom I would have avoided with horror in normal times. I was reckless enough to consider them as possible liberators, to envisage fleeing in their company, on their cart, through a countryside that I wanted to suppose practicable, free of enemies.

"Leave!" I risked. "Leave as quickly as possible—and if you have a spark of humanity, take us with you."

With a gesture, I indicated the location of my wallet, to signify that I was willing to pay for their services.

"One might perhaps see…" said one of them, with a sly smile whose significance, unfortunately, I did not suspect.

The three individuals stepped aside and began to confer. We waited, tremulously, for the conclusion of their discussion. Then one of them approached us. I remember that he was a big, solid fellow, wearing a cap with several flaps, whose mouth was partly deprived of teeth. He reeked of alcohol, and his hands, which he spread in order to converse, were covered in scratches that were still bleeding.

"For sure, my mates and I would like nothing better than to work for worthy bourgeois. It all depends on the price…if there's a means of reaching an understanding. How much do you have on you?"

I took out my wallet, which, in anticipation of an analogous expense, I had taken care to furnish copiously. I counted in front of my interlocutor the sum that I found there, without noticing that the rustle of the bills provoked a particular gleam in his eye. When I had finished my calculation, I confided: "I have three thousand francs. Is that sufficient?"

"For sure, that'll do me!" he said, taking possession of the wad and stuffing it unceremoniously into his trousers.

He turned to his companions, and all three burst out laughing.

Slightly surprised by their attitude, but expecting nevertheless that they were about to execute the agreement, the price of which I had paid in advance, we waited for them to unload their cargo. By contrast, we saw them continuing to heap up the rest of the objects that were on the sidewalk.

"Hey! Aren't you forgetting us?" I exclaimed to my debtor.

He turned round and planted himself in front of me, swaying slightly, his massive silhouette looming over me by a head. With a further smile, full of bestiality, he caused the fangs that still remained behind his lips to gleam. I would never have thought that a human face could acquire such a satanic expression, and my indignation was further increased by the insult.

"What? What?"

"You're loading your cart. It's us who ought to be taking our place there!"

"That's agreed," he said, extending his hand. "But you'll have to wait for the next trip."

"Wretch!"

I had been cheated. His attitude indicated that he would have laid me out with a blow of his fist. I had no hope of any restitution from the nauseating bandit. Oh, if I had only had my revolver! I believe that I would have put a hole in his ugly head without a scruple.

But Suzanne pulled me sleeve. "Let's go...what does money matter? Let's go!" she begged.

"Come on!" her father insisted.

We drew away. All along the avenue we encountered no one but other members of the lowest criminal classes, similarly occupied. All those people were looters, alas! Assured of impunity in a city devoid of police, they were calmly robbing houses of their riches. We saw works of art of the greatest beauty being carried away, sacks full of jewelry, inestimable tapestries: an entire booty of marvels that had been heaped up pell-mell on carts with emaciated horses. The criminal faces of the thieves, their breath heavy with alcohol, their eyes avid, their coarse delight in enriching themselves, inexplicable in those menacing hours, were repulsive, and caused us to hasten our pace toward the Place de la Concorde, and then the Rue Royale, where people had gathered.

Oh why had we entered that human tide that was flowing along the boulevards, and which immediately absorbed us, took possession of us and carried us away!

There was an indescribable swarming, a pressure such that we were suffocated by it at first. One might have thought that the circulation of Paris had flowed back toward its heart, doubtless out of the same need for community in misfortune that we also experienced, and the whole of the vast city seemed to be concentrated in that place.

One cannot form any idea of what that crowd was like. It was not even a crowd, for a crowd is elastic; determination permits it to be escaped; this was a condensation of all the men, all the women and all the children, amassed and compressed between two insurmountable barriers, the walls of houses, subject to surges, eddies and whirlpools provoked by the exasperated gestures of those attempting to make room. For as far as the falling dusk allowed us to distinguish that scene of disorder, we could see nothing but a seed-bed of heads, the majority hatless, a swell of raised arms, brandished canes, frantic gestures, dominated in places by children set on the shoulders of their parents, striving to get them out of the crush.

The ground floor of the buildings opposed implacable resistance to that anarchy with lowered iron shutters, but on the entresol and all the upper floors, crowded windows were disgorging, one might have thought, the living substance of houses filled like anthills. The Place de la Madeleine, the church that erects the antique order of its columns there, the roofs and the chimneys—everything was covered with the human swarm; it seemed that people were stacked one on top of another; clusters caused the trees to bend; and we saw a balcony, succumbing under the weight, plunge into the crowd, introducing death and disaster thereto. As for the howls, the imprecations, the blasphemies that accompanied the fury, I dare not record them.

"We're doomed! Link arms! Squeeze together!" I had shouted to my companions at the very beginning, as soon as I realized that it was impossible to go back. And we had seized one another, knotted ourselves together, in such a way as not to allow ourselves to be dissociated, taking care to place Suzanne between Monsieur Vernet and me, to barricade her delicate person with our tense muscles. I sensed her grip imploring my strength. She did not say anything, she did not cry out; she submitted to the assault of pursed lips, palpitating nostrils.

As for me, all my humanity, my fraternal pity bequeathed by centuries of civilization, had vanished at a stroke; I felt myself repossessed by the savage impulses that engaged our remote ancestors to the ferocious egotism of self-preservation; I would have committed murder to defend us. And I pushed, and pushed back, with a cold rage.

And yet, at times, just as the wind stops blowing and destroying in the midst of a tempest, calms were produced; the human tide stagnated, a relative respite leveling out the crowd—above all, when news arrived, coming nearer and nearer. The cries died down then; the fury declared a truce; a wave of emotion, gaining the anxiety of the people, calmed the delirium. The street-rumors in question were, however, highly improbable, even inadmissible; and what surprised me most of all was that the drama that had unfolded a few kilometers from Paris, and was now displaying its menace around the fortifications, was unknown to the majority.

At times, it was announced that the macrobes had been destroyed by the artillery, and explicit details were given about their anatomy, for it was put about that their autopsy had been carried out by the scientists of the Muséum. I remember that in the midst of the silence, a young man who wore the white smock and black skullcap of a hospital intern shouted details of the scientific examination to us from a window.

"Their stomach," he affirmed, "is as big as a dining room where twenty-four guests could eat in comfort. People have been found there alive who were swallowed two days ago, including a great wood-merchant from Mantes, who had to introduce himself to the deputation, and a peasant pushing a wheelbarrow full of carrots. Yes Messieurs, those poor folk had lived on those vegetables! To tell the truth, the effect of gastric juices had left them in a rather sorry state...they presented the same lesions that burns would have produced, but their lives are expected to be saved..."

A ludicrous invention: delirium or joke? The people welcomed those words open-mouthed, immediately passing them on, and those absurdities passed like a consoling breeze. It would not have taken much for us, who knew the unreality of such fables, to have accorded confidence to them, by virtue of a sort of appetite for reassurance, in order to dissipate momentarily the horrible nightmare of our impotence.

But what astonished us more was hearing, from another window, a grave gentleman who looked like a magistrate, wearing the ribbon of the Légion d'honneur, shout to us: "Don't worry! It's all over! The danger is averted! Tornada is nothing but a vulgar usurper; he had no other purpose than to take possession of the government. And that's now done; the president has resigned. Tornada is installed at the Élysée." He added: "Everything will be restored to order...go home in peace!"

I could not imagine that such implausibilities were being pronounced with so much seriousness.

They reflected, moreover, a state of social enervation, which the present situation could not help but exasperate, and of which trouble-makers were bound to take advantage. I had that conviction when, a few meters further on, I collected the report of events that, on this occasion, appeared to me to offer more truth, by virtue of the fact that were more appropriate to the mentality of a people at bay.

Those rumors were confided to me by one of the journalists of the *Parisien*, Dardant's paper. I knew him; we had studied together, and had not run into one another for a long time when the turbulence suddenly brought us face to face. Having entered the crowd in pursuit of material for a sensational article than he hoped to publish the following day, like us, he had been unable to get out. Cramped, jabbing with his elbows, fighting, without ceasing to hold his notebook in one hand and his pencil in the other, he shouted at me:

"Well, what do you think? This is new! Half of Paris is in revolution, did you know that? There's talk of the Commune! I don't understand anything anymore. Do the anarchists want to seize power? What can you expect, with such a government?"

But a surge of the crowd separated us. I saw him dragged away by the countercurrent, compressed and lifted up, then swallowed up, still finding a means to scribble notes in his book. He waved his arms briefly, as if to swim toward me, and then vanished.

In any case, on our side, a sinister band, mingling men and women, foaming at the mouth, their eyes bulging, jostled us. The cohort in question was howling:

"Death to the bourgeois!"

"Down with the Republic!"

"Long live Anarchism!"

"A blood-letting, to save the people!"

"No more rich!"

"No more owners!"

"Filth! Death! Hou! Hou!"

Evidently, our decent clothing made us an objective of their hatred. They surrounded us, they stifled us; and amid the gesticulations of the fanatics, I thought I saw the gleam of a weapon—a revolver or a knife; I no longer know. I only retain, as a certain impression, my fiancée's fearful expression as she turned toward me, and the memory of letting go of her arm for a moment in order to throw a punch and crush the lip of a hooligan who was trying to lay his hands on hr.

That was an imprudence, for my action immediately determined a red rage on the part of the bandits. And I wondered whether we would be able to get out of it, and what massacre might have succeeded my recklessness if, by a strange opposition of popular sentimentality, a procession of students—oh, how invariably insouciant and cheerful that age is—had not interposed themselves between our aggressors and us. The young people arrived, dragged in a crazy saraband, perforating the crowd, so to speak, drunk on noise and youth, shouting, as if in the midst of a fairground, that inept song of which circumstances had definitely determined the fortune:

"*Viens, macrobe, viens!*"

They did not break the block of our knotted arms. They passed by, carrying the anarchists away, whom their passion guided elsewhere, away from us; and that distance, limited to a few meters of separation, was worth as much as an immensity in the circumstances. The clamors of revolt were mingled momentarily with the inanities of the song, dissolving into them, each translating the base psychology of the crowd. Soon, other angers, other threats and other fears arriving from all directions, caused us to forget them.

And the tide took possession of us again, hugged us, dragged us away, tossing us once again, in the radiant heat of thousands and thousands of people. Squeezed against one another, arms still enlaced, we allowed ourselves to be carried along by a wave that incessantly brought us back to the same place.

It took us, I think, three hours to cover the distance between the Opéra and the Rue Drouot. Night had fallen completely; we could only distinguish the swarm of people by the light of the rare resinous torches that the police had attached to occasional lamp-posts. After areas of dim light, we passed into frightening shadow, in which abominable actions inspired by exasperated instincts were carried out. In order to protect Suzanne from them as much as possible we kept as close as we could to the border of houses.

Occasionally we passed cafés that were still open, but barricaded, and saw customers inside drinking by the light of candles set in bottlenecks. They looked back at us, immobilized and fearful. Once, there was a veritable charge of the crowd toward a brasserie where people were eating. We heard the sound of breaking windows, revolver shots and women's screams, but we got out of the way in time not to have to witness the pillage of the restaurant.

Twenty paces further on, another spectacle immobilized us again. A cinematographic display flickering at the corner of the boulevard announced that it was about to show scenes of the combat of the artillery against the macrobes—but it did not show any of the sinister animals, and concluded its session with an advertisement for a laxative pill. Then the light abruptly went out.

We had just fallen into darkness again when a clamor rose up, while a human flood carried us away, crushing us, bringing us toward a focal point that we could not perceive.

"My God! People are fighting!" Suzanne shouted to me in the torment. "Let's get out of here!"

Her energy, so terribly put to the proof since we had entered into the torment, seemed to me to be on the point of exhaustion. I could feel her weakening. Was she about to fall into a faint there and then?

"If ever..." I began to say to Monsieur Vernet—but I did not have time to finish the recommendation I was about to give, concerning the way in which we ought to protect the fragile child. The riot got worse, inflating the thunder of voices and causing the people to thrash around in an indescribable confusion.

Not letting go of the person with whom I was primarily concerned, estimating that her father, on the other arm, was an additional burden rather than a support, I exasperated my resistance with the sentiment of my dual responsibility. Beside myself, losing all the sympathy that I normally felt for the unfortunate, even if they were strangers to me, I resisted, shoved back and struck out.

Alas, what did I accomplish during those savage minutes? What terrors did I provoke in order to remain standing? What flesh did I trample in order that mine might subsist, in order that my companions should not come to harm? I dug my heels into people who had fallen; I penetrated torsos, crushed limbs and kicked—alas!—I kicked imploring children out of the way.

And the strangest thing about that odious melee in which everyone was led by circumstances to sacrifice his neighbor is that it had no cause. That murderous crowd was obedient to an irrational panic comparable to that which grips a theater audience when a practical joker shouts "Fire!" although nothing is burning. If all those people had kept still, they would certainly have been content with the restricted space that bound them together. The formidable pressure was compounded out of thousands of individual gestures.

I was soon convinced of that, and felt remorse, when I saw the mob suddenly calm down, as waves calm down when a few drops of oil are poured on them. It only required a policeman standing on the shoulders of another, aiding himself with a small electric torch, to begin reading a government proclamation.

The tumult was extinguished; only a quivering, anxious curiosity replaced the clamors of disorder and the fighting. As we were quite close to the official messenger, I did not miss a word of what was emitted through a bushy moustache, whose coarseness was emphasized by the glare of the torch. And this time, the news, at least in substance, seemed to me to be accurate.

"The government," I heard shouted, "meeting in Ministerial Council, is communicating the latest information concerning the danger threatening Paris, and the measures adopted to remedy it. The public ought not to be unaware that the situation is grave, the macrobes occupying the entire periphery of the city. Their movements, precisely monitored since last night, imply that they are following a plan of investment, the strategy of which will, to all appearances, defeat all the measures taken in anticipation..."

"Hou! Hou!" growled the crowd, at the last, evidently maladroit phrase—but as if the heads of State had anticipated that protestation, the policeman continued:

"Nevertheless, the progress of the macrobes has been temporarily suspended, and nothing suggests that they will resume their march before serious protective measures have been undertaken. The government is pleased to announce that a committee of scientists, with Professor Serviat, a member of the Institut, at the head had succeeded in crossing the monsters' zone of occupation and has penetrated into the laboratory from which the animals originated. The committee informs us by wireless telegraph that, having discovered the process of their development, it has already found, within the resources of chemistry, the means of destroying them scientifically..."

"Ah! Ah!" the crowd responded to that promise—whose simplicity, however, worried me.

The agent went on: "The government therefore engages the population to remain calm, and not to yield to the actions of the enemies of the Republic, avid to profit from an exceptional situation to disturb social peace. These troublemakers, by creating further disturbances, can only disrupt the calm of mind that is, at present, more precious than ever to the ministers, in order to calculate the danger and confront it. Measures of extreme rigor will, in any case, be taken against agitators of disorder, and the first, for which the government has taken the initiative, is the declaration of a state of siege."

Cheers, mingles with whistles, greeted that announcement, but the policeman signaled by his gestures that he had not yet finished. His voice rose up again in the silence.

"Although able to guarantee the normal reestablishment of security, as much with regard to political troubles as the invasion of the macrobes, the government nevertheless advises the population to take refuge in the subterranean areas of Paris. Access is authorized to the Métropolitain, the Catacombs, the sewers and the tunnels situated beneath the Opéra. The cellars of the Hôtel de Ville, several monuments and certain churches, lists of which will be pinned up in the Mairies, will, by prefectorial warrant, be delivered to the public. A system of food supply will be organized tomorrow by the municipality..."

"Ha! We'll believe that when we see it!" shouted a street-urchin, in the midst of the silence that fooled the end of the sentence.

Oh, the Parisian people! How fickle they are! Laughter underlined that childish gibe—and that was a good thing, because it downed out the end of the proclamation, which made a further demand for the confidence of the people and announced that the police were on the track of Tornada.

"That manifesto is signed by Durand-Tartapian, the Minister of the Interior," Monsieur Vernet breached, in the momentary calm. He added: "Notice that he's only inspired by political concerns. Isn't that typically modern? So I only grant him a very limited credit. The annihilation of the monsters seems to me to be increasingly improbable. I prefer to retain from that statement only the article that permits us to hide. But where shall we go, my children? You've seen the state of this crowd—its lack of restraint, of wisdom. You've seen its fury. And then, going down into the Metro—will that be possible?"

"Isn't it more prudent to try our luck in the Catacombs?" I asked.

"Evidently, the Catacombs are less well-known, but they're a long way away—the entrance is in the Place Denfert-Rochereau…and my poor Suzanne…"

"I feel capable of going as far as that, Father."

"Let's go then, let's go!"

We were just in time; the crowd was going crazy again. Bawling, screaming and revolutionary songs burst forth not far away. An immense flame, sudden flaring up in the vicinity, revealed that the sedition had not been quieted by the government's fine words. We turned round and saw a column of fire, plumed by millions of sparks, shoot up behind the rooftops of the houses.

"What's burning?" people were asking.

"It's the Opéra!"

"No, it's the Crédit Lyonnais."

"No, it's further away—it's the Printemps or the Théâtre de l'Athenée…"

The guesses were drowned out by the rumors. A horde grouped around a black flag prolonged its stir as far as our group, and suddenly, the terror of a single man dominated the tumult for an instant. I heard the cried of a tortured beast and, standing on tiptoe, I saw in the uncertain light of the distant fire that they were murdering the policeman who had just read the official message. Oh, those clamors that grabbed your guts, that slaughter of a worthy man!

"Run! Let's run!" Suzanne begged.

All our energy from then on was consecrated to moving obliquely to the right, in order to take the Rue Richelieu, which was nearby. The crowd was shoving, stifling us, proffering its futile, desperate rage from a hundred thousand mouths, shouting: "Death to Tornada! Death to Tornada!" The roadway was nothing but a roaring furnace, fueled by hatred. Oh, how urgently we strove to get out of it! What blows we gave and received! What savage precipitation!

Finally, after further actions that I dare not remember, we were finally moving into the desired street when a cry from Suzanne immobilized us.

"There he is! The wretch! The wretch1"

At first, I thought she had gone mad. But on observing the object that had unleashed her anger, I was petrified. There, inside a café, I saw Tornada!

It was him; there was no doubt about it. It was him, because of his ravaged face, agitated by tics, because of his vast beard hanging down to his belt, which his nervous fingers were occupying in buckling and then unbuckling. It was him, sitting in front of a peppermint cordial, the reflection of which, projected by a candle-flame, tinted his sardonic laughter green. It was him, watching with impunity, triumphantly, his vengeance of genius!

At first, anger invaded me, a temptation to launch myself at his abominable person, to break the glass that separated me from him, to wind his long hairy beard around his neck and squeeze, strangling him with it! But a wisdom, a council of moderation that I read in the attitude of my companions, immediately put a brake on my rage. Ill-placed as we were to exchange our sentiments in the midst of that frightful tumult, those clamors stifling our voices, I understood from the gestures of Suzanne and her father rather than their words that they wanted me to get to the madman, and to get him to put an end to the cataclysm.

They would have attempted it themselves, with more chance of influence than I had, if two insurmountable obstacles—firstly the crowd, and then a large barricade of barrels protecting the glazed window—had not separated them from the criminal. I saw Monsieur Vernet's mouth open to shout a recommendation to me, but I could not hear his voice. Then he indicated to me, by lowering his finger, a possible route through an open ventilation-shaft to the kitchens, and with another gesture, his resolution to remain where he was until the negotiations were concluded.

I shivered at those mute orders. Would I ever find them again? Deprived of my support, would they not be borne away?

After that hesitation, which any fiancé will excuse, I released my arm from Suzanne's, cleaved through the human border encrusting the walls, and plunged into the ventilation-shaft, which was only just wide enough to permit the passage of a human body.

IX

I plunged, it is necessary to say, arms outstretched and head first; and it is a pure miracle that I was not badly hurt in that somersault, which an acrobat would have refused to execute. It is certain that great emotions count among the best anesthetics, for, like a soldier who does not feel the bullet that has passed right through his body, I felt neither the violence of my fall nor the tearing of my wrist when my hands encountered the flagstones of the kitchen. Furthermore, my movement of propulsion toward that dark and unknown place was so rapid, so irrational that I dare not affirm that it ended on the floor. It is possible that I encountered obstacles that attenuated its brutality, and that I fell on to sacks or baskets of comestible provisions. In truth, I no longer know.

At any rate, the kitchen was not deserted, and curses greeted me as soon as I stood up again. Directing my gaze toward a corner of the room where an oil-lamp was spreading a light so feeble that it was indistinguishable from outside, I saw half a dozen people sitting around a table covered with victuals, occupied in eating with a serenity and an appetite that appeared to me not to lack irony.

It was a kitchen household of the classic type: the obese man clad in white with a cloth cap tilted over his ear; the fat woman with three chins collapsing toward enormous breasts; in the company of four apprentices as thin as their seniors were blossoming with fat.

"No one can come in!" the man commenced by shouting at me, brandishing his fork.

"It's not allowed!" said his companion, supportively, pausing in her mastication.

"Does Monsieur have his invitation on him?" chaffed one of the apprentices.

"Don't disturb yourselves, my friends," I replied.

That dialogue, whose flavor would have been appreciated by a vaudevillian, but which only revealed a perfectly natural emotion in either side, did not cheer up the diners. At first they affirmed their intention of sending me back by the same route that I had arrived, but they doubtless feared that my example might be followed by others, for, after a conference whose details were inaudible to me, the man got up to go and close the ventilation-shaft by means of a solid iron lid. He cursed at the same time, declaring to me, with irritated eyes, that he was going to lack air now, and that he detested "eating while stifling."

"I beg your pardon," I said, humbly, when I thought he had calmed down slightly. "Excuse me—I'm just passing through. Will you allow me to go and join one of my friends, who is waiting for me in the café?"

But he shook his head. "No one goes through—I told you that, Monsieur. It would take no more than that for us to open the doors to customers. We'd no longer be at home then."

"Listen," I said. "The meeting I have upstairs is important. Do you know who you have upstairs? Do you know who I've just seen, from the street? Tornada!"

"Tornada?"

"Yes, Tornada."

"Who's that?"

"What! You don't know! You don't know the name of Tornada?"

Thinking that I was the object of his mockery, at the height of irritation, I had folded my arms.

"Tornada?" the man repeated. "Unknown, Tornada. Me, I live quietly."

"We only know *tournedos*," confided the female cook.

"But what about the macrobes?" I howled. "You've heard mention of them? Well, Tornada, their inventor, their creator, is upstairs!"

This time, Homeric laughter welcomed my declaration. Oh, the macrobes! What a joke! No, the story of the macrobes was for others! They knew perfectly well that it was only an invention of the revolutionaries, made to deceive the people, to whip them up, to drive them along, as the barking of dogs directs a flock of sheep to a determined point, and no serious man would ever be naïve enough to attach any faith to it. And the apprentices, infected by the chef's explosion, laughed uproariously, clutching their bellies.

"That's fine," I said. "Retain your absurd confidence. I'm not going to waste my time convincing you—but I need to go through and I shall. Show me the way."

I must have looked intimidating, because the man's gaiety suddenly died down. Cowed, he opened a door for me and pointed to a dark stairway. I groped my way up the steps, and, guided by the noise, went through another door and reached the common room.

Immediately, I recognized the madman enveloped by the halo of the green liquid. I slid through the crowded ranks of the customers and joined him.

I paused momentarily to look at him. He seemed even stranger than before, more firmly in the grip of his dementia than during our previous meeting. Folded in two on his chair, having buttoned his jacket over the threads of his beard, it seemed to me that he had scarcely recovered from a convulsion that had furrowed his brow terribly and was still agitating his right arm. The candlelight, gliding over his cranium, emphasized its improbable bumps, and his cheekbones, crimsoned at present, were jutting in the midst of the green tint of the rest of his face.

He stretched, sniggered and stammered a few words; then, picking up a piece of paper that the fit had caused him to drop, he began scribbling on it, and soon seemed to be nothing but a peaceful mathematician or a mild philosopher, transporting through the disaster the passion of a metaphysical problem.

"Monsieur Tornada! Monsieur Tornada!" I said, in a voice that would have softened the heart of a Chinese torturer.

He did not raise his head. He continued to draw the tip of his pencil over the sheet of paper. Leaning toward his work, I perceived that he was drawing a map of Paris, around which a number of little crosses had been marked. In less tragic circumstances, I would certainly have attempted to identify the positions of those crosses, which obviously related to the present calamity, and I would have discovered the emplacements of the monsters investing us. But the moment scarcely inspired my mind to curiosity, and I was intent on another liberating concern.

"Monsieur Tornada! Monsieur Tornada!" I repeated, this time touching him on the shoulder.

He flinched, as if he had been touched by an electric discharge. He covered his drawing with his fully-extended hand, then screwed it up, rolled it into a ball, shoved it in his mouth, and started masticating it. Only then did he look at me, and I judged by his wild expression that he did not recognize me. His breathing accelerated; three times, his eyes disappeared beneath his eyelids in such a fashion as only to show the whites; his hands described a few movements imitating the extension and subsequent retreat of a tentacle, and after having spat out the ball of paper, he finally resumed a normal expression.

During that further fit, I had had time to finish observing the alteration of his features, noting their satanic expression, increased by the surprise of hearing his name spoken aloud. The extension of his vibratile ears, the planes and hollows sculpted in his visage, and the prognathism of his jaw had adopted such reliefs that, in truth, his physiognomy no longer looked human.

"Who are you?" he demanded, in a distant voice, which the ambient noise made even fainter.

"You don't recognize me?"

"No."

"I'm Mademoiselle Vernet's fiancé."

I perceived that that name, thrown into his mind, immediately acquired such an influence there that I thought at first that I could count on its evocation. Tornada must have been going through one of those psychological states in which delirium is still semi-conscious, in which the inspiration of a fact, or a person, can be sufficient to modify the current of a determination, when the brain takes possession of it. His face as imprinted with a very particular softness; tears flowed from his eyelids.

"Oh! Yes, Suzanne…Suzanne…" he stammered. "How glad I am to have advised her to flee! She's far away now. She and my worthy friend are far out of range of my darlings!"

"No!" I protested, violently. "They haven't fled! They're here, nearby. You can see them from here, jostled by that furious crowd! For pity's sake, Monsieur…"

"Yes, I'm glad," he affirmed, rubbing his hands.

He was no longer listening to me. At the same time, I had sown the seeds of another upheaval in his mental ferment, and he was surrendering to it, completely forgetting the first. I thought it prudent to allow that new eruptive lava to flow away before returning to my supplication, and I listened to his rambling words.

"But the others! Oh, the poor people! Are they miserable enough? Look at them! This is a good place from which to observe them. You've never seen anything like it! I had to be born for that! The elements have never given any idea of such a cataclysm! They're mightily imbecilic, the elements! They make the ground tremble, they parade cyclones, stir up tidal waves…but what's that, compared with what I've created? What is it, in truth? An entire people…the most beautiful of peoples…the French people…!"

He laughed sardonically. Then, accentuating the lines on his forehead, clenching his fists, he panted, with such profusion that that I had difficulty divining what kind of ideas corresponded to each of his statements: "Me, in my laboratory…a culture, a simple culture…darlings…soda and chalk combined…atmospheric demi-pressure…and yellow, yellow, yellow…! And then, I had to fix the acidity…then, every day, a little more…I caressed them…I held them in the palm of my hand…oh, what a thrill! What a thrill, my darling!"

He punctuated his speech with special gestures, translating the entire evolution of his phenomenon. Sometimes his hands described circles, sometimes zigzags; sometimes they seemed to be palpating substance, sometimes stoking spines. But he became suddenly suspicious of me, and looked at me warily.

"If you ever repeat...."

"No, no," I protested. "Trust me! You know how much admiration I have for you, for your work...and the bonds that unite me with Suzanne..."

"Have they gone to the Midi?" he asked, anxiously.

It was the moment, propitious once again, to soften him, to remind him of two friends, whom the torment was bringing closer to us. I could, in fact, see through the window that the shadows outside were agitating more violently; the eye of the popular cyclone was moving toward the window of the café. A strident cry that I thought I recognized as that of my fiancée was a more imperious appeal for the rapid execution of my project to save us from death by means of the murderer himself.

"Listen," I said to him. "Listen carefully...leave your dreams for a moment. You love Suzanne like your own daughter, don't you?"

"Yes, my daughter, my poor child!"

"And Monsieur Vernet, you love him too, you hold him in esteem?"

"He's the only brain in the Institut," he affirmed.

"Well, both of them..."

I was unable to go on. A formable crack resounded from the front of the café. The barricade of barrels that was forbidding access had just given way, thunderously. A hurricane of cries, the last plaint of those who were choking and trampled underfoot, unfurled, accompanied by the sound of glass panes shattered by the rush. The human sea invaded our refuge, sweeping away the tables of the original customers, driving as far as the café's counter in an indescribable disorder. A thousand terrified faces, a thousand howling faces, were dancing before my eyes—and among them I recognized, fearfully, the most dear of faces: Suzanne, alone, struggling in the torment, extending the imploration of her hands and the agony of her gaze toward me.

Then, I forgot Tornada, who had just stood up, uttering a burst of insane laughter. I precipitated myself toward my fiancée, and reached her, by means of I don't know what prodigy of force and ferocity. Then, after having drawn her to me, encircling her with my arms: "Your father, Suzanne?"

"Separated! Carried away! Lost!"

"Where? Which way?"

"That way! That way! Oh, let's search for him, Jean, for pity' sake! Let's find him! Him first..."

I drew her toward the outside. Fortunately, a counter-surge facilitated our exit, and we were able to slide along the wall, avidly interrogating the atrocious melee that the sentiment of individual defense was still driving to the worst actions.

To describe my fiancée's despair to you would be impossible. A thousand times she called out to her father in the torment. A thousand times, retained by my hand, she whirled around in the same space of ten square meters, stiffening herself against the tide of men, women and children. We were no longer thinking about Tornada, nor of revenge. We were interrogating the swell of heads frantically, without the beloved white head showing itself therein. Futile efforts! Soon, a more forceful mob swept us back into the street that we had decided to take before being separated from Monsieur Vernet.

"Don't worry, my dear Suzanne," I said to her. "We'll find him again at the Catacombs."

In tears, fearful, in despair, she obeyed me. We had only to allow ourselves to be shoved along the Rue Richelieu. Lighting had not been provided there, unlike the boulevards; the conflagration did not project any light there, and it was pitch black, the haunted night of murders and crimes. Oh, what a terrible odyssey, what instincts, in that darkness! I still shiver at the thought.

Outside the Bibliothèque Nationale, however, I suddenly felt Suzanne stop holding on to me. She weakened; she collapsed in a faint. I took her in my arms and carried her, utterly limp, thinking that I was no longer holding anything but a corpse. The flood threw me out, with my precious burden, in the Place du Palais-Royal, where a torch was burning. Seeing that the crowd was battling furiously to reach the entrance to the Metro, I made a detour and took refuge in the Place du Carrousel, which was dark and relatively deserted. I reached the Gambetta monument and deposited the object of my adoration, who was just coming round, on the stone. I was out of breath, incapable of any further action.

"My father? Where's my father?" Suzanne asked, faintly.

I strove in vain to console her. She wept, and through her tears she stammered the same question, incessantly. Sitting beside her, I rested her head on my shoulder. At that moment, I knew all the distress of hearing her suffer and remaining impotent. Mothers who watch their children die must experience those sharp emotions.

Gradually, however, Suzanne's plaints became spaced out. Soon, I could not perceive anything but regular breathing—child-like breathing. Exhausted, she had fallen asleep. I felt a horrible fatigue myself, which went so far as to dominate the sharp pain in my wrist. I no longer had the courage to do anything but lay my fiancée on the ground and cover her with my jacket.

And under a sky whose implacable darkness was spangled with stars, like a funereal awning, I went to sleep in my turn.

X

The next day, as soon as the livid daylight appeared, the fresh air and the pain in my wrist woke me up.

Was it, in fact, really those factors that recalled me to the ambient reality? Was it not rather a song that pursued me momentarily in my sleep? At any rate, when I opened my eyes, I fund before me an indescribable presence. I would have smiled, on any other occasion, on recognizing the man who was singing *"Viens, macrobe, viens!"*—the same individual who, the day before, had sold us old brioches for an exorbitant price. His Neptunian hair covered by a flat-brimmed hat, his nose reddened by cold, his replete body shivering in a long gray frock-coat, he was strolling with a artificial gaiety through the desolation of others; and with his pipe in his mouth, he never ceased to continue the success of his song. I even believe I remember that he was staggering slightly.

I turned my eyes away with dignity in order to gaze at my fiancée, lying beside me. She was adorably pale, continuing her child-like slumber.

Then I looked at the Place du Carrousel. In that magnificent space, as in the sumptuous perspective of the Jardin des Tuileries, there was nothing but a succession of groups formed by people who had imitated us; the ground was strewn with exhausted people, still asleep. Only might have thought it a desolate field where all afflictions were united, parents with children, husbands with wives. Some were waking up and stretching. Sobs rose up behind me, on the other side of the grille surrounding the Gambetta monument. It was lamentable...

An usher from the Colonial Ministry, recognizable by his blue coat with gold buttons, came down from the Pavillon de Flore and advanced through the heaps, stepping over bodies. Allowing Suzanne to sleep, and without losing sight of her, I went toward the man, as others did, who were surrounding him already.

"Well, what's the news?"

"You're in luck, Messieurs. We possess fresh intelligence, for the telephone service as just been reestablished."

"So, what do you have to tell us?"

"Nothing very cheerful. They're ferocious; they've destroyed the Élysée, taken the Hôtel de Ville, blown up the bridges surrounding the Île Saint-Louis and massacre the troops sent against them—and it's said that they've set fire to the warehouses at Ivry. I noticed a gleam, yesterday evening..."

"What do you mean? Are they setting fire to things too?"

"Oh, they won't deprive us, the monsters!"

"It's their leader, doubtless?"

"A famous scoundrel, Monsieur! He declared the Commune last night! What will become of us, the honest functionaries...?"

"Tornada has...?"

"Tornada!" said the man, looking me up and down, angrily, beginning to think that I was making fun of him.

Only then did I understand that the honest functionary in question had no other concern that informing me of the triumph of the Revolution in Paris. Anarchy had sprung forth from the danger threatening the city; the sectarians had taken advantage of the confusion to change the government. And his first, his gravest preoccupation was what was going to become of his position and his salary, comfortably acquired by eight hours of daily idleness, in consequence of the social upheaval. The other danger did not exist, in the face of that personal anxiety.

"But what about the macrobes, my good man?"

"The macrobes? Well, they're still there."

"Are there any details?"

"No. They haven't budged during the night."

"You're talking as if their presence around Paris doesn't worry you?"

"It might worry me, if Monsieur Serviat, the great chemist, weren't occupied with them, but with him, one can rest assured. Oh, he's a clever one, Serviat!"

"Why? What has he done?"

"You don't know? It's odd that you're so ignorant."

"Speak, speak, my god man!" I pressed him, panting to know.

"Well, he's succeeded in getting into the macrobes' cave out there at Rosny, near Mantes..."

"That was proclaimed, indeed, but I thought..."

"It's not necessary to think; it's necessary to know. Me, I know."

"Speak! Speak!"

He hesitated. The confidences he had imparted so easily in talking about the revolution seemed to grip him at heart now that he had to surrender information of much greater interest. Perhaps, in fact, he did not know anything at all, and was talking to make himself seem important.

He smiled blissfully. "This is it: Serviat has returned, and it appears that he's found a secret to destroy the vile beasts—a kind of chemical product that he's gone to offer to the new government, to curry favor. Oh, he's a clever one, Serviat…he doesn't forget, he's thinking about his situation."

From his parted lips the usher expelled a little jet of saliva. Then, pushing his cap toward the back of his occiput, he said: "Me, Monsieur, I wouldn't have been so confused. I know what I'd have done, if I'd been the government. Yes, it wouldn't have taken long."

"What would you have done, my good man?"

"I'd have gathered all the honest folk underground, and left the surface of the communards."

"And then?"

"Then I'd have sent the army against them—a well-disciplined, strong army, with cannons. We pay enough taxes for that."

"And?"

"Then, naturally, the communards would have been chased out of Paris."

"Naturally," I agreed, with a certain pity.

"And what would have happened?"

"Yes, what would have happened?"

"The macrobes would have wolfed the lot, M'sieu…and that would have been a good thing, M'sieu!"

And the honest functionary, as soon as he had revealed his strategic plan, drew away, rubbing his hands.

I have taken the trouble to record that conversation with the usher, not because of the interest it presents in itself—for in truth, it was rather puerile—but because it is very significant of the mentality that animated an entire people in those hours of fear. It is curious to observe the paltry considerations can result from the instinct of conservation, which is generally believed to be purified, and magnified by centuries of civilizing atavism.

Although the very existence of society was compromised, and a giant ring surrounded Paris, ready to stifle it, the predominant concern among thousands of citizens was to modify the social order, to change the formula of government, and to base individual hopes on political calculations; while thousands of other citizens only envisaged the dispossession with terror. Yes it was expectable, the panic of all the poor people dominated in spite of everything by obsessions of an inferior and purely self-interested order; and every heir having to think about his inheritance, while every businessman was already planning the speculations that the disaster would allow him to stir up. It is said by a reliable source that when Messina began to collapse after a subterranean convulsion, as soon as the news broke, avid businessmen took the train to the destroyed city, running the risk of further quakes, with the sole aim of buying cheap the land diminished in price by the cataclysm—like birds of prey flocking to charnel-house without noticing the rifles aimed at them.

Well, with regard to the drama through which I lived, the same disconcerting psychological observation was recordable.

Certainly, in many circumstances, evidence of admirable abnegation compensated for the vileness of the general egotism. Certainly, there were heroic parents, devoted children, spouses and fiancés, whose altruism was sufficient in itself to ornament the story of such a calamity with the most beautiful nobility—fortunately for human dignity. But I repeat, the vast majority no longer took advice from anything but the dryness of their hearts; the people who were no longer dominated by the fear of the gendarme, and the gendarme too—an honest functionary, in essence—all, I have reason to think, were only obedient in that enormous adventure to the impulses of an eminently shabby self-interest.

That was for me an incomparable lesson in philosophy, and I would certainly have taken longer inspiration therefrom if my anxiety had not brought me back to Suzanne. I went to rejoin her, my heart suddenly calmed, only wanting to remember from the usher's words the intoxicating hope of our imminent liberation. I thought that the pause in the macrobes' progress had been inspired by Tornada, and that the madman, finding his vengeance sufficient, had used his mysterious power over the monsters to prevent them from advancing. A further contribution to the accreditation of that sentiment, moreover, was the presence of Tornada, observed by me the previous evening, which I wanted to consider as a safeguard. Would he expose himself to the risk of being crushed or devoured along with everyone else?

Vibrantly, I came back to Suzanne and woke her up in order to tell her what I knew, and what I had concluded from the usher's words.

"Oh, if it's true, what a liberation!" she sighed. "Only let me hug my father in my arms, and I'll forget this entire drama!"

"Let's go, Suzanne. No doubt we'll find him soon."

Fragile hope! A terrifying noise responded to that remark, and plunged us back into the frightful reality. Oh, that was the moment when we entered more cruelly into that improbable drama. What a frisson suddenly ran through me—for

I was too well aware of the significance of the *Frott...!*
Frott...! Frott...! that we could hear not to begin trembling,
manifestly enough for Suzanne to experience the reverberation
of my emotion.

She did not even have time to question me. An incredible
racket, produced by the collapse of houses, burst forth in the
surroundings, as if an earthquake had shaken the whole city.
The horrified clamor of a people was mingled with it, dominated most of all by the roaring that revealed the proximity of
the monsters. They could be heard arriving from every direction: from Les Halles, from the Saint-Germain quarter, from
the great boulevards, from the region of the Hôtel de Ville.
Yes, everywhere! From all directions the deadly hordes were
running, sacking, swallowing, at the very moment when we
were counting on the pity of their creator. By virtue of what
incredible accord were they making that unanimous irruption,
surrounding the center of Paris with a destructive circle?

To begin with, we ran toward the Jardin des Tuileries.
Then we stopped, like hunted animals, uncertain of which way
to go. paralyzed by the roars that were bursting forth from all
directions. I took hold of Suzanne's trembling hand. A common, infinite distress stupefied us. We stared at one another,
awaiting the event that would annihilate us.

A few minutes were eternalized in that unspeakable terror. Then I saw—did I really see it? was I not delirious? am I
not delirious now in recounting it?—an enormous mass, like
an elongated gray rock that had surged from the entrails of the
earth, fill the sky while accomplishing a forward roll, and fall
directly upon the buildings of the Finance Ministry, which
collapsed under its weight.

The light of day had been suddenly diminished by it.
Dust billowed up from the crushed building, continuing the
artificial demi-obscurity, with the result that the macrobe that
had just introduced itself so fantastically began its devastating
work without me being able to distinguish it clearly. It finally
emerged from its cloud, and I estimated, in spite of my terror,
that it was a little taller than the level of a fourth floor, and that

the area of the Cour du Carrousel permitted it just enough room to crawl along, dilating its body and then shrinking it again. Meanwhile, its trunk, projected in all directions by a rapid rotation and endowed with an incalculable force of suction, collected on the wing, if I might put it thus, all the wretched, tiny people who were running along the ground and drew them into it.

Oh, the unforgettable nightmare! The macrobe went back and forth, turning and roaring—and we stood there contemplating it, a cold sweat on our temples, our limbs limp, petrified, involuntarily uttering little inarticulate squeaks, which we could not repress. We sensed that it was about to suck us in like the others, but we did not budge.

It accomplished a rush to the right, and then it came back toward the Gambetta monument, and stopped there. That pause was lucky for us, at the same time as it signified a new threat for the future. I had thought, in fact, after the failure of the bombs, that Tornada's creatures were blind and moved toward their fodder by means of a simple sniffing of their tentacle, but I was obliged by what I saw then to be convinced that they were endowed with sight in some part of their body that I could not identify. It is impossible to interpret otherwise the act that followed the macrobe's hesitation.

In fact, the latter sniffed the statue of the orator forcefully; then, observing that the bronze did not respond to its attractive force, seized by rage, it wrapped its trunk around it and tore it free. It held it for a moment; then, finally recognizing its error, hurled it into the air prodigiously. I followed the trajectory described by the projectile, and even before the thought occurred to me that it might annihilate us, I saw it fall five meters away from us, digging into the ground and flattening, with a red splash, a poor man dressed in a gray frock-coat, who was singing, in accordance with the whim of a parodist of whom history ought to speak: "*Viens, macrobe, viens!*"

That crushing, so close to us, rendered us all our terror. We fled then, recklessly. Pursued by the whistling of the tentacle, by the broom-like swishing that the carapace made, our ears ringing, carried on by the gallop of others, we reached the flower garden of the Tuileries, and then the bank of the Seine.

I do not know by virtue of what miracle we escaped at that moment. Lifted up twenty times by the air current that the trunk produced, and dropped to the ground twenty times, we struggled with our last reserves of energy against the fury of the torrent of suction. Alongside us, galloping like us, we had already seen the ministry usher disappear, and then a curé who dropped to his knees, and then women, children and a hundred others. It was amazing to observe the facility with which the monster snatched them up and caused them to fly into the flared conch that constituted the tip of its appendage. One might have thought that a magnetic current was drawing them in.

In any case, my senses were so confused at that moment, and my preoccupation to maintain my fiancée next to me so vivid, and my blood, hastened by running, was making such glimmers dance before my eyes, that I dare not affirm anything further about that frightful minute. Certainly, however, other things must have happened during that flight, which took us along the edge of the Place de la Concorde and then the Cours-la-Reine, at the speed of a runaway horse.

I do remember that when we arrived at the Pont d'Alma, after stopping momentarily, and noticing that no macrobe was in view on the other bank, I shouted to Suzanne, in a suffocation: "To the Eiffel Tower! Across the bridge! To the Eiffel Tower!"

For the moment, I was truly inspired. The monster, in fact, did not follow us. Its gray mass continued to snake along the other bank, crushing the trees, disemboweling the buildings, swallowing the unfortunates who had not imitated us.

It seemed to us that we were quitting the torments of Hell to enter into a paradise of solitude. Humans, you who ordinarily walk at a measured pace, you will never know how delightful it was for us to advance with less haste, to let ourselves ease our breathing momentarily, all the more so as we had taken for the objective of our relented course the liberating

127

tower, the summit of which we could see, installed in the warmth of the nascent sun, and we had the certainty that its tall framework would soon be disengaged from its girdle of troops, because the horses of the Republican Guards, relieved of their riders, were galloping toward us. I felt the hoof of one of them brush me, like a caress, as it passed by.

Will I be able to recount what followed without hating destiny? When we arrived at the tower, the situation was scarcely any more enviable. Our last refuge was inaccessible. An entire population was battling to climb up it. Men were killing one another like ferocious beasts, in order to reach safety. The stairways and struts of the edifice, from a few meters above the ground, were black with people, bristling with human clusters. They formed the swarm of an anthill, a feverish swell, rising to the most elevated positions. I saw people hanging on to columns letting go and falling on to their fellows.

As for myself, I no longer knew any chivalrous sentiment, or any pity. Dragging Suzanne, I rushed into the melee, and knew the horrible intoxication of thrusting people aside, striking out, perhaps killing…I can no longer remember. But I retain since that time, the greatest indulgence for crimes engendered by the instincts.

And I shoved, and I struck out, in order to reach the first marble step of the southern stairway; and I was about to reach it when a roar burst forth a hundred meters away from us, and then a second, and then others.

Of course! I was stupid not to have realized that those twenty million preys perched on the tower would tempt our engulfers!

And the macrobes came running from all directions; their gray mass surged forth; their prodigious bounds filled every sector of the horizon, and then landed on the nourishing heap, while their avid trunks, whirling and roaring, ate into the crowd.

Oh, to flee, to flee again! Alas, we no longer had that possibility; the crowd paralyzed us, froze us with its far, by the very suspension of its fratricidal actions.

Momentarily, I had a flicker of hope, for the pressure threw us toward the Pont d'Iéna and I thought it was free and launched myself toward it...ah yes! One last monster, the one that had been pursuing us a little while before, moved on to it.

Then, there was nothing else to do but await the hecatomb. I darted one last glance of distress and love at Suzanne, to which she responded with an unexpected expression, as her face brightened with the celestial exaltation of martyrs.

"It's over, Suzanne! This time, we're doomed!" I stammered, with a shiver.

"Well, let's die in the river—together!" she shouted.

Yes! Any death at all rather than the monsters' tentacle!

In a few bounds, we tumbled down the stairs that led to the jetty. The river, an image of serenity in the face of the disaster, was rolling magnificently. The idea of disappearing into it enveloped me with a sovereign tranquility.

I drew my fiancée against me, and, passing her all my heart in a first and final kiss, surrendered myself with her to the Lethean wave.

XI

I no longer recall exactly what happened during the minute that followed our leap into the Seine, for I was at the end of thought and suffering, and I no longer had any idea in my head but finishing it, and holding Suzanne in my arms. I retain the memory, however, that the coldness of the water seemed beneficent to me, and that my ears filled with a splashing that replaced the noisy clamors from without.

Then...was it the instinct of preservation, superior to my will that brought me to the surface and, in spite of the weight of my garments, forced me to utilize the current that was bearing us away? Was it me who sustained Suzanne, or was it her who, with a hesitation equal to mine, maintained herself intelligently on my shoulder while I swam? I cannot say. I cannot specify anything apart from the moment when, after having traversed the entire width of the river, I saw the people on the quay on the other bank who were making signs to me. I have the perception that someone threw me a rope, and that the rope was terminated by an anchor, which remained on the surface of the water.

With the aid of chance, and also my skill, I succeeded in hooking the spike of that anchor to my fiancée's dress. Without seeing it, for I was now too busy resisting the current, I divined that someone was pulling her ashore and hoisting her up on to the quay. Then someone threw me the anchor, to which I clung, in order to be lifted up in my turn. I vaguely recognized the large wall on which the Pont d'Iéna is seated, and finally fainted, out of strength, into a gentle oblivion.

The dolor of the wound on my wrist, which had reopened during the preceding events, reanimated me. My first perceptions were strange, and continued to give me the impression that I was living in a dream. What could I see, then? What was that dark room, feebly lit by a smoky lamp, in which people were leaning over me, watching my awakening with interest?

What amazed me most of all, though, was to observe that the light was playing over the breastplate of an ancient suit of armor, looming up in front of me. I remained in that vague hesitation, my ears assaulted by noises emanating from the far side of the room. Then, as an individual leaned toward me, I saw on his face the features of Monsieur Serviat, the chemist, the friend of my future father-in-law.

I have not said enough about Monsieur Serviat, who plays a preponderant role in this story. Monsieur Serviat was, as I have already said, a highly placed official scientist whose career had been singularly favored by circumstances and chance. He was also haloed by a legend, and during gala days at the Élysée he never failed, as he pointed to the commander's cross pinned to his lapel, to declare that twenty-three years before, he had only been a humble pharmacist's errand boy, sweeping the shop and delivering bottles of medicine all over the city. One fine day, in the middle of an epidemic—it was a good day for pharmacists—he had stood in for the sick apprentice, crushing potassium chlorate and adding julep syrup with such joy that his employer had been amazed and, having taken him under his protection, had sent him to study the art dear to Monsieur Purgon.[15]

No one suspects the fortune that a man thus launched into science might acquire. Knowing that he is unsupported, everyone takes an interest in him; devoid of protection, everyone protects him; and devoid of esteem, everyone admires him, and admires themselves at the same time. If the sons of Papa succeed easily, the sons of many Papas have even greater chances of success. No one will be astonished, therefore, that the député for Carcassonne, from which young Serviat hailed, obtained a bursary from the city for him, and that old ladies clubbed together to add the dessert dishes to the city's beef-steaks. There was a Serviat Committee, and the child of Carcassonne, glorious in his examinations, became the glory of

---

[15] A character in Molière's *Le Malade imaginaire* (1673), physician to the hypochondriac who gives the play its title.

the entire Midi when, a little later, appointed a professor of chemistry, he praised the alimentary vale of alcohol—but, it goes without saying, the good alcohol, the sole inoffensive alcohol, that the vintners distil. From then on, having become a great citizen of the region, all meridional political influences coalesced to aid him to pass through the doors of the Institut while still young.

Never did any man wear the green coat so valiantly. He put it on for all occasions. When anyone had need of that color to embellish a wedding or garnish a table, he immediately came running. He paraded himself, strutted, put on airs and flirted merrily. He did not lack, moreover, either the appetite for work enjoyed by those who have begun work too late to have used up their intellect, nor the faculty of assimilation the brains possess which are spared the multiple and confused registrations of childhood. He gave lectures; he was a kind of commercial traveler of science. His few discoveries got a lot of publicity, without being absolutely new—but they passed for such, in consequence of the fortunate death of a few insignificant collaborators. And we know the results of the fracassite, which he had invented without anyone's aid. All things considered, a charming man.

Well, my friend, are you feeling better?" he asked me, as soon as he discovered the reactivation of my gaze.

"Yes...but what has become of Suzanne?" I asked, immediately.

"Have no fear, the young woman is here," he replied.

I sat up, and distinguished my fiancée lying on the ground in the middle of another group, in the halo of another lamp. She woke up just in time to send me a sad smile with her lips, and began asking for her father insistently. At that moment I lost consciousness again.

A little later, the energetic flagellations of a wet cloth on my face rendered me the use of my senses definitively. Then, my eyes adapting to the place, I recognized that I was in a kind of stonework gallery between fifteen and twenty meters long and about three wide, about one and a half times my stature in height. On one side, to my right, the tunnel opened to the outside, so far as I could judge by the daylight filtering through the base of a grille placed over a door; while on the other side, to my left, the conduit plunged steeply into the earth, extending into an obscurity disturbed by clamors. A confusion of voices was buzzing in that refuge, dominating a sound of water that I could clearly hear running in the darkness when the voices died down. When I extended my led to stretch it, my foot collided with something hard, like a rail.

"Where am I, then?" I asked Monsieur Serviat, who had just addressed a few words to the heroic armor.

"You're at the entrance of the sewer that opens on to the Quai de Billy, my friend."

That response allowed me to get my bearings. I had, in my time, visited the underground regions of Paris, and I knew that there exist in places, communicating with the Seine, galleries known as "outlets," facilitating the clearance of sewers. By that means, the sandy debris that accumulates in the drains can be collected and transferred to boats which transport it some distance away. The same conduits, in addition, permit collectors to disgorge their overflow into the river in times when abundant rains provoke sudden floods.

That explained all that I had just glimpsed, including the illumination of the wan service lamps, the presence of rails under my feet, and the nearby wagons. It was an unexpected freak of chance that the plunge into the Seine that Suzanne and I had made had terminated just at the entrance to one of those galleries, and that we had had the good fortune to be picked up there.

Good fortune? Was it necessary to give so much thanks to fate? Should we not rather, on the contrary, have cursed it for having snatched Suzanne and me from the oblivion to which we had reconciled ourselves? What would become of us in the midst of these people that hazard and fear had assembled in this subterranean duct? Who would feed us? What would permit us to wait until our enemies had gone away? Would they ever go away? Would Tornada, taking his vengeance to the ultimate limits of cruelty, employing his mysterious power over his creatures, ever order them to retreat? Even supposing that he avowed the same hatred against the rest of the nation that he had heaped upon Paris, and that he launched his army on further ravages, would he not organize matters in such a way as to complete the extermination of the capital by leaving a rearguard of monsters there? Would there not emerge from his powerful brain—had he not already anticipated—a means of clearing out the places in which the residue of the people, thus far spared the gluttony of the macrobes, had gone to ground? I could suppose anything of such a terrifying individual.

A thousand other considerations were still jostling in my imagination, already exhausted by so much anguish. The physiological inferiority in which I found myself gave them a confusion of which terror was the principal agent. I supposed, by turns, everything that one can invent of the most deadly and the most salutary. Soon, however, only one obsession subsisted, the tenacity of which ended up oppressing me. I saw Suzanne and myself, and our companions in distress, chased from our refuge by virtue of the air suddenly having become unbreathable, Tornada having arranged to project toxic elements into each issue of the sewer.

In truth, I expected no more than that logical conclusion of a great crime, the methodical destruction that would precipitate us outside in the fashion of rabbits chased from their warren by ferrets. I believed that I could already sense the action. And now I think about it, I think that idea was suggested to me by the unhealthy emanations with which the atmosphere of the sewer was charged. How many thousands of lungs were respiring there, in that obscure and narrow network?

My head was aching; I could feel the pulsations of my heart throbbing in my temples. Overcoming the faint that still threatened, I dragged myself over to Suzanne, who was lying a few paces away. The people who had supervised our rescue had stood aside momentarily. I extended my hand toward her, and her wet clothes, clinging to her flesh, initially gave me the most painful impression—but my distress increased further when I observed the diminution and the weakness of her poor body.

She tried to speak; her voice barely vibrated. I understood, however.

"It's you, Jean, isn't it?"

"It's me, Suzanne."

"I'm not dreaming? You're really there?"

"You're not dreaming, and I'm really beside you."

"Why did you save me just now? We were sinking…it would have been very easy to die."

"It would have been frightful to be separated, Suzanne."

"Those who love one another aren't separated by death."

"I still wanted to believe there was a chance!"

"Oh, chance!"

"I wanted to cling to a hope."

"Oh, hope!"

"It's necessary."

"I have no more chance and no more hope. My father..."

After lifting herself up slightly on one elbow, she had just let her head fall back on to the ground, betrayed by her strength. That movement permitted her to receive the vague light of a lantern hanging on the wall; and I found her so livid, with the bone-structure of her face so evident, that I thought of the physiognomy that she would acquire once dead, and I understood the vanity of the words that I was employing to reassure her. To attempt further explanations, to invent other hypotheses of salvation, would only increase her disappointment, for the time being, adding a further torture to the anticipations that her common sense established clearly through her weakness. Anyway, she no longer seemed disposed to talk. She was at the limit of exhaustion, and her hand, of which I had taken hold with the precaution with which one touches fragile objects, was cold and soft in mine; only occasional nervous tremors revealed the persistence of life therein.

I also succumbed to numbness and think I would have fallen asleep if singular noises, which soon took on the amplitude of a din, had not been produced in the more remote part of the sewer. In my demi-torpor, I saw four individuals come to place themselves in front of me. They conferred in low voices, and I heard their words, which seemed at first to be rather incoherent.

"No pity," said one. "Pity's all right when..."

"Better to let them be!" growled a second, who wore the blue smock and wide-brimmed hat of Les Halles.

"We could roll dice for the guard?" suggested a third, whose clothing, with metal buttons, must have been some kind of military or watchman's uniform.

"For sure! Then it's not always the same ones to strike!" approved a fourth, whose silhouette I could not make out.

And all four of them repeated in chorus: "No! No pity for anyone!"

But a revolt of voices, coming from a distance, interrupted their conspiracy. They were shouting:

"Leave us alone!"

"We have as much right to be here as you!"

"We were here first!"

"Back!"

"I warn you that I'm armed!"

"I want to pass!"

"Back! Back!"

Then the protestations were lost in a furious scuffle. A detonation burst forth, which suddenly quieted the tumult. The noise of a mass falling in the water occupied that temporary silence—after which an irritated voice proclaimed: "I have enough for five!"

And the plaints, maledictions and exclamations of hatred resumed, duller and more attenuated.

I understood then what was happening, and I don't repent of having felt my generosity awakening. In other circumstances, perhaps, I would have appointed myself the champion of the unfortunates who, less fortunate than us, had found their retreat in the collector itself, while we were occupying a relatively spacious diverticulum. Oh, the poor people! Coming from the gallery directly below ours, I could hear the poignant expression of their distress and bitterness. How could I dare to complain when, on reconstructing accurately enough the ovoid structure of the sewer, I knew that they must be cornered at the side wall, perched on a narrow sidewalk forming a border to the drainage channel; and that they were only protected from falling into the water by a fragile rail—all that in the horror of darkness!

Soon, I no longer had to wonder why they stayed there instead of coming into ours, which was connected to theirs by a small iron ladder. Nothing would have been easier for them to lodge there, for there were no more than twenty of us, and, furthermore, another tunnel, leading from out refuge to the outside, gave access via a few stone steps to a fairly large space constructed immediately beneath the road surface, and which, to judge by the voices I could hear arriving from there, was not overcrowded. But the feeble reflections of a lamp revealed to me that some of our companions in adventure had gathered in front of the steps leading to the conductor, and their egotism was opposing the sharing of our space.

Implacable in their cruelty, I saw them strike redoubtable blows again, and throw back into the sewer a poor man who tried to join us by climbing up the shaft of a hoist near the iron stairway, which facilitated the removal of sand. I heard the unfortunate man's body fall into the water, amid cries of hatred exchanged between the people in our gallery and those filling the sidewalk of the collector tunnel.

Nevertheless, my natural generosity soon dissipated in the face of the present contentment of still being alive and having Suzanne, also alive, by my side.

I was huddled against her, and I passed through a new, rather pleasant cerebral phase, doubtless resulting from the torpor succeeding the unusual physical expense demanded by recent events. I rested from thought, anticipation and attempting to comprehend what was happening around me. I think that I even slept for a while. Then, my annihilation dissipated progressively; the ambient phenomena recovered their value,

137

and I surrendered to my curiosity. I sat up, with my back to the wall, and found that I was next to Monsieur Serviat.

The great scientist was very absorbed at that moment with an individual clad in ancient armor, the breastplate of which I had perceived when I awoke. He was making noble gestures as he spoke to him; he seemed to be letting his words fall from the height of a pulpit, and his southern accent acquired the amplitude of a declaration of doctrine, with the particularity that he adopted simultaneously a nuance of respect and sympathy whose motive I could not comprehend. I was obliged to tug on the flap of his frock-coat twice to attract his attention to me and for him to satisfy my need to know by virtue of what sequence of events the sewer had also collected him.

"My dear Master," I began, "you've saved us: what gratitude!"

"Don't mention it, my friend," he protested. "But let's confess that hazard sometimes works for the best, since it was at the very moment when I was risking a last glance at what was happening on the far bank that I perceived you as you threw yourselves in the water. That act of audacious despair, to which the events, surprisingly enough, only seem to have inspired you, had the interest for me that any struggle incites. Although urged to come back in here by those surrounding me, I could not take my eyes of the couple who were fleeing so bravely."

"Oh, my dear Master, bravely…"

"But yes! Yes!"

"We wanted to die…"

"I approve of your having sought death elsewhere than in the stomach of monsters. At least Tornada won't have had your skin!"

He did not hold back the expression of his old rancor in the manner in which he pronounced that last sentence. I detected therein all the rage of scientific rivalry, improbably persistent at that moment when danger had cornered us.

"The swine, eh? Can you believe it?" he added. Then, dismissing the hated image with a gesture, he went on: "Yes, I was there, on the bank, watching the plunge without being able to identify the plungers, when I suddenly recognized you. It was then that I ordered that someone throw you an anchor. Oh, you were very skillful in catching it, my friend—it was a veritable feat; and that Tornada..."

He did not finish. He understood that his insistence was about to become distasteful, and seemingly decided to revert to good manners. I thought I divined that his respect was commanded by the presence of the ancient suit of armor, which had just drawn closer to us and was listening to us.

"But you, my dear Master, how is it that you found yourself here? So many various rumors have been circulating in your regard that I don't know what to think. Has it not been proclaimed that you had found a means of breaking through the circle of monsters and reaching Tornada's laboratory? There, it was affirmed, you had discovered the secret of the macrobes' creation—a secret that has no connection with what our enemy has published—and that you had brought back a method of destruction that your first action was to submit to the new government. Is there any truth in what has been said? Excuse my impatience, and pardon me for interrupting your conversation with Monsieur..."

I pointed at the ancient armor, but Serviat paid no heed to my pause. If my questions were pressing, he seemed to be in just as much haste to inform me.

He raised a finger in the air. "Fantasy!" he said. "Everything that has been communicated—fantasy! The governments, both the former and the new, were making use of my name in order to reassure the public. In truth, I haven't moved from Paris. I had no need to penetrate into Tornada's laboratory to figure out his macrobes, and I had only to remain in mine to conceive a means of destroying them—and it's done, my friend...*Eureka!*"

Carefully, he removed from the pocket of his frock-coat a bottle that was creating a bulge there, and raised it into the air. I was able to make out that the bottle did not present any tragic appearance. It was filed with an opaline liquid, which reflected in blue the rays of the lamp before which he held it up. Immediately after having exhibited it, however, he replaced the bottle in its hiding place with the same precaution.

"*Eureka!*" the scientist repeated, buttoning up his frock-coat. Then, suddenly gripped by anger again, frowning ferociously and shaking his jowls, he exclaimed: "Oh, it's high time I avenged myself on that blackguard! It's time I put an end to his machinations! He's behaved toward me like the worst of fraudsters. He's stolen from me, Monsieur! He's stolen my discovery!"

"What discovery?"

"Why, *Micrococcus aspirator!*"

"I thought, Master, that you denied its existence?" I dared to suggest.

"You need to understand—I haven't denied anything!" he protested. "on the contrary, long before Tornada presented his paper to the Académie, I was the first to claim that all bodies are capable of giving birth, or, at least, favoring the evolution, of parasites specific to their species. That is, moreover, a general law; it's sufficient to look at what happens in nature to convince oneself of it. It's evident that the life of some is grafted on to the death of others…yes, that life is engendered by death…"

It would have been easy to adapt that philosophical phrase to our present situation, but it did not provoke any retrospective despair or lamentable anticipation, for the chemist did not leave us time to reflect upon it, continuing: "I had, therefore, foreseen this *Micrococcus aspirator*, and I can thus affirm that Tornada has robbed me."

It is, assuredly, an excessive pretention that assimilates a rather vague and quite commonplace general idea to a discovery that is more than ingenious, but the scientific mores of our era are accustomed to these arbitrary procedures, and I did not comment on its injustice, inasmuch as another question was burning my lips.

"All right," I conceded, indulgently, "But what about his other discovery?"

"What discovery! I deny it! Tornada is incapable of discovering anything!"

"However, Master...!"

"What?"

"His abnormal development favored by..."

"I deny it!"

"Damn! However..."

"I deny it! I deny it!"

"Ah! I could swear, myself..." I completed my sentence with an abrupt gesture toward the exterior ravages.

The scientist became conscious of the ridicule to which his obstinacy was giving rise. He suddenly calmed down. He turned to the person in the armor and bowed, with a smile. Then he addressed himself to me.

"When I say that I deny it, it's necessary to understand what I mean. I don't deny the phenomenon, of course—you'd think I was as mad as Tornada! But I deny that he has found the principle of it. Long before him, I and Dar..." He interrupted himself, and then resumed: "I and Darwin thought about anatomical modifications capable of presenting themselves in transplanted organisms. It only remained to find the method. That was the affair of a good workman, not a genius. Certainly, I don't refuse Tornada the qualities of a good workman, but the idea isn't new. Oh no, it isn't new!"

He rubbed his hands, delighted at having made things clear.

"Assuredly," I approved, meekly. "But my dear Master, your own discovery? Your method for saving us from the monsters?"

"Ah! There, I've got it!" he announced, proudly, radiant this time. He spun toward the individual encased in iron and bowed again. He said, mistaking his designation, doubtless in the heat of his revelation: "Listen carefully, Madame. What I have to tell you is quite prodigious."

He turned back to me. "You listen to me as well, Gérard, and remember this date, for it will be celebrated tomorrow. When I found out that Tornada had launched his macrobes against Paris, I said to myself: 'Serviat, people are obviously going to count on you; what can you do for these worthy people?' Then, quivering with the hope that I inspired, I went to my laboratory and shut myself up there, alone—all alone, that's my best fashion of creating. Then, my friends, I thought of it! Ah, what a seething there is, beneath this cranium. What accolades of neurons! What accolades, my good friends!"

He fanned his forehead, doubtless to calm the ardor still simmering there, and then went on: "Yes, everything is vibrant behind there; all the hypotheses racing tumultuously; and I had to choose from among a dust of ideas, as an astronomer has to select a single star from the Milky Way. I had rapidly eliminated from that confusion the cumbersome notions, and I remained in confrontation with two solutions—two, no more. And my ingenuity had been to borrow them from biology."

Privately, I approved of the Master's admission of his borrowing. It was probably the first time he had admitted to having borrowed anything.

He continued: "Being a chemist, I could easily have thought of something else, but I thought about biology. For, with what phenomenon were we dealing? A biological phenomenon. And also pathological. Follow me carefully."

I thought I was back on the school benches, so professorial was the tone of voice he had adopted. He pinched his nose and declared: "What are these macrobes? Large microbes, my friends, nothing else. How does one destroy microbes? Yes, how does one destroy them? You know, Gérard, but you, Madame"—again he was mistaken in his appellation!—"you, Madame, don't know."

And, raising himself up to his full height, sticking his thumbs in his waistcoat, he went on: "One destroys microbes in several ways. I'll pass over the mechanical and antiseptic methods. I'll even pass over the agents favorable to phagocystosis.[16] And I arrive immediately at the new therapeutics..."

"An antimicrobial serum?" I exclaimed.

"Ah, my good friend Gérard, that's where I was quicker off the mark than you! What is the serum of malady? It's a liquid taken from the blood of healthy animals, resistant to the malady, or sick animals previously immunized by an infection or a vaccination, isn't it? And the hypothesis was, indeed, elegant, of making an antimicrobial serum. Ha ha! Not banal...not banal..."

He swelled up with pride at the idea, and continued: "But how could a serum be injected into those dirty beasts? Can you see me setting out, syringe in hand, to confront those giants and saying to them: lend me your scale so I can introduce something into it? *Viens, macrobe, viens!*" He ventured a smile, and then resumed his gravity. "And then again, a serum isn't manufactured in twenty-four hours. Then I thought, quite simply, of a toxin."

"A toxin isn't manufactured in twenty-four hours either, Master."

"My dear Gérard," he said, swelling with pride, "for me, twenty-four hours is sufficient."

He took out his bottle again. He consulted the troubled fluid amorously, and said, with great simplicity: "And here it is."

"What toxin?" I persisted. "Is it a derivative of albuminoid? What is its molecular grouping? Is it radioactive? Does it contain mineral materials, manganese...?"

"That, my friend, is my business," the academician riposted, his expression suddenly firm. "That's chemistry, and

---

[16] Phagocytosis—the process by which a phagocyte engulfs a solid particle—was named and described by Élie Metchikoff on the Institute Pasteur in 1882, initially observed in single-celled creatures, although the possible importance of the process in the working of the immune system was gradually realized.

it's my business. Let it suffice for you to know that with a few drops from this little flask, I have enough to poison a kilometer of the Seine. It's a violent destructive agent, which I've extracted from my brain, and I intend to distribute it in the river when the monsters come to slake their thirst there."

He put the bottle back in his pocket, with the same jealous care, without further explanation.

He adopted his easy-going attitude again, and added: "And that's when, emerging from my laboratory, I was surprised by the arrival of the macrobes. Slightly anxious, I admit, I precipitated myself into the mouth of a sewer that happened to be open—and do you know to whom I had the honor of offering my hand in order that she might descend at the same time as me? My old and great friend, the Baronne d'Abila, to whom I introduce, in these strange circumstances, Mademoiselle Suzanne Vernet and Monsieur Jean Gérard."

Suzanne had stood up to listen to the scientist's explanations. Amazed, we turned our eyes toward the person indicated to us by our interlocutor. In truth, we hesitated at first to bow, for we had just realized that the armored knight was a woman.

Now that those frightful hours have passed, I can smile at the baroque idea that the Baronne d'Abila had had, in the hope of protecting herself against the macrobes, of putting on an ancient suit of armor ornamenting her antechamber. Her considerable breasts and stout calves were escaping in adipose pads from the iron plates that she had precipitately placed over her chemise, whose fabric surpassed them. Plant on that warrior apparel a little tousled russet head, which would have been obliged, half a century before, to put on the make-up then generously reparative of the outrage of the years, and you will have a picture of the caricature that Monsieur Serviat was offering to us. Nevertheless, we were not unduly astonished. We knew that the Baronne was very eccentric, often celebrated by the newspapers for her sporting achievements and dangerous voyages of exploration, and we were at a moment when such details do not surprise you. Although she bore the name of a purgative water,[17] and perhaps by the very reason of that particularity, she was very popular in France.

She greeted us politely with an inclination of the head and a gesture with the helmet that she was holding under her arm.

"Alas, Madame," I felt obliged to say to her—for one feels constrained to condolences in all the frightful events of life—"what a frightful adventure!"

"But no!" she protested. "I find, on the contrary, that it's very amusing. I was nearly collected a little while ago by a macrobe, and it was the most exciting moment of my life. I've never experienced anything similar, even on the day when cannibals took me to their grill-room in order to feast on me..."

"Ha ha! They had good taste!" quipped Monsieur Serviat.

"Oh, shut up, Master!" said the Baronne, coquettishly, slapping him gently on the hands.

Soon, however, the chemist's discovery having rendered us some hope, our natural curiosity, invincible in spite of the gravity of the moment, drew us toward the people who were our companions in distress. The majority, plunged in the darkness, were unrecognizable, but by the dubious clarity of a sewerman's lamp, recently hung on the wall, I distinguished among the nearer ones, first, a female collector for the Salvation Army, wearing the distinctive cap of the sect, who seemed to me to be very pretty; then a clean-shaven actor with a sonorous voice, emphatic in his gestures; then an American clad in a loud suit, who was pluming his drooping moustache

---

[17] This slightly cryptic reference probably refers to solutions made from the plant *Citrullus colocynthis*—commonly known as bitter apple or vine of Sodom—used as a purgative since antiquity and commonly harvested in the vicinity of Abila in Jordan, although the Baronne's name is more likely to refer to Avila in Spain, the name of which was occasionally rendered as Abila.

with puffs of smoke from a pipe stuffed with Richmond to-bacco; then a concierge who was weeping unstoppably; then a sewerman shod in boots and dressed in waterproof cloth. There were others, too, whose status was difficult to define— including an astonishingly dark-haired elegant man of the "old rake" variety, and a very young blond man—all exhausted, and supporting very lamentably, to judge by the bitterness of their conversation, the menace of the microbes.

But how dare we criticize the attitude of others when Su-zanne and I felt so desperate ourselves? My poor fiancée, her garments still soaked from her immersion, was shivering, and although I drew her close to me, I was unable to warm her up. Fortunately, moved by pity, the sewerman had the inspiration of lighting a coke fire that was prepared in one of those perfo-rated braziers that road-menders use for making macadam. The smoke it gave off provoked protests at first, but, the heat it radiated soon being appreciated by everyone, we were able to dry ourselves there without remorse. In the end, I was obliged to give thanks for the devotion of which people are capable, for the brave man shared a bread roll with our group, which gave us some comfort. His alms were inappreciable, and he refused the louis that I offered him.

And the time went by, immeasurably long. When I was not employed in consoling Suzanne, I could not help being invaded by a philosophical astonishment that the attitude of my companions inspired in me. I judged, in total lucidity, how irreparable and inveterate the poisoning of our civilization is. We had not been in that tunnel for half a day, and social life was already recommencing its work, with the same motives, the same passions and the same defects, as if events assured us of our continued existence. A glance was sufficient to con-vince me.

Monsieur Serviat was playing the gallant with the influ-ential Baronne d'Abila; and while the young recruit of the Salvation Army, as pretty as an angel who might also be a demon, started preaching and collecting, the American, com-fortably installed on a bed of sand provided to him by one of the small wagons, never ceased smoking, and demanding whisky, proclaiming that he would give his fortune to have a glass. His offer seemed to me to be as extravagant as his passion for alcohol. Did he not inform us, the next moment, that he was a billionaire in consequence of a trust in calves? He was, he affirmed tranquilly, "the emperor of veal."

After that, I heard the concierge bragging about the tyranny she had exercised over her tenants, before those "satanic pimps"—as she called the macrobes—made their appearance, and the actor declaring that Monsieur Guitry could not hold a candle to him.[18]

Perhaps, though, those boastful things were only said superficially, in order to counter intimate dread, for, although we supposed that we were protected from the monsters' devouring rage, and could no longer hear anything overhead that revealed their presence—neither roars not the creaking of carapaces—we could not suppose, even so, that their work was concluded. Sometimes, too, the name of Tornada was pronounced, and there was then a further consternation, a hatred proclaimed by all mouths. Then everyone fell silent, listening, in anguish. We feared those giant leaps, which, by provoking the collapse of our tunnel, would have given access to the gluttonous giants.

At other times, news, transmitted along the human chain filling the collector and communicating with the entire subterranean network of Paris, reached our ears, confirming the total destruction of the city, the annihilation of its people.

Suddenly, however, what a contrast! What a breath of liberation!

"They're destroyed! They're destroyed!" transmitted voices arriving in tumult from the tunnel below our own.

---

[18] The reference is to Lucien Guitry, father of the eventually-more-famous Sacha, who left the Comédie-Française in 1902 to become director of the Renaissance, where he established his reputation as the leading French exponent of contemporary drama.

One might have thought it a rumble of triumph, a thousand clamors welcoming the birth of a god.

And almost immediately: "Long live Serviat! Long live the savior!"

"Have I saved someone, then?" the chemist asked me.

That was the exact moment when the actor, shouting more loudly than the others, came to tell us the news.

"Yes, Monsieur," he said, addressing himself more specifically to the chemist. "Yes, Monsieur, Serviat has saved us!" And raising his arms to the heavens, his mouth wide, he went on: "Serviat is a genius, you hear, Monsieur! Serviat is the man of the century!"

"Thank you," said the scientist, swelling up with pride, "But..."

"And let no one contradict me!"

"I wouldn't dream of it...but what has he done, your Serviat?"

"He's found a lethal malady, which he's transmitted to the monsters."

"Ah! What is it?"

"The plague! Yes, Monsieur, a sort of plague! And they're dying of it, they're dying of it!"

"Really?"

"Really."

"Well, Monsieur, tell these poor people to wait a little before shouting. They're going too quickly. Certainly, the nation can count on Serviat..."

"A man of genius!"

"Indeed, but who hasn't yet had the opportunity to make use of his invention."

"How do you know, Monsieur?"

"I know."

"Because?"

"Because, Monsieur, I am Serviat...that's me!"

I have no need to insist on the actor's confusion—a confusion that rebounded on the ambient frenzy, reached the human cordon transmitting the news, extinguishing the cries of enthusiasm with the same rapidity, to replace them with tears.

And the bleak wait resumed.

Like the others, I had allowed myself to be taken in momentarily by the illusion of deliverance, although I did not know yet what to make of it. It is curious to remark how contagious the puerility off a crowd at bay can be. Is there is that circumstance a manifestation of cerebral anemia?[19] Possibly. But I was obliged, like the others, to bow down to the reality, and I soon had no other resource to occupy my mind, relaxed by drowsiness, than to interest myself in the dramas unfolding at the two issues of our tunnel, where the macrobes were not threatening people directly and were allowing them to deliver themselves to scenes of abominable violence.

To be sure, I only saw those scenes through a dim light, and I was too weary to philosophize about their psychology, but for which I would not have failed to endorse the verity of all the ages that might makes right. Did the poor people imploring us from the bottom of the stairway leading to the collector not have as much right as us to share our space? Did we ourselves not have the right to take the few steps leading to the subterranean room that was only occupied by a few individuals? No: on either side, a ferocious guard was maintained, arbitrarily limiting everyone's right of abode, and distributing blows of a cudgel to those who wanted to exceed its limits. I saw the powerful market porter devoting himself to that task with a particular mastery.

"No one passes!" he howled. And his fist, raised to the level of his hat, fell upon a skull. The noise was audible, the crash of the body, which fell with a splash into the water.

---

[19] The distinctive features of crowd psychology, developed at such length in this narrative, had become a hot topic of debate in fin-de-siècle France because of the pioneering investigations of the subject carried out by Gabriel Tarde and Gustave Le Bon.

At one time, weary of striking out, he detaching himself from his group and came over to me.

"It's time the idlers did some work," he said. "Your turn!"

I refused. His fist clenched; I feared his crushing blow, and assumed a defensive stance. I could have crushed me between his fingers, but Suzanne threw herself upon me, making a rampart of her weakness, and the brute relaxed his fist, and went away, grumbling.

How can I continue to translate those long minutes of anxious uncertainty? Silence was progressively established; everyone rested in their own distress. Suzanne had gone back to sleep, babbling vague words testifying to her nightmare. I took advantage of that to stretch my legs a little, and started pacing back and forth, like an animal in a cage with other animals.

My room for maneuver was by no means comfortable to travel, as can easily be imagined. I was hindered by recumbent bodies, which I had to step over, by the presence of wagons blocking the tunnel to the extent that it was necessary for me to slide along the wall to get past them. As for risking myself at the external opening overlooking the Seine, where daylight, visible through the bars of the closed gate would soon be replaced by terrifying darkness, I truly did not dare. For the moment, all the menace seemed to me to lie in that direction, and, not knowing what surprise that orifice might reserve for those who approached it, I judged it more prudent to keep my distance.

Soon, it was completely dark outside. Our redoubt, in the wan light of the lamp, took on a particularly lamentable aspect. Silhouettes stood out in a fearfully suggestive imprecision. Faces could no longer be seen; their angular contours, their sculpture of distress and dolor, could only be divined.

At times, there was a fulgurant glimmer in the shadow; that was the American, the "emperor of veal," relighting his pipe. "Whisky? Whisky!" he demanded, with an insistence neighboring on delirium. And the atmosphere filled with the perfume of his tobacco, while the young collector for the Salvation Army, his neighbor for the moment, waved the smoke away from her nostrils with indignant protective gestures, similar to those of the astonishingly dark-haired old gentleman and the very blond young man.

"As if it's permissible to poison the air like that!" agreed the concierge, with disgust, sweeping the air with her apron. And she added: "Just try that in my house! I'd have a policeman on you in three minutes, and out you'd go, Englisher!"

That "Englisher" summarized all her ethnographic notions, all her age-old hatred of the invader. She had, besides, already heaped that denomination on the "satanic pimps"—and Tornada for her, was also an "Englisher."

"Necessary not to get your blood up for so little, Mother," said the worthy sewerman, placidly. "Necessary to think how lucky we are to be here."

That consolation had no other result than reestablishing the concierge's flood of tears, and the apron dabbed her eyes to collect the moisture therefrom.

In another corner, I observed the truly warm friendship, emerging from the disaster, that was being established between Monsieur Serviat and the Baronne d'Abila. Would they have thought of finding one another charming in normal life? My God, what admirable resources the genius of the species has! Yes, while everything around us was collapsing, perishing in a frightful cataclysm, those two individuals were embarking upon a regular flirtation. I saw them, each as picturesque as the other—I say picturesque because of their social status, although I could as easily have employed a less indulgent expression—him, the great scientist, the national glory, with his bottle making a bulge in his frock-coast; her, the grand dame, squeezed into her stifling suit of armor, using all the graces, flatteries and coquetries they would have deployed in a drawing room during a formal reception. My word, did the member of the Institut not push seduction to the point of opening a box of candy and offering a piece to the explorer?

"It's not the toxin this time, Master?"

"No, trust me."

But, as the fingers clad in an iron gauntlet could not take one, I believe I remember seeing the scientists seize a bonbon and place it in the Baronne's lips. I heard the latter's teeth, still pretty—perhaps an artificial beauty, but let's not dwell on that—crunch upon the delicacy…which issued a violent appeal for the satisfaction of my hunger.

"Oh, give me one! Give me one!" I had a desire to cry out. But I was timid, still reserved, and I dared not think about my starvation, and Suzanne's, and turned my gaze away from the temptation in order to interest myself in other psychological states, which the situation unveiled, as malady lays bare the soul of an invalid.

Among all those poor stranded individuals whom destiny had accumulated in that subterranean tunnel, I had not failed to be intrigued by the appearance of one particular individual whose silhouette remains astonishingly clear in my mind, although the circumstances had scarcely caused my gaze to pass over him. He was a man of indeterminate age, nothing about him indicating whether he was young or old. He was neither fat nor thin, neither tall nor short, wearing garments of a respectable cut, gloves and decent shoes. Everything about him would have made him one of those neutral individuals whose paths one frequently crosses in the streets without noticing them, had a certain eccentricity not been acquired by the aristocratic quality of his face, in which a monocle and an extraordinarily fetching beard, trimmed with absolute symmetry, with not a single overlapping hair, reigned triumphantly.

To judge by the care that he took of that superb beard, by the worshipful manner in which he raked it incessantly with a small pocket comb, one divined that it was his sole claim to fame, and one forgot that it was dominated by a commonplace nose, eyes devoid of brightness, and a restricted forehead, half of which was covered by a gray felt hat.

Imagine, moreover, that the individual was striving to give the beard and monocle thus planted in a banal face an air of superior irony—that he often mingled in groups occupied in discussing our frightful situation, but that, without saying a word, once the news was acquired, he retired, shrugging his shoulders, accompanying his retreat with a satisfied clucking and a pressure of his hands, one against the other, so energetic that the joints of his fingers cracked.

And yet, a manifest need to talk gripped him; that was evident from his attitude. Doubtless, on the other hand, he did not want to confide his noble reflections to common mortals.

After a long hesitation, he apparently judged me worthy of receiving them, for he began to prowl around me, and soon, without my having given any signal to provoke his testimony, he came up to me and engaged me in conversation with a quiet, colorless voice.

"My dear Monsieur," he said, "this is a very strange event, and for myself, I'm curious to know what its consequences will be. Don't believe, however, that I'm as distressed as the others by the dire fate that is reserved for me! Oh no, that base terror is by no means mine!" Accentuating the cracking of his knuckles, he added: "I am, on the contrary, delighted by what is happening."

"What! You're delighted by this disaster?" I exclaimed, without moderating my surprise and indignation. "Can you confess that at such a moment?"

"Understand me clearly. Listen to me with deference. I don't confide my thoughts to just anyone. If I've chosen you for a confidant, it's because I don't know you, and because I can believe you to be of a moral caliber superior to that of the others."

He caressed his beard with both hands, with the back of one and the palm of the other, and then continued, sententiously: "I find in this adventure of the macrobes a supreme lesson in energy. I was waiting for the time that would finally permit me to express my sentiment, and I deliver it with all the more satisfaction because I predicted this catastrophe."

"What! You anticipated that Paris would one day be delivered to the voracity of these monsters, Monsieur?"

"Understand me clearly: I don't mean that I foresaw that a scientist would one day bring the disaster out of a culture medium, I simply mean to express that I was counting on a great public calamity to regenerate our people, which is truly in need of it. People no longer make war, my dear Monsieur, because the nations fear the bloodshed and the destruction; they no longer tremble before epidemics, because hygiene stops them with sterilizers; they're protected from heat and cold; and mechanical tools do the work of arms. Add that a legion of humanitarians has invaded our globe, that savages are being civilized and that the tsar bows down before the Duma. So, what means remain for Immanent Cruelty to do its work? What means remain for the soul to draw the elements of virtue from dolor? Alas, humans no longer have to relax into the egotism of their happy lives; they go to sleep without enjoyment, with the concern of cultivating the heart, and there is a universal decadence. Well, no! It's too much! Bless the lesson of fear! Lift up hearts! Let us fortify ourselves! Let us become virile!"

In the ardor of his discourse his monocle had escape from his eye; he was sketching broad gestures; and I listened with amazement to the strength prophet. A thousand objections, inspired by my present distress, rose to my lips, and I would have presented them to him had I not sensed that his flood of words still had some way to expand.

In a voice suddenly transformed, which hissed with envy, he continued: "I tell you that the present moment is eminently salutary! Let us obtain the confirmation for that, if you wish, from the study of all those around us, who have gravitated to this sewer. Let us observe them in turn. I have some of them at my fingertips; to every lord his honor. Let us look first at Serviat, who is pretending not to recognize me, although we have collaborated in the past. He's a man of science honored to the point that, on gala days at the Élysée, he sports decorations and sashes of ever color and form, so numerous that, finding no more room to pin them on his chest, he's obliged to hang them over his buttocks! Come on, Monsieur, I ask you—is it decent to pose like that in a display of tinsel?"

I saw that he was caressing the lapel of his jacket with the tip of his finger, and leaning over, I noticed that his own modesty prevented him from wearing anything except a little red ribbon, which I mistook at first for the Légion d'honneur.

He continued: "Alas, Monsieur, Serviat has invented fracassite. Has he invented it? No matter. At any rate, once his discovery was made, he dared to deliver it to the artillery, with the result that now, if what is said about the power of that explosive is true, war will become impossible, and we shall be deprived henceforth of a source of necessary calamity. What would you have done in his place, Monsieur? What did I do, myself, when I discovered the formula of my own explosive? I hastened to bury it in a drawer, imitating my disinterest on the day when I found the serum for tuberculosis. Ah, that's the way I am!"

His momentum carrying him away, he had dropped his monocle again. He was obliged to search for it on the ground for some time. He finally discovered it, after groping around, and replaced it in the orbit.

"And that Baronne, whom I've encountered many times in society, and who is also pretending not to know me, doubtless because I haven't spared my sentiments in her regard in my newspaper..."

"Your newspaper?"

"Yes—you've surely read the *Justicier*, my weekly publication?"

"Certainly," I acquiesced, obligingly, although I was completely ignorant of the rag in question.

"Well, that Baronne, let's talk about her! Would you believe that she takes baths in goat's milk? That she covers her entire body in beauty cream at sixty-six francs a pot, and that she has devised a system of suspenders with which she stretches her face at night in order to avoid wrinkles? She poses as a charitable woman! She's president of the Association for the Protection of Feeding-Bottles—to replace the milk in

her baths, perhaps. She sits on the committees of twenty societies, each more benevolent than the last to vicious infancy and
spoiled old age—and she explores Africa in order to care for
the ophthalmia of little cannibals! Wretch! Wretch!"

He shook his fists.

"Well, Monsieur, I tell you this: charity is baleful work.
To the proposition that work should be given to the poor, I
consent; but the proposition that they should be maintained, I
reject. It's contrary to dignity, to social intelligence! It's also
contrary to the will of Nature, which wants everyone to develop strength in the service of the instinct of conservation! Let
us follow the example of Nature does! Let us follow the example of Death! They are excellent selectors! They are being
disturbed in their harmonious dispositions; the prey they have
decided to sacrifice is being snatched from them; the swing of
their scythes is being paralyzed—and it's evil work to oppose
them. I understand that so well that when I was sought out to
be placed at the head of the Association of Bone-setters, even
though my position, my name and my antecedents designated
me to do that work triumphantly, I flatly refused, Monsieur; I
slammed my door in the faces of the delegates who were imploring me; and there was an almighty fuss!"

"Oh, I thought...?" I said, interrogating the color of his
decoration more carefully; noticing this time a minuscule yellow stripe bordering the red of his ribbon. It was the distinction of some negro king.

He divined my astonishment at seeing him ornamented
by it, and, wanting to dissipate the deplorable effect of my
discovery, he added: "I refused the Légion d'honneur. They
squander it too much."

Proud of that further gesture of disdain, he took a small
comb from his pocket clad in a leather sheath, opened it, and
engaged it delicately in his beard.

"And the others, Monsieur! That concierge, who was
once mine and with whom I quarreled because she made her
lodge a hospital for all the stray cats in the street! And that
actor, who has seen me many a time applauding in the front

row of the orchestra stalls—with a certain sincerity, I must admit, for he's not denuded of tradition—but whom I couldn't go to see again after the day when he interpreted the plays of Brieux![20] And that dainty child who wears the costume of the Salvation Army, and whom I had to threaten with the police one day for wanting to slip me her newspaper, which I consider as a kind of begging. Yes, all of them, Monsieur, all of them, I consider as baleful servants of a benevolence contrary to the broad designs of Nature, which demands that one experiences strife, that one suffers, for the greater elevation of character!"

He concluded his diatribe with an expression of anxiety, which I thought at first attributable to the problems that were agitating him. It was nothing of the sort, however, and I soon perceived that his preoccupation was engendered by a personal detail, for, having caressed his beard, he had just observed that its elegance was opposed by the defective alignment of a few hairs. This time, he brought out a pair of scissors from his pocket and snipped the undisciplined hairs—and his physiognomy resumed its fine implacable tranquility.

I was then able to get a word in.

"I find you unjust, Monsieur. To struggle against evil, in whatever form, is the finest employment of the civilizing faculties. In my own case..."

"What do you do?" he interjected, immediately.

"I'm in charge of a laboratory at the Institut Pasteur..."

"The Institut Pasteur! You're at the Institut Pasteur?" he cried, thrusting me away with a manifest horror. "You've gone

---

[20] Eugène Brieux (1858-1932) was the leading realist dramatist of his era in France. His play *Les Avariés* (1901; filmed in English as *Damaged Lives*), public performance of which was banned by the censor, but which was read by the author in private to a select audience, followed hot on the heels of Couvreur's *Les Mancenilles* (1900), which similarly deals in a didactic fashion with the danger to society posed by syphilis.

astray in that place? You work on serums? On vaccines? Have you no shame?"

"No, Monsieur."

"You ought not to be proud of yourself, my friend. The Institut Pasteur is an abominable factor of decadence. It's me who's telling you this!"

I was beginning to get indignant. "But who are you, Monsieur, who find it so easy to heap such criticism on humankind?"

He took off his hat. I expected to hear him pronounce the name of some important Parisian personality.

"I'm Célestin Lebon."

"And what is your business?"

"Insurance, Monsieur."

After which he turned his back on me, in order to go and snigger somewhere else.

I had soon forgotten his ramblings. I took some pleasure in conversing with the sewerman, possessed of a candid soul, in complete contrast to the one whose bile I have just been respiring. He talked to me about the macrobes with a surprising tranquility. He was brave without being boastful. He listened to the story of my nocturnal expedition to Mantes, and seemed surprised that the monsters were phosphorescent.

"What's happened certainly isn't ordinary," he concluded, when I had finished.

At about ten o'clock a new racket began, which woke Suzanne. Once again, the illusion of deliverance was being passed along. As my fiancée no longer believed it, the sewerman, who had decidedly taken a liking to her, proposed to go out and ascertain whether the monsters had retreated.

He was surrounded.

"It's dark; you won't be able to see anything..."

"But yes, since they're green, the darkness..."

And the brave man went to the door that gave access to the Quai de Billy, opened it, stuck his head through, inspected the bank, and then came back in. And I shall never forget the joyful fashion in which he shouted to us: "For sure, because there's nothing more to scoff, they've gone!"

With what irony destiny was playing with us, in making the worst realities succeed the most cheerful hypotheses! The sewerman had not taken four steps away from the door, which he had just carefully closed behind him, when the door, pulled from outside, exploded furiously. At the same time, an invincible current of air extinguished our lamp, and the celestial shadow disappeared from the orifice of the tunnel to be replaced there by a green phosphorescence.

"Get down! Get down! Lie down!" I shouted to Suzanne, forcing her to flatten herself on the ground beside me.

I understood what had happened. One of our engulfers, evidently on watch in the roadway above our heads, must have been attracted by the imprudent reconnaissance of the sewerman. Sniffing the man, it had lowered its appendage toward the entrance, and, not being able to get into it by virtue of the narrowness of the orifice, it had applied its conch to the opening, like a sucker, in order to produce a vacuum in our tunnel and such in anything that was there.

I was even more convinced when I heard the fatal roaring, to which the inter-collision of wagons responded as they slid along their rails, like children's toys, toward the monstrous tentacle, and were then rejected by it when they were found to be inappropriate for alimentation.

That gigantic suction had provoked a formidable displacement of air, which I sensed that Suzanne and I, placed among those nearest to the door, would be unable to resist. Although we were still clinging to the ground, the improbable force rolled us over at times. It was a cyclone unleashed over our few cubic meters with all the furious impetuosity of the great unleashments of nature. We felt people passing over us like projectiles, going to be engulfed by the green phosphorescence. And we would have been subjected to the same fate if my hand had not been fortunate enough to encounter a mooring ring sealed into the wall, and had I not clung to it with a desperate energy, while my other hand prevented Suzanne's displacement.

Then the phenomenon vanished as quickly as it had appeared. Darkness resumed possession of the orifice of the tunnel, and we heard nothing more. One might have thought that nothing had happened.

It had, though. When the lamp was lit again, and when we counted ourselves, some were missing. Five victims—five immolated individuals—had served as prey for the monster. The sewerman and Célestin Lebon were among them, and the American had left us too. Oh, the poor devil wouldn't be demanding his whisky any more. We found his pipe, still smoking.

Night set in above us, in consternation. We had gathered in the most distant corner of the tunnel in order to escape any similar attempt, in case it was repeated. Nevertheless, sitting against the wall and huddled together, Suzanne and I succumbed to fatigue.

It might have been two o'clock in the morning when we were woken up by the noise of a collapse nearby.

"It's the Pont d'Iéna crumbling!" guessed Monsieur Serviat.

We went back to sleep. We had arrived at a certain fatalism.

XII

A sob uttered by Suzanne snatched me from my heavy inertia. I cannot describe the sadness that the plaint in question caused me, combined with the malaise of waking up in the cold and damp. The fire had gone out some time ago for want of fuel.

My flesh felt bruised and mortified. A glance toward the livid dawn showing through the entrance to our tunnel further increased my torment. My entire horizon was limited to a stretch of river drowned by rain. There were tears in nature, as in me, as in the still-closed eyes of my fiancée. What cruel dream must the poor child be going through, for her sweet face to be manifesting such anxiety? Her parted lips were stammering incomprehensible words; her hands, folded over her body, lying on the ground, were trembling; her entire being testified to a horrible interior drama.

I woke her up to extract her from it. I strove to offer her a reassuring smile. With the aim of replacing her alarm with a more immediate and less grave preoccupation, I asked her to adjust my dressing. She lent herself to the task with the bravery of a young nurse.

Around us, the first impression of that morning was quite different from what I expected. Our companions stretched their limbs first, and loosened themselves up by swinging their arms. Then—I don't know why, perhaps because of that incomparable character unique to Parisians—they began to crack jokes. A few humorous rockets were rapidly transformed into a veritable firework display for which the attitude of the Baronne provided a pretext.

The latter, her bosom being decidedly too cramped, had taken off the breastplate of her armor and handed it to Monsieur Serviat, who had put it on over his frock-coat to warm himself up. But as she was in her chemise beneath her protective disguise, and as she had retained her helmet on her head

161

and her thigh-guards on her legs, I confess that her accoutrement did not lack hilarity, and that the grand dame on the one
hand, and the great scientist on the other, were rather reminiscent of two clowns in a vaudeville theater.

Inspired by the example, the actor turned his jacket inside out and started composing verses about them, which the
audience repeated in chorus. Cases are cited of nervous, almost demented gaiety, at the most tragic moments of history.
The funniest thing of all was that the chanted refrain followed
a tune that had been adopted, with other words, into the reper-
toire of the Salvation Army, and the pretty follower of General
Booth joined in ardently. She thought we had been converted!

I observed that she had, at least, inspired the religion of
her beauty in two of us, and that the old excessively dark-
haired old gentleman and the very blond young man were de-
ploying a furious rivalry in adoring her as their new idol. The
hostile glances that they darted at one another were harshly
appreciated by the concierge. The latter, sitting apart in a corner, superb in her dignity in the midst of the racket, opined
that all those people were well worthy of living in a sewer; she
could not even conceive that they had been born elsewhere.

Soon, however, that artificial gaiety melted away. We
had had no more news of life outside, nor of the macrobes,
when terrible information reached us thanks to the unfortunates who had taken refuge in the nearby collector. The poor
people, still prevented from joining us by those who had posed
themselves at the stair-head, opposing a human barrage to
them, were uttering more emphatic plaints.

I deplored all the peril of their situation. I, the rare moments of silence, when they ceased to cry out, we heard the
current of the water, increased by the external downpour,
flowing more impetuously. The level was riding in the corridor, and a particular odor was emitted by it, fetid in the extreme, the reek of which also filled our tunnel, scarcely com-
bated by the air from outside. We attributed that odor to the
detritus that the rain had brought into the drains, subsequently

drawing it into the sewer, which was making the entire network a veritable charnel-house.

We soon had proof of the verity of that explanation, for toward midday, as he concierge was proposing that it might be possible to extract something to eat from the things that the collector was carrying, a mocking voice emerged therefrom, replying:

"Madame is hungry? Let Madame permit me to offer her breakfast..."

At the same time, an object wrapped in paper as thrown up to us from the gulf. There was a battle around the projectile, but when its envelope was removed, a cry of horror went up. What had been sent to us was the hand of a little child, still bearing a modest golden ring on the ring finger.

"Alas, what mother must have had the despair...," Suzanne murmured, turning her eyes away.

From then on, the certainty of danger resumed its full value within us. The memory of that human debris had dissipated the gaiety and the appetite of the captives. Two live rats, which had been captured when the more impetuous waters chased them out of the collector, were also disdained. We knew only too well, alas, on what they had been nourished!

The result was that the day, the third since the appearance of the macrobes, ended in pangs of hunger. Dusk fell on the bank visible from the orifice; the twilight darkened, and eventually disappeared.

I hollowed out a bed for Suzanne in the sand in one of the small wagons, and installed her in it. Still fearful of an attack by the monsters that the vehicle and its precious contents might have attracted, I took care to moor it with a powerful iron chain that was passed to me from the chamber communicating with the roadway. And night reigned in absolute obscurity, for we saved the few drops of oil still remaining in the lamps, in case their light became useful later.

That was a night of terror, which I traversed initially without being able to sleep, occupied in watching over the repose of the object of my adoration—a night haunted by phantoms, of which the water growling in the collector echoed the lugubrious, melancholy song. Then, as the surface of the great city fell silent, I allowed myself to be borne away into a reparative oblivion.

I scarcely dare remember my first sensation of the following day, so atrocious was it. I was woken up by a clutching hand posed upon my stomach and, one might have thought, uprooting it. I truly discovered, that morning, what the starving endure—but, disdaining my own suffering in order not to think about anything but Suzanne's, I got up and leaned over her bed of sand.

At first, my anxiety was extreme, when I thought I had discovered nothing more than a cadaver, so inert was her body, so silent her lips and so icy her hand. To dissipate my horrible dread, at the risk, if she were only asleep, of causing her to quit the slumber that was soothing her existence, I shook her gently.

"I'm hungry…! I'm hungry…!" she moaned, in an exceedingly wan voice.

She repeated her plaint, with a childish insistence. I had never cursed the genius of Tornada and the cruelty of destiny, which were submitting my beloved to such an ordeal, as I did at that moment. And my rage was further increased when daylight, imposing itself on the orifice of the tunnel, showed me the adorable contours of her face, suddenly so thin, so slack and so corroded.

"Today, my beloved, today we'll eat," I assured her. "This situation can't go on! The monsters will go away. Hold on! Can you hear what people are saying? They're saying that the macrobes are drawing away, eastwards."

A more vivid gleam in her eyes persuaded me that she was smiling at that hope. I refrained from dissuading her from that, although I remained convinced of the improbability of such a retreat.

I imagined, on the contrary, how terrible our death would be in that redoubt, which was increasingly filled by the fetid odor. I recalled the description of a long agony given by

No monstrous presence; no threat; one might have thought it the awakening of Paris on a splendid morning. But on raising my eyes toward the Eiffel Tower, I saw it still swarming with people, and a dirigible, which I recognized as the *France*, was detaching itself at that precise moment, and started flying into the azure, toward the west.

Those observations persuaded me right away that the macrobes had not left Paris. I would have gone back right away to announce the sad news if the ardent desire to bring back some nourishment for Suzanne had not inspired me with the temerity to go on. I therefore started climbing the stairway leading to the Pont d'Iéna.

Having reached the top, the possessor of a vaster horizon, I was finally able to take account of the disasters caused by the giants. In fact, improbably, the right campanile of the Trocadéro had collapsed, and its central dome was staved in. I calculated fearfully the height of the leap accomplished by the monsters, and their formidable weight in falling back, in order that such a monument could be smashed to that extent. On the other side of the Seine, the devastation was similar; all the houses were reduced to rubble, exposing lamentable fragments of walls, to which morsels of masonry still clung in places.

I shivered before that spectacle. I hesitated to take my perilous adventure any further. What could I do, what could I find among those ruins? Would I not be exposing myself quite needlessly? Furthermore, signals were being addressed to me from the tower whose exact significance I could not understand, because of the distance, but which were certainly not encouraging me to continue.

However, as the image of Suzanne, dying of hunger, did not cease to obsess my mind, I plucked up my courage, crossed the bridge at a gallop, went around the foliage framing that side of the Champ-de-Mars and reached the Avenue de La Bourdonnais. My idea was that I would end up finding something to eat there. It was impossible that an entire quarter could be devoid of provisions and that I would not succeed in unearthing some from beneath the rubble—all the more so as I remember the presence of a grocery near the beginning of the long artery.

I was soon forced to retract my hopes, though. The road was virtually non-existent; there was nothing but an extraordinary confusion of heaps of stone, wood, twisted iron, windows and chimneys, mingled as if every house had been dynamited. Shading my eyes with my hands, however, I saw in the distance that the Galerie des Machines, which had not yet been destroyed, was still standing, and that in the middle of the avenue, one single-story building—only one—also subsisted, spared by the scourge. Its shop-front, painted bright blue, sprightly in the sunlight in the midst of the disaster, immediately became my objective, and I headed toward it, going around obstacles, and sometimes jumping over them in order to go more rapidly, immediately getting to my feet again if I tripped.

And still no macrobes on the horizon. Nothing. It was a solitude that troubled me as much as the giant apparitions. I can say without boasting that I showed proof at that moment of a certain courage, given that the silence of the people perched on the tower, by whom I felt that I was being observed, also frightened me.

Oh, what a journey! Well, would you believe that I was not the only one making it? Suddenly, I perceived accompanying me, disappearing only to appear again, an adorable little dog, one of those spirited black English terriers, as amiable as can be, who are in ordinary life better than friends to us. At times it stopped in front of me, and stood on its hind legs, bringing its front paws back against its torso, begging. I can assure you that with its upright ears and its shining eyes visibly inspired by a soul, it was pleading the cause of its famished instinct irresistibly.

Irresistibly? No, alas, for I lacked humanity on this occasion. I called to the charming little animal with my most encouraging voice, but my secret design was not to nourish it—quite the contrary!

It must have divined my ferocious intention, however, for it ran away just as I was about to seize it. Then I continued on my way toward the blue shop-front.

When I reached it, I observed that it bore the sign of a wholesaler of wines and vinegars. Unable to account for the fact that it had been spared by the scourge—perhaps because of its lesser dimensions, after all?—and astonished by the contrast between its fresh paint and perfect alignments and the surrounding collapses, I introduced myself into the building without difficulty. After having passed along a corridor I found a bourgeois dining-room, to which a kitchen was adjacent. I ran into it, and there, in the larder—O marvel!—I found food.

No, the miser recovering possession of his money, the near-dead shipwreck-victim who sees the savior vessel appearing, the criminal who hears his acquittal pronounced—what do I know?—none of those fortunate individuals ever blessed circumstances as much as I did before my discovery. Imagine it: on that bourgeois shelf there were two cold roasted chickens, half a ham, languorously pink, red wine, butter and bread! Yes, bread too—stale bread, but bread! Oh, the truculent emotion!

And I began "stuffing myself up to here!" I started chewing, chewing voraciously, and drinking, drinking recklessly. O Suzanne, my beloved, forgive me; I believe that I forgot you in that paradisal minute. Forgive me, on learning that it was for you, immediately my hunger was satisfied, that I put two chicken-wings in my pocket; for you that I heaped the rest of the provisions into a basket; for you again that I made a rapid tour of the shop, and stole at hazard six bottles of white wine with which I completed my provisions.

Infinitely pleased with that booty, I loaded the basket on to my shoulders and headed back outside. That unexpected meal had completely transformed my psychology. I found the sight of the rubble cheering. The street was so calm, so deserted, and I was now astonished by the facility of my expedition. And I started marching briskly, vivified by a new energy, listened to the bottles clinking merrily on my back, and thinking joyfully about the joy that I was about to cause, when, perhaps a third of the way along the avenue, a familiar sound—a hated sound—made me turn my head.

Frott...! Frott...! Frott...!

It was coming from the direction of the Galerie des Machines.

They were still there, alas. They had discovered me!

Climbing on to a heap of rubble, I saw them in the distance, coming out one by one from the vast hall, which they had doubtless adopted as a lair, where they must have been lurking like dogs in a kennel after breaking down the doors. They were coming, crawling, raising their tentacles, roaring, their frightful gray mass scarcely impeded by the border of rubble.

I got down again immediately in order to run away. Turning my head again, I could only see one of them, for the others were masked by the formidable dimensions of the first. Nevertheless, I sensed ten behind it—ten that were about to surround me, to seize me, to swallow me.

Then I started a mad, reckless race, far more terrible and perilous than the one I had undertaken three days before, along the quays, for this time I was alone, the only prey. I bounded over the rubble with the agility and skill of a gymnast, and took advantage of the open spaces to recover my momentum, and ran in a vertigo, obedient to the illusion that I was gaining ground. I had not let go of my basket, though; I kept it stuck to my shoulder by a miracle of equilibrium, and I heard the bottles bumping into one another, accompanying with the gaiety of their clinking the frightful rumble of the monsters, who were gaining on me.

And what irony! Suddenly, a bottle broke, and I felt liquid inundating me from head to toe—and, surprised by a strong acidic odor, I perceived that it was vinegar that I had carried away, not wine.

Damn! The monsters were going to eat me *à la vinaigrette!*

Realizing that escape was impossible, I put down my basket and waited, with sufficient composure still to witness a poignant drama that unfolded fifty meters away from me. The little dog that I had wanted to kill a little while before had come back, frightened and trembling, as if hypnotized, into the middle of the street. It stood on its hind legs, pulled back its forepaws, and started begging in front of the macrobe, with an attitude of delightful supplication.

Futile graces! I saw it lifted from the ground, and, still maintaining its adorable attitude, fly into the aspiratory tentacle. I was all the more upset because its disappearance signified my imminent fate. In fact, I could already feel the violently-displaced air causing me to oscillate.

Then the tentacle came closer. It was whirling. I contemplated its frightful gray gyration, stupidly. My last thought reached across space to the tunnel where Suzanne was waiting for me.

XIII

By virtue of what inexplicable phenomenon did the monster suddenly veer away from me, as if my presence inspired the same horror in it as it did in me? Was it caprice? Was it the disdain of a satiated animal? But in that case, the ones that were following it would not have spared me, and my death would have been no less certain.

Utterly terrified as I was, I had hardly had time to ask myself that question, and to observe that my first pursuer had executed a leap into the air that left the way clear for the others, than a second macrobe surged forth. It sniffed me, less avidly than the preceding one, and then seemed to be repelled by my person, by virtue of the same invisible force. It retreated backwards, allowing me to hear the collision of its carapace with those of its fellows; then it disappeared.

And seven other macrobes presented themselves thus before the prey that I was, then vanished in the projection of their entire mass, accomplishing a perilous leap, and subsequently falling back deafeningly in the vicinity. From the direction of the racket, I understood that they were fleeing toward Grenelle.

I remained alone.

Stupefied, having no explanation for my incredible immunity, with a mad bound, I resumed my race toward the Pont d'Iéna. I tumbled down the stairway leading to the quay and went back into the tunnel. A sublime cry from Suzanne welcomed me; her arms wrapped around me frantically. The sweet recompense for my audacity! I would have liked to respond by reassuring her, and promising her imminent liberty, but I had to confess, to her and to the others who were pressing me with questions, that the danger still persisted. Then, as they noticed the odor of vinegar on me, I was obliged to give the explanation, recounting my adventure, and the breaking of a bottle of that liquid on my shoulder. It was unbelievable, and yet, in spite of the implausibility of what I said, those minds debilitated by hunger believed me.

Finally, waiting until my interlocutors had been distracted by the Serviat-d'Abila flirtation, which was being closely observed, not without malice—oh, the genius of the species; everything gives way before it!—I handed my fiancée the two chicken wings that I had taken care to pocket. She was so imprudently hasty in raising them to her mouth that she was seen. First the actor, then the concierge, and then the disciple of the Salvation army, and others, threw themselves upon her like wolves, mouths agape, to snatch the victuals away from her. I did my best to defend her property, striking out at the gang of marauders, trying brutally to drive them away; it was no good. She was knocked down and dispossessed before even having been able to swallow two mouthfuls.

That brutality inspired me with the most vivid rancor against the humans assembled there. I judged them well worthy of their fate, and I promised to avenge myself on them and to disdain all sentiments of compassion in future.

That incident, that violent battle over a scrap of food, had only served to inflame the appetite of others. The most ludicrous and unrealizable projects to procure something to eat were proposed. Eyes were gleaming, and the young Englishwoman from the Salvation Army ate dirt before my eyes.

"My God!" the Baronne suddenly said. "Why not demand from the sewer that which Heaven, truly too unjust, refuses us at present..." Then she added, making her teeth grate a little more: "I believe that once, when I was living among the cannibals..."

I turned to Suzanne. She was on the brink of fainting. I could not, however, allow her to die of hunger. I equipped myself with a bucket and, parting the ferocious guardians of our gallery, went down to the bottom of the iron stairway leading to the collector.

It was the first time I had ventured that far, and I was able, by the light of a match, to convince myself of the privilege of our situation, those of us who were living in the broad corridor.

As far as the light of my match dissipated the darkness, I could see people sitting on the ledge above the channel of the sewer. The majority, huddled against the cement wall, were asleep, exhausted, their legs dangling in the water. Others were moaning, and I saw some who were already in advance of us, biting into pieces of flesh pulled out of the black water at hazard.

What impressed me the most, however, was the odor that filled the place. Whereas, in our location, the air renewed by the vicinity of the exterior was relatively breathable, here there was an unspeakable atmosphere, vitiated by the crowding of people, and by all the horrors that the sewer, swollen by rain, was carrying.

Not lingering over those sensations, I plunged my bucket into the current, without catching anything at first. I repeated the maneuver and, encountering resistance, pulled harder, and eventually found myself loaded with a heavy booty.

I went back upstairs, but, having reached the summit, I ran into new difficulties, for those who had appointed themselves the owners of the tunnel no longer wanted to let me back in.

First, I negotiated in vain; I invoked justice, right and reason. Then, as they remained deaf to my arguments, I ended up flying into a frightful rage and declared that I was determined to throw into the water, along with myself, any inhuman individuals who continued to oppose my passage. Then the latter stood aside before my threats, and I finally returned to my friends.

Oh, what we pulled out of my dipper then! I cannot think about it without shivering. There was a human foot, a fragment of shoulder, a vertebral column and a few other items of quivering flesh. My fiancée turned away from them in horror, and I no longer care to remember that the actor devoured a piece of sausage that was lying in the bucket with those anatomical specimens.

"Listen, Jean," Suzanne said to me, her eyes dilated with distress. "Listen: I can see that we're condemned to die of hunger. It's frightful, and I want no more of it. Let's hasten our agony, shall we? Ask Monsieur Serviat, who possesses a violent poison, to give us a few drops—and let's drink them together, my Jean!"

The poor child! It was the only time, very excusably, that she lacked courage. I tried at first to dissuade her from her project, to make her envisage a possible deliverance—but she was obstinate, and I consented.

I transmitted my request to Serviat, who refused flatly, on the pretext that individual interest had to cede to the salvation of all, and that he would not surrender an atom of his precious liquid.

When I returned to Suzanne after that discussion, I perceived than she had fallen into a kind of torpor due to weakness and emotion. Then I lifted her into the wagon and laid her down on her makeshift bed, and, having covered her with sand to shield her from the cold, I waited for darkness, which returned, atrocious and eternal.

Around me there were plaints, gasps and delirium. As he went to sleep, the actor declaimed the story of Theramenes.[21]

The next day was the fourth of our claustration. Our despair, on awakening, foundered before our exhaustion. We were no longer thinking; we were no longer anything more than anemic whimpering animals. I calculated that human resistance has limits, and that several among us would undoubtedly die that day. Alas, would my fiancée also be subject

---

[21] Theramenes was an Athenian statesman and general continually caught up in political upheavals in which he apparently attempted to play a moderating role; he was eventually executed for his troubles, remaining a highly controversial figure after his death, whose actions and motivations created a dissent among historians that continues, albeit esoterically, to the present day.

to that fatal decision of fate? I anticipated the blow that I would suffer, that would strike me down over her body.

She was lying in her bed of sand, her eyes closed and her hands joined, like a wax Madonna. Her lips were employing their scant breath in calling to two individuals whom she confused in the same devotion, the last glimmer of a heart in the process of extinction.

"Papa…! Jean…!" she repeated.

Oh, that poignant appeal, the anguishing litany of her virginal tenderness! I picked up her head gently, like a precious trinket, and drew it to my shoulder; I talked to her, and I was surprised by the widening of her gaze, which searched for me without seeing me. The poor child! How I adored her, that morning!

But I must get back to the tragic adventure, and the fashion, as extraordinary as everything else, in which it ended.

I remember that Suzanne had fallen unconscious again, which permitted me, with the aid of the triumphant daylight at the orifice, to measure the weakness of the other disaster-victims. It seemed to me that the same instinct had reckoned with the sentimentality of all of them. Faces emaciated, features drawn by suffering, they were no longer attentive to anything but their hunger. Their eyes admitted that they would have devoured one another.

I heard the actor and the concierge proposing, as if it were perfectly natural, selecting by drawing lots the person who would serve the others as nourishment, and I wondered whether the covetousness of the excessively dark-haired gentleman and the very blond young man, still directed toward the pretty collector for the Salvation Army, was still addressed to her charms or to the delicate snack that she promised.

Monsieur Serviat was slyly sucking his last cocaine pastille, and the Baronne d'Abila, the only one who was still striving to find the situation amusing, had just tightened her leg-armor by two notches, declaring that she would come out of it with an admirable figure.

Yes, we were at that point when, suddenly, someone directing his gaze toward the exit shouted: "Look what's happening in the Seine!"

We drew a little nearer to the orifice, still haunted by the fear of tentacles, and perceived that an enormous wave, propelled in the opposite direction to the current, like a tidal bore, had suddenly raised the level of the river. The water, which we had been unable to see a little while before because it was framed by the quays, was now visible; foam was seething on its surface, and we estimated that it must have risen by about a meter. We expected to see it fall back again, or at least remain stationary, but on the contrary, it continued to swell, to the extent that it soon reached the bank, over which it began to extend, turbulently.

Alarmed by that phenomenon, so seemingly unnatural, but for which I found an explanation without difficulty, I turned to Monsieur Serviat.

"Is it, perhaps, the macrobes?"

"Go and see, my friend! Go and see!"

Forgetting the danger of risking myself outside, so impassioned was I by the other danger, I bounded on to the quay. And what sudden anxiety! To the west, the direction from which the flood was precipitating, shortly before the Pont du Passy, a giant floodgate was blocking the Seine. One of the animals was lying across the bed of the river and filling it almost entirely.

If I had not been familiar with the monsters I would willingly have compared the one that was bathing to a metal dam disposed for a subfluvial endeavor, two-thirds submerged, whose upper part, heaving adopted the form of an elongated dome, dull gray in color, was surmounted by a mobile chimney—the animal's appendage. I saw the tentacle plunge into the liquid, sucking in a considerable quantity, and raising it up again, squirt the jet a hundred meters. My fear increased further when I observed that other macrobes were coming from the direction of Grenelle, ready to imitate it.

"This time, it's the end," I came back to say to the scientist. The animals are bathing. One has already invaded the Seine and the others..."

"Well, perhaps it's time to offer them a little liqueur!" exclaimed Monsieur Serviat, brandishing his bottle of toxin.

He had scarcely announced his plan when a second wave disturbed the river, overflowing the bank and projecting a torrent into our tunnel. A horrible human clamor, mainly coming from the collector placed beneath us, where the mass of liquid had found its natural direction, responded to the voice of the roaring wave. The imprecations of men and the desperate screams of women rang out; there was a frightful din compounded of all the noises reverberated by the cement walls along the dark tunnel.

I understood that another macrobe had plunged into the river, upstream from the first. That explanation, however, did not serve to moderate my terror, because I foresaw that, even if the other animals had decided to take up their positions behind the first, we would be no less condemned to perish submerged, given that the river would not stop In its inexhaustible course, and that its elements, repelled by the monstrous barriers, would inevitably accumulate between the quays where the drain was hollowed out. Indeed, after having dropped momentarily, the level was already rising again, less impetuously but without respite, and we had water up to our knees.

All that formidable chaos, that panic in the face of disaster, those plaints and gasps, had extracted Suzanne from her inertia. She raised herself up in her wagon, gazed at the tide dazedly, and turned her hallucinated face toward me.

"Jean!" she stammered. "Is it possible? Is it true?" Then submitting to the reality, she held out her arms to me, with the distress of a child at the end of so much suffering, after seeing fate play with her, and me, so stubbornly, before carrying us away. I seized her swiftly, and pressed her to my heart.

"Oh, Suzanne!" I cried. "My Suzanne, don't forget..."

But a third wave cut me off, passing furiously through our refuge, and went to be engulfed in the collector, definitively extinguishing the lamentations of the unfortunates who were down there.

Oh, what agonies there were in that black liquid! And what a spectacle in our tunnel, where people, howling their terror, were struggling to resist the current that already possessed us up to the waist!

And what I saw then, unconsciously, in a last glimmer of observation, before preparing to die myself and to feel Suzanne dying in my arms!

First there was a mother who, escaping from the collector and having reached the top step of the iron ladder, incapable of opposing any longer the forces dragging her away, holding out her child toward men who disdained her plea. She begged someone to take the child, that at least her treasure might be saved. She was swept away, disappearing along with her poor burden.

Then, in an extraordinary confusion, in a haste paralyzed by the water, there were people striving to reach the other stairway, the stone steps departing from the middle of our tunnel toward the roadway. Reaching the bottom, they ran into the implacable egotism of those who were already occupying the steps, who, further delaying the danger of going outside, defended their position with terrible actions, hitting, stabbing, strangling.

I saw the collector for the Salvation Army, her whole face illuminated with an ecstatic joy, open her mouth and intone a hymn, while the actor, suddenly going mad, was gripped by inextinguishable laughter. I saw the Baronne strip off the rest of her armor once and for all, and get ready to start swimming, beside Monsieur Serviat, who was taking the stopper from his bottle with a tremulous hand.

As for me, all my energies deployed toward the sole possible issue, I gripped Suzanne tightly in my arms, and resolved to attempt a last near-impossible salvation, to reach the submerged quay, then the steps to the Pont d'Iéna, and then the streets. Briefly, I gave her a few last instructions, recommending her to hang on to my shoulder without impeding my movements. She was scarcely listening anyway; her eyes, dilated by fright, were still protesting, more than any possible speech, against the imbecilic cruelty of destiny, which was obstinate in battering down the door of our happiness.

She must have judged, as I did, the futility of our efforts, suspecting that, at the exit from the tunnel, the fatal current would carry us away, to steer us toward the macrobes' tentacles. Even if we were spared by the fury of the waters, even if we reached dry ground, was our end not assured by the voracity of the monsters?

And the water rose, rose incessantly, under the inexhaustible momentum of the river. Stiffening myself nevertheless. I took a few strides toward the exterior light.

I had arrived very close to the exit, but a fourth wave, more impetuous than the others, immobilized me. A fourth macrobe had just plunged into the river, again upstream of the preceding ones.

The liquid mass swirled and foamed, and then leveled off, leaving me shoulder-deep in the water, while Suzanne, whom I was carrying, was waist-deep. I took a few more steps, and arrived in broad daylight, before the unforgettable spectacle of the flood, agitated by the swell of the successive gigantic immersions.

"Look out! Don't swallow a drop! I'm poisoning the Seine!" shouted Monsieur Serviat, who had followed us, hanging on to the Baronne at the moment when she plunged bravely into the torrent.

He was solemnly brandishing his murderous bottle. Although I was conscious of the puerility of his action, thinking that he would condemn us to be poisoned too, given that one cannot ask a swimmer not to open his mouth, an absurd hope nevertheless invaded me at the sight of what was about to happen.

"I'm poisoning! I'm poisoning!" he repeated, excitedly, his vessel unstoppered, both arms raised.

"It's futile, my poor Serviat!" a voice replied to him, coming from our left. "My lovely macrobes adore your toxin!"

Oh, that voice! That accursed voice! Where was it coming from? I thought I recognized it, and yet, was it possible that it came at that moment to insult our misery? What macabre joker was emitting it, then?

I turned my gaze toward the place from which it was echoing, and what I saw inspired the most emotional moment of the entire adventure, fertile as it was in *coups de théâtre*.

Standing in a rather frail dinghy, which was moving alongside the wall of the quay, was an improbable individual. Was it really a person? Was it not rather an unreal apparition, engendered by my delirious brain? Everything led me to believe so, for no human being had ever been decked out thus. The phantom was, in fact, covered, from the occiput to the toes, even hiding the face in such way as not to leave room for anything but the eyes and a long black beard, by a chestnut-red envelope similar to those rubber fabrics that are manufactured in order to make artificial sponges. And the improbability of the costumes was completed by the object that he wore slung over his shoulder: a bucket like those used by bill-posters, equipped with its brush.

Quite at ease, in spite of his burden, he brought his dinghy forward by pressing with his feet on two pedals that doubtless controlled the thrust and orientation of some kind of automobile engine.

Then I remembered something: I had seen that spongy silhouette before, from the height of the dirigible *France*, on the day when Junisseau had pointed out the individual guiding the macrobes with the broad sweeps of a holy-water sprinkler. I was, therefore, in the presence of the Almighty of the monsters, the genius that controlled them and led them to destruction!

And suddenly, after having recognized a tic that had just convulsed one of his free arms, I launched toward the apparition a stupefied cry: "Tornada!"

It was Tornada! It was the god of the macrobes, their creator, their inspirer, so deadly to Humankind! It was Tornada, at the height of his madness, taking a boat trip on the

Seine, doubtless in order to savor, in the spectacle of his work, the intense voluptuousness that maniacs experience in the realization of their crime. And the more we looked at him in terror, the more he laughed, and the more agitated his tics became.

"How little scientific intelligence you have, my poor Serviat!" he contrived to shout, nevertheless, above the fury of the waters.

Stupor had stopped the chemist's gesture of salvation. He considered Tornada, in bewilderment. I remember that he unthinkingly replaced the stopper in his bottle, but continued to hold it up in the air, probably preserving it for his moral enemy. Then, suddenly, seized by rage, he stammered:

"Just wait, scoundrel! I'll take away your appetite for the Académie!"

Drunk with wrath, forgetting that he could not swim, he came forward, cleaving through the flood, toward the madman. But the latter did not even seem to notice him. He had returned his interest to the group formed by Suzanne and myself, to my efforts to resist the inundation, which was reaching us again, coming up to my shoulders.

He was moved to pity. "What! It's you, my dear children! It's you, imprudent little ones! You didn't follow my advice, then? You stayed in Paris?"

"Oh, Monsieur!" my fiancée implored, in a sudden surge of hope. "Save us! Save us!"

I saw that that appeal had suddenly softened the strange individual. Using his skill and a surprising strength, he brought the boat closer to us, and with a firmness of grip that one would not have suspected in such a small man, he first grasped my fiancée, lifted her up and drew her into his boat. Then he extended his hand to me, in my turn. That was fortunate, for the river was continuing its inexorable rise, the turbulent waters had already exceeded human height, and I was on the point of succumbing to the engulfing flood.

Then, as soon as we were in the dinghy, Tornada picked up the brush contained in his bucket, and sprinkled us with a liquid that had a strong odor of vinegar.

"Wretch! Wretch!" Monsieur Serviat was still howling, hanging on to the boat with one hand and trying to climb into it.

Tornada did not seem to hear him. He was sitting down next to Suzanne and gazing at her with a profound tenderness. His eyes filled with tears, but I was unable to determine whether the cause that provoked his emotion was the fact of seeing my fiancée so exhausted, with the lividity of a corpse, or whether, on the contrary, the acid vapor given off by his receptacle and his clothing was irritating his eyes and determining the apparent sadness.

He remained thus, unmoving, contemplating her, for several seconds, which seemed to me to last for an eternity.

"Speak, my child," he said, finally—and that last word took on an extraordinary softness on his lips. "Speak, and you alone I will obey."

"Halt the disaster, Monsieur!" Suzanne moaned. "Save those you can still spare!"

"Even Serviat?"

"Yes, him too! All of them! All those who remain!"

That request seemed to make him hesitate. He began grimacing again, and his limbs sketched further convulsions. A last supplication from Suzanne who had thrown herself on her knees, finally made up his mind. He gripped his rival, who was still clinging on to the edge of the boat, by the wrist and pulled him in.

"You! If you move...!" he said, dumping him on to a banquette, like a parcel.

In response to an ardent prayer from Suzanne he repeated his maneuver for the Baronne, just as a fifth bore, produced by the irruption of a fifth macrobe into the river, had descended upon her and was about to drag her away. The socialite was in quite a state! Her wet chemise was clinging to her vast flesh, her long hair was loose and sticky. Oh, I swear to you that it was not a pretty sight! But how much more dolorous was the disaster that had swept over our erstwhile companions, who had all drowned, annihilated by the irresistible flood. The orifice of our refuge was invisible now, alas!

Trembling with horror, I sat quietly in the boat, hugging Suzanne. The drama had taken such a stupefying turn that I no longer knew what to think. Tornada's conduct promised us salvation, but what enigmas did it still reserve for us? The madman was liberating us, after having destroyed an entire people, but what was he going to do with us now...inasmuch as the macrobes had detected us?

I saw their colossal masses moving sinuously along the driver, toward our freely drifting boat. On the other hand, more were arriving, bounding from every corner of the sunlit space, accumulating on the bank, raising their frightful roaring conches. Tornada, however, did not seem to be alarmed by their approach. He planted his little sponge-silhouette in the boat, derisory before so many monstrosities encircling us, and he spoke.

"Serviat," he said, "You're a pretentious idiot and an incomparable ass. Do you still deny the presence of *Micrococcus aspirator* in alkaline environments?"

"I don't know..." the scientist stammered.

"You don't know? And yet I'm showing them to you, the darlings! Look around you—they're visible enough. And do you still deny that they can develop abnormally, in an appropriate culture medium? Eh? Do you still deny that?"

He twitched triumphantly. He clucked, in a victorious snigger.

The chemist, as frightened as us in seeing the circle of animals draw tighter, did not reply.

"Monsieur!" Suzanne begged. "They're arriving! They're here! There!"

"Have no fear, my child."

Our boat continued its atrocious drift. It had arrived about fifty meters from the first immersed macrobe; seized by the eddies produced by its mass, it spun, contrary to the direction of the river's flow, imposing on us successively the view of all the giants circling us—but which, however, remained on the bank, trunks elevated, held back by an incomprehensible dread. Our anguish reached its extreme. How were we going to escape them? By means of what magic power was the genius of Tornada going to save us from the monstrous horde? Or was he simply bringing us to the hecatomb, with a refinement of cruelty?

I thought so at first, at the further signs of evident dementia that Tornada was then showing. He had picked up the brush from the receptacle suspended from his shoulder, and began sprinkling us again, like a priest blessing the dead, while his lips murmured obscure words. What did that action signify, after all? What power did it have over our destiny? Was it merely a macabre ritual prior to the sacrifice?

The fabulous circle was still tightening. In every direction, there was no longer anything to be seen but raised trunks, prolonging their horrible whistles. Nothing, this time—no divine or terrestrial power—could enable us to avoid the fatal air current. I gave Suzanne my last glance of adoration. Around us, the thousand sunlit facets of the water were palpitating.

"Watch carefully, Serviat!" proclaimed the madman.

He resumed his position at the pedals, and activated them with a few light pressures. The boat moved off, going up the Seine with an amazing rapidity. We seemed to be flying over the water, whose surface was now flooding the quays, with the result that, whichever way we turned, we perceived the lamentable expanse of devastated Paris, while the macrobes, attracted to the banks by our presence, directed their progress in our direction. Pitiful heaps of rubble, and fragments of the walls of palaces, the Chambre des Députés, the Légion d'honneur and the Gare d'Orsay filed past.

Between the Pont des Saints-Pères and the Pont des Arts, however, the boat suddenly stopped. What an astonishing contrast! The Cité had been spared; the towers of Notre-Dame, the Palais de Justice, the Sainte-Chapelle, defied the abolished city with their splendor, and the crushed Louvre opposed its ruins to the still-intact Institut.

What did Tornada want? Why that sinister excursion? Did he want to contemplate, one last time, the cupola that the incredulity of men had refused him? Did he want, one last time, to carry away the vision of his disastrous power, or to pass his magnificent and fatal army in review? It was there, arranged along the two banks, having immobilized at the same time as us, and yet, it seemed to me, still retained by I knew not what mysterious power.

"Look, Serviat!" howled the maniac. "Look at the Institut! If I wanted, eh? In pieces, the Institut. But there's Vernet...where has he gone, then, Vernet? And then, there's his daughter...oh, oh, oh, my daughter, where is she, too? My daughter!"

He sniggered. He spat in the direction of the monument. Then he leaned on his pedals again, and the boat, still accompanied by its formidable cortege, resumed its route toward the Trocadéro. Soon, we found ourselves back at our point of departure. The waters, further increased, were swelling around the masses installed there.

"What is life, if it isn't oblivion?" reflected the madman, aloud, twisting the two halves of his beard together.

Mad—yes, indubitably, he was mad. Unhurriedly, he took from the inside pocket of his strange garment a small pistol barely twenty centimeters long, like an child's toy. He secured it in his hand, and pointed it at the nearest macrobe in the river. I observed that he was aiming at a fairly distinct patch situated beneath the monster's tentacle, which I had not noticed until then. Was it with that vain implement that he expected to breach the mass that fracassite had been unable to scratch?

"*Vade retro, macrobe!*" he pronounced, pressing the trigger.

The shot was fired. A light smoke evaporated in the firmamental purity. And the miracle was accomplished: as soon as the animal was touched by the projectile, we saw it quit the water, turning a prodigious somersault, Instead of carrying it forward, however, the leap took it backwards, with the result that the colossus, having obstructed the sky momentarily, fell back toward Grenelle in a clap of thunder.

"And one!" Tornada counted.

The water displaced by that immense void had drawn us toward the second macrobe. After an instant of further peril provoked by the unstable equilibrium of our boat, when the level had stabilized again, Tornada raised his arm again and subjected the second animal to the same fate as the first.

This time, the leap finished on the Pont de Passy, which resisted, and the gigantic carcass remained there, motionless, belly up, its tentacle hanging down. We could no longer doubt the mortal power of the projectiles.

"I bow down, Tornada!" cried Serviat, as stupefied as us. Then, lowering his head, he added. "Yes, I'm defeated. You're the Master! Explain it to me now, Tornada—explain it!"

"How did I do it? Oh, my poor fellow!"

He turned to Suzanne. In truth, it was to her that he replied; it was her that he attempted to dazzle. He disdained his rival—and that disdain spared us necessarily abstract scientific reasoning. While taking aim methodically at the other animals, which his boat, skillfully maneuvered, passed along the river's edge, periodically reloading his ammunition clip –whose cartridges, each enclosed in a brass detonator, were constituted by thick glass ampoules, he continued.

"It's to you that I'm addressing myself, my child, for, if I except your father, the brain of an academician is too obtuse to comprehend. This is what I've done. I cultivated in special media, entirely appropriate to their growth, microscopic animalcules that I had discovered in bicarbonate of soda. I had the idea that they would develop there abnormally, and that I would be able to make them do so rapidly, by subjecting them to appropriate conditions of air, light, nourishment and social exigencies—yes, social exigencies too, for a chemist must double as a sociologist. As I said, I had the idea that I could subject them, within a year, to the transformations that Darwinism attributes to centuries of evolution. What? Does function not create the organ, eh? Ha ha! I made functionaries! Who do not belong to the Institut!"

He paused to take aim, extending his arm.

"Leap, macrobe! Bang! *De profundis!* Yes, out there in my laboratory at Rosny, I plotted a tasty revenge against those cretins. Out there, I grew these villainous beasts. If you knew what voluptuousness there was in seeing them, every day, growing larger—and my joy increased too! Bang! *Ave macrobe!*

"And destroying them, now, I can confess to you that it's breaking my heart—bang! I kill you too, lovely macrobe!— and it required, my child, your meek suggestion, and the imperishable memory of my daughter, which your grace has reawakened—bang! will you, macrobe, ever reawaken?—for me to decide to immolate my pretties. Bang!... Bang! Bang! Bang! Bang!"

Gripped by a destructive rage, with an extraordinary skill, he now accelerated his fire, which was succeeded by the immeasurable leaps of the macrobes, and the thunderous din when they fell back, out of our sight. Perhaps fifty had already been carried away by their agonized leap, and the bank was now free of them, while only one remained in the water, which continue to block the watercourse, and that one was still too far away from us to be an immediate preoccupation.

But what was he going to do about the others, the scientific genius? How was he going to get to them? Already my imagination was setting off on a hunt, in Tornada's wake, through the streets of the devastated city, or rather the surrounding plains that were also subject to their ravages—and that pursuit, favored by an evident security, was already making me smile when my attention was absorbed by a new maneuver of the man clad in sponge.

"Pass me that object," he said to me, pointing to a long case on the floor of the boat, which I had not previously noticed.

I held it out to him; it was rather heavy, in spite of its re-stricted dimensions. As soon as it was in his possession he held it up vertically; then he pressed a spring that gave birth to the three limbs of a tripod, which he established solidly on the floor. Another pressure on a second spring caused a kind of little metal tube to emerge at the upper extremity, surmounted by an ampoule similar to those he had employed to destroy his macrobes. Without him even having to touch it again, a suc-cession of sparks set the base of the tube ablaze; then an al-most insignificant explosion occurred, which launched the ampoule into the air.

"Close your eyes!" Tornada ordered, at the same time.

I made the mistake of not obeying him. Curiosity made me look up into the sky, following the supposed trajectory of the ampoule, until an extremely vivid flash of light seared my retinas. Although blinded by that extraordinary radiation, I nevertheless retained the impression that its color was an or-ange-red and that its form was akin to the spray of a firework.

That light, so special, and its expansion in the form of a bouquet, was not new to me. I remembered having observed it several times before, from the height of Mont-Valérien, on the day when the Committee of National Defense had made a fool of itself with the plan to destroy the macrobes with cannon fire. Why was Tornada reproducing it? In what interest?

I soon had an explanation from the words with which the inventor accompanied his maneuver, and once again I had to admire the more than ingenious fashion in which the whole affair had been planned.

"Run, my lovelies! Run, my darlings! He murmured, ad-dressing himself to our invisible enemies, which were incapa-ble of hearing him. Then, in a louder voice, gesturing toward the deserted banks, he added: "Run! Come! The light is calling you! Don't you recognize your light of orig..."

He suspended his phrase, but I had understood. Their light of origin! That was it! Tornada had made use of an or-ange-red light to cultivate his microorganisms, and that was doubtless the reason why the experiments carried out at the

Institut Pasteur, for lack of that detail, had failed. And that orange-red light, he was reproducing in their air with an exceptional intensity; he was making use of it to rally his creatures, to attract them, as if by a magnetic fluid, to the sacrifice to which his new pity commanded him.

Indeed, at his celestial command, the bank soon resonated with a formidable *Frott…! Frott…! Frott…!* and was garnished once again with a host of gray enormities.

All the rest of the flock was there, fifty meters away from us, roaring, brandishing their tentacles, and yet, still retained on the bank but I still knew not what terror of their shepherd.

Meanwhile, Tornada continued to direct his weapon against the successive targets offered to his skill. It was no longer anything but a continuous crepitation, and to every one of his infallible shots, a formidable leap responded, an obscuration of the sky soon followed by the distant fall of a monstrous cadaver. We were no longer counting his victims, but he seemed to have the number in his head, for he proclaimed, at a certain moment:

"Seventy-two! Keep coming, my darlings! Come! Bang! Bang!.... And Bang!

"For pity's sake, explain," Serviat groaned. "Explain!"

But Tornada continued to address himself to Suzanne, while reloading his weapon.

"How inferior he is! What a nonentity he is! It's true that he's a member of the Institut! But you, my child, you, who aren't, tell me: how does one neutralize acids?"

"Acids?" asked my fiancée.

"Yes, acids."

"With alkalis."

"Of course! She knows! She isn't a member of the Institut! And she knows, too, that acids are the enemies of alkalis! So, you can grasp, Serviat, you utter ass, that in order to destroy creatures emerged from alkaline environments, it requires…what? Bang! Bang!...it requires a few drops of acid…simple vinegar! And bang! Bang!...and that it's sufficient

190

to strike there, at the original cell, the vital navel of my lovely microbes, their only vulnerable spot. Bang! Bang!...that it's sufficient to strike there, to kill them, the poor darlings! And to think that Serviat has prepared a toxin! A toxin! Ha ha ha! Bang! Bang!"

He was no longer clucking; he was growling; he was uttering howls toward his hecatomb.

Then, a flash of revelation shot through me. I understood then why I had been spared by the monsters, two days before, in the Avenue de La Bourdonnais; why they had even moved away from me in evident horror. Fate had aided me singularly, by inundating me with the immunizing liquid, the vinegar from the bottle broken in the haste of my flight. I understood, too, everything that had previously seemed inexplicable to me: Tornada's costume, a sponge steeped in acetic acid; and his actions in sprinkling us religiously; and method of herding the macrobes by inspiring them with the terror of the murderous fluid. All that I had put down to the count of incoherence became the logic of a powerful brain, and I criticized myself, in my spirit of scientific deduction, for not having suspected it.

Mad, however, Tornada was! It was sufficient to contemplate him at that moment, rolling his wild eyes, intoxicated by his murderous gestures, shouting and howling, to be convinced of it.

Nevertheless, he soon relented his fire; he no longer launched his projectiles without hesitation. He proclaimed the repeated "Bang! Bang!" that accompanied the death of his creatures more faintly. His final shots were spaced out.

Our boat had brought us close to the macrobe that still occupied the river, the waters flowing around it to resume their course beyond it, after having passed over the height of the quays, giving it the appearance of a gray rock in the midst of a tormented sea. As soon as it saw us, its tentacle began to gyrate.

"We're at ninety-nine," said Tornada, in a whisper. "That's the last!"

He was weeping. To destroy his work like that, for a child's grateful smile—was that not a sacrifice to which it is necessary to attribute a certain measure of grandeur? Had Suzanne not extracted from him the testimony of his genius? Was it not his brain that she was tearing out of him, at the same time that she was forcing him to extinguish his creation?

And Tornada's hand trembled, when he aimed his weapon for the last time. Nevertheless, he hit his target, and an enormous displacement of the river, companying the monster's leap, after nearly causing us to overturn, finally signified our liberation.

I cannot describe our jubilation here.

"All! All! Adieu, my pretties!" sobbed Tornada. Then, turning to Suzanne: "You see, my child, what I've done for you! Will you now forgive a poor, desperate man who wanted to rediscover his daughter in you?"

He held out his hand to her—but she shivered with such fright; she had, at the memory of the distress that hand had accumulated, the disasters it had engendered, the innocent deaths that it had caused, experienced such a surge of disgust that Tornada understood that he had committed irreparable sins. He grimaced, and twisted his beard. He convulsed in a tic that was reminiscent of the tentacular movement of his monsters. Finally, he took another revolver out of his pocket, and before we could do anything to stop him, he applied the barrel to his temple.

"Bang!" he repeated.

And he collapsed, in a red splash. The madman disappeared with his work.

But now that I am finishing this story; now that, having relocated Monsieur Vernet—among what transports you can imagine—Suzanne and I are married; and I can hear, interrupting the joyous sounds that those little devils our children are making, the ringing of the bell that is announcing the arrival of Monsieur Serviat and the Baronne—can you imagine that they're married!—now, truly, on thinking about it, I wonder whether everything I've recounted was real, and whether Suzanne and I, and everyone we know, an entire people, were not atrociously delirious for a week...

THE ANDROGYNE

I

At the moment when I quit the smoking room, leaving my last cigar, in order to obey the imperative gestures of Rolande, who had just ordered me to rejoin her in the drawing room, I sensed the strange gaze of Professor Tornada weighing upon me for the third time.

Strictly speaking, that gaze was interrogating me rather than weighing upon me, but it fascinated me at the same time, and I was obliged to protect myself against all the attraction, contrary to that of my mistress, in order to detach myself from it and not to submit myself once again to the extraordinary doctrines of which the scientist had made me the reluctant auditor during the meal.

In other circumstances, perhaps I would have considered it as good fortune to have been his neighbor at table. His biological discoveries were impassioning opinion; his operatory skill placed him in the first rank of surgeons; his originality distinguished him even further. Many others, in order to occupy my place at his side, would have overlook the malaise inspired by his ugliness, comprised by a face that might have been molded by the evil, all flat surfaces beneath an entirely bald cranium from which, by contrast, an Absalomian beard hung down, extending in waves half way down his chest.[22] But it was the first time that Rolande had invited me to her

---

[22] The Biblical Absalom was killed after his abundant hair became entangled in the boughs of a tree, so "Absalomian" is often used in French literature to refer to long hair, although very rarely to a beard.

home; she had recommended me to avoid any manifestation that might have led her husband to suspect our liaison; and my mind had been more occupied in forbidding myself the joy of being her guest than in listening to Professor Tornada talk.

Once I had passed through the zone of influence I mentioned therefore—of which the scientist's eyes were the focal point—I drew near to my mistress, in the middle of a circle of ladies, and sat down with a feigned indifference in the chair that she indicated to me.

"Bravo, my Jo!" she muttered to me between her teeth. "You've been admirable. Be sure that I'll be able to recompense you for conducting yourself so well."

"Tomorrow?" I asked, in the same discreet fashion.

"Tomorrow," she approved. "Tomorrow, a five o'clock, your Rolande will arrive, fervent, at our love-nest."

"And then, in a week?"

"In a week's time, I shall bid farewell to my tyrant, and I shall breathe freely. I shall breathe, my Jo, through your lips."

I followed the direction of her eyes. They would have struck Monsieur Variland down, if looks could kill. Her rancor against that man with the cold and glabrous face, pinched by a lorgnon, with a square jaw revealing egotistical appetites, was clearly legible therein. His silhouette, all worldly correction, modified the impression of his face slightly. He was a financier. He had obtained Rolande by throwing into the conjugal balance the weight of ten millions, and she had allowed herself to be convinced by submission to parental will.

In three years of marriage, not only had he not succeeded in making himself tolerated, but had further crushed by mental torture that poor child-like heart, which only required a smile in order to be happy. Authoritarian, vindictive and suspicious, with no compensatory qualities, he would certainly have driven her to suicide, she had often told me, had I not intervened.

Dear Rolande! My entire reason for living! I had met her for the first time at the home of mutual friends, the Chabrols, where her husband had left her in September in order to go hunting—but it was said on the quiet that the hunt in question

196

was not in the forest, but at the most in a poultry-yard. I had, therefore, had no more to do than collect that poor suffering heart. Oh, the awakening of a love that cannot be confessed, but that the blush on a face betrays at our approach! Oh, the first confessions that are merely tacit accords, sometimes murmurs, but of such a divine harmony!

She had given me all those virginal first fruits of the heart, and I was sufficiently grateful for them to have delivered myself subsequently to the treasures of her body. As soon as we had returned to Paris, she had run to my home and offered herself with a kind of sacred transport. Far from calming us down, our encounters only exasperated our need to share life—with the result that we had recently taken the resolution to attempt happiness together. The reason she had wanted me, in spite of my resistance, at that dinner, was precisely in order for me to strike up a friendship with the Chabrol household, where she was counting on staying for a while once she had returned to her parents to institute divorce proceedings.

"The Chabrols," she reminded me.

I headed toward our future hosts, in order to reach an understanding with them, but I was unable to get to them. They were part of a circle forming at that moment around Professor Tornada, who was being taken to task by a corpulent lady of an ultra-masculine appearance, dressed like the gentlemen in a frock-coat and wearing a golden-blonde wig—a truly hilarious picture—the Baronne Nirvâne des Illeuls, Nirvâne being her forename. She was, fortunately for her husband, a widow. She was tolerated as such, and some people even sought her out, because, bitten by the literary tarantula, she had produced a number of novels claiming the social superiority of women.

"Come on, Doctor, what are you telling us!" her contralto voice was saying.

"Absolutely, Madame," affirmed the shrill and insistent voice of Tornada, impatiently.

"Change sex at will? You must be joking!"

"I don't joke, Madame. Were you joking, the day when you wanted to give the illusion that your own had changed?"

"Me! My modification, alas, is merely in the costume; it's only a reaction to fashion," the Baronne riposted, with a burst of laughter that propelled adipose waves along her upright neck. "But to transmute a male animal into a female in the flesh, that surpasses the imagination! How is it done, then? Tell us that. Oh, do tell, Doctor!"

It was obvious that the question interested her prodigiously. She was not the only one, moreover, to find that interest therein, given that matters of generation have the gift of impassioning humans universally; all ears, including mine—and even Rolande's, I then perceived—were curious to collect the professor's explanations.

But Tornada would not satisfy our legitimate desire to learn. To all evidence, the subject raised by the Baronne, although it concerned a recent biological discovery, was extremely importunate to him. He manifested his impatience by a tic that twisted the corner of his mouth and caused his eyes to tilt backwards in their orbits, which rendered him hideous, and after which, relaxed by that nervous manifestation, he spoke calmly.

"I detest talking science in a drawing room, Madame. Only know that these operations have been carried out on inferior animals, and accord me the credit of being sincere." With a smile that was a rictus, he added: "Furthermore, if you continue to doubt my word, entrust yourself to me and perhaps I shall be able to make you, in reality, the person that your ridiculous accoutrement has the pretention to indicate."

"I'm not an inferior animal," stammered the Baronne, vexed.

That quarrel cast a chill. To avoid a scene, I thought it as well to say something in my turn. I wanted to generalize a debate that, left to those two excessive characters, was taking on a disquieting tone. Although a painter, and by virtue of that fact accustomed to precision, I nevertheless possessed a facility of elocution worthy of an advocate, and anyway, the prospect of shining in front of Rolande did not displease me.

"These experiments are certainly curious, Doctor," I affirmed. "I've read the communication to the Académie des Sciences—it's the tadpole, isn't it, whose sex can be inverted by placing it, at a certain moment of its development, in appropriate alimentary conditions."

"That discovery is not mine," Tornada declared. "It was presented to the Académie by Edmond Perrier.[23] But I've taken things much further..." He smoothed the strands of his beard, caressing the slowly, and added: "Much further...perhaps people will laugh one day..."

After that, he did not unseal his lips again, as if he feared having said too much. The field was then open for me, and I addressed the audience.

"What a pity," I exclaimed, "that these practices are limited to batrachians and can't be extended to humans! Then we'd see some strange swaps, wouldn't we, ladies?"

My question provoked a debate. Everyone had an opinion about the opportunities provided by such modification, and in the racket of voices I distinguished the Baronne's contralto, which was naturally in favor of the virile personality—while the Chabrols, a tenderly united couple, expressed their desire to retain the status quo. I also heard Mademoiselle Blanche Férette, a young universitarian equipped with several diplomas, declaring that men were more privileged. Blanche Férette was, however, very pretty, and her grace and charm gave her a power of which she must have been unaware in order to state

---

[23] Edmond Perrier (1844-1921) was an invertebrate zoologist, and never presented a paper to the Académie on changing the sex of tadpoles. He had a strong interest in evolutionary theory, comparing and contrasting the Lamarckian and Darwinian accounts in *Lamarck et le transformisme actuel* [Lamarck and Contemporary Evolutionary Theory] (1893), but his citation here, in the context of the ongoing discussion, might have some connection with his study of *La Femme dans la nature, dans les moeurs, dans la légende, dans la societé* [Woman in Nature, Mores, Legend and Society] (1910).

that principle so categorically. Then there was Madame Savari, the beautiful cantatrice of the Opéra-Comique; she boasted without reserve of the good fortune of being a woman. A flower blossoming splendidly in an outrageously low-cut dress, her gaze, as she spoke, never quit the fashionable young composer with the blazing eyes, Rimeral, whose lover she was. Her sparkling teeth were presently consuming the royalties of the author of numerous operettas as light as they were banal, but favored by success.

When the sound of voices had calmed down somewhat, I took a malign pleasure in interrogating a few other couples individually, and everyone declared their regret in not being a batrachian—from which I concluded that all of them were unhappy in their amours.

"But what about you, Monsieur Sigerier?" Rolande asked me, maliciously.

Paradoxicality was a familiar amusement of mine. I plunged into it wholeheartedly, savoring in advance the effect that it would have on my mistress.

"Me? My dear Madame, I'm a little hesitant, for a reason that has nothing to do with reason"—Rolande's heart was bound to understand that it was the cause in question—"but, if I set aside that personal consideration, it appears to me that the weaker sex is much the more privileged in life. In truth, one is never content with one's lot, but I ask you, what more agreeable manner is there of traversing our brief existence down here than being a pampered, adulated and fêted creature, of only having to think of oneself, while all charges and concerns are reserved for men? Women invoke their weakness, but that it precisely their strength. A smile that reveals pretty teeth, or a dimple in the chin, is far more powerful than an arm wielding a valorous sword; and the conquests of men, in whatever domain they extend, invariable end up in the service of women!"

"An example: the law!" protested the Baronne. Raising her voice, she went on: "The law is made by men and for men. It is the worst organ of slavery. It enslaves women entirely!"

"And that is lucky for them, Madame"—oops! I nearly said Monsieur—"because, if moral constraint did not exist, would women have the joy of tasting forbidden fruit? The entire secret of happiness is there—in vanquishing difficulty! Most of the time, what drives spouses apart is precisely the fact that the law assures them of their tranquility and their harmony. You would often see two people who detest one another as a household adore one another if they were living separately and had to overcome the impediments of amour."

In response to this theory, people nodded or shook their heads, in accordance with their conjugal accord or disaccord, and I divined, in Rolande's mime, that she was criticizing me for saying such things about the future legal proceedings that we were preparing. But she doubtless thought that my comments were designed to deflect her husband's suspicions, if he might have any, for her moue was soon transformed into an ambiguous smile.

In any case, I anticipated so many valid objections to my fragile arguments that, in order not to drag out the discussion I hastened to conclude. "In fact, if only from that point of view, I bitterly regret not being one of those exquisite little monarchs at whose feet men prostrate themselves. And hurrah for the scientist who, will, some day or other, raise me up on to the pedestal of weakness!"

Those last words being an ironic homage to Professor Tornada, I turned toward him to observe the impression they made on him—but I was surprised to discover him plunged in an armchair, soundly asleep, as if the nonsense had had a soporific effect on him. He was even emitting little explosions through his fleece, akin to snores, and in the silence that followed my speech, those explosions reminded the guests of the time and gave them the signal to depart. People got up to go, went into the vestibule and hurried along the valets who were helping them with their overcoats. I was ready to follow the movement, heartbroken at having to tear myself away from Rolande's company so soon, when her husband pointed at the sleeper and asked me: "And what are we going to do with the

201

transformer of tadpoles?" He thought he was giving proof of wit in shaking him by the shoulders and saying: "*Il est tard, têtard.*"[24]

"I know. I was waiting for Monsieur Sigerier to retire, in order that I could take a little walk in his company," said the professor, standing up with an astonishing liberty of his senses.

We went into the street. As soon as the heavy batten of the door closed, I tried to separate from the scientist, who lived a long way away, whereas I lived in a bachelor apartment in the Rue du Général-Foy, near my studio in the Rue Lepic. But Tornada had taken me by the arm, authoritatively, and dragged me in his direction without saying a word.

Once again, for the fourth time that evening, I felt submissive to an influence that the man was exercising upon me. Not that the influence in question was hypnotic in nature, for I am perfectly familiar with those phenomena, of nervous origin, to which I am refractory; his power was something else, indefinable, not yet observed in occult science—as if my individuality, although I was able to progress with a normal equilibrium, had been carried away in a crazy gyration around Tornada, the central point of my orbit.

Yes, what happened at that moment is inexplicable, as was the rest that followed therefrom. Yes, now that I am recalling to memory and transcribing that extraordinary adventure, I cannot yet find any possible interpretation, either in the practices of magnetism or those of physics, in that physics cannot yet touch the supernatural.

All I can remember is that several times, while we were walking—and we walked for a long time, along streets I did not know, which must have run parallel to the fortifications—his beard, which the folded under his cloak, became phosphorescent. Was he hiding some sortilege of modern science therein? Did his fleece mask a fluid accumulator that was

---

[24] i.e., "It's late, tadpole."

drawing me along, or was it an accumulator itself? I am too ignorant of such things to risk a hypothesis.

After an exceedingly long time, we reached a broad and cold façade whose lights were extinct. There were two doors, one large and one small. He opened the smaller one, and pushed me into an open space, in which I vaguely distinguished a funerary vehicle, introduced me into an obscure building and had me climb a staircase on which I stumbled over every step—after which, suddenly, a magnificent light inundated a sumptuous study. Bookshelves ran along the walls; thick woolen carpets scattered a thousand delightful flowers; expensive item of furniture laden with papers and pamphlets indicated the efforts of a brain always in gestation; deep divans upholstered in sable must sometimes have substituted for a bed.

He sat me down on one of the divans and handed me a gilded lacquer box. "A cigar?"

I had to accept; it was an order.

I lit the cigar at the flame of an old flint lighter whose spring he had activated.

Was it the smoke? Was it fatigue? My ears were ringing and I could not resist a drowsiness that lay me down on the divan, as if I had been hit over the head with a club.

II

When I woke up, I was no longer in Professor Tornada's study. I was in a bed, which I first mistook for my own, to the extent that, in order to combat the reigning obscurity, I put out my hand to grip the electric light-switch that was ordinarily within reach, on the nightstand next to my bed-head. My hand did not encounter anything but empty space, however; there was no nightstand.

I could not understand that disappearance. My mind was functioning imperfectly, as after one of those long beneficent slumbers, when the intellect has difficulty getting back into gear. I was even falling asleep again when, suddenly, a vivid natural light, dispensed by a large bay window whose opaque curtains had just been drawn back, forced me to take stock of the place where I was.

It was an entirely white room with rounded corners, floored with varnished tiles, in which a pale green frieze ran along the junction of the walls and the ceiling, depicting little amours pursuing one another. Of furniture there was none—nothing except a wheeled cart with crystal shelves, on which stood bottles full of polychromatic liquids and several nickel-plated instruments, so bizarre in their form that it was impossible for me to define their function.

I had given the comfort of my visits to convalescent friends often enough to have no doubt that I was in a surgical clinic. But what the clinic was, and what circumstances had led to my hospitalization there, surpassed my faculties for the moment. My brain was sill so numb that I did not even think of connecting my new situation with the profound, evidently artificial, sleep by which I had been gripped on Professor Tornada's divan. Moreover, the presence of a feminine silhouette beside my bed deflected me from any effort of comprehension.

It was, believe me, a very pretty nurse, clad in a appropriate costume—with the difference that the red cross normally accrediting those who wear it had been replaced in this instance by a T embroidered in green silk on the smock, in the position of the heart. My nurse also presented the notable feature that, beneath her elegant cap, her hair was cut short, at the level of the neck, which gave her physiognomy a slightly boyish ambiguity. What surprised me most, however, was the particularity of her gaze.

To the extent that once can recount something as confused and indefinable as the antecedents of a gaze—which is to say, all that the information of life that a gaze has harvested and stored—what was reflected in the mirror of my nurse's eyes had left an indelible expression of gravity, prudence and wisdom. I have thought a great deal since then about that gaze.

She was evidently watching out for my awakening. As soon as she had perceived glimmers of intelligence she passed a sponge steeped in perfumed alcohol over my forehead. She accomplished that gesture with the solemnity of a baptism, but she touched me even more by the sympathetic manner in which she pronounced the first words that I heard.

"You too, poor child! You too shall know the destiny of transmutation..."

As I was about to interrogate her about those enigmatic words, she closed my mouth with a hand that was both gentle and firm.

"No, don't talk yet...don't even think! Thoughts will come to you soon enough. Wait a moment...wait for his visit...he'll explain..."

Then she left me to go to stand at the window, and examine herself at length there with the aid of a portable mirror. I had a confused notion that she was not obedient to a sentiment of coquetry. Nothing about her gave that impression. She seemed, rather, to be yielding to a sentiment of curiosity.

I dozed off again for an inappreciable interval, and was then recalled to contingencies by a draught of fresh air from the door, which had just opened. Someone came in, whom I had difficulty at first recognizing as Professor Tornada. He was clad in a smock tightly gathered about his thin frame; his abundant fleece was gathered into a white linen sheath, which also covered, like a hood, the top of his head. All that was uncovered, in fact, was his face, where the eyes were animated by a mobility so singular that I found it disturbing.

With an abrupt gesture, he beckoned to the nurse, who went to him, blushing. He caressed her face, and then said: "You're very pretty you know, my dear. Indeed, I'm content with myself. People will say: 'That Tornada is definitely an ace!'"

After which, he sent her away with another mute command.

It was from that moment on that I veritably entered into the unreal. Now that I am writing this memoir of an implausible period of my life, my hand still trembles with emotion.

Tornada repeated on me the same caress that he had given the nurse, and as to her, he declared: "And you too, my dear, will be quite beautiful!"

That gesture and those words troubled me. Having now found all my presence of mind, I judged that he must be passing through a mental crisis—which, in fact, was not impossible, given the signs of derangement that he had already manifested in my presence. The most elementary prudence therefore counseled me to proceed carefully with a madman.

As cordially as possible, I said: "I beg your pardon, Doctor, but you must be mistaken. I'm Georges Sigerier, the painter you met at the home of our friends the Varilands, and there's nothing about me, I presume, that permits you to attribute femininity to me."

"There you're mistaken," he retorted, sniggering. "There's everything necessary about you, since it's a week since I've attributed femininity to you."

An inveterate obsession, I thought, *and let's leave it at that, since that's the way it is. But that doesn't prevent me from trying to obtain information from him about my presence*

in his house, and for what reason my health has required re-
course to his science without my will having intervened.

"It's a week that I've been here, Doctor?"

"Exactly."

"I must have been very ill, then, to have remained un-conscious for so long."

"Not at all—you were the fittest man in the world. I've rarely encountered an organism as perfectly healthy as yours."

"So?"

"So what?"

"Since there was nothing wrong with me..."

He enjoyed my incomprehension momentarily, twisting the threads of his beard, which he had just freed from its enve-lope, around one of his fingers. Then he said: "There was nothing wrong with you physically, but you were afflicted by a mania to which I have given satisfaction by attributing femi-ninity to you, as you put it just now."

"Which means?"

"That you were a man, and that I've made you into a woman."

Oh! He was even more obsessed than I had imagined. Talking to a man whose tells you insane things with an air of tranquility always provokes a malaise, but this time, the idea was so ludicrous that, at the risk of exciting him further, I could not help bursting into laughter.

He too was gripped by hilarity. "Ah! You thought I was asleep the other night, at the Varilands, when you were show-ing off in front of the ladies, by declaring to them—I'm quot-ing your own words—that you 'bitterly regretted not being one of those exquisite little monarchs at whose feet men pros-trate themselves,' to which you added: 'hurrah for the scientist who, will, some day or other, raise me up on to the pedestal of weakness!' Well, no, I wasn't asleep; I registered your wishes precisely! And be satisfied, like a vulgar tadpole: you have now become an exquisite little monarch. You are there, squarely on the pedestal."

Under that flood of words, a slight anguish began to invade me. Not that I believed in what appeared to me to be a fantasy, but it could have been the case that the demented surgeon, in whose hands I had been since my outburst of eloquence, had carried out some surgical operation on my person.

In fact, a sensation of discomfort and envelopment that I felt in the region of my loins, compressed by a bandage, added further credence to that hypothesis. Furthermore, without being able to define it exactly—for it was in the domain of psychology, and was imprecise—I had a vague feeling that my mental personality was no longer the same, that something had changed in myself, as if my character had become weaker, and, on the other hand, endowed with a more acute sensibility.

"Come, come, Doctor…stop this joking."

"You think I'm joking?"

With a bound, Tornada went into the bathroom adjacent to the room, and with a strength that I would not have suspected, he brought me a vast lacquered mirror, which he held at arm's length in front of my face.

"Look!"

Oh my God! It was incredible! The mirror reflected a woman's face, in which my eyes were shining and my nose described its curve, in which my chin presented its customary design, but in which my moustache was lacking, without leaving any trace of having been shaved, although a slight down persisted, while my brown hair descended to the base of my neck. In the ensemble there was a grace, a charm and a delicacy entirely special to women; my complexion, ordinarily quite vivid, was content to be pink; my cheeks had thinned and my forehead extended, very pure, without a shadow or a groove, to the hairline.

And I contemplated that other self dazedly, disposed to soften and be charmed, for I could not refuse to admit, at that moment when I made the acquaintance of my new appearance, that it was seductive.

"Well, darling, are you satisfied?"

Darling…that term suddenly unleashed a magnificent memory from my heart. Extraordinarily enough, due no doubt to my week-long obnubilation, I had closed my mind to traces of the past; I had not yet given a thought to Rolande. But that word *darling*, imprudently emitted by Tornada, a word that we had reserved to the caress of our hearts, suddenly inspired me with the fear that I was lost to her, that our love had just expired in front of the mirror that the scientist was brandishing. For a second, I relived our embraces; I heard the echo of our amorous cries.

What! The sinister individual had killed all that, and buried it under that grotesque denomination!

"Darling! You'll see whether I'm a darling!" I cried, exasperatedly, wanting to leap out of bed to give myself the intoxication of feeling his throat crushed beneath my fingers.

Alas, my fingers were long and delicate! I no longer had the masculine strength that fells an enemy…and in any case, my dressing riveted me to the bed.

Poor weak creature that I had become, my revolt dissolved in sobs.

"Don't distress yourself so," Tornada advised me. "You'll see that there are advantages in your new anatomy. In any case, you agree with that. Have your ideas changed, then, because I've given you the sex you wished for?"

"Oh, it's not that," I sighed, with a desire for sympathy, such as women experience after tears.

"What, then? Are their complications? Don't worry; I've taken care of everything. Is it amour? One can love as well when one is a woman as when one is a man, and I've anticipated everything in that respect too. Oh, certainly, it won't be the same; in the beginning, you might find it a little disconcerting…and in any case, if you knew how preferable purely psychical relationships are to the others…how they spare chagrin, jealousy, resentment, and sometimes hatred, all the inevitable consequences of the base satisfactions of instinct! You're no longer an animal, you're a kind of demigoddess! You're floating in the azure of tenderness: what more could you want?"

He emphasized what he was saying with airy gestures, but I was no longer listening. I had only retained one phrase, important to my amour, and one question was burning me. I submitted it to him: "You've taken care of everything, you say?"

"Yes. I've had your friends informed that you've departed on a long voyage, in order to collect an inheritance in India, that they're not to worry about you, and that you'll write to them—that will be easy enough. Agree that I'm obliging. I've added that in your absence, your sister..."

"My close friends know that I'm an only child!"

"That's of no importance. There are mysteries in families, and you can arrange one. So, I've added that your sister will come in your absence to take possession of your bachelor apartment in the Rue du Général-Foy, and also your studio in the Rue Lepic, on the pretext that, like you, she's a talented artist. You'll also be able to continue to satisfy your tastes...am I not obliging?"

I agreed that he had been touchingly attentive. My revolt had died away completely, and I was only slightly astonished, by virtue of a vague echo of my former virile resentments against anyone who harmed me, by the facility with which I accepted my fate. I was, however, no longer subject to the mysterious influence, emanating from Tornada, which had acted upon me on the evening when he had drawn me away in order to commit his crime.

Yes, I could, and ought to, have confidence in a genius who could change one's sex so easily and so safely. And that confidence encouraged me to ask other questions, inasmuch as Tornada appeared to me, for the moment, to have become normal again, his attitude having become grave and reflective—that one could, in brief, converse with him.

"Professor," I said to him. "It's an accomplished fact; your prodigious talent has mutated me into a woman. I can

210

only bow down before it, and we won't talk about it any longer. Dare I, nevertheless, to ask you for a few clarifications?"

"Entirely at your devotion, darling. About what?"

"About the method that you've employed.

"The method? Why, the most purely scientific."

"I don't doubt it. Nevertheless, let's see…this is very difficult to express..."

"Come on!" he encouraged me. "You may consider that this is still between men..."

"Well, Professor, you're certainly familiar with the story of Abélard?"

"Who isn't?"

"Am I completely…comparable to Abélard?"

"Absolutely not. You're not an incomplete man—you're a complete woman."

"How is that possible?"

"It's possible by removing your creative organs and replacing them with those of a woman."

"Those of a woman! But then…you've employed another victim!"

"It was necessary."

"Alive?"

"Alive."

"On to whom you have..."

"Grafted what I removed from you; it's quite simple."

"And that other person has supported..."

"The operation? As well as you."

"Ah! Of course!"

So, that fantastic thing had happened! I was carrying within me the generative apparatus of an unknown woman, and somewhere, perhaps in the next room, there was a stranger who was recovering, like me, from a monstrous substitution, and would be launched toward a new amorous destiny, taking advantage of my means!

"And the functions?" I stammered. "The functions have been retained…?"

"Integrally."

211

I sat there stupidly. I had forgotten about Rolande. I was only thinking now about the other, Tornada's phenomenon, who was about to take me into society. The sentiment that dominated me was, above all, that of jealousy toward the unknown profitess, a rancor similar to that one feels against an invader who has taken up residence in your homeland, living in your domain, exploiting your wealth, without having to serve your interests. I had other dreads too, confusedly, determined by the fanaticism that I had always had regarding my health. What an abomination! What a usurpation! I shivered in revolt.

But one might have thought that Tornada understood everything that was troubling me. As if he wanted to quiet that new surge, he obligingly offered further information about the originality of his intervention, about what science would be able to extract from it in other domains, for the greater good of humanity. He could already for see admixtures of blood obtained in that fashion, races exhausted by civilization obtaining their regeneration by means of exchanges with primitive races, without anything being changed in their intellectual acquisitions, their mores, or, he hoped, in their anatomical structure or the color of their tegument.

In the ardor of his declaration, he picked up a pencil, and he traced drawings, diagrams and sections of organs for me on the white wall of the room, by means of which he demonstrated to me the logic of his conceptions and the facility with which he had realized them.

"You see? Here, on the one hand, are our ovaries, our uterus and our Fallopian tubes, enveloped by the peritoneum, and here, on the other hand, our prostate, our *vas deferens*...."

But I was having difficulty following him. Our educators leave us in such a criminal ignorance of the phenomena of generation that I could hardly understand his drawings.

"Oh!" I interjected. "What do your hieroglyphics and your operating techniques matter to me? I'm a woman; that's sufficient. I'll only ask you for one more item of information:

will I experience the monthly inconveniences of my new condition?"

"Certainly?"

"And will I have to fear maternity?"

"I'm certainly counting on it."

"Oh! That's rather inconvenient!"

He abandoned his demonstration, put down his pencil and came closer to the bed.

"Well, admit that, in a way, it's your turn. Thus far, all the pleasure of prolonging the species has been for the man, all the burdens for the woman—it's time for a change. Isn't it the case that, from that viewpoint, my discovery will at least have one consequence of equilibrium, of justice!"

I would have wagered that he was already dreaming of extending that justice to all of humanity.

"One more thing," I said. "What you have uprooted and transplanted is a matter of surgery, and I understand that—but that you have give me this form, which appears to me to be perfectly feminine, I can't see as clearly. What about these breasts, which I didn't have before?"

"Injections of extracts from the mammary apparatus of a heifer. Opotherapy."

"The hips?"

"Mechanotherapy, massage, phosphates, injections of paraffin."

"And this long hair?"

"Lotions, vibrations."

"And the vanished beard?"

"Radiotherapy." He smiled. "There persists, however, a suspicion of down that I wasn't able to efface. There, nature has been stronger than me. It has left you a souvenir, as the appendix is the vestige of an intestinal tube. But you'll be all the more charming for it...and the men... Oh, you'll see, the men!"

But he changed suddenly. He had just consulted his watch. A concern was imprinted on his face.

"We're chatting...and I still have to take off your final dressing..."

He rang a bell, replaced his white hood over his head, sheathed his beard and, as soon as the nurse he had summoned had come in, he began, with her aid, to attend to me. I surrendered to his procedures, closing my eyes. I felt him taking off the adhesive bandages, whose removal caused me a momentary burning sensation, and then a sentiment—I nearly said a sensation—of emptiness, which I immediately hastened to verify. In the meantime, he uttered grunts that were his fashion of expressing his contentment with the absolute success of his work. He replaced the bedclothes.

"It's finished, and it's perfect. I have no further reason to keep you here, my dear Georgette. You can get up and go home." Before going out, he added: "Adieu, my darling. Don't forget me in your prayers."

Then he left, followed by the nurse.

Alone again! Alone? How should I express myself now? Should I employ masculine or feminine forms in referring to myself?[25] I still experience such difficulty in recounting that amazing adventure...

Anyway, for the comfort of my writing, I shall maintain, with regard to my readers, my masculine gender. I shall continue as the Georges that I was and not the Georgette that Tornada had just made of me.

Alone again, as I was saying, my first impulse was not, as one might think, to stir profound thoughts with regard to my transformation, nor even to try to imagine the future that was reserved for me in my relationship with Rolande, but rather to deliver myself immediately to purely esthetic observations.

I leapt out of bed with a surprising vigor for someone who had recently undergone an operation and went into the

_____

[25] This difficulty disappears in English translation, in which adjectives are not gendered to agree with the nouns they qualify.

214

bathroom next door, to which Tornada had returned the mirror. In addition to that mirror there was one with three faces, which permitted me to examine myself from every angle. I hurriedly stripped off the pretty pink silk slip with lace trimmings in which I had been decked, and my new form was revealed in a perfection well calculated to impress the artist I was—an artist fond of lines.

What splendor! I offered the harmony of a most perfectly-contoured Eve, to the point that if I had not been a painter I would immediately have dreamed of becoming a model. My structure was deployed in accordance with the sovereignly beautiful harmony of the nymph that Boucher realized, with perfect legs, tapering hips, breasts that were rounded without being excessive, and a neck that was simultaneously delicate and incomparable forceful.

Oh, what long wonderment I promised myself in contemplating myself. At that moment, I blessed Tornada! Of his profanation there was no trace—or, at least, nature had taken charge of veiling it. I admired his science and skill unreservedly, which had succeeded in such a short time in fitting me with foreign tissues, rejoining the flesh, and, above all, in remodeling the rest of the organism in accordance with the partial modification. I was a masterpiece! And my esthetic sensibility rejoiced in it!

Moving closer to the mirror, I made my hips jut out proudly, felt my neck and my rump; I made my eyes flash, my teeth sparkle; I believe that I even smiled—and that all of the smile was for Tornada.

When I went back into the bedroom, however, my excitement faded away. There, on an armchair, arranged in order for me to put it on, was a woman's winter outfit; it had been brought in which I was examining myself next door—and the sight of that fur mantle, the perfectly tailored jacket and skirt, the wide-brimmed hat fitted with an expensive plume, the gray deerskin boots and the long black gloves reanimated my dolor at having to appear like that before Rolande. How should I conduct myself with her? What should I do, what should I say,

215

what should I imagine? What about the cherished plans of liberation that we had made together? Poor beloved! How she would suffer—perhaps more than me—as a result of Tornada's insane action!

I fell into a chair and began to weep. A hand was placed on my shoulder at that moment. I looked up and recognized the nurse. I forgot that I was a woman. An instinctive modesty that was also my habit caused me to make a gesture of chaste protection, placing the costume that was waiting on the chair in front of me.

"Mademoiselle needn't be alarmed. We're from the same gynaeceum... and Mademoiselle shouldn't worry... it's all right."

I did not realize, at that moment, the implications of those mysterious remarks, and did not seek to understand.

"What are you doing here?" I asked, sharply.

"I came to dress Mademoiselle, who might not know how to do it on her own."

I had entered far enough into the skin of a woman—or, to put it more accurately, the woman had entered far enough into my skin, for me to accept being dressed by one of my peers.

She exhibited, moreover, a surprising awkwardness, while smiling sadly.

III

I left the clinic without seeing Professor Tornada again, or any other living soul. The entire establishment seemed deserted. I easily found my way through the grounds, reached the little door—which opened automatically in front of me—went out and walked along the imposing façade. I was on the boulevard that borders Auteuil.

Oh, that first reacquaintance with the outside world! Nature was scarcely smiling, though: no adornment on the trees, a sky heaped with dark clouds, muddy ground…and yet, I looked at the empty spaces fondly, and took deep breaths of the damp air. The imperious need to go home was stronger, however, and, not seeing any carriage, I headed for the nearest stop of the Auteuil-Madeleine tram. One was just about to leave; I got on and sat down.

I immediately found myself the objective of the gazes of the gentlemen who were there. It is a rather curious impression to receive the tributes of a discreet admiration of which one has previously only been the purveyor. I felt some pleasure in it. I observed readers incessantly peeping over their newspapers, abandoning the interest of the information in order to contemplate me.

One of them, a fat man whose belly bounced every time the tram moved off, was the most ardent in observing me. He was wearing spectacles, and had to squint in order to accommodate his long sight to them. As he was, in addition, monitored by a wife as large as himself, the suspicion he exercised in one direction and the admiration in the other combined in a maneuver so comical that I could not help smiling. He took that smile for a consent, with the result that, when the tram arrived in the Place Saint-Augustin, where I got off in order to go home, he left his wife on the tram and followed me.

I walked without looking back. I heard his emphysema purring behind me, increased by the pursuit. He finally caught up with me.

"Mademoiselle...Madame..." he wheezed. The, sticking his jowls close to my face: "Mademoiselle or Madame?"

"Neither, Monsieur."

"Ah! No matter; let's say goddess, then. Where are you taking me?"

Nowhere, Monsieur."

"Oh...I thought...I don't please you, then?"

"No, Monsieur, you disgust me."

"Oh!"

He immediately turned round, saluting me with the word by which one designates a ruminant quadruped with two humps on its back.

Finally, I reached my door. It required a species of heroism for me to go through the porch. It appeared to me that I was crossing the demarcation line of a new destiny. To what would it lead?

Forward ho! I strode resolutely toward my ground-floor apartment.

"Where are you going?" cried a pitiless voice.

The concierge! He emerged from his lodge. Only having seen me from behind thus far, the man was anxious—but when I turned round, his face was impregnated with a perfect bewilderment.

"Oh! How much you resemble him!"

"Who?"

"Your brother. Like two peas in a pod!"

Then he stated waxing lyrical, in florid terms, about the inheritance that had so suddenly required Monsieur Georges' departure.

"I didn't even see him, Mam'zelle, can you imagine? He decamped by night, without even saying goodbye! He was so good to us; we miss him, as you can imagine! But he'll come back soon, we suppose?"

As he opened the door, he added: "Mam'zelle's baggage has arrived."

"Ah, my baggage! Let me be, I beg you."

I felt the need to be alone at that moment with a sacred emotion, as I went back into the nest where Rolande had so often come to take shelter. How many objects evoked her memory! Everything was impregnated with her.

There was the Chinese vase, still containing the flowers that she had brought me on her last visit: mauve irises, retaining a hint of brightness among other, dead flowers, as if they had been waiting for me to return before dying, in order to remind me of her one last time.

There was the fine candy-box from Venice, half full of chocolates and almonds, which we chewed mouth-to-mouth, while she struggled with her sparkling teeth to carry away the larger part, and mad laughter rose up when she succeeded. A sweet preparation for the intoxications that led us to the large bed, quickly stripped of its covers...

And there was also her portrait, traced by my fervent hand, in which I rediscovered the tender smile in her eyes, which she only had for me, when she surrendered her entire soul to me.

All that happiness was, therefore, destroyed; soon, nothing would remain of it but the skeleton, as of those faded irises.

Suddenly, however, my heart began to beat as if to burst. There, in the bowl where the mail was usually placed, were two letters in her handwriting. I pounced upon them, and opened them.

Alas, they were not for me—or, at least, for the lover I had been—but for the sister I had become. They both commenced with a formal "Mademoiselle," and both expressed the desire to make my acquaintance rapidly. The reasons for that desire were banal, pure social courtesy, but I was able to read between the lines the anguish that had dictated them, the need to have an explanation of my sudden flight, and to maintain a link with a vanished friend.

One detail surprised me, however. The more recent of the two letters mentioned that Rolande had received a postcard from me, sent from Bordeaux, in which I had briefly give the reasons for my voyage as well as notifying her of the arrival of my sister. It was in consequence of this information that Rolande had written.

No doubt Tornada had a hand in this matter, as well as in the letter that the concierge had received. But by what method? Had he been able to imitate my handwriting to the point that Rolande had been deceived? Or, abusing the artificial sleep with which he had kept me unconscious for a week, had he succeeded in making me write the missives unconsciously? What others might he have demanded of my enslaved hand, in order to ensure the success of his tenebrous experiment?

All those reflections were dispelled, however, by the joy that I was promised of soon seeing Rolande. I kissed those sheets of paper fondly, as testimonies of a dawn, when I was in despair of the night.

The sound of the doorbell brought me back to the disconcerting reality. It was my concierge again.

"Sorry to disturb Mam'zelle, but since the domestics have been dismissed..."

"Dismissed? By whom?"

"By M'sieu Sigerier, of course. Even though he paid them with a crossed check and they had a hard time getting hold of it, as they had no bank accounts..."

"Get on with it!" I urged him.

"I'm getting there...it's to tell Mam'zelle that I have letters for Monsieur Georges—one of them from the Mairie—and it's to ask what I'm to do with them?"

"Give them to me. I'll forward them myself."

He handed me a voluminous stack of correspondence, and then handed me a card. It was an elegant engraved Bristol simply bearing the name: *Robert de Lieuplane*, surmounted by a comtal crown.

"Is this for my brother?" I asked.

"No, Mam'zelle—it's you he wants to see."

"Another day...another day..." I said, increasingly surprised, and not finding any other way to get out of it.

The concierge left again, and I rapidly scanned my correspondence, a week out of date: business letters, invitations to dinner, a commission for a portrait...the customary bills. But one of the papers impressed me more; it ordered me, on the part of the Mairie, to fill in a census form that same day. I stood there thinking about that banal request for some time. It characterized the social complications that were going to result from Tornada's practical joke.

As if I did not have enough social complications to worry about! Some could be sidestepped, but all sorts of difficulties and embarrassments were going to present themselves continually, stemming from the sudden irruption of a man into the material life of an elegant woman! Trivia, little practicalities—but ignorance made mountains of them.

First of all, there was my baggage. It consisted of three trunks, two hat-boxes and a dozen parcels of various sorts, bags, toilet necessities, jewel-cases, hot water bottles, etc., etc., even including a box of pharmaceuticals. Oh, Tornada had not neglected anything. Where had he collected it all, then?

What also intrigued me was that they seemed, judging by the excess of labels, to have traveled a great deal. The effort to be made to open them, unpack them and arrange their contents seemed to me to be insurmountable. And in addition, even though it was only three o'clock in the afternoon, a great lassitude, doubtless the repercussion of my emotions, combined with the fatigue of my first excursion outdoors, was already overwhelming me. I no longer had any but one desire: to lie down, go to sleep and await events.

For want of a night-shirt, what sweeter envelope could there be than Rolande's kimono? The silky fabric, still impregnated with her favorite perfume and the perfumes of her being, which had always awaited her and awaited her still, was carefully hung up in a wardrobe. I took it out, bathed myself in it as if in carnal water, and allowed myself to sink into the voluptuousness of forgetfulness.

IV

I sat up with a start. Was I emerging from a dream, then, or was I, rather, still plunged in one? Four raps had just been struck on my shutters, distributed according to a conventional rhythm that was the signal employed by Rolande to tell me that she had arrived and that I had to let her in.

At that blessed appeal, soon followed by the ring of the doorbell, I leapt out of bed and went to open the door.

It was her! The door having immediately closed again, by virtue of an automatic obedience to our former customs of prudence, she stopped, gasping for breath, leaning on the door-jamb. Her silhouette in the semi-darkness emphasized the elegance of her discreet coat and skirt, and her broad-brimmed hat, beneath which a thick veil rendered her unrecognizable.

My heart studied her more avidly than my eyes. Oh, if only I could allow myself to take her in my arms and stammer, as before: "At last! At last, it's you, my beloved!" But my attire—negligee and kimono—reminded me that things had changed, and immediately took me back, modestly, into my bedroom, and even into my bed.

She followed me, without being asked.

"Forgive me, Mademoiselle, for forcing an entrance so early in the morning. I know that you arrived yesterday, and my two previous letters have, I assume, reached you. Yes, I'm Madame Variland…Madame Variland…"

She repeated her name several more times, like a person who has lost the thread of what she is saying, under the pressure of another powerful thought.

I understood her emotion. The concierge had just opened the exterior shutters and, as the daylight struck me directly, my resemblance to myself must have struck her suddenly. Looking at a feminine portrait of the man she loved had astounded her.

"Oh my God! Oh my God!" she stammered, putting her hands together in surprise and admiration.

But the memory I evoked became so painful to her that she could not hold back her despair. She burst into sobs.

"What! You're weeping, Madame...?" I played my part, in spite of the difficult I had in controlling myself. "You're weeping, and I must witness your chagrin from the very start! Tell me, oh, tell me what is troubling you so much! Perhaps I shall be fortunate enough to be able to console you."

But she pulled herself together immediately, and, dabbing her eyes with a lace handkerchief that I knew well—for I was the one who had given it to her—she said: "Excuse me...I've been a little nervous for some time...later, perhaps, I'll confide in you...but for the moment, know that I have only come this morning to enquire about you, as my brother asked me to do."

It was at that moment that I began to understand the mechanism that controls the heart of women tested by amour. She had come, she said, only to occupy herself with me, as a woman, but she was, in reality, speaking, acting, proposing and concerting purely to conduct an enquiry about me, as a man. Poor dear heart! Could I blame her for her ruse, which was, fundamentally, a tribute to the lover I had been? Who, in order to defend a grand passion, would not employ such a lie?

"Ah!" I said. "My brother has asked you..."

"Yes, in a letter that I received from him.

"You know him well enough, then, for him to write to you?"

"We were in continual communication. My husband was a particular friend of his...so his departure, in a gust of wind, without warning anyone...no one at all...surprised us greatly. Tell me, is it conceivable that someone can disappear like that, without even informing the closest of his friends? He sent the same letter to all the people he knew."

"All of them?"

"All, in the same terms—like a circular, a prospectus."

"Do you have that letter?"

"No...my husband kept it. It announces laconically his departure to collect an inheritance in India. India! He had never told us that he had family there...and he informed us your arrival in Paris, and asked us to give you a good welcome."

"I'm glad," I remarked, "that Georges had mentioned you to me some time ago..."

"A long time," she confirmed.

"Which proves to me that our separation had not disunited us, and that he had not ceased to think about me." And I persisted: "He spoke to you about me, then?"

"Often." And, plunging deeper into her lie: "He even gave me a hint about your engagement."

"My engagement!" I started.

"Not categorically, in truth. He mentioned it...without naming anyone, without precision.... It was only in his letter that he told us that it was a matter of the Comte de Lieuplane."

The announcement of my marriage to the individual who had sent me his card the day before must have imprinted a certain tragic expression on my face, for Rolande lost the assurance of a candid liar and examined me with a certain anxiety. As for myself, that extravagant news, by which Tornada's fantasy was amplified and further developed, in accordance with a plan of which I was beginning to suspect the scientific interest—had he not said to me: "You are a virgin, but you will not be spared maternity?"—the news revolted me. So, I was not rid of that sinister operator. Free, I would continue to be his slave, in those essential functions in which human beings are most determined to retain their free will.

Again, I thought about telling Rolande everything, in order to ask her to take my side, to be my ally, and to stand up with me against the ambushes that were going to be extended for our amour. But the singularity of my situation threatened, first of all, that I might pass for a madman in her eyes; she would never believe in the transmutation of a man into a woman; and even if she did believe it, I feared even more the ridicule that she would inevitably heap upon me: the ridicule that kills the noble sentiments, particularly love.

Furthermore, curiosity, even more than prudence, bade me to secrecy, advised me at least to wait, in order that, having become the entire confidante of my mistress by virtue of the parity of our sex, she would progressively yield to me the verity of her heart, and introduce me completely into the flower-bed in which the bloom of our tenderness had grown.

Perfectly united as we have been, I reflected, *sharers of our souls and our senses, there are nevertheless impressions, nuances and criticisms of which she has left me ignorant, and since there is no longer any peril in my dwelling on them, if I might put it like that, well, let us await he amity that is in preparation, in order to know them in their entirety.*

What man in love would ever blame me for having made that little calculation, and for having concluded therefrom my silence, at that moment?

I therefore suppressed the confession that was burning my throat and waited until the intervention of Monsieur Robert de Lieuplane was revealed more clearly. For the moment, I wanted to concentrate entirely on the windfall of Rolande, to abandon myself uniquely to the intoxication of her presence.

"I believe I understood from what you said just now," she said, "that you were separated for a long time? Is there some dissent between your brother and you? In truth, that would surprise me. Monsieur Sigerier never manifested any rancor in talking about you."

"Did he often talk about me?" I interjected again, in order to know exactly how far she would take the candor of her lie on that subject,

"Sometimes...when he allowed himself to evoke the past...when he talked to us about his family, his friendships...his amours..."

Dear child! I could easily see where she was trying to get to...and, indeed, the interrogation I expected flowed quite naturally from her lips.

"He was a very handsome man, very distinguished...very chic, in sum. Because of that, women noticed him a great deal, and he flirted with them a little, in consequence. Oh, without conceit…but, all in all, he liked the fact that he was noticed…"

Oh, how well I had done to stay silent! I was going, progressively, to know all about myself. It was not much to start with, to be sure, but how far that slight criticism was from displeasing me, since I could distinguish a retrospective jealousy therein!

She continued: "And, aided by his notoriety, you can imagine the harvest of his success. Did he mention it to you occasionally, his success?"

"He was very discreet."

"That was another quality of his. But with you, whom he loved, perhaps, in his letters…"

"No, never," I affirmed

"However," she persisted, obstinately, "he must have loved someone. A man of his age cannot devote himself entirely to his art. For my part, I think there must be some feminine reason for this precipitate departure. Perhaps he's eloped with a woman. It happens!"

Oh, quickly, quickly, calm that poor creature overwhelmed by suspicion! Relax that forehead tensed by suspicion; destroy the scaffolding erected by that heart in disarray! For I understood her anxiety, remembering my own emotional turmoil.

I poured out the sovereign sedative: "You're mistaken, Madame. There's much less romance in my brother's life. He certainly did not confide the details of his escapades to me, but I can affirm that there were hardly any, and you astonish me greatly by suggesting that he maneuvered to attract the admiration of women, for he was hostile to that kind of behavior. He had so far as I know, one serious liaison, but he was very careful not to compromise it with any reckless action. And if, as you imagine, he were ever to take the decision, always very grave, to remove the woman he loved from her hearth, believe that it would only be after mature reflection, and with the formal determination of offering his life in compensation."

I made that declaration of principle in a solemn tone that must have contrasted with the frivolous spectacle I offered: my kimono, my bare arms, my tousled hair. She did not taste the spice; she drank in my words like a philter, lying back in her armchair, her eyes closed.

"Moreover," I continued, "I can assure you that in the circumstances, it is not permissible for me to think of any folly on Georges' part. His voyage was exclusively dictated by matters of interest..." And I added, by virtue of an unconscious obedience to Tornada's recommendation, and to give an appearance of plausibility to the arrival in society of the demoiselle that I was: "Yes, the same reasons that have kept us separated until now, and which have ensured that many people, if not you, were ignorant of my existence..."

"May I know what they are?"

"Know them..." I hesitated. Help, great Courteline![26] "I regret, Mademoiselle, not being able to confide them to you. It's a family secret."

She was content with that reason, in the style of Boubouroche. A frown-line still subsisted on her forehead, however. I assumed that it was inspired by astonishment that her dear lover had not sent her any word via the *poste restante* via which we communicated when circumstances prevented us from meeting.

I promised myself that I would give her that further security as soon as she had gone.

But all those emotions had exhausted me. Furthermore, I had not had anything to eat for twenty-four hours, and hunger,

---

[26] The reference is to the dramatist Georges Courteline (1858-1929), famous for his blithe satirical comedies, which Couvreur doubtless appreciated. The sex-comedy *Boubouroche* (1893), in which the eponymous husband is convinced by his faithless wife, by means of a complex web of lies, that he has not been deceived, even though he has caught her *in flagrante delicto*, was one of his greatest early successes.

reacting on my nervous system, caused me to yawn. I immediately offered my apologies.

"What! You're dying of hunger and you're letting me ramble on? You must order you breakfast to be served immediately."

"I don't have any staff. My brother dismissed them all."

"No staff!" she commiserated. "But I don't want to leave you like that. I'll find you some myself! In the meantime, I'll make you breakfast. We'll surely find something here.

And when I protested, declaring that I wanted to take care of it myself, she said: "No, no—stay in bed. You'll see. It will be very amusing."

Oh, I can well imagine the value she attached to those few moments of domesticity, in which she was about to revive the sweet intimacy of our afternoon snacks, in the appeasement of our senses. It was me who served her then; I brought her pastries, fruits, ice cream, liqueurs, hot tea; and she, her hair unkempt, one shoulder emerging from her kimono, crunched away heartily, drank with the hesitation of a kitten; and my feast was in watching her more than savoring the delicacies...

"I'll certainly find something," she repeated.

She pretended conscientiously not to know where to find our provisions. She left as if to search the apartment, reached the kitchen, where I heard her opening the cupboards, and went to the dining room, where she continued bustling.

"There! This will make you feel better!"

Triumphantly, she brought our dry cakes, our Samos wine, and arranged them on our plates.

And I divined at that moment the adorable gourmand that she was; my hair was unkempt, my bare shoulder was emerging from the kimono, and I had her gestures when I ate and drank.

"Look at that pretty little mouth—how it gets stuck in!" she murmured, looking at me delightedly. And it was something else I had said that she was repeating to me.

Sated, I got up to get dressed. When my ablutions were concluded, I accepted her aid to put my clothes on. Precious aid! Without her, I would certainly have been mistaken regarding the attribution of the undergarments.

In the meantime, she had opened my trunks and unfolded my garments.

"Mazette! You have beautiful lingerie! And this lovely blouse! And this champagne two-piece! Put it on!"

I obeyed. I was soon clad in champagne. The costume suited me marvelously.

"How pretty you are, Mademoiselle!"

Yes, I was decidedly a beauty. I felt an entirely feminine pride. And Rolande would not have wearied of contemplating me, if we had not been interrupted by the concierge. He handed a card to me.

"It's the gentleman from yesterday who's come back…"

"I'll leave you," said Rolande, with a malicious smile, for she had been discreet enough to read the card. She added: "I'll leave you, but I won't abandon you. From today on, I'm adopting you. You'll come to the house, often. You'll meet my husband. He's a slightly cold man, but he'll be pleasant to you: he loves pretty woman."

She squeezed my hands tenderly. "Would you like us to become friends?"

"With all my heart, Rolande," I replied, eagerly.

"That's right: call me Rolande, and I'll call you Georgette. *A bientôt.*"

She carried my reality away. Alas, I fell back into the fantastic with the one who followed her.

It would take me a considerable number of lines to translate the diversity of my sentiments during that first meeting with Robert de Lieuplane. He was an aristocrat about thirty years of age—my age, in fact, if I had not been rejuvenated by Tornada's spell—who adopted without distinction a bright beard and a costume cut in the latest fashion.

That was all I distinguished of him at first, I was so disturbed; I later had the leisure to remark other particularities, which I shall relate in due course. He seemed to be in perfect health and a disenchanted smile was grafted on to a eucrasic physiognomy, revealing lovely teeth.

Perhaps it was his sad expression, or perhaps my new sensibility, but I felt myself gripped by a mixture of suspicion and irrational sympathy in his regard: two incompatible sentiments that I nevertheless felt concurrently.

He was carrying a bunch of flowers that he seemed embarrassed to be holding, at the same time as his cane and his gray felt hat. He deposited all of them on a sideboard and sat down gravely in an armchair without being invited to do so. I could only do likewise.

"What do you desire, Monsieur?"

"You ought to know."

"I know absolutely nothing."

"He didn't tell you anything?"

"Who's *he*?"

"Well, our friend, Professor Tornada."

"Nothing," I stammered. "Nothing..."

"Well, that's because he must have forgotten to talk to you about it. He's so busy, that man... I'll tell you what brings me here, then: it's to pay court to you a little, and to discover whether it sticks.[27] I want to marry; he tells me that you do

---

[27] I have translated *coller* literally as "stick," although the English term does not carry the same range of familiar implications as the French term when used as slang; in this sense the phrase implies "whether it works out." However, the character uses *coller* further on with reference to the protagonist's dress, with a more literal intention, and it crops up throughout the novella, almost as a kind of leitmotiv. There is a further implication here and elsewhere, which the reader is presumably intended to infer, although the protagonist fails miserably to jump to the conclusion in question. The fact that the English term carries an additional range of reference adds a further dimension of crudity, but one that is by no means inappropriate in the circumstances.

too, so I've come to put myself at your disposal. To be sure, the mistake he has made is to announce our engagement before we know whether it sticks. It's necessary never to marry people without knowing whether they stick. But since it's done, it's done, and we're on our way to the conjugal state, since your brother hasn't said no."

I was suffocating! Even more than Tornada's despotism, the vulgarity of the man, his suggestion that it was merely a matter of knowing whether we "stuck" or not, his manner of emphasizing his statements with futile and common gestures, shocked me in the extreme. I got the impression from him of a lack of education and *savoir faire*, of which I had always been scornful in others and which, particularly in this case, disconcerted my penchant for distinction. And yet, he had a "de" in his name—he was even titled! It is true, I attenuated almost immediately, that certain noblemen like to frequent stables, for love of horses, and that naturally, filthy language inevitably follows...

So, this was the man who was destined for me! I knew nothing about him, about his family, about his mores or about his blood, and the arbitrary power of my forger was being brutally imposed upon my opinion after being imposed on my flesh! What! So I was to become Madame de Lieuplane, share the bed of this gross individual, and perhaps have his children! It was so ludicrous that I could not help smiling—to which my fiancé, who decidedly exaggerated everything, responded with lewd laughter.

"You'll see that it sticks," he said, complacently. "And if it doesn't, well, there's still time to break it off. In the meantime, I'll whisk you away so that we can have a little jaunt in the Bois. I have my old banger at the door. Get a move on, my little Georgette. Put your walking shoes on. Hang on, though—let me take care of you—your dress isn't sticking."

He had noticed a crease on my champagne two-piece. He had me turn around, and deemed that a tuck in the fabric was required.

"That's all right," I said. "I'll have my chambermaid modify it as soon as I have one."

"No needed for the maid…I'll take care of it."

I was surprise to see him take a small sewing-kit from his pocket. He chose thread, a needle and a thimble. He knelt in front of me, reduced the flaw and started to sew. He deployed a professional skill, his hand maneuvering like that of an expert seamstress.

"Oh! So you've been a tailor?"

"No, but I've always been interested in couture. The proof…"

He showed me his fingers, rather delicate but peppered with needle-marks. Then he finished his work.

"There! It sticks now." Don't forget to powder your nose."

I obeyed. My will no longer existed. It was necessary for me to submit.

We finally went out. As I passed under the arch, the concierge slipped me a discreet compliment on my engagement. It did not astonish me that Robert had talked to him.

We climbed into the two-seater sports car that my companion drove like a beginner. He must have been more familiar with horses. We reached the Bois without any mishap, however. Radiant sunlight had brought out a good many strollers. We left the car in the Allée des Acacias in order to take a short walk.

My fiancé did not appear to be known to anyone. However, as we went along the pathways he kept tipping his hat and making gestures of sympathy, to which I noticed that everyone responded with astonishment. By contrast, I obtained a certain success. Gentlemen turned to look at me; ladies did the same. I took pleasure in observing it. Feminine pride was awakening in me.

At midday, we returned to my home. What did fatality have in store for me?

"My chick," my fiancé said to me, "I hoped to have lunch with you, but it can't be done; I have business to attend to. And this evening, I'm going away for two days. It's bad luck. But I'll be back on Thursday and we can have dinner."

"What business are you in?" I asked.

"I'm in the wine business. And just now, I'm opening a shop in Lille. Yes, that's where I'm going to do it. For want of capital, you know. So, our marriage is a stroke of luck—your fortune will be useful to me. I'd even like you to call in at the bank this afternoon to sign a power of attorney. I've warned them—they're expecting you."

"Oh! At what bank?"

"Yours—the Crédit du Nord...one might think that you didn't know?"

"Yes...yes..."

He was awaiting my response with prodigious interest. I sensed his venality.

"You'll sign?"

"Certainly."

What was I doing? Anything he wanted. I was only rich in my talent, and my own savings were in a different bank.

He bade me adieu, took the steering-wheel again and disappeared. What deliverance! What a windfall—two days of liberty! And yet, by virtue of that same inexplicable emprise, completely alien to the heart, entirely physical—but again, a physicality into which amour did not enter at all—I regretted our separation. I watched him draw away as if he were taking away a part of my being.

When I went back into my bachelor apartment, a fairy had passed through; the housework was done, the table laid, and a genteel soubrette was waiting, who told me that her name was Anna and was expecting her sister to start as cook the following day. I recognized Rolande's initiative and thanked her secretly. I had a few mouthfuls of the succulent repast sent from her home, and then sat down at my writing-desk in order to write to her.

What should I say? How should I commence that corre-spondence destined to put her to sleep, in which I was to be an absentee while my heart and my hand were present. It was necessary, and would be necessary, to be very watchful. What would be appropriate?

For now, I set aside the difficulty by addressing an ante-dated letter to her to explain my absence. The *poste restante* would take the blame for the delay. I did not spare either my sadness or my persistent fervor.

I was finishing the letter when two nuns called, collecting for an orphanage. It was not my habit to refuse; ordinarily, I gave in order to get rid of them, but this time my donation was combined with a previously-unknown pity for the disinherited children. In thinking that they had no family, my heart suffered with a maternal anguish. Was I now, then, bound to desire a child?

I emptied my purse into those benevolent hands; then, out of money, I thought about going to my bank. But that was something else that would involve me in social complications: what would be given to the painter Georges Sigerier would be refused to his unknown sister!

Let's go to the Crédit du Nord, then, I decided, *inasmuch as I have to sign a document there.*

As Robert had informed me, my visit to that important establishment was expected. I was immediately introduced into the office of a senior employee, who greeted me with great politeness, demanded a few signatures and asked me if I needed money.

"Certainly. How much do I have in my account?"

"Two million liquid, which it would be wise not to leave dormant."

Two million! This was beginning to become interesting. There could be no doubt about their provenance. Tornada was the purveyor. He earned vast sums and lived ascetically. He only had to pay his operating expenses, of which I was the experimental subject. But two million was quite a sum, and I wondered how many citizens, at that price, would refuse a change of sex...

"I'll cancel that power of attorney," I said, immediately. "Let me have one million, and prepare documentation for the investment of the other, in Mère de Famille shares."[28]

My tongue had slipped, but the employee was only startled by my dispositions. "You're taking away a million! In a check?"

"In bills."

The package was bulky. I transported it to my own bank, where it was welcomed without difficulty into my account.

Right! I had enough to indulge my caprices, and the future was less bleak. In any case, did I not still have my art? Did I not have therein the supreme resource and the sovereign consolation? I felt an imperious need to work, to serve Beauty—and to make sure that my inversion had not diminished my talent.

I went back to my studio in the Rue Lepic with a sacred emotion. I could have hugged my palettes and brushes to my heart. I blew kisses to my canvases, my drawings and my sketches. All my effort, all my life! And in a corner, under the light of the bay window, filleted by yellow silk, the full length portrait of Rolande, hidden from the profane by a curtain: the cherished image, which I kept for myself alone, for my wonderment, for my worship! I drew the fabric aside, prostrated myself before the altar, and I adored the idol.

But I hid my treasure swiftly; someone had just knocked on the door.

It was a model, a young man of Roman beauty that I had hired to sketch before my adventure and who had come every day for news.

"Undress...take any pose you like."

Oh, the intoxication, the limitless intoxication of rediscovering the lines, of fixing the harmony. If I was dead for amour, I remained fully alive for my art, and I had never

---

[28] *A la Mère de Famille* is a confectionery company, still active, which claims to be the oldest chocolatier in Paris.

drawn better—with the particularity, however, that my strokes, while remaining as form, had a new delicacy.

At eight o'clock I was still working. It was necessary for the man to declare that he was tired for me to abandon my charcoal.

I walked home, blessing the consolation of work. Two eggs, and I went to bed, ready to sleep for twelve hours.

IV

It smacked of prodigy! I found myself, a little while later, as a woman, in the same drawing room in which, as a man, my extraordinary adventure had begun. I was sitting beside Rolande. Our recent amity, and her protection, permitted me to hold her hand. There were the same people around us as at the previous dinner: a circle of women, among whom were the soft-spoken Madame Chabrol, the thunderous Baronne des Illeuls—the latter still in masculine attire—Mademoiselle Férette and the cantatrice Savari, chatting idly, while the gentlemen were finishing their cigars in the adjacent smoking room.

Their discussion was audible in puffs, still rolling around the same subject of transformism, in which I had taken up such a regrettable position. Successively, we overhead the common sense of Monsieur Chabrol, the irony of Monsieur Variland and the tempestuousness of Tornada—for he was there, the monster! He had even been my neighbor at table, but he had not even unclenched his teeth for me, neglecting even to look at me, as if I did not exist. By contrast, my other neighbor, Rimeral, had shown considerable gallantry, wanting to me to recognize his voice, insisting that I should go to sketch him at his home, promising to compose a piece for me—an entire performance that caused Mademoiselle Savari to look daggers at me.

Only one guest was absent: Georges Sigerier. Only one was new: Robert de Lieuplane.

With regard to Georges Sigerier, in general, only benevolent comments were made. In some sections of Parisian society, it is not considered overly malevolent to say of an artist that his work is "a load of tripe"—that was the beautiful Savari's appreciation—and of a citizen that he must have left Paris in order to avoid the consequences of a moral scandal; that was the Baronne's certainty, and the idea did not displease

237

her. I owe it to the truth to say that these opinions changed radically when it became known that I was the painter's sister, and my brother was praised from then on for having come into an inheritance that would spare him further commercial endeavors. In sum, I was liked, and reputed to be a gallant fellow.

But with regard to Robert de Lieuplane, the silence was crueler than opinion. He had conducted himself at table with an evident intention to be a good companion, but he had eaten chicken-legs with his fingers, wiped his glass before filling it himself, and laughed so liberally that he had splashed the tablecloth. I also heard Madame Chabrol confide to Rolande that she had been obliged to be wary of her neighbor's feet throughout the meal, and that neighbor had been none other than my fiancé. Furthermore, the word "stick" had not ceased to decorate his conversation, and I discovered that the word had been adopted by two young men, who repeated it while accepting a glass of liqueur from Rolande.

If I had been a young woman and my own mistress, those details would have separated me forever from such an inappropriate suitor, but I was only an artificial virgin and I felt the atrocious experimental power of Professor Tornada weighing upon me.

He came back into the drawing room. Of what mysterious force was he the dispenser, then? As soon as the satanic individual reappeared, who had not paid me any heed throughout the meal, I felt myself circumscribed once again by his gaze, magnetized by the phosphorescence of his beard, which could not be seen in the light, but which must have been active. With one bound, I was beside him.

"Well, Georgette," he said, "are you content with your lot?"

"Yes, Master."

"You've welcomed your fiancé politely?"

"Yes, Master."

"And the two million?"

"That too, Master."

"All's well, then. By happy, my daughter."

He withdrew, in the English fashion. I immediately felt liberated—but Rolande had followed that interlude with an anxious curiosity. She drew me to one side, and gave me the benevolent caress of her hand again, as if she knew that she had to console me.

"What was that man saying to you, Georgette?"

"Nothing in particular, Rolande."

"He scares me! I would have preferred not to invite him this evening, but my husband insisted. I don't know why, but I was fearful of is presence on your behalf. Above all, never confide yourself to his care!"

"I don't have any reason to do so, Rolande; I'm in good health."

"The guests are leaving…your fiancé is smoking his pipe with my husband. Come on—we can go and talk about your brother.

From the joy that brightened her expression, I judged that my recent letter, sent to Bombay by an agency and sent back to France from there, had reached her *poste restante*. She must have learned it by heart, doubtless before destroying it, for she repeated to me involuntarily the expressions that I had put into it, mentioning the local customs, the beauty of the women, the unexpectedness of the décor. I had copied all that out of Larousse.

"He must have arrived, mustn't he? And I imagine that he's ecstasizing over the marvels of the Dravidian or Chalukyan architecture, or making sketches of the silhouette of some Deccan woman....so noble in stature, it appears..."

"You're so very interested in him, then?" I risked, for the first time.

She blushed. "Oh, yes! Your brother, you see, I find him so different from others, so superior! He's radiant, with his intelligence, his delicacy of heart, his talent. He has strength and charm. I could understand that a woman might love him to the point of abandoning everything to become his companion, his associate—his slave, if he wished. And what renders you so precious to my heart, Georgette, is that you resemble him in all points. Tell me about your childhood together."

I was obliged to invent things, and I must say that they were not to my disadvantage. I described the family milieu, the large park with spreading trees, reading, with blonde heads poring over the same book, and prayers, hands joined at the foot of the bed, before sleep rocked by the angels.

Rolande palpitated, like a child listening to a marvelous story. "More! More!"

And I invented, and invented, finding puerile memories so far from my reality—for, as an only child, neglected by an invalid mother and a father entirely devoted to difficult business affairs, it was from within myself, and nature, that I had drawn the elements of my emotions, my sensibility, and the first awakenings of the love for painting that had determined my career.

Rolande was impassioned by it. Never, in our conversations after love-making, had I ever undertaken to reanimate my childhood, and she had never asked about it. Everything had been left to the intoxication of moments that were too brief. Now, the sister purified the brother, and, on finding her so attentive to those puerile stories, so captivated by that novel from the Bibliothèque Rose, that I could scarcely remember the vibrant mistress she had been.

Our intimacy was, moreover, now limited, since I had become a woman, to purely sentimental exchanges: on her part, absolute slavery to her menaced dream; on mine, no reawakening of the senses that would have given rise to an impossible delirium. One might have thought that Tornada, in giving me carnal virginity, had simultaneously reforged a virgin heart. Was it the affect of a cicatrization, an internal adaptation reacting upon my nervous system that was maintaining me in that calm? Was I waiting for a new puberty?

No matter; I passed by, insensible to the original suggestions that life never ceases to display. Lovers tenderly enlaced in the street, posters casting their equivocal scenes on walls, animals obedient to the force on instinct, masculine gazes coveting me—nothing, none of it, succeeded in reawakening the ardent appeal within me, of reanimating Eros, once my dominator.

I was often disconcerted by that.

Rolande and I, increasingly united, never quit one another's company, so to speak, except when her husband required her at home. We went about our business, went shopping, took tea, and went to exhibitions, as ethereal and frivolous comrades. Her husband, after having welcomed me with suspicion, now admitted my company with an evident satisfaction, Several times, the couple had invited me to share a box at the theater; I was at the front, squeezed against Rolande; the perfume of her blossoming lily-white flesh, which had once intoxicated me, exalting my desire to the heights of passion, reached me from her cleavage—and I did not have to struggle, to hold myself back; I was no longer provoked by it. And there was an infinite sweetness in that harmonious, tranquil liaison, spared the jealousies, suspicions and rancors that spoil amour.

One sole shadow: Robert de Lieuplane.

Many a time, with discreet solicitude, Rolande had attempted to interrogate me about that fiancé, unworthy of me, on the nature of the sentiments I bore to that man, of a different essence than myself, when my fortune guaranteed my independence. But I had always deflected her enquiries, and the mystery subsisted for her, as it did, moreover, for me.

At least, with a secret accord, we maneuvered in order to avoid him. Otherwise, he might perhaps not have "unstuck" himself whenever his dealings in wine did not call him out of Paris. He sent me an abundance of flowers and bonbons; Rolande and I sniffed them and crunched them; that was my compensation.

He was, however, so solidly installed in my future that he did not understand why I had retracted the power of attorney for which he had extracted a promise from me. He saw it as a violation of the rights established by the mysterious force; he came back to it constantly, and his bitterness had even occasioned a few scenes in which, without explaining ourselves—for it there was no basis for reasoning—he exerted an authority, a conjugal power, that frightened me.

One day, I had even thrown him out, but he came back that same evening, like a man driven by fatality. And, an inconceivable phenomenon, I had welcomed his return with gratitude, as if, in finding him again, I were reentering into possession of a part of myself.

All these reflections had momentarily suspended my conversation. I fanned myself weakly, my gaze directed toward my enigma.

"What are you thinking about?" Rolande asked, touching my bare arm.

"Nothing…or, rather, yes: that you might think that I'm flattering my brother's character. What do you expect? That's the way I see him…but I realize that others have the right not to be as benevolent as me. He certainly has his little faults, he flaws…who doesn't?"

"You!" she affirmed, giving me a kiss. "As for your Georges, you don't praise him too much. No, your admiration for him isn't excessive. Fortunate will be the woman he'll distinguish in the course of his voyage…and if he has left a friend in Paris, well, veritably, I feel sorry for her."

Her voice and her face expressed her distress; never had the fervor of a woman for the memory of a lover been so vividly betrayed. Oh, wretched instability, and how necessary it is to refrain from demanding the absolute!

Someone who came in to bid her farewell suddenly disrupted the enthusiasm that I had seen in her. It was the composer Rimeral: a handsome, elegant man with a fire in his eye that might have passed for inspiration if his music had contained any. Seconded, moreover, by the aureole of a facile glory, he had a considerable effect on women, and did not stint himself in making use of it.

His assiduities toward Rolande had already been, on several occasions, the occasion for quarrels between us. She had ended up fearing them to the extent of avoiding, in her relations with the lady-killer in question, anything that might wound my susceptibility. Without expelling him from her drawing room, she had no longer given any pretext to my jealousy.

Well, on seeing his appear this time, her features suddenly became serene again, provocative coquetry prevailing over the interior drama. She leapt to her feet, leaving me there in order to go and talk to him. I heard them plan a cup of tea, in private, in order that he could play the best parts of his next operetta for her—a certain success, he affirmed.

And that man was the lover of the comic-opera star Savari! He was ruining himself for her, and Rolande knew it!

And Rolande, a moment before, in the penetrating tone of her questions, her religious attention to my words, had manifested to me the passion of a heroine!

I was even more astounded than wounded. When she came back to it down beside me again, her complexion animated and her voice still vibrant, I could not help saying to her, dryly: "Is he your lover?"

But she riposted, in the same wounded, haughty tone that she used when I suspected her: "What are you suggesting, Mademoiselle?"

"You've arranged a dangerous rendezvous, at any rate."

"Is that any of your business?"

We separated coolly that evening. Taken home by car by my fiancée, who, under the influence of wine, criticized the vintages to which he had done generous honor, I meditated my vengeance on the way.

Oh, little wretch, you betray me thus! You're going adventuring in the home of that music-manufacturer, that supplier of barrel-organs, scorning the sacred memory that you owe to me! Well, we shall see. You'll be punished. I know a good way of getting you back on the leash...

It was not rage that transported me, as before. The chagrin surpassed anger. My exasperation lacked the support of a blow to masculine pride. It also lacked the fear of being dispossessed of a carnal property, with all the ugly spectacles that a lover forges when he imagines his mistress succumbing

elsewhere. That was now a dead letter for me. I could no longer conceive that those torturing visions might repossess me.
No, my bitterness was not removed from the purely psychic
domain. In betraying me, it was my soul alone that Rolande
was about to sacrifice; her outrage only ate into my tenderness.

"Until when, my chick?" Robert asked, as I pressed me
doorbell.

"As soon as possible...tomorrow...don't leave me," I
astonished myself by saying to him, in my resentment.

V

Our quarrel did not last. Two days later, Rolande came to my apartment and threw her arms around me.

"My dear," she said, "I've come to beg your forgiveness. I realize that I've been wicked with you and imprudent with Monsieur Rimeral. I ought not to go to his rendezvous, but a promise is a promise. Be assured, nevertheless, that if I can fear his audacity, I have nothing to fear of myself. I want to remain an honest woman."

"Don't go, Rolande!" I begged. "One never knows where surprise, violence, a moment of direction or weakness, might lead. Then, what bitterness, what regret! You've often spoken to me about my brother Georges; you value his esteem. What would he say if he learned that you were about to risk yourself in the company of a man unworthy of you?"

Magical invocation! I had touched the sensitive spot.

"You care as much as that?"

"For Georges...for you, yes."

"Well, it's settled; I won't go."

I clapped my hands, and she sealed our reconciliation with another kiss.

"To compensate you," I said, "I have a surprise for you; you're coming with me."

"Where?"

"To a secret garden, of which you're the magnificent flower.

"I can guess! Oh, how glad I am!"

We went up the Rue Lepic slowly. It was the day of the open air market, with stallholders shouting and the bustle of shoppers. Insensible to the picturesque movement of that corner of Montmartre, Rolande climbed the hill, leaning on my arm, as if making a pilgrimage. It was indeed a pilgrimage, an act of devotion; she seemed to be praying as we went into my studio, the sanctuary where our lips had taken communion for the last time...

"Someone has been in here since he went away, then?" she reflected, with an imprudence that I did not underline.

"Certainly—me."

"I meant that someone has been working here.

"Again, me."

"That's true—you're a painter."

She set about inspecting the studio. I watched her. She passed without blinking before the complicit divan, and her portrait. Then she stopped in front of a canvas on which I had recently been working. I had been unable to resist the temptation to copy the masterpiece that Tornada had made of my anatomy. I had represented myself in the simplest attire, clad only in a black velvet mask.

"Who is that woman?" she queried, with an anxiety that I was glad to observe.

"Me, again."

"Painted by?"

"By me."

Oh! Of course...of course!"

She took a few paces back, half-closing her eyes in order better to study the details of the work, which could count among my best. I noted her professional attitude, imitating my fashion of looking at paintings.

"Do you know, my dear, that you're wonderful?"

"As a painter?"

"That too...in terms of figure, I don't believe there exists in Paris, and perhaps anywhere in the world, a nude as perfect!"

"Your opinion won't change before the model?" I said, stepping behind a screen in order to undress, and proceed with a few retouches.

When I reappeared before her, evoking Eve before the original sin, she had sat down on the divan, in her favorite spot, and was sending for the spirals of an Oriental cigarette. I had inculcated sufficient respect for my labor in her for her to

allow me to arrange the mirror and perfect my work. She followed all my movements silently, without even daring to
budge, her eyes wide with wonderment.

That went on for two hours.

"There!" I said, laying down my palette.

"Come here now."

I went to her, emotional. She made room for me, moving
aside slightly. She touched the marmoreal contour of my arms.
She caressed my hair, long enough now for me to put it up.
Then, drawing my head toward her breast, she murmured:

> *I could stay here for hours, or for years,*
> *Without exhausting the sweetness of feeling*
> *Your dark-haired head weighing upon me*
> *As if dead among the faded gleams...*[29]

The song with which I lulled her after sex—she was now
charming me with it in her turn! With no possible equivoca-
tion, certainly: nothing but a prayer in which her memory was
palpitating...and I was on the point of continuing it. But prudence immobilized the divine music on my lips, and also the
desire to learn.

"Whose are those lines, my dear?"

"Samain's."

"Do you like that poet?"

"I'm not familiar with his work."

"Then, for to you recite the verse, someone must have
taught it to you."

"Obviously."

"In similar circumstances...when you came to offer
yourself, in similarly simple apparel, to the admiration of
someone you loved?"

"Obviously..."

"Who?"

---

[29] The words are from "Elégie" (1894) by Albert Samain,
which was set to music by Gabriel Fauré.

"Am I not married?"

"So unhappily, Rolande…to a man who surely cannot know that music!"

"No…no…"

Oh well! We were not yet sufficiently intimate. She was maintaining her façade…I felt proud of her for that. I got dressed again, and we left.

In the days that followed, several events opposed our meetings. First of all, I was gripped by a fever for work like those I had experienced in my virile days: a veritable fever, by which I was excited, in which my work alone obsessed me, in which, like an invalid, I needed isolation in order for the illness to pass. It was a nervous transport that augured well, which gave me confidence in my destiny and inspired by with the conviction that I still had what I needed to avoid mistakes, of whatever nature.

All my effort was focused on my masked portrait, and I had the strange ambition to offer it to the admiration of crowds. The Salon was drawing near; there was still time to send my canvas there; I took the necessary steps. They were facilitated by a birth certificate that was delivered to me one morning in a registered envelope. By means of what subterfuge had Tornada—for it could only be him—been able to have me inscribed at the Mairie of my birthplace? How had he found witnesses to establish my presence in society? It is true that with money, one can achieve anything.

In brief, *Masked Woman* by Georgette Sigerier, was welcomed with a favor that gave rise to the anticipation of a rich reward. I learned from Rimeral, who was always on the lookout for gossip, that the jury, of which I was to have been a member, had taken advantage of the success of the sister to denigrate the work of the absent brother pitilessly; the seat in the Académie refused to Georges was predicted for Georgette. Reporters and photographers were bumping their noses on my door on the eve of the private view. It was a triumph.

If Rolande savored it fully with me, in a veritable artistic joy, Robert only counted the surplus value that I would henceforth represent. My fortune was already large, but thousand-franc bills conquered with a few strokes of a paint-brush would permit us to live in luxury. He no longer held back from making sumptuous plans. The wines were no more than an accessory, a pastime. We were "stuck" so firmly, in his anticipations, that he was talking about publishing our banns without further delay. I did not revolt. Fatality bound me to him, more than I imagined.

He disappeared several times without legitimating his absence. I was still incapable of defining my sentiments, in which relief was mingled with anxiety: nothing of the fiancée for her future spouse. I accepted that we were marrying authoritatively, as princes once did, for reasons of State, to associate realms. I did not imagine that I would ever be able to exchange any other testimonies with him than we exchanged at present: the acceptance of a banal kiss on the fingertips, or sometimes, on his part, a pressure, or rather an observation, of the firmness of my bosom, to which I normally responded with a disapproving slap. A barmaid explored by a client defends herself thus, without either party attributing any importance to it.

We lived therefore, it seemed, in a perfect physical indifference. And yet, I was distressed by his disappearances. In vain I attempted to explain it to myself; in vain I reacted against his faults, his vulgarity and his roughness, which rendered him undesirable to me; in vain I persuaded myself that, once we were married, the total lack of attraction would quickly turn to bitterness, and even to hatred. I could not, however, bear the idea that he might hazard another adventure in love, that his absences might result from his paying court to someone other than me. It was not jealousy; it was something inexplicable, like an attack on my instinct of property: the dispossession in favor of someone else of something that belonged to me.

This time his eclipse was prolonged beyond measure. On the fifth day, I could no longer bear it; I set out in search of him. I went to his house; no one knew where he was. At his garage, the same ignorance—and the automobile, moreover, had disappeared with him. The idea naturally occurred to me to address myself to his family and his friends, but on that point, as on others, I knew nothing about him, any more than he did about me. We had never even bothered to seek the primary instructions of those who are intent on founding a hearth.

What, then? Address myself to the police? I was repelled by that kind of investigation, which gets one's name into the newspapers, prey to reporters. Can you imagine that, just at the moment when I was about to triumph at the Salon, the author of *Masked Woman* should also impose notoriety upon herself by a scandal? Oh no—the worthy colleagues would be only too happy to drown a rising star!

Then I thought of going to find Tornada, in spite of the dread he inspired in me, and seeking information from him. He had thrown Robert into my life; he had imposed him on me; no doubt he surrounded him, like me, with solicitude, an obscure benevolence that he did not manifest but whose constancy I sensed.

That day—it was the eve of the private view—Rolande came to collect me at the Grand Palais. We were to go to a dress-fitting, and then go to Fouquet's, the jewelers, where I was having a necklace altered. I liked looking at clothes with her, giving her advice, receiving it, becoming smitten with an item of jewelry on her suggestion, which I sent back later with the same frivolous inconstancy as the generality of women.

As soon as I saw my friend appear, without noticing that she was as careworn as I was, my anxiety overflowed.

"I don't know what's happening. It's five days since I had any news of Robert. It's inconceivable, and I'm truly wondering..."

"I can't believe that you're missing him to that degree," she said, bitterly. "But who can predict love? Some individual that seemingly ought never to enter into your heart suddenly reveals himself the master of it, and that's the case with you and Monsieur de Lieuplane."

"You're mistaken, Rolande..."

But she did not allow me to protest. "While some other, in whom one has invested all one's faith, one's entire future, and who has since then responded to all your sentiments, reveals himself, in the first absence to be the most distant heart, the most perfect stranger, that one might believe that nothing had ever happened between you..."

"And that's your case with?"

"With no one!" she said, wildly.

She had been waiting for two weeks for a letter from me. More in order to know the exact depth of her passion than to punish her for her coquetry with Rimeral, I had resisted taking pity on her progressive anxiety, on the suffering that was beginning to affect her health, replacing sleep with bitter hypotheses, leaving her devoid of appetite before the tastiest dishes. Above all, I was counting on her disarray finally to become her confidante, for it is in periods of doubt that the best tempered hearts surrender themselves, and the consequences of the stratagem legitimated that sentimental anticipation. True lovers will pardon my cruelty.

"You're wrong not to believe me sufficiently your friend, Rolande," I declared softly. "Don't imagine that I haven't observed your distress, and your changes of mood in recent days. To tell you the exact nature of it would be impossible for me, but there's scarcely anything except love that could trouble you to this exactly. Come on! Abandon yourself entirely to me, and believe that if there is any way that I can help you..."

I offered myself at the psychological moment. Abandoning our planned expeditions and that auto that was to take us, she drew me, arm-in-arm, to the Cours-la-Reine, relatively deserted for the moment. Birds were singing. In the spring warmth, oh, how sweet it was to feel the other warmth of her arm, tugging me more forcefully as she surrendered her secret to me, as her emotion increased, at the story of her own tor-

251

tures, translated by a physical need to seek aid and consolation from me!

She narrated the entirety of our liaison, from the first day when I met her at the Chabrols, and I learned how I had seduced her—a source of astonishment for me, because it was not by my talent, my wit, my beauty, or my vigor, but by numerous insignificant little details, such as having well-manicured fingernails and appearing to her one day at a costumed dinner dressed as a Venetian doge, evoking for her the follies and perhaps even the dramas of the Italian masquerade. She did not, however, take her confessions so far as to reveal our physical communions, and I knew that she wanted, at that moment, not to have profaned our secret memories.

"And now," she concluded, "you know everything. It remains now for you to be as honest as me, and respond without evasions to the question I've already asked you: what was the real reason for Georges' departure, and why is he abstaining from cabling me from time to time to reassure me?"

I responded as required, calming her alarms, and her dear arm squeezed me more forcefully at each further reason that I found to reassure her.

"Oh, how good you are to me! How happy I am now to have something better than my piano to which to confide my torments. Music consoles me, though…but you, you my very dear…you, his sister…almost himself…!

Almost, in fact, I reflected, with a bitter irony, in one of those reversals of my state of mind that the improbable acceptance of my fate did not spare me, in my opinion, often enough.

But hazard is the source of unexpected information, and what happened almost immediately after Rolande's confidence demonstrated to me that I still had at least the energy of a virile resolution. In our walk, we had arrived at the Place de l'Alma; we had forgotten to turn around there and we were crossing the Rue Marbeuf when I suddenly perceived an automobile singularly reminiscent, in its color and form, to the one in which Robert had transported me so many times.

Yes, it really was his white sports car, with the comtal crown. It was parked outside one of those bars frequented by an equivocal clientele.

"Let's go in!" I ordered Rolande.

"In there? Oh, you're crazy!"

"Let's go in! Let's go in!"

She understood immediately. Robert was there, installed in front of his saucers, the only man in a crowd of young women. He was enlaced with one of them, a rather appetizing redhead.

As soon as he recognized us, without being taken aback, he abandoned his conquest and came to meet us.

"What a coincidence," he said, smiling stupidly.

"What a coincidence," I riposted. "What are you doing in this hole?"

"As you see, I was meeting up with a few friends..."

"And you haven't quit them for five days, whereas I...but this isn't the place to discuss it. Let's go—come with me."

O my innocence! The girls had decided to join in. Their thick voices derided the crestfallen attitude of my fiancé, with appropriate epithets. He hesitated, and then took a step to return to them."

"You don't want to come with me?"

And bang! With the back of my hand, I slapped the individual who was offering me the good fortune of being able to break with him. I was purple with rage; Rolande was pale with it; and he went a bilious green.

We installed ourselves in his car; he took the wheel and took Rolande home. After which we dined in a cabaret as if nothing had happened.

My anger had died down. He proposed finishing the evening at a café-concert—he pronounced it "caff-conce"—and I accepted. I detested exhibitions of that sort, but Robert took an infinite pleasure in them. And that was another opportunity for a scandal, which shows the extent to which his behavior was villainous.

We had taken a box. Disappointed by the stage, I was looking into the hall, astonished by the number of pairs of opera-glasses aimed at me, when, in the stalls directly below our box, I noticed the brazen insistence offered by a spectator who never quit me with his monocle. On finding myself the focus of the gentleman's attention, I was unable, by reflex, to detach my gaze from him—so he thought me complicit. He soon took a card out of his wallet in order to scribble a few words on it, signifying to me by gestures that he was about to send it to me.

Indeed, at the intermission, an usherette presented herself with the message and attempted to slip it to me—but it was Robert who took possession of it. While pretending to be interested in the performance, he had seen the whole thing. And that man, who was only interested in me for my millions, flew off the handle with the same violence as if he loved me.

Then, coarsely, he shouted at the gallant who had just returned to his set, brandishing the card: "Hey, you! Yes, you, the idiot in the monocle! I have your card, you know? Your name is Monsieur Laspique. No! Take a look at that fat swine who permits himself to make eyes at my fiancée and send her a love-letter! You, who don't attract any eyes, you poor old sap. With that retouched noggin, one goes to bed early! I'm Robert de Lieuplane, and if you want to be sorted out, I'm at your disposal!"

The audience was madly amused. I would have been too, in my normal state, but my feminine impregnation modified my way of being, and at first I had no other recourse than to hide my confusion behind my fan, and then to tug Robert's smoking jacket in order for him to cease the stupid quarrel. He obeyed me meekly.

Once we were outside he said, proudly: "I shut him up, didn't I?"

"You would have done better to shut yourself up, my friend. That's not how one behaves in such circumstances. One is scornful, and one keeps quiet. What stable were you born in, then? You've never talked to me about your family or your education; perhaps it's the moment to make the confession."

He lowered his head, reflected, and then looked away. "Don't interrogate me. I don't know any more."

In any case, I didn't really care. The mysterious chain again: I was bound to that fiancé as one submits to the force of the waves, to atmospheric pressure, without defense, without any possible reaction. And he, to the extent that I could penetrate him, similarly appeared to be accepting a yoke that it was necessary not to interpret.

What conciliated my reason with my indifference most conveniently, for the moment, was the notion that Tornada had set some mediocre fellow, embarrassed in his business, on my heels in order to complete his physiological experiment. He wanted to see what the creation of a transsexual being, with an undeniably sound collaborator, would yield.

As for Robert, the question of money preoccupied him more than anything else. He raised it more audaciously that same evening, as he deposited me at home.

"Come on, my little Georgette, it's necessary to make a decision soon. We can't remain in the preliminaries all our lives. It's May now—what if we were to marry in July."

"It's very hot in July," I reflected. "Wouldn't September be better for our honeymoon voyage?"

"All right, September. I've seen the notary who'll draw up our contract. What do you say to a settlement in which subsequent assets are held in common?"

"If you wish. Common property."

"That sticks."

I was glad to find myself alone in my apartment again. Anna, the chambermaid, had prepared me a cold snack, which I ate. I idled before going to bed. I let my thoughts wander over all the small charms of a home: trinkets, portraits, items of furniture, as many objects coming, by virtue of the force of memory, to constitute the bread of the soul. They had become even more precious to me since Rolande had also caressed them with her gaze. And they would become his!

But the flagging frills, Robert's flowers in a vase, a hat-box on a sideboard, reminded me that, alas, my beautiful dream was over, sunk in the frightful modification of my person.

VI

Private views have lost all solemnity, and even all artistic physiognomy, since the societies began to invite not merely everyone in Paris who is anyone but everyone in Paris, and grocers can get in as easily as art critics, with the same liberty—and sometimes the same competence—to praise "a load of tripe" or denigrate a masterpiece. The crowd that one meets there these days is the same that one sees, indiscriminately, at important funerals, balls at the Hôtel de Ville, military exhibitions and parades of sovereigns—anywhere that idling is gratuitous. It comes to see, and even more to be seen, and God knows what it shows.

That was the reflection that, once again, Rolande and I made when we penetrated, at about three o'clock, under the immense glasswork. As escorts we had her husband and my fiancé. With common accord we left them behind and hurried toward the great staircase, going around the pieces of sculpture. We advanced like two queens through the compact human mass, which parted, dazzled, to let us through: she rendered even more blonde by the azured mirror of her gaze; I evoking by my lofty stature, my proud and supple stride and my ardent teguments, those splendid creatures of the Orient of whom it is said that the body has become the tabernacle of the sun.

For that second debut in glory I had put on a golden tunic that showed me off marvelously; my hair, now long, was gathered up into two shells over the ears; a little ocher powder on my cheeks further heightened, by contrast, the pomegranate hue of my lips. A single pendant, formed of two large clusters of rubies, bleeding from my throat, signified my cleavage. The impression we made was such that we collected, at one moment, one of those eulogies that count in a woman's life: the stercoral exclamation of an artist lighting his pipe. Wonderstruck, he even forgot to blow out his match and burned his fingers.

"It seems to me," I said to Rolande, "that we're causing a sensation."

She did not reply, and I rediscovered the furrow on her forehead that signaled her obsession. The previous year, in the same circumstances, it had been with the other me that she had accepted the tributes of the crowd. She had been proud then; today she was sad.

"Come on. Hold on until tomorrow. Tomorrow, you'll have a nice surprise. I've had a letter."

"For me?"

"For me. Georges asked me to give it to you."

A pious lie...she was maddened by it. Her husband and Robert, catching us up, found her stamping her feet with joy. They drew us toward the grand staircase leading to the paintings.

"Would you care to take my arm," Monsieur Variland asked me, departing from his polite and glacial manners.

I accepted, and he sketched the first smile that I had ever seen appear on his face. Was it the pure satisfaction of escorting to her work the probable triumphatrice, of sharing the incense of tributes, of admiration? I don't know; but it seemed that he held me more tightly against him than was appropriate. He had, moreover been changing for some time, not in his relationship with Rolande, but in his behavior toward me, which was becoming increasingly intimate. It was evolving toward a good grace, significant of a prestige that I exercised over him. There were long gazes, mute coquetries of which I was not yet woman enough to estimate the gallant measure, but which astonished me in their novelty.

Rolande was unaware of all that maneuvering; she was, in any case, totally disinterested in it. I was waiting for it to become more manifest in order to reveal it to her and laugh at it with her.

If the fashions of that discreet courtship remained unperceived by Rolande, however, they did not escape my churl—

by which I mean Robert. With the neglect of worldly custom that was characteristic of him, he approached us with a suspicious gleam in his eye and said: "Pardon me, but isn't it me who ought..."

"Leave me the honor," insisted Monsieur Variland. "Here, by way of compensation, offer your arm to my wife."

O mystery! On seeing him obey and take Rolande, as they say, "under his wing" I felt a little needle run through my heart. But let us be clear; it was not the man in me who was offended, the jealous lover observing in another a manifestation of intimacy with the woman he adores; it was the woman, the fiancée—and I stress that word, which defines better than any other the strangeness of my sentiment—the proprietress, stirred by a contravention of a pledge of fidelity. Yes, that was what it was.

It was a fugitive emotion, at any rate, on either side; for, after having hastily traversed the first two rooms of the exhibition, we arrived in the third, where my painting was. In front of *Masked Woman*, at least six ranks of spectators were standing, and I heard exclamations saluting it, such that I blushed with pleasure beneath my ocher. "Admirable! Magnificent! Moving!" were the only words that expressed enthusiasm. They might have been emitted by grocers, but they always give pleasure.

No! But it's the model, after all!" cried a man in a large felt hat to a friend. "Where has she found those tits? And those hips, old chap, do you believe that they can exist? There are no figures like that! That curve, that purity—it's necessary to go back to Greek antiquity! Civilization has spoiled the form. They don't make them like that anymore!"

"Forgive me, but they do still make them!" protested a shrill voice at which I shuddered.

It was Him. He was perched on the central bench. Modestly, he was savoring his success, running his fingers over the hanks of his beard. Yes, *his* success, since I was that perfection of nature, emerged sublimely from his scalpel and his practices. The painter, astonished by that repartee, turned to

259

him, ready to reply hotly, when Tornada perceived us and bounded toward us, taking off his hat. Then he kissed Rolande's hand and mine.

"Well, Doctor," said Monsieur Variland, "you too have come to see the marvel! You know that it's Mademoiselle Sigerier, that *Masked Woman?* And what do you say, you who are an anatomist?"

"I say," Tornada proffered, slowly, "that I would gladly perform her autopsy."

I shivered. But he immediately went on, addressing himself specifically to me: "Oh, don't worry...later...much later...when she's dead...and I'll add: having died a natural death."

He changed the subject immediately, deploring the mediocrity of the submissions, the kindness of the jury, the decadence of art—except when revealed in a painting like mine. After which, leaving Rolande and her husband in front of the canvas, he took Robert and me aside, familiarly.

"Well, lovers, is everything arranged? Do you know how glad I am to find you together? You're both such darlings! You're going to make one of those couples! Tell me when is the marriage? It's necessary not to let things drag on, you know...and as soon as nature permits..."

We confided our recent decision to him: for September.

"September," he accepted. "That's a good limit. But it's necessary to be good until then, my little Georgette. You hear me? Even more virtuous than the Virgin Mary...who didn't sin but conceived...and conception, damn it, should never be precipitate."

He pinched my cheeks. "Right! She's adapting very well, the darling!"

We went back to the Varilands, who were still listening to people pontificating before my work. Then Tornada took us to the buffet and had some champagne uncorked.

"To the health of the artist!" he toasted, raising his glass in the air—but I shall never know for sure whether it was himself he was celebrating, or me. On reflection, it must have been himself. And we all drank wholeheartedly.

Joy reentered into every one of us. Personally, with the aid of the champagne, I experienced for that extraordinary being a kind of gratitude. He was not, however, at that moment, using any kind of supernatural influence on me. I thanked him secretly for having given me the opportunity for a triumph, and for having facilitated my intimacy with the Varilands. Although my organism remained in that neutrality, although no other solicitation led me to want anything more from Rolande than a pure and profound affection, well, that was perfect! But would it last? Would I remain eternally in that gray tenderness, in which the senses were abolished?

One of the things that Tornada had said made me anxious. It was with regard to my adaptation. What significance did he give to that term, exactly? Was my adaptation physical or mental? And if it was physical, what did it have to do with the modification that Tornada had produced in me?

I would gladly have asked him the question, at that moment when I considered him a kind of spiritual father, since he had transformed my mentality as well as my body. At least, I believed so. But it seemed that nature took charge of answering for him, and I received, at that precise moment, for the first time since the surgeon's operation, the advertisement that the field of maternity was open to me.

I was so far from that idea that I had not thought in recent days of interpreting an abnormal nervous state: mood changes, fantasies, lassitudes, and a heaviness in my loins. I had attributed those disturbances to Robert's misconduct and the legitimate emotion of a debut at the Salon. But this time, it was necessary for me to yield to the evidence, and nature advised me copiously. Need I confess that no noble ideas connected with the prolongation of the species passed through my mind, and that my only thought was to preserve my golden tunic...

I leaned toward Rolande's ear,

"Let's go, my dear, let's go; otherwise, there'll be a disaster!"

Rolande divined what I meant. Women have no need of explanations for matters of that sort.

Robert, naturally, protested. He made one *faux pas* after another. "What an idea, to run away like that! What's wrong with you, then?"

"Nothing out of the ordinary; everything comes to she who waits," riposted Tornada, with a satisfied authority. He had understood.

Accompanied by Rolande, I went home. She put me to bed, and filled hot water bottles for me. With the ease and the fraternity that dissipated all constraints between women, subject to the same unpleasantness, she cared for me without modesty, shamelessly asking me questions about my health that she would not have tolerated me asking her at one time, and which would have made her blush with shame. Very embarrassed in my responses, I attributed more suffering to myself than I was really experiencing, both to avoid her inquisition and to prolong the dear moments of her assistance.

"How lucky men are!" she reflected.

"Oh, yes," I agreed, with a conviction increased by my former immunity.

She only decided to leave me when she was entirely convinced that my soubrette would take the usual precautions, but her departure brought me another divine joy, when she addressed me as *tu*, which she had never done before, even in the most forceful of our past effusions. Oh, the freemasonry of the eternal wound!

"You understand that it's necessary that you don't fall ill. What would Georges say? You promise me to rest?"

"I promise, my dear."

"That's good. I'll telephone my doctor now."

I started. "Oh no! No doctor!"

"He's a specialist. He's young and charming."

"I don't want one!"

"Yes, yes! You'll see him—for me, for Georges and for yourself."

The Trinity! The Holy Trinity...and we were, in fact, only two. I smiled sadly, and waited for the disciple of Aesculapius. My God, what would he make of me?

He soon arrived. He was, as Rolande had said, a practitioner of rather seductive appearance, dressed in the latest fashion, with a distinguished receding hairline and a fan-like beard scented with opopanax. He interrogated me a little, palpated me discreetly, like a man who took no pleasure in it, smiled at Rolande's alarm and wrote a prescription, for form's sake, whose principal component was mint.

He might not have liked his profession, but he liked flirting. As soon as his consultation was over, installing himself at my beside in a comfortable armchair, he started talking about racing, dancing, coving and clothes, passing on tips, gossip, technical pointers and the process of fabrics.

What! This was the scientist to whom Rolande confided her health! A frightful suspicion occurred to me.

"Have you known Madame Variland for a long time?

"Two years, perhaps. We hit it off right away. She's a charming friend." Observing my amazement, he went on: "Oh, no...not what you might think. Perhaps it wouldn't be necessary to try too hard...she's so unhappy in her marriage, the poor thing, and had so much need of consolation—but with my clients, never!" He smiled. "And then, even if it were the case, only she and I would ever know. My discretion is proof against anything."

That information was for me. The inflection of his voice and his suggestive expression indicated as much. But I did not like his effrontery, and I harvested the crop of his implications internally. Assuredly, I did not suppose that Rolande would ever abandon herself to that quack, whose presumption and conceit could only make a bad impression on her—but she had doubtless deployed with him the provocation, the need for seduction, the ignition, if I might put it thus, that she had hidden from the jealousy of the lover but no longer repressed in the presence of the friend. That irritated me. Was it the action of a genuinely smitten woman also to cede to the vain satisfactions of vanity—to compromise, with games of such easy empire, the grandeur of a passion sworn to be eternal?

"That's all right," I said to the doctor. "I have no further need of your talents for the moment, and I think I shall get better without further care. How much do I owe you for your visit?"

He got up, accustomed to such rebuffs on the part of nervous women, and slipped on his yellow gloves. "I never ask for anything from pretty women."

A final scorn, a final insult. I took them aboard, tearing up his prescription. I got up and marched impetuously back and forth in the room. My nerves were bad. I was agitated by a thousand contrary thoughts. Doubtless the natural spring, that flood of life, which had just welled forth so unexpectedly, was also affecting my mentality and opening up new horizons to me, akin to what happens to everyone at the moment of puberty.

Of all these physical phenomena, as I have already said, I was in crass ignorance—the inconceivable ignorance of all men for whom the educator at college deliberately suppresses a part of the anatomy—and what a part!

Then, in a frantic desire to clarify the mystery that had just occurred within me, I ran to my bookshelves. I discovered a treatise on anatomy there and began to devour it. In truth, I knew exterior beauty, but what beauty, power, method and ingenuity there is, too, in those depths, in that productive factory of the race where one of the elements of being is regularly distilled, to be subsequently liberated as a red torrent—while other elements, the male, the sperm, race hectically to at the first opportunity, to encounter the egg, to fuse with it and commence the prodigious work of life!

It was an entire romance, a story of chivalry, perhaps with its jousts and battles between microorganisms among the anfranctuosities of the route—who can tell? Already, there were multiple rivalries before the unity; already, in the unknown folds, destructive wars, the eternal epic of Nature, the cruel stepmother.

Oh, my surgeon must be a prestidigitator of genius to have thus transported, from one body into another, and reciprocally, such a delicate mechanism, without any appearance remaining, without any loss of function...for my creative mechanism was entering into activity, as the day's adventure testified.

And certainly, the element of me that he had grafted on to someone else must also be commencing its fecund work.

Someone else...that was the dominant idea of my meditation after the reading in question. In the resignation of my subjugated being, fallen back into administration since the operation, not thinking about my fate any more than a child who emerges into life and accepts all is fatalities, I had only reflected in brief glimmers on Tornada's transmutation. But now that my "femininity" had awakened, I was also taking on a new mental personality; now that my conscious individuality was beginning to be reborn—and it appeared to me, save for a few details, almost identical to the preceding one—I heard troubling interrogations rising within me.

A surgeon finds it necessary to remove one of your arms: it is a sacrifice you make to health; you know that that sectioned part of you will disintegrate, return to humus, serve as pasture for other lives; you close that little tomb and the mourning is only partial. But a surgeon removes that same arm in full vigor, and, far from interring it, takes it into his head to make a gift of it to another individual, with all its resources of strength, energy and vitality, in order that it can resume its useful functions at the dictation of other inspirations...that was as arbitrary as if a Tornada of painting had stolen one of my canvases in favor of an unknown, and the latter had added his signature to it and obtained an exceptional recompense for it at the Salon. I make use of that comparison because it was the one that came to mind at that moment, and because it appeared to me to express my renewed indignation most clearly, by virtue of its professional nature.

O matter that had been stolen from me, where were you at that moment? O my graft, on what stock were you continuing me? O my health, to what were you being exposed? O my ever-respected property, under what influences were you persisting, and were you not being profaned in frightful company?

By virtue of an anxiety of the same source, I also interrogated myself as to the origin of the substance that I bore within me. From where did that exchange come, from what flesh had it been claimed? That mystery tormented me as much as the other. Tornada might have guaranteed to me the immaculacy of his truck, but I could not take his word for it without reservations. He was capable, with his skill, of having repaired the outrages that had been inflicted on it—those outrages that are said to be final but are in reality the first. He was capable of having bleached that which had been blackened; and in that case I could only be proud of a false virginity; in that case, a degrading epic was dormant in my loins!

Furthermore, although science is beginning to distinguish the influence of the mind on the body, it has not yet defined the measure in which the body can act upon the mind; and I wondered whether the solicitations, and perhaps the habits, of that region newly imprisoned in my organism might not lead my brain, previously moral in that kind of regard, to the worst aberrations.

"Let's wait and see," I began reflecting aloud. "Let's wait, and inscribe on a calendar, in all prevision, the date..."

And I added, bitterly, while making the memorable day with a cross: "Let's go! I've now passed from chick to hen...a hen![30] I mustn't forget..."

---

[30] I have translated *poule* literally as "hen," partly because it connects with Robert's previous habit of addressing the protagonist as *poulet* [chick], but in French, when the word *poule* is applied to a woman, it usually implies loose morals, as in the earlier reference to Variland's hunting expedition only taking him to a poultry-yard.

Neglecting the prudent advice that I had been given to stay in bed, I sat down at the table to write the letter to Rolande that I was supposed to have received.

I made it long and passionate. The further my pen ran over our mauve paper, the more I set aside the doctor's nasty suggestions and found phrases appropriate to calm her alarms and maintain her sacred fire. I needed to believe in her, in her constancy, in her fidelity. I could not, however, any longer demand of myself the wherewithal to serve the prolongation, in her and in me, of fervor that my extraordinary destiny condemned to annihilation. And, all things considered, I was only continuing the legend of my absence in order to soothe my sentimentality.

When I reread my letter I marveled at its form as much as its foundation. I had realized a delicacy of style, an elevation of sentiment that was entirely new and unexpected, with light touches of feminine expression. Was it the case, therefore, that Tornada's graft was extending its roots all the way to the brain?

VII

I was now taking at least one meal a day at the Varilands—lunch, for preference, in order that Rolande and I might have the leisure to run thereafter to the futile employ-ments of the afternoon. I liked to arrive early, to surprise her during her toilette, emerging from a perfumed bath, surrender-ing her hair to her chambermaid, her blonde flesh blossoming in a peignoir.

As soon as she saw me appear, she clapped her hands. "It's you, my dear! How nice it is of you to give me all your time! How fresh and pretty you are this morning! How do you manage to be ready so early? Have you had your bath? Would you like me to have one run for you?"

She did not give me the time to put in a reply, and each of her remarks was mingled with a kiss, which she gave me on my hair, on my veil, on my gloved hands, as if the idol of her amity were worthy of being embraced even in its vestments. When her initial enthusiasm had passed, she sent her soubrette away and it was me who replaced her. I anointed her with *eau de toilette*, I trimmed and polished her fingernails and toenails. I rediscovered thus every detail of her adored being, her sump-tuous flesh, and discovered others that I did not know, such as a beauty spot hidden under the fawn down in her right armpit.

"Would you like to help me with my gorget? I'm taking care to maintain myself, you see…it's necessary that he finds all this in good condition when he returns, the wretch, who will probably have been able to make comparisons out there…"

While I occupied myself thus, an odor of her reached me, which troubled me, not because it reanimated the memory of my defunct enthusiasm, but because I received new delights therefrom, previously perfectly innocent. I loved to run my fingers over the delicate grain of her skin, over the contours of her legs, and then to place her in against the yellow light of the window, in order that her hair would be even more radiant. I also loved to cover her bare shoulders with kisses, because I embraced the health, beauty and life erupting therefrom; because, even so, there was weakness under that splendid form: a distraught heart that was beating for me, the protector of which I still wanted to be. The homage of a slave, the empire of a master, the admiration of an artist, and the tenderness of a sister, there was all of that complexity in my happiness in being with her: the entire symphony of love, save for the love of the lover.

She lent herself unreservedly to those ingenuous caresses exchanged under the aegis of the dear exile, of whom I had become the unique messenger. To spare myself the complications of the agency, expeditions following re-expeditions, and also to spare Rolande the petty shame of the *poste restante*, I arrived periodically, in accordance with delays in transit, as the bearer of the expected missives. I had usually written them that same morning. I posed therein, as if at hazard, questions related to Rolande's confidences, or any event of which I wanted an explanation. I thus put her good faith to the proof, and observed that a woman can, in her replies, dissimulate the truth from the man she loves—for a confidante is often, in that respect, more favored than the individual for whom one would die.

We opened the letters together; we commented on them; we drafted the replies together.

That day, she stopped writing, and raised her beautiful azure eyes to me.

"He says that a woman truly in love, as he knows me to be, owes it to her distant lover never to flirt. What shall I reply to that?"

"Well, the truth."

"The truth is that I don't flirt with anyone."

"Do you believe that, Rolande? When I caught you again, the day before yesterday, sitting in the little drawing room next to Rimeral, bursting into laughter while telling him

I don't know what scandalous story of the theater? You didn't even resist when he put his hand on yours."

"You saw that?"

"I saw it—even though, as soon as I appeared, Rimeral immediately resumed a posture less compromising for you. Isn't that flirting, then?"

"I don't love Rimeral. I love Georges."

"All the more reason for your conduct to be inexcusable, unworthy of the absentee who is certainly maintaining all his fidelity to you, in thought and action, and would never permit himself such liberties, even with a black woman."

Contrite, not challenging my indignation—a greatly attenuated reflection of a solid anger of the day before last—she ventured: "Oh! You won't betray me?"

"No, you'll do that yourself."

"How?"

"By honestly confessing the truth to him."

"Perhaps you're right. He'll have more confidence in me."

And she began her confession, but she deployed such feminine guile that by the end of the explanation it was Rimeral who was guilty of having recounted the scabrous story and of having taken hold of her hand by force."

"You're not telling the truth, Rolande!"

"Almost…almost…why upset him? I love him so much! I would sell myself for him."

"Be careful of giving yourself, in the meantime."

"Oh, Georgette, what are you suggesting?" she protested, putting her hands together. And she added, gravely: "If that ever happened, there would be nothing left to do but kill myself."

And she was telling the truth, at that moment! She was not exaggerating. Her remorse dissolved in tears, and I had to console her, to take her in my arms, to dry the furrows traced on her cheeks with my kisses.

"Go on! Send your letter anyway. Perhaps, indeed, ignorance is better that the truth."

Once more I had ventured into that chaos of summits and gulfs that is a woman's heart. I discovered singular shadows there, beneath the eternal lights! But after all, is the heart of a man any different?

We went into the dining room, where Monsieur Variland had already been waiting for us for a while. I observed that his grave person was undergoing a progressive evolution in harmony with his heart. Having passed through the severe frock-coat with the correct waistcoat, now he was adopting a newly-fashionable jacket with a handkerchief in the pocket. The fabric was still somber, but it was to be expected that it would brighten before long as his attempts to seduce me continued—for it was for my sake that he was following the progressive decrease in the austerity of his costume. It was for my sake that his crown of hair was bearing the waves of a timid undulation due to the artifice of a hairdresser. It was for my sake that his upright collar was now relaxed and that he could fold it over, at the conclusion of his reports on the financial crisis and foreign politics. It was for my sake that he drank slowly, avoiding the lurches of his Adam's apple and the gurgling of the liquid brushing it. It was for my sake that, after looking at me for a long time, he finally turned his eyes away, uttering, at fifty years of age, the sighs of youth.

Look for an amorous reason when a third person intervenes in the intimacy of a marriage. That principle had guided the curiosity of the friends of the family, and from Monsieur Variland's behavior, with my aid, they had quickly concluded, if not my misconduct—which my fortunate situation, my success at the Salon and my now-official engagement rendered more inadmissible—at least a deliberate and misplaced coquetry on my part.

I must confess that their opinion was not without foundation, for it amused me sometimes to reply to Monsieur Variland's long gazes with a smile, and to observe how easily men take possession of such misconstrued testimony of simple social familiarity in order to support their dream and rebound into desire. I therefore divined, from the reserve of the

271

Chabrols, the pity of Blanche Férette, the young universitarian, the excessive interest of Baronne Nirvâne des Illeuls and the insolence of the composer Rimeral that my trial was taking place in their minds and that they were convicting me of troubling their hosts' hearth.

Even among the domestics that opinion acquired credit. In particular, Louis, the *valet de chambre*, treated me with the protective consideration that one has for a stranger who might one day or other, by virtue of divorce, become one's mistress. He was secretly scornful of me beneath his attentions. When he served me at table he indicated the morsel that I ought to take, but he shrugged his shoulders when taking away the dish. One day, when he had been sent to me by Rolande, he had said to Anna, my soubrette—who repeated it to me—that his "old boss" was in love with Mademoiselle, and that Madame had better watch out, for at the rate things were going, Mademoiselle and Monsieur would not be long in "taking a walk" together. We had laughed about it, but my merriment was mingled with an aftertaste of vexation.

Generally people felt sorry for the innocent fiancé and the abandoned wife. They were the only ones not to have interpreted Monsieur Variland's new style in that fashion. Robert was, in any case, too rarely invited to acquire suspicions by observing his rival's behavior. Business affairs—serious, this time—had taken him away from Paris again, and I had blessed his absence, for his lack of tact, the jealousy that he experienced in my regard without loving me, would undoubtedly have led to a scandal, regrettable because it would have disrupted my easy relationship with Rolande. What would I do, I often asked myself, if that master, whom I ought to obey, forbade me henceforth the company of the Varilands? Would I then be reduced to secret meetings with Rolande? No more of the openness so comfortable to our mutual tenderness; no more of the sweet slavery of the mornings, when she was at her toilette; no more chatter about the absentee?

As for Rolande, she attributed her husband's embellishments to some infatuation external to the house, and, moreover, rejoiced in it, thinking about the liberation for which she had always hoped. For my part, I was very careful not to tell her that I was the cause of it. I feared that I might remain profaned in her eyes if ever my extraordinary destiny took a further turn and made me a man again. I wanted that man to present himself without a past, without a stain.

The pleasure and simplicity of my relationship with Rolande was, however, not without reservations, and there might be ambushes in preparation in all regards, for which I was determined to watch out.

Monsieur Variland kissed my hand cheerfully and the three of us took our seats. As soon as the hors d'oeuvres, he declared: "I've just seen that charming Robert de Lieuplane. In parentheses, he made me take half a dozen hogsheads of a wine of which I had no need, for your sake, Mademoiselle, because you appreciate it…yes, it's his famous Lur-Saluce, do you remember?[31] And we decided something by common accord."

"What?" I said, fearing a blow of precisely the kind of which I have just spoken.

"We have decided that my wife and I are abducting you."

"You're abducting me?"

"Yes, to take you to stay, for a few months, at our château in Touraine."

"But what about Robert?" I asked. "Will Robert be coming with me?"

He went on, while chewing a jellied egg: "Robert won't be accompanying you. He's very busy, the poor fellow, and has no time to idle. He can, in any case, come to see you as often as you desire—the journey only takes a few hours by automobile…and I'll add that you'll find our friends there. That amiable company will, I hope, convince you to accept."

He plunged his head back into his plate, and I was able to comprehend, by the vivacity of the winks that Rolande was

---

[31] The Lur-Saluce family own the Château d'Yquem, under which label the wine in question is better know.

273

addressing to me, the price that she put on my sojourn out there. Dear Rolande! I would have liked not to have to resist her—but the indefinable necessity, devoid of attraction, that I experienced for Robert's company caused me to hesitate over my acceptance.

Not knowing what to add, Monsieur Variland had recourse to his wife. "You insist."

"I hope," she said, "that there's no need to insist. Georgette knows only too well the pleasure she would give us, especially if she would paint my portrait during our sojourn."

"That's right!" agreed Monsieur Variland. "And when she's finished yours, I'll offer myself as a model."

"With a mask?" Rolande suggested.

That extravagant image, of a Variland costumed as Adam before the fall, with a black mask over his austere face, made all three of us burst out laughing, and secured my acceptance. We were still laughing when Robert was introduced. He had the scent of a base alcove; I believe that I even remember that he was slightly drunk, that he did not take his hat off and that he swished the air with his cane as he spoke.

"Well? Is it sticking, our plan?" he said to Monsieur Variland—and when the latter confirmed it, he added, disdainfully: "She needs it, the darling; it'll do her good."

He had never disgusted me so much, and I never found myself as close to afflicting Rolande by reversing my decision in order to remain in the vicinity of the cad. Explain that...!

We left the following week. I had, as an orderly woman, packed my trunks arranged my cupboards, and set up mountains of naphthalene to deter mites—to the amazement of Anna, who had never seen a mistress get her hands dirty. I had the clear conscience of a housewife when the Varilands' forty-horsepower came to pick me up.

On quitting the Rue du Général-Foy, which had so often sheltered our now-compromised amours, Rolande could not contain her emotion. I saw her discreetly wipe away a tear.

When we were in the country, Monsieur Variland, who had been perorating until then, identifying the important

274

dwellings we were passing and their owners, an entire holiday Gotha, went to sleep. Then I was able to take Rolande's hand.

"I can see that you're sad, my love."

"He'll come back! You swear to me?" she said, interrogating my eyes.

Oh, the sovereign charity of lies! To calm her down, to lull that heart at bay: the heart that was mine, in spite of its inconsequences, effusions and levities with Rimeral; in spite, perhaps—who knows?—of a weakness on the day when the appeal of tenderness might be too imperious; the day when nature, the accomplice of sin, would drive those poor nerves weary of waiting with the force of instinct...

"I swear to you, Rolande."

Then her cheerfulness was reignited, and no longer had any occupation but one: to wake Monsieur Variland up at every château we passed, in order for him to identify it, along with its style, and name its owner. Alone with his wife, the poor man would scarcely have savored that curiosity, but for me, he wiped the sleep from his eyes, gazed while blinking, recognized the edifice, cited its location, its style and its owner, and went back to sleep. I experienced a girlish joy in such mischief, but that was primarily because Rolande was enjoying it with me.

We went through Tours and, twenty kilometers further on, we arrived. Monsieur Variland had recovered consciousness and had recommenced his perorations, like a horse whinnying as it approaches the stable. He sat up straight, smoothed his hair and adjusted his hat, intent on entering his domain as handsomely as possible.

A grand appearance, the château—"what style is it, Monsieur Variland?" but he was no longer answering—a seventeenth-century dwelling outlined its façade and massive towers at the end of a long avenue, in the frame of a park with age-old foliage, in which the laws, delicately carpeted, sloped gently away toward a glimpse of profound countryside. A lively stream babbled incessantly over pebbles toward a little lake where boats and canoes were moored to the piles of a

Swiss chalet. Behind it were the glazed arches of a vast orang-ery, and further behind, the outbuildings, the busy stables and the automobile garages. All of that for one man!

All of that, which Rolande, a few months earlier, had been ready to leave in order to share my uncertain life: the life of an artist barely emerged from hackwork, the yoke of mer-cantilism, at the mercy of an accident! I understood her emo-tion, her disappointment at returning to this place, which she had hoped never to see again.

She smiled even so at the staff assembled in front of the perron to welcome the masters; she extended her hand to the head gardener, the gamekeeper; she kissed the florid cheeks of the children of the farm. Oh, she was not proud, those humble folk must have thought of her—but the same opinion certainly did not greet the rigid, affected authority and curt orders of her husband, who had become once again, after the fantasy of the journey, the shark in confrontation with his prey.

His prey, the château, which he owed to a coup on the Bourse, conceived in one night, executed in a few days, at the time of the threat to Agadir.[32] I attributed to Rolande alone the power to retain me in that ostentation. At that moment, in any case, I would have crushed the entire human race for her—for she had just run to a flower-bed in order to pick a rose, and to present it to me.

It was the flower that, as a man, had been my favorite, and which, as a woman, I was going to adore even more.

---

[32] In 1911 Germany sent warships to Agadir, the capital of Morocco, to protect the interests of its nationals there, and triggered a major international crisis, provoking fierce reac-tions from Britain and other nations and causing stock markets to fall steeply throughout Europe. The threat of war between France and Germany was only narrowly averted, with France being able to confirm her protectorate, postponing the Great War for three more years.

VIII

Monsieur Variland had to return to Paris almost immediately for important financial discussions. He would not return for a week. Robert, for whom my jealous concerns attenuated with his absence, did not reappear for some time either. A postcard with these simple words of love: *Gone to Marseille, sale in Provence of the next harvest*, assured Rolande and me of complete tranquility.

Liberated from those importunate individuals, the sojourn at the château became delightful for us. It was July; all the vegetation was expanding joyfully. Getting up early, putting on short skirts and walking boots, after a snack of milk and fresh eggs, we set out at hazard in the vast estate. We avoided the parlor, the stables and the garages where the obsequious servants lived who reminded us of civilization. We preferred the company of healthy rustic individuals: in the farms, whose inhabitants had, it seemed to us, a rudimentary mentality, little distinct from that of the animals confided to their care, and were thus incapable of interpreting my presence; or in the kitchen garden, where the gardeners scarcely noticed our passage and did not look up when we asked them questions.

The great work of nature impassioned us, whether it was offered to us by the creative endeavor of livestock or the emergence of plants from the humus.

On the very first morning, Rolande paused, her eyes brilliant with desire, in front of a cherry tree weighed down by its red burden. I understood.

"I'll go!"

"No, me!"

"Both of us, then."

I made her a ladder with my hands. Once she was sitting on a branch, she helped me to climb up in my turn. We settled down face to face. At nature's banquet, one only has to reach out one's hand.

"One might think we were in an aerial private booth," she joked.

"You've done this before, then, Rolande?"

"Alas, no...I would have liked to very much, with Georges, but every time I asked him, he refused."

That was untrue! She had never expressed that desire to me, to which I would have consented wholeheartedly. Why that petty lie? A mystery. But I was no longer keeping count of her inexactitudes. Ordinarily, I sought an explanation, but not this time.

Without noticing my astonishment she continued her feast. The fruits crunched in her avoid mouth and she experienced a little fit of folly. Collecting the moist stones from her lips with her fingers disposed like pincers she threw them at me, and I responded in kind. When one of the projectiles, after hitting my throat, fell into my cleavage, her joy reached its peak. She laughed furiously, in the sunlight, and I saw the pure arcade of her teeth, on which my kisses had once become intoxicated.

"You seem a little out of sorts?"

"No, I assure you."

But the woods attracted us particularly. At intervals, there were stone benches arranged concentrically around a table. We neglected them in order to go lie down on the moss, the better to relax under lust vaults. We drank the fresh breath of the foliage and listened to the thousand confused sounds that are the harmony of forests. Our closely-positioned bodies exchanged their fluids. She made a pillow of my breasts, for it was always me who retained the predominance, me who served her more with the thousand protective attentions that men usually reserve for women.

"Do you like having me with you?" I asked her one day, when she wound her arms around me more tenderly.

"I don't *like* it...like isn't a strong enough word...I have an eternal need for your presence...you're becoming as necessary to me as air, or bread..."

"Why, Rolande?"

"Because you pacify me...you envelop me...you lull me to sleep. When you're here, it's as if it were him...my heart, to use a technical term, a scholarly word that he employed with me, enters into a euphoria...it's quieted to the point at which I can no longer feel it beating...a calm that I experienced when I gave myself. Nothing more existed then...it was the divine annihilation...I was as if I were dead..."

"But Rolande, you didn't limit yourself, then, to these sentimental exchanges?"

"Oh no...he was rather avid, you know."

"And you?"

"Me? Not at all."

I nearly cried: "Liar! Liar!"

But she went on: "Myself, I attached all the importance to the heart; the rest didn't matter to me, any more than it does with you." She drew away slightly: "I'm not saying that...if you were your bother instead of being his sister...I'm not saying that I wouldn't feel differently attracted...you resemble him so much! Your gaze is the same, with the same manner, as one might put it, of going to search for the truth in my brain. You have his way for forming a moue...yes, the same pursing of the lips. I don't need to hear myself criticized to know that I've done something worthy of criticism...I only have to look at your mouth. And even your handwriting is his! Yes, I've taken your letters and shown them to Rimeral, who divines character from handwriting...well, on listening to his analysis of you, it was Georges he was describing..."

She sat up. "Give me your left hand." With the gravity of an Egyptian priest, she interrogated my destiny in the slight lines that attitudes had imprinted on my palm. "No! The same lines...exactly the same line of Apollo, the love of art, of beauty! With a nonexistent Mercury...and a feeble Mars, courage...very feeble..."

279

"But Georges was wounded in the trenches!" I protested.

"Oh! Did the shells pick him out?"

"Pardon me! It was while emerging for an attack!"

"Don't insist…for I can still see, at about the age of thirty-five, as in him, a malady in which you'll need courage. But don't worry—I'll be there. I'll be able to care for you, my poor dear…"

And, lying down beside me again, she pecked my cheeks and my eyes with little kisses.

In order not to hide any of the truth, I ought to report that that was the first time that I emerged from the perfect indifference to the corporeal suggestions in which I had languished since the day of my transubstantiation.

To what could that be attributed? To the awakening of my creative faculties, of which nature had already given me notification three times? To our conversation, which evoked our moments of passion, and ignited once again under the pressure of her hand and her innocent facial caresses? I did not know how to respond; but I could not suppress a tremor of my entire being, and a penetrating languor—which she did not perceive, fortunately, for I immediately summoned up all my will to suppress them.

Oh, why not hold to that sweet psychic sharing? Why regret manifestations in any case impossible of renewal? Man, as everyone knows, becomes at a certain moment a sad animal, when desire no longer exalts form in his eyes, when he is satisfied, sated by a coarse act. It is then that is born in him, along with the lassitude, the troubles of the imagination, the unhealthy suggestions, the injustices toward a wealth that his appetite no longer pursues…and I had the admirable privilege of being able to spare myself those disconcerting reactions, in remaining a woman before the woman I loved.

But then, I could no longer see my happiness—the happiness that is not to desire to thrust away thereafter, to abandon oneself to the idleness of the senses, to float in the limbo of amour…the limbo, what am I saying?…in the paradise of amour, before the trinity of Purity, Virginity and the Ideal!

Go and dominate the impulses of a new puberty, then! When, that same day, after a ride on horseback, in which Rolande revealed the horsewoman in her of whom I was as yet unaware, she prepared go for a swim in my company, I had to feign a sudden illness to spare myself the sight of her undressing. I swiftly left the kiosk where she was putting on her bathing costume, and waited until she was in the water to taking off my riding-habit in my turn and follow her into the water.

Its coldness was a benefit, calming my impossible desire. I swam so intently that I did not see her reappear, fully dressed, on the shore. Furthermore, our chambermaids had arrived, which contributed further to my moderation. She held out her hand to help me out of the water, enveloping me in a peignoir.

"You're an admirable naiad!"

"You're another, Mademoiselle!"

"Yes, but...you possess something that I don't, and which suits you marvelously."

"Which is?"

"Your bosom. The bathing-costume reveals it even more. You could give points to the Venus de Milo...and can you imagine..." She leaned toward my ear and, arranging her hand like an acoustic funnel so that her confidence could not go astray, she said: "Can you imagine that Georges also had a bosom. How many times did I not say to him that he'd make a very pretty girl?"

She had never said anything like that. Even so, I was retrospectively flattered.

We went back to the vast drawing room populated with furniture, paintings and expensive trinkets, which, at the very least, did honor to Monsieur Variland's eclecticism. But the place weighed upon us. It was solemn, overwhelming. Disposed by the owner, it retained a kind of reflection of his correct coldness, his pretention to be imposing rather than to charm or seduce. We quickly deserted it for Rolande's small drawing room. Hung with an old *toile de Jouy* representing playful amours, with Louis XVI wall-mirrors and a triptych painted by Watteau, it also offered a profound divan uphol-stered in karamanie, crammed with faded silk cushions, where one could appease the voluptuousness of reveries. We lay down on it and stayed there for some time without speaking—after which she intoxicated me with a few lines from our dem-igod:

> *It is raining flower petals.*
> *The flame bends in the arm wind;*
> *With my eyes I possess you,*
> *And my eyes have need of tears...*[33]

Oh, that music! That music via her voice! She drew tears from me.

"What do I see, my poor love? You have a pain in your little heart? Is it Robert's absence? No, it isn't, is it? I'm not disputing your love, but I don't think..."

"It's not him."

"Who, then? Tell! You can't tell me? You have a secret from your Rolande, then?"

"Georges," she extracted from me, enigmatically.

"Yes, Georges...," she accepted, confused. And she add-ed: "Georges—I sometimes reproach myself for forgetting him for Georgette...but that's not a great sin, is it? For Georges and Georgette, I put beneath the same crown...a crown made of the diamonds of my heart..."

Thus our dear days of isolation passed. Of her portrait, there was no mention. In the evening, after a little music and a little more reading, we separated at the door of my room. For the tranquility of my nights, she was resident in another wing of the château. Monsieur Variland, doubtless obedient to a secret hope, had wanted it that way. And I did not have to hear her moving about, attending to her toilette, murmuring her

---

[33] Samain again, but a different poem from the same collection as the one previously cited, titled for the first quoted line, this one set to music by Henry Kimball Hadley.

song. I did not have to think that a simple discreet rap, struck on her door, would permit me to be in her arms. A long corridor to traverse can become the signification of a mental barrier. I respected it.

IX

Monsieur Variland came back. The château was about to fill with guests as well. In the big limousine he brought the Chabrols, Rimeral, Mademoiselle Férette and the Baronne des Illeuls, Others would follow later, for the hunt. Robert had also notified me of his imminent arrival.

Our intimacy was so sweet that, in order to prolong it further, Rolande, who was suffering slightly from a chill contracted during our walk, exaggerated her illness and kept to her room. I was thus obliged to stand in for her in some of the duties of mistress of the house and welcome guests as they disembarked. It was an opportunity for me to take note of the traces I had left in hearts.

"Not too bored?" Monsieur Variland said to me. "Oh, how I deplore these accused business affairs that have kept me away from you. I hope so much for your sympathy."

"But you have it already, Monsieur Variland."

"That's understood, but by sympathy, I mean…anyway, we'll talk about it later. For the moment, I'll telephone the doctor."

When he had gone it was the Baronne's turn to offer her condolences, with modulations of sadness in her *basso profundo*…

"So, my pretty, our friend is suffering and I wasn't here to assist in caring for her!"

"What would you have done differently, my dear Madame?"

"Call me Nirvâne," she insisted, squeezing my hand. "What would I have done? I don't know. I would have brought my woman's heart. Women always have a compassionate heart, while men—oh, don't talk to me about men!" She was still squeezing my hand. "There's so much to do for our own. You'll help me, my pretty? We'll be friends?"

"Certainly, my dear Madame."

"Call me Nirvâne..."

Her soft chemise reverberated gelatinously. Her smile evoked the asperities of a rock espoused by seaweed. She seemed, moreover, to be endowed with a double chin... Oh, no...!

Rimeral's compliments were even more intolerable, however. In him, I sensed, for the moment, my true rival. There was no doubt about it; that fop had come exclusively for Rolande. Weary of paying for the luxury of his chanteuse, he hoped to find a gratuitous replacement in the woman I loved. And I could not forget her encouraging behavior toward him.

He came up to me after the others. "So, your charming friend is in bed. How annoying! Tell me that it's not serious? We'll see her this evening, I hope? No? Ah! Tomorrow, then?"

"Don't count on it, Master," I declared, deciding on a tactic that jealousy had just awakened on me. "Rolande's condition is much more serious than Monsieur Variland imagines, who has not even been to say hello to her. The doctor has been summoned. I fear a bronchitis consecutive to the chill. For a few days, at least, therefore, you'll be reduced to doing without her company and tolerating mine."

"I couldn't hope for a more agreeable replacement," he said, "and however little you like music..."

"I believe, Master, that I would love it with you."

And *bang!* He started, as if he had received an electric shock. His gaze was impregnated with slyness, surprise and commiseration. *Another one!* he seemed to be saying to himself. *How I pity her! But she isn't disagreeable...* Then he put his hand to his moustache and smoothed it, with and expression that was both conquering and conquered. I was very familiar with all those little reflexes of donjuanesque conceit; I had observed them in others before him, and perhaps I had even manifested such absurdities myself...

"Will you paint my portrait?" he asked.

"Yes," I breathed, with perfectly feigned joy.

I immediately went up to Rolande's room. She was still asleep, I woke her up.

"My dear," I told her, "your malady is taking on unexpected proportions. A physician is coming; He'll find you troubled…between now and then, learn to cough…you might even have a little delirium…"

She promised all that I wished. I made her rehearse a few coughing fits, and she was so adorable that, yielding to an unreflective impulse, I kissed her recklessly—but I had miscalculated the surge of my kiss, and it was on the lips hat it landed. She did not seem overly surprised, but I had to run away in order not to yield to the temptation to persist.

From then on, with regard to my admirers, I used my charms with the expertise of a courtesan of old. I realized how easy it is for a pretty woman to turn men's heads. It only requires a very rudimentary observation of their psychology and a few well-placed remarks. Conquerors of our sex are truly inferior who cannot cultivate that facile artistry, contenting themselves with a kind of empiricism of amour, surrendering themselves to the favors of hazard or of momentary impulses. If they knew their power, the world would no longer belong to the stronger sex. And I made a note of those precious warnings for my own benefit in case, however improbable it might be, I might one day revert to my initial condition.

The seigneur Variland came the very next day to present himself to my tender snare. He had, it is true, already stuck his neck half way in of his own accord. I had only to encourage him a little to tighten the noose completely. Certainly, that situation, by virtue of the gentleman's enterprise and assiduity, was going to become importunate—but who could tell? Rolande might be able to obtain an advantage from it, and that decided me.

I inaugurated the orangery that day, placed at my disposal for work; I was arranging it as a studio, setting up my easels and canvases, when there was a knock on the door. I called out: "Come in!" and he appeared, in a bright, youthful costume, following the logic of his metamorphosis.

"Can you imagine, my dear Georgette, that your fiancé has just written to me to ask me to be his witness! Well? It's necessary that I know definitively..." I saw him go pale. "Are you seriously thinking of marrying?"

"Very seriously."

"With that tavern-pillar? Do you love him?"

As I did not reply, pretending to be interested in cleaning a palette, he came closer to me and took me by the shoulders, I allowed it to happen.

"You can't love him!" he exclaimed. "He's unworthy of you! What you need is a companion who understands you, who shares your tastes, who would be capable of being useful to you in the development of your talent...a brain, finally, to whatever branch of intellectual flight he might belong..." After a short silence, he added, shamelessly: "A man like me..."

"You're not free."

"One can...one can render oneself free! Come on, my child...it's my habit to speak frankly, and not to let even a sentimental question drag on. You must have perceived the effect that you have on me, no? Rolande has become completely indifferent to me...so...if Rolande were out of the picture...what would you think about a divorce, in order to consecrate my life to you thereafter? Will you encourage me?"

"Poor Rolande...!" I sighed.

He took that plaint as a promising formula and withdrew, enfevered by hope, asking me to think about it.

I had not expected that he would arrive at that extremity right away. It drove my mind to distraction. To think that I had just received a kind of marriage proposal from a man whose wife I had wanted to abduct a few months before, and that the man in question might perhaps be anticipating his wife's death! That was mad, hilarious...tragic! It made me regret the scruples that had delayed Rolande and me for so long in making the decision to run away, in order to avoid hurting the husband. Less hesitation would have spared me Tornada's crime. We would now be free, different in sex, on the shores of some Italian lake..."

With that fop Rimeral things moved even more swiftly. Oh, he did not pause over sentimental bagatelles, that one; he led the ritornel of love with a thrust of the bow as jolly as his orchestral folderols. He counted on trussing me up in the tromboidal fashion in which he had bowled over so many actresses before his adhesion to Savari.

The two of us were alone in the gilded small drawing room; he had just played me, in a susurration, two touching and banal melodies from his next operetta, which would win him the honors of the barrel-organ yet again, when, judging that his music must have brought me to the boil, he abandoned the keyboard and precipitated himself on to the sofa where I had stretched myself out to listen to him. He seized me round the waist with his muscular arms.

"I'll tell Rolande!" I exclaimed, struggling.

"What does Rolande matter to me?" he exhaled. "It's you I love, you I want, you I shall have!"

In a holy revulsion, I scratched his face. But he paralyzed my arm with one hand, and groped at my collerette with the other. I felt something like a warm animal armed with tentacles crawling over my bosom. And I saw the two bloated leeches of his lips descending upon my face.

It was a mute struggle, for I had not dared not cry out, in which my resistance was exhausted at the same time as my disgust. My God, what was happening? What decline, what fall, what debasement—considering my androphobia of yore, which persisted in my new structure—would have occurred, if there had not been a sudden noise in the next room...

My violator stood up just in time for Blanche Férette only to perceive my disturbance, and my precipitation in tidying my hair. Without saying a word, she picked up a book forgotten on a side-table and withdrew.

"You see, your imprudence has compromised me!" I lashed out. "That silly woman suspected your violence; she believes me complicit; in two minutes, the whole château will know. How are you going to repair that assault on my honor? Are you going to offer me marriage?"

"One might think about it," he said, meditatively.

"But I'm already engaged!"

"That's not irremediable."

Nevertheless, he had cooled down. He let me leave without attempting anything more.

I was gleaning spouses! Oh, my conjugal future was solidly assured!

If I had only had to record those proposals—quite natural, in sum…but I received another a few days later, even more extravagant.

The hot August day was coming to an end, and I was taking a short walk around the lake, I the shade, before dinner, preferring solitude to the company of the château's guests—some because, like Variland, Rimeral and the Baronne, they were too interested in me and others, by whom I mean the Chabrols and Mademoiselle Férette, because they were now giving me the cold shoulder. Suddenly, I heard cries of fright coming from the summer-house, and I saw people leaning over the balustrade, pointing at an overturned boat, next to which someone was drowning, of whom nothing could be seen but arms agitating desperately in the water.

My abilities as a good swimmer remained intact; I hastily rid myself of my dress and sandals, and clad only in my underclothes, which clung to me like a bathing suit, I dived into the water and headed straight for the victim. I had soon caught up with her.

It was the Baronne. I recognized her, firstly by the fact that, when I tried to grab her hair, her wig came away in my hand, and then because, at the second attempt, it was by mans of the lapel of her masculine jacket that I succeeded in dragging her to the shore. She was revived without anyone having to pull her tongue, copiously vomiting up the draught that she had just swallowed. Then I took her back to her room, in order to exchange her wet clothes for a smoking jacket.

"You saved my life, my pretty," she said, before going downstairs again, "and my affection for you is doubled by a real admiration. In addition to your charm and beauty, I find in

289

you the virtues of audacity, courage and sacrifice, which our natural enemies, men, do not have, although they attribute them to themselves, while women possess them but do not show them. We are henceforth inseparable. Tell me, are you having a good time here?"

"That depends on what you call a good time, Madame."

"Call me Nirvâne…I don't want to hear you call me anything else again. Do you find this environment interesting?"

"Not very…Nirvâne."

"Well, I'll take you away with me."

"Where to?"

"Brittany. I own an island there. There, no neighbors, no satyrs…the immensity for us alone…natural grottos, of which we shall be the nymphs…for one can relax there…and the gentle murmur of the waves to accompany out tender words. Is it agreed? Will you accept, my pretty?"

"But how can I, Nirvâne?"

She tried to kiss me to seal our pact, but the bell rang for diner, and I took advantage of it to slip away from the nirvana she was offering me.

I forgot these ridiculous and ugly things when I was with Rolande. For five days she had been feigning pneumonia, and I had appointed myself her nurse. In sum, I spent the greater part of my time at her bedside. I had arranged with the country doctor, whom she had deceived along with everyone else that her door should be forbidden even to Monsieur Variland. He only showed the tip of his nose in the morning, to enquire about her night, and in the evening to enquire about her day, and was not seen again.

While he was there, Rolande buried herself under her bedclothes, presenting a mask of asphyxia, proffering incoherent phrases. As soon as he had turned on his heel and retraced his steps the door was locked with a key, and the joy reappeared immediately. She threw away her pillows, and we savored our malice. I carefully refrained from telling her about my intrigues downstairs; her natural prudence might perhaps have found them excessive, but I took pleasure in aggravating the consequences of her chill, which were winning me the prolongation of the comedy, and, in consequence, our isolation.

All the troubling symptoms that I had collected with regard to her character, I no longer wanted to remember. I divided them up, rejecting her flightiness, her inconsequentiality, her morbid need to please, only to remember the passionate lover that she had been, and still was in the depths of her heart.

What troubling information, though! As our abandon progressed, she no longer had any reserve. Now that I acquired her confidence entirely, she was sure of my fidelity to the secrets she surrendered to me. Every day, she lifted a little further the modest veil that women maintain, sometimes even in their overflowing.

At first, she had proceeded by means of hints, and silences that were explanations. Now she no longer moderated her language. She did not wonder whether the virgin to whom she was telling these things could accept such confidences; she talked, and talked, as if we only had a single brain. She laid out curiosities that I would not have tolerated at one time. A further letter I had written to her from India, in which I had intentionally evoked our amorous pleasures, became another pretext for more audacious confessions. At every suggested phrase she drew me toward her neck and whispered: "Can you imagine, my dear..."

Thus far, I had been the sole object of her confessions, but one morning, she told me about her husband, with disgust. And the next day, she told me about a third, and then a fourth, with whom she had consoled herself before me. In vain I strove to discover who they were—wasted effort. She did not want to let go of a discretion of which I could not approve, having already interrogated her on that subject. Every time, she had replied to me with saintly assurance that I was her first lover. Oh, the charity of her proud gaze, the candor of her expression, when she affirmed that! I had blessed her! Now, I could have strangled her. Fortunately, I was able to repeat to myself that one is not the master of a past...

But all those remembrances, all those images, inevitably had an effect on my re-summoned nature, on the creative instinct. I no longer approached her, and no longer touched her, with the same serenity of my prepubertal phase. When she proceeded with her toilette in front of me, when she asked me to lend her a hand in getting dressed, and when she displayed without constraint her divine flesh and I breathed in its blonde aroma, an intoxication invaded me to seize that healthy pulp like a wild fruit, to bite into it, to bruise it, to feast upon it...

Then again, when she gave me innocent caresses, kisses to transmit to my distant brother, I could have cried out to her: "But don't you sense, then, that he's before you, that Georges is me?" And I pushed her away, angrily, only to pull her toward me again immediately and seek her kiss.

She did not understand; she abandoned herself to me innocently...and I had to flee, to seek the cold shower of frequentations downstairs.

Alas, in another domain too she disconcerted me. Until now I had thought her completely disinterested; she had seemed to consent to follow me without worrying about her material fate; she had paid no attention to the money that my talent assured me, and even protested in a dignified fashion at every insignificant gift that I offered hr, only accepting them after much insistence on my part. Yes, she had appeared to me, in that aspect of her character, perfectly independent and noble. Well, one morning when we were chatting about her husband's fantastic profits, her face suddenly filled with gravity.

"And Georges?" she queried. "Do you know how much he earns, per year?"

"I don't know, my dear. It must vary."

"How much do you think he'll be able to give me for my clothes?"

"I don't know."

"At least twenty thousand, I hope. One can't get by on less. There are questions, you understand, that one doesn't

292

bring up…but one has to think about them…as well as insurance for my old age…"

"And if he didn't have enough…if he were to lose his right arm, for example…what would you do? Would you go with him anyway?"

"That's true—I hadn't thought of that. Bah! He could use his left arm!"

"And if he lost both of them?"

"Oh, then…"

The spontaneous protests I expected did not come. She thought about it…

Oh, Rolande! Rolande, venal like all the rest?

In fact, in my new identity, I informed myself much more fully about her life. One hides a great deal from men, and they do not have time to observe. What I discovered saddened me.

Downstairs, I was still the coveted woman, who reigned over all—even, I was obliged to accept, the mild Monsieur Chabrol. He had declared his belief in my innocence and taken my side enthusiastically when that shrew Blanche Férette recounted, with some amplification, what she had seen with regard to the composer and me. As for the others, Variland and Rimeral were unsparing in their demonstrations and planning their future with me. Their attitudes denouncing them to one another, a rivalry was born that was expressed in sly attacks and incessant denigrations. A competition ensued. Only the Baronne had confidence. Others' games in my regard did not worry her. She had seen many others played with women who were her friends. Serene in her trousered obesity, she waited patiently for me to give the signal for the departure.

The result was that when Rolande, who could not extend her deception eternally, reappeared among her guests, she fell into a full-scale ferment. She quickly perceived the disturbance that I had cast into all hearts.

A further surprise: her initial sentiment was cold anger.

"What! That's your perfidy, while I was in bed! You've stolen my husband!"

293

"But you don't love him! You were going to run away from him!"

"What does that matter? I'm still his wife. And as long as I'm his wife, I won't allow anyone else to steal him from me. But that's not all—you've stolen my flirt too!"

"Rimeral? But you don't love him; you love Georges!"

"It doesn't matter; he was my flirt, and I need affection."

"Oh, take them—take back those men! They're yours; I won't dispute them with you...but my God, how naïve Georges was!"

Alas, my idol was gradually crumbling. It was time that Robert returned. In him, at least, there was the unknown, and perhaps I would succeed in reconstructing with him the sacred temple of dreams that was falling further into ruins with every day that passed.

X

He reappeared, flag flying. two days later—consequentially, long after he had announced his arrival. I clapped my hands when I saw him, not because my heart was missing him, but because I was missing him corporeally, if I might thus express the lack that he made me feel, A better analysis of his influence over me had now established that, without him, I was in some way incomplete. There are no words, and perhaps no circumlocutions, to translate it more accurately.

"It's stuck!" he darted, as soon as he disembarked. "I've done some superb business deals! Three thousand hogsheads, with a ten franc profit on each. Count it!"

He had forgotten to kiss my hand. I remarked on it. He did it without enthusiasm.

Then he continued: "So, how's it going, darling? Have you been daubing while Robert was slaving away? I've sold three of your paintings, you know."

"To whom?"

"To clients, of course! Oh, I know business, me."

Around us, lips were pursed. Rolande was laughing frankly, without resentment. Robert? Not worrying, Robert. He reassured all my lovers. That beautiful woman, that artist, with that mercantile lordling? No, it wasn't possible. And yet, some force riveted me to him.

I felt my chain more imperiously still when having gone to his room a few hours later to thank him for the candy he had brought me, I found him with Anna, my soubrette, sitting on his knee.

I sent my rival away with an angry gesture. "So! What does this signify, Robert? You're lowering yourself to the dish-rag now? When I'm next door? When we're due to be married in a month? Do you think I'm going to follow those hussies?"

He smiled and shrugged his shoulders. "Don't get excited. It's of no importance. She's neat and tidy, that girl…what more to you want for a quarter of an hour of pleasure? As for following her, you know full well that you can't avoid it. So why make such a fuss? Let's both take things as they come, since there's no way of doing otherwise?"

"That's your whole morality! Why isn't there any other way?"

"Because it's necessary?" he said, obstinately.

"And why is it necessary?"

"Because he wishes it."

"Who's he?"

"The master."

"What master?"

"Tornada, of course…Professor Tornada."

He had lowered his voice fearfully in pronouncing that terrible name. I was conscious that he had made the response that I would have made to the same questions and that we were both, and in the same fashion, under the yoke of that incredible man.

A deduction followed, but so rapid, and still so confused, and yet so redoubtable, that I hesitated to take possession of it. It was, however, necessary that the strange phenomenon be clarified.

"Come on, Robert—an abnormal situation exists between us, and it's time we obtained an explanation of it. I'm going to ask you to answer frankly, in your interests as well as mine. You don't have any sort of affection for me, do you?"

"Not a drop."

"You much prefer whores and maids."

"Much."

"And yet, you hold on to me."

"Yes."

"Why?"

"I don't know."

"Well, I'll tell you—because what you feel for me, I feel for you. But don't hide anything from me." I adopted my most authoritarian tone. "How long ago did you meet Professor Tornada?"

"Six months ago."

"Where did you meet him?"

"Where? At his clinic."

"So you've had an operation?"

"Yes, he operated on me."

"At his clinic in the Boulevard d'Auteuil?"

"Yes, there..."

"On what date? Can you remember the exact date? It's very important. Was date?"

"The fifteenth of February."

"And for what reason did the professor operate on you? For what illness?"

"I wasn't ill."

"Any more than me! So? In that case...well...!"

We looked at one another dazedly. We had understood one another. The same work of assimilation that had been accomplished in me had done its work in him. He was suddenly, brutally, able to explain an entire ensemble of questions that had been haunting his unpolished mind since the operation, which he had previously been no more able to solve than I had, but which, crystallizing in response to my questions acquired, at that precise moment, the form of certainty.

"Bloody hell!" he exclaimed, looking at me from head to toe, but with a particular emphasis on the region in which he knew that he had been dispossessed. Stammering, he went on: "Then Tornada's swap...was with you? Between you...and me? Both of us! Oh, no, that's a lot more than popping a cork!"

"Tell me! Tell me the whole story!" I ordered, in a frenzy to know everything.

"Well, this is it," he said, calming down. "My name is Robertine Lieuplane. I'm the daughter of a wine-merchant from Nevers, in the Nièvre. I can't complain—my parents were good to me, I wasn't unhappy. But what do you expect? One has one's temperament...at twenty, the heart moves you, doesn't it? It's difficult to resist. And when Jules ran after me…he was so handsome, my Julot! Slanting eyes, like a Chinaman, a blond goatee…so nice…but utterly good, utterly honorable, you know? Wouldn't have touched me. I was good, went to confession…but I loved him! Then, as my parents didn't want Jules, because of his position…he was a butcher…too bad! I left my family to come and get a job in Paris, until we were married…"

"Go on! Go on!" I insisted, seeing that he was getting caught up in his memories.

"Wines were what I knew, so I got a job in a bar. It isn't fun, you know, serving in a bar…necessary to get along with the clients…a glass to the left, a glass to the right…while you're serving, some of them pester you…that disgusted me. I wanted to stay good for my Julot…so I handed in my apron. Well, just my luck…on my last evening in the bar, I was chatting with the clients: I was telling them how difficult it is for a woman on her own in Paris, how much better off the men are, that they have a much better deal…when some kind of mechanic with dark glasses and a big overcoat that hid his face came in and asked me for a mélé-casse.[34] I served him…he didn't drink it but he listened to me while I jabbered on, making eyes at me…oh, those eyes! 'We'll talk again,' he said, when he paid me. And he went.

"An hour later, I came out in my turn, and who should I meet? My mechanic, who opens his overcoat and shows me his beard…a long beard that threw off sparks, like electricity. From that moment on, I don't remember too well…except that that mechanic was Tornada, and that he took me to his place, to his clinic…where I fell asleep…and that, when I woke up, I was no longer the same…oh no…not at all…now I understand…!"

I had already stopped listening. It was my own story that he was telling me, in such a vulgar fashion: the same origin, the same futile pretext for a madman's action, the same conse-

---

[34] A briefly-fashionable mixture of eau-de-vie and cassis.

quences. Robert was the other subject who had served, at the same time as me, for Tornada's stupefying biological experiment. That mad genius had transplanted into him what he had uprooted from me, and vice versa. I did not even have to interpret the sequel to the surgical adventure, so evident was it that Tornada, wanting to marry me to my co-operaté—or rather, my co-operatée; I'm getting lost, grammatically, in all these interventions—had no other objective than to observe how his neosexuals comported themselves in the great work of creation.

I could now explain to myself all the psychic particularities that had always confused me when I had thought about the mixture of attraction and repulsion that I felt for Robert: that need to have him in proximity, under my surveillance, when his company was odious to me; and, above all, my anxieties when he was absent and offending, by virtue of his absence, my sense of property.

Of course! He really was taking away a part of me!

So I, Georges Sigerier, a reputed painter, winner of the grand prize at the Salon, supposedly bound for the Académie, who had become a woman at the dictation of Tornada, had been alimented, in the mysterious sources of life, by a barmaid in love with her Julot!

And thus, that fragment of my being, grafted on to the daughter of a wine-merchant from the Nièvre, had been let astray by her into I knew not what low company, delivered to I knew not what degrading liaisons, exposed to I knew not what dangers!

And I could not even hold it against the creature, who had been equipped with it against her will!

"This Jules," I gasped. "Yes, this Julot...your Julot—have you seen him since?"

"Naturally. He's in my blood, under my skin!"

"Like me, alas," I reflected.

"So, I ran after him. Every time I said that I was going on a business trip, of course, it was also to take a trip to the Nièvre, where he's still a butcher..."

"And what happened?"

"Come on! Nothing could happen!" Bitterly, he added: "He didn't even recognize me."

Still my story, in fact! Which proves that in all the echelons of society, humans obey the same ineluctable forces...

"However, my lad, if you've abandoned all physical hope with regard to Julot, damn it, you've compensated yourself abundantly elsewhere. Oh, you've made fine use of me!"

"From the moment that I had to renounce Julot," he explained, "I no longer had any reason to deprive myself elsewhere...and as you've said, my nature is rather passionate...very passionate, even..."

Very passionate—that was incontestable. So passionate that, under the suggestion of my remark, his eyes had suddenly lit up, and he drew nearer to me with an intention about which I could not be mistaken.

"Don't you think," he snorted at me, "that it's not worth the bother of waiting for the Maire and the curé? And that...it would be more fun...if the two of us...?"

So! Was I about to let myself be violated? And by myself, to boot?

He was able to see his beautiful fiancée suddenly strike the virile pose of a boxer. Fists forward, Georgette Sigerier was only waiting for one more gesture to knock Robert de Lieuplane out. I was about to stick him with one of those uppercuts that would even lay the daughter of a Nièvre tavern-keeper out cold...

He understood, and went out, with his tail between his legs.

XI

The auto that was taking us—Rolande, her husband, Robert and me—on the excursion suddenly came to a stop as the brakes were violently applied at the entrance to a little village.

Monsieur Variland put his head out of the window. "What is it?" he asked the chauffeur.

"I'm no longer in control of the steering, Monsieur."

"See to it, then..." He pulled his head back in. "A breakdown! And we're still thirty kilometers from the house...and it's already six p.m. We certainly won't be back for dinner. What will they think, back there?"

"They'll suspect," Robert reassured him, "that we're in a sticky situation, and we'll send someone to look for us..."

"With what? The forty's in Paris; the big limousine has been out of action since yesterday..."

"There's still Robert's torpedo," I said.

"I've forbidden anyone to touch it," my fiancé informed us.

"Well then, we're in trouble," Rolande grumbled. Taking out her bad temper on her husband, she added: "Your idea of the four of us going out together was so absurd, my friend, that I'm still wondering why..." Her tone signified: *I know why; it's Georgette; you did it so that Chabrol and Rimeral, your rivals with regard to her, wouldn't be with us...*

She fustigated me at the same time, as she had done repeatedly in the last few days, with a scornful grimace.

Was it necessary for that stupid rancor to possess her? Under an ideal sky, in a gentle warmth rarely offered to poor humans, with the exciting visit to the old château, the day might have been one of those that count, but Rolande had sulked the entire time, keeping watch of her husband's behavior toward me. Of her sacred dream, of distant Georges, nothing remained. There was nothing but the jealousy that

301

Georgette excited in her, over two men that she did not love, one of whom horrified her to the point that she was prepared to leave him. That was all. Oh, confusing female mentality! A box of surprises!

And yet, that evening, nature summoned appeasement, tenderness and languor. The village, at the bottom of a hill, was cheerful, with all its faded tiled roofs and the foliage of its orchards. To our right, the fields stretched away toward harmonious hills already tinted with the blue that announced the veils of night. To our left, beyond a pool dormant under water-lilies, was the peace of a wood, a mysterious vegetal poem...

"I can't do it on my own," the chauffeur protested.

While Variland and Robert took off their jackets, I took Rolande away.

"Come on, my dear," I began, taking her arm. "You've been sullen with me for three days, and you're wrong. No, I can't explain it. It can't be the case that your animosity comes from the behavior of those imbeciles toward me. Setting Georges aside, you know what those men are, don't you? Frivolous, superficial, light-minded individuals, for whom love is a kind of sport, and woman an instrument of vanity. Aren't we above such miserable exercises? Aren't there, in our relationship, enough elements of tenderness for you to be able to satisfy your heart, until Georges returns your former happiness to you?"

"Will he ever come back?" she yielded.

"Yes—you know that; he tells you every time he writes. It's merely a matter of patience. But for pity's sake, in the meantime, let's not spoil our beautiful affection with stupid female rivalries! Don't you believe in me anymore? Do you want me to reassure you, by going away?"

"Oh, no!" she said, holding on to my arm more tightly.

"Oh, I sense that you're coming back to me! And I experience an infinite joy in that, because I love you..." My voice became musical. "I love you, you see, more than you can imagine, and more than I'm able to express. It's not necessary to be a different sex to love! Don't you believe that two women can devote their hearts together as well as lovers? Love between lovers, you see, always has a disconcerting, diminishing conclusion. Once desire is satisfied, the man and the woman become momentary enemies, or at least indifferent to one another. Nothing any longer remains of the ideal, the intoxication: just two sated beasts who, for two pins, would tear one another apart like beasts. While between women, for whom instinct is a dead letter…oh, I'm not talking about madwomen, and I not talking about sick women…well, between women, there's an eternal Eden for the heart—the Eden into which I'd like to enter with you, Rolande…"

"That's curious," she reflected. "You're talking to me like your brother…it's true that he applied those arguments to a man and a woman, and served them up to me when, as you put it, the beast was satisfied…but I find in your words not merely his ides, but even his expressions…"

"All the more reason for you to bring back to me, entirely, the affection that you gave to him…the same affection! And together, from now on, let's scorn the rest of humankind…the Varilands, the Rimerals, the Lieuplanes! Would you like that? Will you promise to do that, until Georges comes back? I'll fill the interim in your heart, my love, and it will all remain in the family. Will you promise?"

"I promise," she said. "Because it wasn't of those men that I was jealous—it was of you."

She was lying—but what did it matter? She offered me her lips to seal our reconciliation. O demon! Our kiss escaped the pure ideal that I had just invoked as the supreme argument of our new mode of union. We tore ourselves apart, happily, just in time. Monsieur Variland arrived, waving his long arms.

"Bad luck!" he howled. "Disaster! Can you imagine that that animal of a chauffeur has broken the steering? We can't get back. We'll be obliged to eat and sleep here. Is there even an inn?"

All four of us, abandoning the auto, went down to the village. Yes, there was an inn. It even had a name that did not lack a certain propriety, so far as Robert and I were concerned:

303

the Hôtel des Mutilés. The name was legitimated by the serious injuries suffered by the owners, two brothers, during the war. One of them was missing an arm, the other a leg, and those two limbs, crudely painted on the sign, evidently attracted custom to the establishment, since that evening, there was only one room free.

"We'll give it to the ladies," Variland declared, "while Monsieur de Lieuplane and I will bed down somewhere else."

"Yes, yes…one can always sort something out," Robert agreed. And I observed that he was thinking about "sorting something out" with the barmaid. She was a slattern two meters tall; he was already looking at her with an incendiary gaze that she did not misinterpret. Such a handsome gentleman! Alas, I was about to be exposed once again!

Even for a painter, these exhibitions are rather painful, I said to myself, in bitter jest.

We dined summarily, on an egg and a slice of bacon. I hardly touched the food anyway, so great was my apprehension about having to spend the night with Rolande. I ordered myself sternly to let her have the bed and content myself with a chair, My nerves, exasperated by a long continence, further disturbed by the tenderness of our reconciliation, might perhaps have led me to bad behavior that could have no conclusion, and uneasy presentiments advised me to be prudent.

At ten o'clock, the one-armed landlord came to bring me a candle with his remaining arm. It was to notify us that it was time to retire. Monsieur Variland protested; he would gladly have taken a brief walk—doubtless to draw me into a conversation relative to his intentions toward me, and his divorce from Rolande—but they were about to shut up shop; the wagoners were already asleep and everyone needed rest. Then again, nowadays, the arrogance of a high financier cannot stand up to the determination of a mutilated innkeeper. He gave Rolande a peck on the forehead, kissed me passionately on the hand, and we went our separate ways. Robert had disappeared, and I had already reconciled myself to a carnal sacrifice, the origin of which was now clearly defined for me,

A creaking stairway took Rolande and me to a neat room overlooking the street. The mutilated proprietors had gone to some trouble for clients of our importance. The narrow bed was adorned with white sheets scented with lavender, and a fake Oriental rug had been unrolled; the washing facilities were abundantly supplied with water. Behind a blue plush screen, there was even a discreet item of furniture, carved by a local carpenter, bearing an astonishing resemblance to the Trojan horse—every modern convenience, in sum.

While getting undressed, Rolande, cheered up by the adventure, ecstasized: "No! It's quite chic here! Look at this, my dear—a bridal crown in a glass case! A panoply with a trench-helmet and mortar-shells. And a portrait of Monsieur Grévy![35] Oh, no, not that! Look away, Monsieur Grévy...I don't want him watching me sleep..."

She topped beside the bed. "But how narrow this bed is! We're going to be a trifle cramped. Oh, that won't displease me...you have such soft skin. And then, you know, I've often thought that it would be nice to have it against mine. What are you waiting for? Why aren't you undressed? Why are you sitting there, as stiff as a mummy?"

I was, in fact, sitting in an armchair, waiting for her to go to bed. I was watching, wonderstruck, the ritual of her undressing, the fall of the veils, one by one, that revealed the splendor of her body. There were her arms, their full firmness, their delicate wrists, the gilded fleece in the armpits; there was her back, sumptuous marble, emerging from the corset like a shell, toward the pure contour of the nape; there were the legs, harmonious in their black silken sheaths, joined to the slender foot by thoroughbred ankles; then, once the corset was un-

---

[35] Jules Grévy, elected in 1879, was the first President of the Republic who was not committed to restoring the monarchy. His successful first term was followed by a disastrous second, from which he was forced to resign, after peripheral involvement in a scandal involving trafficking in honors, in 1887.

laced, the hips, beneath the delicate chemise, displaying their grave and powerful curve.

I scarcely dared look at her! Every one of her gestures, every one of her beauties, took me back six months, to the ecstasies of my bachelor flat. Desire—the same desire, the master desire of the race, with all its energies, transports and furies, invaded me as before. My ears were ringing; there was a strange taste in my mouth. A long frisson ran through me.

"What are you waiting for?" she repeated, astonished.

"No!" I resisted. "No, Rolande. You can see that it's impossible…we'll never fit into it together. We'll prevent one another from sleeping. No."

"And you intend to stay there?"

"Yes, in this armchair."

"All night?"

"All of it, yes."

"Oh, you're crazy!"

She sprang out of the sheets into which she had already slid. She came to kneel by my chair, and put her arms around me.

"Yes, you're crazy. Can't we put up with a little awkwardness for one another's sake? And then again, will it be awkward? When we can stroke one another, gently…when we can breathe one another's scent…when we can feel one another's hearts beating…for one another. Come on, my love, come on. I'll go to sleep on your shoulder, as with Georges, when I was weary…and you'll see…you'll see how good it is."

All the fluids issuing from her splendid being, all animating my covetousness at once, expanding, penetrating the fibers of my being, transported me toward the impossible intoxication. I could no longer resist; I got undressed with a flick of the wrist, and followed her to the bed.

"Oh Rolande! Rolande!"

From that precise moment on, I no longer dare recount what happened. Oh, not for the reason that certain minds, too curious about exceptional situations, might imagine with regard to my actions in rediscovering the adored body of my mistress. No, it's because from that precise moment on, my mind no longer belonged to me.

And this is why.

I had heard, without paying any heed to it, so much was I the victim of my own emotions, an automobile purring in the street, blows struck on the door, and a shrill voice shouting: "Open up! Open up!"

Then there were footsteps in the corridor, which stopped at our door, and someone had said: "This is it."

Then, just as I embraced Rolande, a sudden force separated me from her. Oh, I knew it well, that force, since I had been possessed by its several times before. It enveloped me, gripped me, took possession of my will as a magnet does of iron; and I was obliged, without any possible resistance—to Rolande's amazement—to tear myself away from her arms, quit the bed, get dressed and go to the door. I knew that behind that door there was a frightful man, whose long beard was, at that moment, phosphorescent, and that, a moth hypnotized by that green light, I was invincibly bound to follow him.

"Let's go!" said Tornada, buttoning up his ample overcoat to hide his luminous fleece.

We went along the corridor. The battens of the door closed behind us. A powerful roadster was panting in the street. Robert was already sitting in one corner.

"Be careful, don't get close to him. Sit in front with me…he must have lice. Do you know where I picked him up, the slut? In the barmaid's bed!"

He padded himself with blankets, grabbed the wheel, and stepped on the accelerator.

Oh, that nocturnal journey! We were probably doing a hundred and fifty an hour; the headlights were swallowing up the countryside, we were breathing in a cyclone.

Where was he taking us? Toward Paris—but why? I did not think about that, though. It was necessary.

At one time, he braked so hard we almost overturned. He seemed to want to explain something to me. But he set off again immediately, and only spoke thereafter as if to himself, in disjointed phrases that he cast to the wind.

"Imbeciles!... Tradition!... Mores!... And that prosecutor!... The stupid police!... Oh, the Sûreté... But me, I was remaking the world!... Choice of sex, universal happiness! Ten couples already!... Twenty transsexuals!... All successful!... Perfect!... Couldn't they even wait nine months?... At least we'd have seen!... Who could have complained?... Not them, certainly?... Who?... Colleagues, jealous... Donkeys, fornicators!... What about professional secrecy?... All undone now!... All to do again!... Oh, pooh!....rotten humanity!... As before!"

Volcanic lights were now advertising the great city. Tornada went through the customs like a whirlwind, without stopping, and then along the fortifications. I soon recognized the black façade, the two entrances to the clinic. We went through the grounds, we were in the sumptuous study.

Once he had sat us down on a divan he said: "A cigar, my darlings?"

"Master, I no longer smoke since..."

"Yes! Yes!"

I lit up. My head spun. I slumped on Robert's shoulder... We slept.

XII

A week later, Professor Tornada had arranged every-thing. I reentered into possession of my property. That which had not belonged to me was restored to me. By virtue of his satanic procedures, I had recovered the appearance I had be-fore his burglary.

I had been remaled! I could return from India. I don't say that without pride, because men place their pride in the pre-dominance of their sex. But I say it with even more content-ment, for my feminine phase had been fecund in precious in-formation.

As soon as I returned to the Rue du Général-Foy, the first thing I did was run to the telephone and ask for the Varilands' number. Louis, the valet, appeared at the other end of the line.

"Are Monsieur and Madame in Paris?"

"Only Madame," the servant replied, in a discreet, mournful voice. He had recognized me, and was commiserat-ing with the chagrin that I ought to be experiencing.

"Would you ask her to come to the apparatus?"

A few seconds of waiting, and then, indistinctly, the sound of footsteps, and a brief order to Louis: "Leave me…," and finally, the dear vibrations of the beloved.

"Jo! It's you, my Jo! Oh, how could you?…without warning me! No matter! I'm glad! Yes, in our distress, it's good to know that you're here. But what a business, my friend! Do you know anything about Georgette?"

"Yes, everything…come quickly; we'll talk about it."

"I'm on my way!"

The time for her to leap into an automobile, and she was in my arms. Oh, what transports! What delirium, in spite of her incoherent conversation, in which she threw all the recent events at me, pell-mell—the abduction of Georgette and Rob-ert, her husband's complaint to the police, the Sûreté's search for a crime in the manner of Landru,[36] and her own panic, under the threat of the reproaches that I would surely address to her for having looked after my sister so poorly.

I reassured her: "No, no! That's insane. Why so many stories? The truth is quite different..."

"Oh, so much the better, so much the better!"

I explained that Robert, worried by the passion toward his fiancée of which Monsieur Variland was giving evidence, had simply taken her away, as was his right. His error was to give that departure an appearance of scandal, but that was not surprising in a man devoid of education. The letter that I had just found on my return said that they were both in the process of traveling happily in Corsica, and it was certain that it was with Georgette's consent, since she told me so in her letter.

"That's what astonishes me the most!" Rolande remarked. "But after all, on reflection, women are so bizarre!" Then, swiftly: "Telephone these details to the prefecture, urgently."

"Later, Rolande. The police have other fish to fry."

"That's true," she said. "Tornada must be keeping them busy..."

"Tornada?" I queried, anxiously.

"What! You don't know? He's been arrested, this morning. The newspapers are full of it. Special editions are being cried on the streets."

Tornada banged up! After the removal of my final dressing, then? Immediately after my departure from the clinic? Oh, I had been lucky!

---

[36] The serial killer Henri Landru, who seduced eleven women he met through "lonely hearts" advertisements in the newspapers, killed them once he had access to their assets, and allegedly burned their dismembered bodies in his stove, was tried for murder in November 1921, in spite of the lack of physical evidence, and convicted; his execution was still pending when this story was published in January 1922.

But Rolande, stimulated by the singularity of the story, told me what the surgeon had done to warrant being taken away in handcuffs.

"Can you imagine it, Jo? It's frightful! Can you imagine that he was amusing himself changing people's sex—and without consulting them, which makes it worse! Is that credible? Is it possible? Can you see yourself, my Jo, in skirts? What would become of us…and our love? Then there were complaints—but they've been retracted, because he succeeded…he must have been skillful, at any rate…in putting things right in all the people he'd operated on. And the rumor's going round that a hermaphrodite, whom he's also fabricated, didn't make any complaint…"

"A hermaphrodite!" I shivered with retrospective terror.

"Yes, that's what the newspapers are saying…but I didn't understand very well. Explain that phenomenon to me…it must be monstrous, my Jo!"

She was manifesting a prodigious interest. Undoubtedly she was counting on obtaining some benefit from my explanation, but as I now had to go through a long period of respite before the reestablishment of my normality was complete, and I would certainly have disappointed her, I put off the explanation until later. I drew her sagely to an armchair and knelt down before her.

"So, while poor Jo was traveling, you've been good?"

"Perfectly!"

"You haven't forgotten me?"

"I never stopped thinking about you."

"No flirts?"

"Not the shadow of one."

"You swear?"

"I swear."

Oh, the limpidity of her gaze, the honesty of her tone, the tranquility of her conscience when she perjured herself! But I was no longer astonished by it.

She added: "I'm still worthy of departing with you, and am only waiting for you to say the word."

"Ah, as to that, my dear Rolande..." I took her hands. "Listen...I've observed a great deal and leaned a great deal during my voyage. Do you know that there's a land where witchcraft still exists? Well, I met a sort of witch out there—or rather, an enchantress...yes, a young enchantress...as pretty as you are...as seductive as you..."

"Who was your mistress?"

"No! On my honor, believe me...but who was so interested in me...in us, for I told her about our liaison, our plans...and she told me, that enchantress, in prophetic words that I'll never forget: 'Be prudent; be prudent...for the sake of the persistence of your love, leave that woman to her husband; don't take her away; only remain her lover.'"

"What right had she to interfere?"

"Wait. 'Because,' she added, 'separation, the difficulty of meeting, ignorance of one another, illusions, are the gusts of wind that stimulate the flames of love...while perpetual contact, possession without reserve and, even more so, reciprocal penetration into the character and soul, are the ashes that stifle the sacred flame!'"

"And you're going to listen to that stupid prophecy?"

"We're going to think about it, at least."

She went away in tears; but I had no remorse. I knew full well that she would stop at the first street corner, take a little mirror, rice powder and rouge out of her handbag, and repair the outrage of her dolor to her face, before the image of her irreparable self.

And we would continue, as in the past, to magnify our dream of salutary deception!

In that fantastic adventure, I had learned what woman are—but I had also learned what men are. Oh, they're scarcely more brilliant, and I would no longer boast about belonging to their kind. All, all of them, companions of St. Anthony...

And me? An egotist, at least—a ferocious egotist, to judge by the fashion in which I was disinterested in the fate of my co-metamorphosee, Robert. Had she gone back to serving in a bar? Had she "stuck" again with Julot? Had she taken refuge, a virgin once again, with her family?

I really and truly didn't give a damn.

Well, that's men for you.

SF & FANTASY

Adolphe Alhaiza. *Cybele*
Alphonse Allais. *The Adventures of Captain Cap*
Henri Allorge. *The Great Cataclysm*
Guy d'Armen. *Doc Ardan: The City of Gold and Lepers*
G.-J. Arnaud. *The Ice Company*
Charles Asselineau. *The Double Life*
Cyprien Bérard. *The Vampire Lord Ruthwen*
S. Henry Berthoud. *Martyrs of Science*
Aloysius Bertrand. *Gaspard de la Nuit*
Richard Bessière. *The Gardens of the Apocalypse*
Albert Bleunard. *Ever Smaller*
Félix Bodin. *The Novel of the Future*
Louis Boussenard. *Monsieur Synthesis*
Alphonse Brown. *City of Glass; The Conquest of the Air*
Emile Calvet. *In a Thousand Years*
André Caroff. *The Terror of Madame Atomos; Miss Atomos; The Return of Madame Atomos; The Mistake of Madame Atomos; The Monsters of Madame Atomos; The Revenge of Madame Atomos; The Resurrection of Madame Atomos; The Mark of Madame Atomos; The Spheres of Madame Atomos*
Félicien Champsaur. *The Human Arrow; Ouha, King of the Apes; Pharaoh's Wife*
Didier de Chousy. *Ignis*
Jules Clarétie. *Obsession*
Michel Corday. *The Eternal Flame*
André Couvreur. *The Necessary Evil*; *Caresco, Superman*
Captain Danrit. *Undersea Odyssey*
C. I. Defontenay. *Star (Psi Cassiopeia)*
Charles Derennes. *The People of the Pole*
Georges Dodds (anthologist). *The Missing Link*
Harry Dickson. *The Heir of Dracula*
Jules Dornay. *Lord Ruthven Begins*
Alfred Driou. *The Adventures of a Parisian Aeronaut*
Sâr Dubnotal *vs. Jack the Ripper*
Alexandre Dumas. *The Return of Lord Ruthven*
Renée Dunan. *Baal*
J.-C. Dunyach. *The Night Orchid; The Thieves of Silence*
Henri Duvernois. *The Man Who Found Himself*

Achille Eyraud. *Voyage to Venus*
Henri Falk. *The Age of Lead*
Paul Féval. *Anne of the Isles; Knightshade; Revenants; Vampire City; The Vampire Countess; The Wandering Jew's Daughter*
Paul Féval, *fils. Felifax, the Tiger-Man*
Charles de Fieux. *Lamékis*
Louis Forest. *Someone is Stealing Children in Paris*
Arnould Galopin. *Doctor Omega; Doctor Omega and the Shadowmen* (anthology)
Judith Gautier. *Isoline and the Serpent-Flower*
H. Gayar. *The Marvelous Adventures of Serge Myrandhal on Mars*
Léon Gozlan. *The Vampire of the Val-de-Grâce*
G.L. Gick. *Harry Dickson and the Werewolf of Rutherford Grange*
Edmond Haraucourt. *Illusions of Immortality*
Nathalie Henneberg. *The Green Gods*
V. Hugo, P. Foucher & P. Meurice. *The Hunchback of Notre-Dame*
Romain d'Huissier. *Hexagon: Dark Matter*
Jules Janin. *The Magnetized Corpse*
Michel Jeury. *Chronolysis*
Gustave Kahn. *The Tale of Gold and Silence*
Gérard Klein. *The Mote in Time's Eye*
Fernand Kolney. *Love in 5000 Years*
Paul Lacroix. *Danse Macabre*
Louis-Guillaume de La Follie. *The Unpretentious Philosopher*
Jean de La Hire. *Enter the Nyctalope; The Nyctalope on Mars; The Nyctalope vs. Lucifer; The Nyctalope Steps In; Night of the Nyctalope; Return of the Nyctalope; The Fiery Wheel*
Etienne-Léon de Lamothe-Langon. *The Virgin Vampire*
André Laurie. *Spiridon*
Gabriel de Lautrec. *The Vengeance of the Oval Portrait*
Alain le Drimeur. *The Future City*
Georges Le Faure & Henri de Graffigny. *The Extraordinary Adventures of a Russian Scientist Across the Solar System* (2 vols.)
Gustave Le Rouge. *The Mysterious Doctor Cornelius* (3 vols.); *The Vampires of Mars; The Dominion of the World* (w/Gustave Guitton) (4 vols.)
Jules Lermina. *Mysteryville; Panic in Paris; To-Ho and the Gold Destroyers; The Secret of Zippelius*
André Lichtenberger. *The Centaurs; The Children of the Crab*

Jean-Marc & Randy Lofficier. *Edgar Allan Poe on Mars; The Katrina Protocol; Pacifica; Robonocchio; Return of the Nyctalope;* (anthologists) *Tales of the Shadowmen 1-10*
Xavier Mauméjean. *The League of Heroes*
Joseph Méry. *The Tower of Destiny*
Hippolyte Mettais. *The Year 5865*
Louise Michel. *The Human Microbes; The New World*
Tony Moilin. *Paris in the Year 2000*
José Moselli. *Illa's End*
John-Antoine Nau. *Enemy Force*
Marie Nizet. *Captain Vampire*
C. Nodier, A. Beraud & Toussaint-Merle. *Frankenstein*
Henri de Parville. *An Inhabitant of the Planet Mars*
Gaston de Pawlowski. *Journey to the Land of the 4th Dimension*
Georges Pellerin. *The World in 2000 Years*
Ernest Pérochon. *The Frenetic People*
Pierre Pelot. *The Child Who Walked on the Sky*
J. Polidori, C. Nodier, E. Scribe. *Lord Ruthven the Vampire*
P.-A. Ponson du Terrail. *The Vampire and the Devil's Son; The Immortal Woman*
Edgar Quinet. *Ahasuerus*
Henri de Régnier. *A Surfeit of Mirrors*
Maurice Renard. *The Blue Peril; Doctor Lerne; The Doctored Man; A Man Among the Microbes; The Master of Light*
Jean Richepin. *The Wing; The Crazy Corner*
Albert Robida. *The Adventures of Saturnin Farandoul; The Clock of the Centuries; Chalet in the Sky; The Electric Life*
J.-H. Rosny Aîné. *Helgvor of the Blue River; The Givreuse Enigma; The Mysterious Force; The Navigators of Space; Vamireh; The World of the Variants; The Young Vampire*
Marcel Rouff. *Journey to the Inverted World*
Han Ryner. *The Superhumans*
Angelo de Sorr. *The Vampires of London*
Brian Stableford. *The New Faust at the Tragicomique;The Empire of the Necromancers (The Shadow of Frankenstein; Frankenstein and the Vampire Countess; Frankenstein in London); Sherlock Holmes & The Vampires of Eternity; The Stones of Camelot; The Wayward Muse.* (anthologist) *News from the Moon; The Germans on Venus; The Supreme Progress; The World Above the World; Nemoville; Investigations of the Future; The Conqueror of Death*
Jacques Spitz. *The Eye of Purgatory*

Kurt Steiner. *Ortog*
Eugène Thébault. *Radio-Terror*
C.-F. Tiphaigne de La Roche. *Amilec*
Louis Ulbach. *Prince Bonifacio*
Théo Varlet. *The Golden Rock. The Xenobiotic Invasion; The Castaways of Eros; Timeslip Troopers* (w/André Blandin); *The Martian Epic* (w/Octave Joncquel)
Paul Vibert. *The Mysterious Fluid*
Villiers de l'Isle-Adam. *The Scaffold; The Vampire Soul*
Philippe Ward. *Artahe*
Philippe Ward & Sylvie Miller. *The Song of Montségur*

MYSTERIES & THRILLERS

M. Allain & P. Souvestre. *The Daughter of Fantômas*
A. Anicet-Bourgeois, Lucien Dabril. *Rocambole*
A. Bernède. *Belphegor; Judex* (w/Louis Feuillade); *The Return of Judex* (w/Louis Feuillade); *The Shadow of Judex*
A. Bisson & G. Livet. *Nick Carter vs. Fantômas*
V. Darlay & H. de Gorsse. *Arsène Lupin vs. Sherlock Holmes: The Stage Play*
Séamas Duffy. *Sherlock Holmes in Paris*
Paul Féval. *Gentlemen of the Night; John Devil; The Black Coats ('Salem Street; The Invisible Weapon; The Parisian Jungle; The Companions of the Treasure; Heart of Steel; The Cadet Gang; The Sword-Swallower)*
Emile Gaboriau. *Monsieur Lecoq*
Goron & Emile Gautier. *Spawn of the Penitentiary*
Rick Lai. *Shadows of the Opera: Retribution in Blood; Sisters of the Shadows: The Curse of Cagliostro*
Steve Leadley. *Sherlock Holmes: The Circle of Blood*
Maurice Leblanc. *Arsène Lupin vs. Countess Cagliostro; Arsène Lupin vs. Sherlock Holmes (The Blonde Phantom; The Hollow Needle); The Many Faces of Arsène Lupin*
Gaston Leroux. *Chéri-Bibi; The Phantom of the Opera; Rouletabille & the Mystery of the Yellow Room; Rouletabille at Krupp's*
Richard Marsh. *The Complete Adventures of Judith Lee*
William Patrick Maynard. *The Terror of Fu Manchu; The Destiny of Fu Manchu*
Frank J. Morlock. *Sherlock Holmes: The Grand Horizontals; Sherlock Holmes vs Jack the Ripper*

Jean Petithuguenin. *The Adventures of Ethel King*
Antonin Reschal. *The Adventures of Miss Boston*
P. de Wattyne & Y. Walter. *Sherlock Holmes vs. Fantômas*
David White. *Fantômas in America*
Pierre Yrondy. *The Adventures of Thérèse Arnaud*

SCREENPLAYS

Mike Baron. *The Iron Triangle*
Emma Bull & Will Shetterly. *Nightspeeder; War for the Oaks*
Gerry Conway & Roy Thomas. *Doc Dynamo*
Steve Englehart. *Majorca*
James Hudnall. *The Devastator*
Jean-Marc & Randy Lofficier. *Royal Flush*
J.-M. & R. Lofficier & Marc Agapit. *Despair*
J.-M. & R. Lofficier & Joël Houssin. *City*
Andrew Paquette. *Peripheral Vision*
Robert L. Robinson, Jr. *Judex*
R. Thomas, J. Hendler & L. Sprague de Camp. *Rivers of Time*

NON-FICTION

Stephen R. Bissette. *Blur 1-5. Green Mountain Cinema 1; Teen Angels*
Win Scott Eckert. *Crossovers* (2 vols.)
Jean-Marc & Randy Lofficier. *Shadowmen* (2 vols.)
Randy Lofficier. *Over Here*

ART BOOKS

J.-M. Lofficier & D. Taylor. *Tongue Lash*
Jean-Pierre Normand. *Science Fiction Illustrations*
Raven Okeefe. *Raven's L'il Critters; Rave's Faves*
Randy Lofficier & Raven Okeefe. *If Your Possum Go Daylight...*
Daniele Serra. *Illusions*